THE MAMMOTH BOOK OF
TALES FROM THE ROAD

Regimiento = 2000 soldiers

용기리

Also available

The Mammoth Book of 20th Century Ghost Stories
The Mammoth Book of Arthurian Legends
The Mammoth Book of Astounding Puzzles
The Mammoth Book of Awesome Comic Fantasy
The Mammoth Book of Battles
The Mammoth Book of Best New Horror
The Mammoth Book of British Kings & Queens
The Mammoth Book of Chess and Internet Games (New Edition)
The Mammoth Book of Comic Fantasy II
The Mammoth Book of Elite Forces
The Mammoth Book of Endurance and Adventure
The Mammoth Book of Eyewitness History 2000
The Mammoth Book of Great Detective Stories
The Mammoth Book of Haunted House Stories
The Mammoth Book of Heroic and Outrageous Women
The Mammoth Book of Historical Detectives
The Mammoth Book of Historical Whodunnits
The Mammoth Book of Humor
The Mammoth Book of Jack the Ripper
The Mammoth Book of Legal Thrillers
The Mammoth Book of Locked-Room Mysteries and Impossible Crime
The Mammoth Book of Love & Sensuality
The Mammoth Book of Men O'War
The Mammoth Book of Murder and Science
The Mammoth Book of New Sherlock Holmes Adventures
The Mammoth Book of Nostradamus and Other Prophets
The Mammoth Book of Private Lives
The Mammoth Book of Pulp Action
The Mammoth Book of Pulp Fiction
The Mammoth Book of Sex, Drugs & Rock 'n' Roll
The Mammoth Book of Soldiers at War
The Mammoth Book of Sword & Honor
The Mammoth Book of Terror
The Mammoth Book of the History of Murder
The Mammoth Book of True War Stories
The Mammoth Book of The West
The Mammoth Book of the World's Greatest Chess Games
The Mammoth Book of True Crime (Revised Edition)
The Mammoth Book of Unsolved Crime
The Mammoth Book of Vampire Stories by Women
The Mammoth Book of War Correspondents
The Mammoth Book of War Diaries and Letters
The Mammoth Book of Women Who Kill
The Mammoth Encyclopedia of The Unsolved
The Mammoth Encyclopedia of Science Fiction

THE MAMMOTH BOOK OF
TALES FROM THE ROAD

Edited by
Maxim Jakubowski and M. Christian

CARROLL & GRAF PUBLISHERS
New York

Carroll & Graf Publishers
An imprint of Avalon Publishing Group, Inc.
161 William Street
NY 10038-2607
www.carrollandgraf.com

First published in the UK by Robinson,
an imprint of Constable & Robinson Ltd 2002

First Carroll & Graf edition 2003

ISBN 0-7867-1069-1

Printed and bound in the EU

Contents

Acknowledgments

REMOTE VIEWING by Mat Coward, © 2002 by Mat Coward. Used by permission of the author.

MIGRANT PEOPLE by John Steinbeck, © 1939, renewed ©1967 by John Steinbeck. First appeared as Chapter 17 from THE GRAPES OF WRATH. Used by permission of Viking Penguin, a division of Penguin Putnam Inc.

DIVERSION by Elizabeth Counihan, © 2002 by Elizabeth Counihan. Used by permission of the author.

JUST DRIVE, SHE SAID by Richard Paul Russo, © 2002 by Richard Paul Russo. Used by permission of the author.

THE ROAD TO CEDAR RAPIDS by Greg Beatty, © 2002 by Greg Beatty. Used by permission of the author.

KICKS ON ROUTE 66 by Sylvia Rose, © 2002 by Sylvia Rose. Used by permission of the author.

24 HOURS FROM TULSA by Martin Edwards, © 2002 by Martin Edwards. Used by permission of the author.

SUMMER CANNIBALS by Maxim Jakubowski, © 1996 by Maxim Jakubowski. First appeared as Chapter 4 from IT'S YOU THAT I WANT TO KISS. Used by permission of the author.

TINA AND LUCILLE by O. Z. Evangeline, © 2002 by O. Z. Evangeline. Used by permission of the author.

THE FLYING LADY DINER by Debra Gray De Noux & O'Neil De Noux, © 2002 by Debra Gray De Noux & O'Neil De Noux. Used by permission of the authors.

THE ROAD CALLS ME DEAR by Cory Doctorow, © 2002 by Cory Doctorow. Used by permission of the author.

ON THE ROAD by Jack Kerouac, © 1957 by Jack Kerouac. First appeared as Chapter 4 from ON THE ROAD. TM/ © 2001 The heirs of the late Jack Kerouac, under licence authorized by CMG Worldwide Inc. www.cmgw.com.

THOSE VANISHED I RECOGNIZE by Tom Piccirilli, © 2002 by Tom Piccirilli. First appeared in THE MUSEUM OF HORRORS by Dennis Etchison. Used by permission of the author.

THE VOLCANO DANCES by J. G. Ballard, © 1964 by J. G. Ballard. First appeared in THE TERMINAL BEACH. Used by permission of the author and the author's agent, Margaret Hanbury.

WEASAL AND THE FISH by Peter Turnbull, © 2002 by Peter Turnbull. Used by permission of the author.

HORIZONS by Colleen Anderson, © 2002 by Colleen Anderson. Used by permission of the author.

JOURNEY'S END by Carol Anne Davis, © 2002 by Carol Anne Davis. Used by permission of the author.

ORPHANS by M. Christian, © 2001 by M. Christian. First appeared in TALEBONES. Used by permission of the author.

Introduction

"I see nobody on the road," said Alice.

"I only wish I had such eyes," the King remarked in a fretful tone. "To be able to see Nobody! And at that distance too! Why, it's as much as I can do to see real people, by this light!"

Lewis Carroll, *Through the Looking-Glass*

Two roads diverged in a wood, and I
I took the one less travelled by,
And that has made all the difference.

Robert Frost, *The Road Not Taken*

"solo tome
el camino menos
travitado"

This is a book about going, about travelling from point A to point B, although there are more often than not fascinating and devious side roads taken on the same trip. The destinations aren't important here: the people in these tales could be looking for something, running away, or just aimlessly wandering the highways and byways of this world (or other worlds even), playing tourist or innocents abroad. What is important about these stories are the routes they take, the ways they move, the travelling, their unique journeys – the roads they travel and the encounters that occur: joyful, scary and full of so many contradictory epiphanies.

Robert Frost, in the quote above, said it too well: "I took the one less travelled by, and that has made all the difference." When we conceived this anthology we envisioned a travelogue of journeys, a tour guide of ways less travelled, a selection of stories highlighting the different ways writers have viewed the highway and roads in fiction: two lane, white line, nightmares; monotonous journeys in which the dark night of the soul emerges with awful clarity; touching vacation reminiscences; tales of truck stops and gas stations; cops and crooks barrelling down midnight boulevards; rock and roll radials moaning on a concrete snake's back; stories of great wheeled migrations; anguished tales full of sound and fury of love on the run; and others a view out of the window, so to speak, at the various stories and writers who have gassed up the car and headed out for parts unknown with anguish and expectation in their heart.

As writers, the two of us have long roamed the fictional highways of crime, erotica and science fiction, fantasy and horror, and this blend with striking tales of ordinary life has, we feel, come up trumps and opened up the already crowded landscapes of the book and its singular theme. We, of course, were also under the magic influence of the movies, in which a car zooming down an empty road is not just an archetype but an indication of adventure to the nth level (indeed, Maxim curated a major season of road movies for London's National Film Theatre some years back), but we must confess to being amazed at the variations our contributors brought to the party (and, further, the absolutely enormous amount of submissions that made the final choices agonizingly difficult).

We quickly discovered the road trip is more than arriving at the destination. We may have had a map, our plans, but we never foresaw how the travelling, the journey, changed this book and us. The road is here – the asphalt, diesel, the endless parade of telephone poles, and a foot on the accelerator – but something else, something special has also hitched a ride along the way: human nature.

These are road stories, that hasn't changed, from authors famous and established but also many newcomers or visitors from neglected genres, but they are also stories of redemption, of change, of examination, of growth, of doubt, of leaving What

Was on the highway to What May Be.

This book started with a full tank of gas, a new game of Auto Bingo, an itinerary, and a bagful of potential thrills and awkward, enforced relationships, but a mile, then two, then twelve down the mythical road we, and the authors of these stories, discovered things about ourselves and what a good – a really good – road story is all about: not where you're going but what happens to you on the way.

We are grateful to the wonderful writers who went with us on this trip – and who are waiting in just a few pages to play tour guide for you: we hoped for great, but we got excellent. In particular we'd like to thank the estates of John Steinbeck and Jack Kerouac for allowing us to include two undisputed classics of the American highway – for, after all, what Road book could be complete without THE GRAPES OF WRATH and ON THE ROAD? We also wished for variety and were delighted by a spectacular assortment of tales: barrelling big rigs, *noir chases* across alkaline flats, roads beyond Earth, trips full of tears, trips of laughter, trips of terror, and voyages across landscapes recognizable from AA maps and within the human psyche.

In fact, this collection turned out so fascinating and pleasing that it's very tempting to tell too much here, to reveal all the great sights you're going to see along the pages as you read this mammoth book of road tales. Every story is moving in many different ways, inspiring all kinds of feelings – the least of which is to pack your own bag, pick a direction, and start off.

But we won't tell. Like any good book or road trip, you shouldn't know too much about your destination, the end of the trip: the discovery inside yourself and out in the world, is in the travelling itself.

So, buckle up, roll down the window, pack some spare clothes for all weather possibilities, pick a direction and just go. Who knows what you'll find along the way? And that's what makes the road, and this book, so special. And take your time! Speed is not of the essence.

Remote Viewing

Mat Coward

"Whatever you need, you carry it on your back. If you can't carry it on your back, you don't need it." That was my uncle's motto, when I was a kid and he and I used to run away from home together, which we would do about once a month in the summer and very rarely in winter. I got my love of aimless travel from Uncle Raymond – aimless travel disguised as journeying. Whether I got anything else from him, I suppose time will tell.

In the army, a similar principle applied: if you hadn't been issued with it, you didn't need it. At 0800 hours Tuesday morning, I'd been issued with a road atlas of Great Britain, ten shillings in cash, and a Ford Cortina.

"Driving a civilian VIP," I was told. I was to consider myself under the command of the VIP, I was to wear civilian clothing, and I was to report back to my sergeant at 0900 on Saturday with, if I knew what was good for me, most of the ten shillings intact.

I didn't care. I was not quite nineteen, and driving around in a civilian car, wearing jeans and a T-shirt and sunglasses, sounded like a much better way of spending a summer's week than marching and attending training lectures and cleaning weapons. Even with a civilian in tow.

I was laid low with lust for her from the first moment I smelled her. I'd been leaning against the car, the road atlas open on the bonnet in front of me; not planning the trip – I had no idea where we were going – but browsing, running my finger along curvy roads, letting my head rest in unvisited market towns and unheard-of villages. It was a lovely travelling day, the sky blue but without glare, the morning air warm but fresh. A day of sweatless sun. Everything I needed was on my back, or in my pockets: ten shillings in cash, a full packet of cigarettes, the keys to the Cortina. And my youth. I can say that now, though I wouldn't have believed it at the time – my youth was all I needed, and that was in my pocket too.

You don't smell women's perfume very often in the armed forces, so when the tendrils of her orangey scent hooked into my nostrils and my tongue, I turned and stood to attention in one movement.

She had her hands in the pockets of her white woollen jacket, and her head on one side, and for a moment I thought she'd been looking at me – looking at me, that is, in the same way that I looked at girls when I found myself standing behind them, unobserved. Even as the thought half formed, I knew it couldn't be true. She was a woman, I was a man. She was a civilian VIP and I was a boy soldier. Why would she look at me?

"You'd be Joe," she said, and for a moment her voice – the accent American, the tones far from smooth – so excited me that I couldn't reply. "You *are* Joe? I hope you are."

"Yes, Miss. I'm Joe."

"Not Miss," she said. "Sondra. I'm a civilian, remember? And so are you, today."

"Yes, Miss," I said, and I said it at least partly because I knew it would make her laugh. I don't know how I knew, but I was right.

"OK." She put out her hand and I shook it – a little clumsily, because hands aren't used much for shaking in the army, and I'd been in the army more than a year by then. "They tell you what we're doing, Joe?"

"I'm to drive you wherever you want to go."

"That's all they said? Well, that's OK. Let me see that map, will you."

I stood aside to let her get at the road atlas. She turned to the contents page at the front, told me to hold it open for her against the slight breeze that blew uninterrupted across the parade ground, then reached into an inside pocket of her jacket and came out with a blue oval crystal hanging on the end of a knotted thong. She held the crystal out over the map, and closed her eyes.

Needless to say, I hardly noticed the crystal, let alone wondered about it. She had her eyes closed, which meant I could study her at my leisure.

Appropriately enough, as I relate this Cold War footnote for the first time, I find myself looking at the nearly nineteen-year-old soldier, this boy Joe, as if through a telescope attached to a time machine. Turning a memory into a narrative is a completely different process from simply remembering; when I remember that Joe, I'm him, thirty years on. But when I make him into a character in an anecdote (anecdote, I think, is a fitter word than footnote, in all honesty), I view him remotely, from a distance. I can tell you things about *him* that I couldn't know about a younger version of *me*.

For instance, I can analyse why he was so stricken with wanting for Sondra. She was about forty, with untidy, darkish hair pushed back from her face. Her features were somewhere between pleasantly nondescript and moderately irregular. Her figure was ordinary; slim for her age, but ordinary. She had busy, intelligent eyes, and she wore nice perfume. I can analyse his attraction to her, which was immense and immediate, and I have no trouble identifying its basis: she fancied him. His body knew that, even though he didn't, and sometimes that's all it takes.

Joe, naturally, did not analyse the matter. What was there to puzzle over? He was nearly nineteen and male. She was younger than his granny and older than his niece. And female, and not ugly. Joe was unaware of the existence of – could not have imagined, at his age, the existence of – any subtler criteria than that.

And she wore nice perfume and her eyes smiled.

"OK," said Sondra, after dangling the crystal for a minute or so. "Turn to page eleven, Joe, will you." I did. She closed her eyes again, dangled some more. I noticed that the crystal travelled in circles on the end of its thong; anti-clockwise for a few turns, then clockwise. When it stopped altogether, she opened her eyes and winked. "Righty-ho, Joe – you about ready to go?"

I drove east, under her orders, in the direction of an old wool town in Suffolk. (I don't think I'll say which one. I've been out of the army a hell of a lot longer than I was in it, but old habits die hard, and some of them for good reason.) We went with the windows open, and we didn't hurry because Sondra said she didn't need to hurry or want to hurry. As soon as we cleared the base, she lit a long American cigarette and asked me if I'd like one. I told her I wasn't allowed to, because I was on duty.

"This week you're a civilian, remember?"

"Well – OK, thanks."

"And if anybody asks, you're my nephew. OK?"

She asked me why I was laughing and I told her that I only had one aunt, and she was an agricultural worker in Devon, who measured four foot in all directions and had worn false teeth since she was seventeen, following a fall from a hayloft. "What did she fall onto?"

"My granddad."

"Oh *God*," said Sondra, her eyes wide with laughter. "And was he – "

"Don't worry. His were already false."

So she lit another cigarette and reached over and slipped it between my lips, and I tried not to let her see that I'd tasted her lipstick in case that might offend her.

"Well," she said, "I'll take your hilarity as a compliment."

I didn't look at her. I didn't dare.

"But if anyone *does* ask us, that's who you are. OK?"

"Your nephew."

"Right." She sniffed extravagantly, and waved her hand in front of her face. "You know, the air really smells of shit a *lot* around here."

"Mostly farmland along this road. If you don't like it, I could go onto the motorway."

"If I don't like it? Joe, who would *like* the smell of shit?"

"Actually, it's one of the things I like best about driving on country roads. You get the smell of cows, then a second later there's the cow parsley from along the hedgerow. Then the exhaust from a lorry going the other way, then – "

"Then back to the cow shit. Lovely." I noticed that she didn't close her window, though. She might not like the smell of cows, but she liked being on the road. Just like me.

After a while, Sondra said, "She a good person, this Devon aunt of yours?"

"She's smashing."

"Well, I'm your other aunt. Aunty Sondra from New York. OK?"

"OK, Aunty Sondra."

"And I'm smashing, too. I don't want to have to get jealous of a woman with no teeth."

There was *so* much less traffic on the roads thirty years ago, that it's almost impossible to imagine, let alone remember. I don't suppose there's any such thing as a quiet country road in Britain any more, unless you're somewhere fantastically remote in the highest Highlands, in which case where would you be driving to?

I don't drive much today. I don't need to, and I don't choose to. We have two cars, of course – everybody has two cars, and yet no-one can understand why the roads are so crowded – but my daughter's the only person who ever uses them for anything more than shopping or commuting. It's years since I've done any actual *motoring*.

Extraordinary to think that as recently as the early 1970s, even in southern England, away from the main roads you could drive for miles without worrying about overtaking or being overtaken or getting stuck in a jam. I once drove halfway from Somerset to Yorkshire with my headlights on in daylight, because there was no-one coming the other way to flash me to tell me that they were on.

Extraordinary to think of Joe, on that journey, as happy as he'd ever been in his life; as happy as he'd been when he was a kid, and he and his Uncle Raymond used to run away from home in the summertime.

About ten miles short of the town Sondra had told me to head for, we got stuck behind a slow tractor and trailer on a narrow, hedge-lined road curling between big, flat fields. After five minutes of crawling along, I apologized.

"Don't worry," she said. "I told you, I'm not in any hurry. Is the weather always this fine in England?"

"Always," I said.

"Tell you what, next crossroads we come to, pull over for a moment."

After another five minutes of the tractor's bum, I pulled onto the verge.

"All right," said Sondra. "Let's see what we see." She had the pendant in her hands again, and her eyes closed.

"Don't you need the map?"

"No, not this time. Hush now, let me concentrate."

She was wearing a denim skirt. It wasn't especially short, but I could see her knees and the lower stretch of her slightly plump thighs. I looked at them for a few minutes, while a wren barked at us from a holly tree. The driver of a post office van clicked me a wink as he passed us, and Sondra opened her eyes.

"You don't ask many questions, do you? For a nephew."

"I'm in the army," I said.

"So you are." She took the road atlas out of the glove compartment, and laid it open on my lap. "Here – this village. Should be about a mile away."

"Right you are."

We drove slowly through the village's one main street. Sondra loved the patch of common with the big oak tree, and the sagging old cottages that looked as though one good door-slam would cave them in.

She told me to stop outside a newsagent's. While she went into the shop, I stood by the car enjoying the noisy stillness character-istic of a living village on a weekday. A breeze brought the unmis-takeable suet smell of school dinners, and then a moment or so later another breeze carried the shouts of children echoing on tarmac.

"That one cottage we passed on the outskirts of the village? Standing on its own? Let's go there." She'd been gone ten minutes. She hadn't bought a newspaper, or anything as far as I could see.

We parked a little way down from a small, white cottage, which was surrounded by a buzzing, riotous garden. Sondra took out her crystal, and let it circle above her lap until it changed direction. There seemed to be less ritual involved than there'd been when she was working with the map; she didn't even close her eyes.

After a while, an elderly man wearing a waistcoat and old suit trousers came out of the cottage and began deadheading roses. "OK," said Sondra, taking a camera out of her patchwork shoulder bag. She snapped a few photos of the old man, then she said, "That'll do for today. Let's find lunch. You know what I'd like? A real olde worlde English village inn."

"All right."

"First, I need a telephone kiosk."

The pub we settled on was more old than olde worlde, but Sondra seemed satisfied. Lunch consisted of a ploughman's with mustard pickle, and a pint of Watney's each.

I watched her eating. I watched her drinking. Her lips were small and her tongue was large.

"You don't have to commit me to memory," she said. "I'm going to be around all week."

"Sorry," I said, covering my blush with my beer glass.

She patted me on the arm – the left arm, just above my watch-strap, with four fingers above and the thumb underneath, like a doctor taking a pulse. But nothing like that.

"You can ask questions, you know. It's up to me whether I answer them or not."

I tried to think of a question, because I thought it would please her. "Are you really a civilian?"

"Not exactly, but yes. You understand?"

I chewed a small piece of rubbery cheddar. "That phone call – what'll happen to the old man?"

She smiled over her glass. "You *are* quick, aren't you? You're my quickest nephew. I must've had a real smart brother."

The way she said it irritated me. "You did say I could ask."

"OK. Well, I don't know – what does happen to communists in this country? They get put in charge of labour unions, as far as I can see."

"How do you know he's a communist?"

She widened her eyes, and swilled the beer around in her glass. After a moment, she reversed the motion, so that the beer circled clockwise. I must have looked shocked, or impressed, or something else inappropriate, because she put the beer down and shook her head. "No, listen. You know in the newspaper shop? I showed the owner a letter signed by your Home Secretary, and asked him for a list of everyone in the area who subscribes to the *Morning Star*. Seems sensible, no? You buy a communist paper, you've got to be a commumst. There was only one guy on the list, but one is enough."

I had to bolt my bread and cheese to catch up with her. "Where to next?" I asked, as we got back into the car. "More wrinkly Reds?"

"Just drive," said Sondra. "How about that?"

I just drove. The afternoon oozed away. We stopped to watch some old geezers playing bowls, somewhere in the Midlands. "We seem to be heading north," I said.

She shrugged. "You're the driver."

We found a hotel – a pub that did rooms, really – in a market town in Lincolnshire. Sondra paid cash for two rooms, for "me and my nephew".

For dinner, we went to a Chinese restaurant. She said she'd never had such bad Chinese food in her life, a fact which seemed to delight her. I said I preferred Indian anyway, and she said, "Ooh, what a sophisticated nephew!"

"Look, I wish you wouldn't keep saying that. Frankly. About the nephew thing."

Under the table, she tapped my knee with soft knuckles. "Don't be impatient."

I told her a lot about me, and she told me a little about her. She was a New Yorker, Jewish, and from what she called "a blue-collar background".

"There aren't many of us in the company I work for, you know what I mean? And those that there are tend not to get the choicest assignments."

I wasn't entirely sure what she meant. I could guess what blue collar meant, but I've never been someone who likes guessing. I prefer to know for sure. In the army, especially, guessing is rarely a good idea.

"Blue collar? You don't know what blue collar is? Let me see, what parallel term do you use in Europe – oh yeah, that's it: peasant."

From the restaurant, we walked to the local cinema. She took my arm, the way an aunt might. During the film she held my hand. We had a nightcap in the bar of the hotel, then we went to bed. I stayed awake as long as I could, but whatever I thought I was waiting for it didn't occur.

There's something about driving for the joy of it that makes it a very *immediate* experience. So much of life is nostalgic, even when you're doing it, but driving – perhaps because of the motion, or the concentration it requires, or the never-quite-absent risk – always happens in the present.

At breakfast the next morning, she said, "Scotland. Can we get to Scotland in a day?"

"Sure."

"I'd love to go to Scotland. Can we see Loch Ness?"

"I'm not sure if we'll get that far north in a day," I said. "But Edinburgh's nice, so I've heard."

"Edinburgh! They got a castle there?"

"You know they have, Sondra." I *wasn't* her nephew.

She rapped the table. "Hey, Joe – let me take my excitements how I choose, OK? So: do they have a castle in Edinburgh?"

"Yes," I said. "A big one."

In the car I offered her the map, but she shook her head. "You're not using the pendulum today?"

"I will if you want me to."

"Why would I want you to?"

"So you can cover your ass."

"Cover my arse?"

"Listen. On Saturday, back at your base, you'll be debriefed. They're going to want to know exactly where we went, who we saw, what we did. Specifically, what *I* did."

"OK," I said. "Let's get a picnic."

We stopped at a little supermarket in the suburbs of a city and bought some French bread, some fancy cheese, some apples and a jar of pickled onions.

"The thing is, Joe," she said, as we drove on, eating the apples, "I'd prefer it if you told them what I tell you to tell them."

"Rather than anything as olde worlde as the truth, you mean? So, for the purposes of my debrief, what *did* you do?"

She crunched for a while, and I tried not to notice the juice on her chin. "You know what a Parapsychological Surveillance Programme is? I hope you don't, because if you do you're a spy and I'll have to kill you and bury you in the woods."

I didn't know, of course.

"Why I'm here, Joe, is British security have been told by a defector that there are secret ammo dumps all over this country, maintained by British Reds, fifth columnists. Yeah? For sabotage work, when the Soviets invade."

"And are there?"

"My people don't take it seriously. Which is why they've sent me to dowse for them. Dowsing – that's the thing with the pendulum, OK? Now, the British don't yet know that's what I'm doing – they just think I'm some kind of expert."

"In what?"

She chuckled. "Good question, honey. In finding secret commie ammo dumps by driving around the countryside in a Ford car with a handsome young chauffeur, I guess. Anyway, it all cements the special relationship between our two great free nations. The British think they're getting the benefit of the latest thing in experimental counterintelligence, my guys get to justify the budget for my section – which takes some doing, believe me – and me, I get a vacation. Which, incidentally, I've been owed since Nixon was in short pants."

I threw my apple core out of the window. "This is your idea of a holiday?"

Sondra turned in her seat to look at me, and she smiled and kissed me, with her lips slightly apart, on my neck just below my left ear. "I'm enjoying it," she said. "Or, what – you have something *better* you'd rather be getting paid to do on a Wednesday morning in midsummer?"

We were passing through an ancient, stone-built village at that moment, going so slowly that we could hear a toddler's cry of fearful delight as a large duck erupted from an old millpond to snatch a bread crust from his hand.

Our first kiss. Even if it was only one-way. I concentrated on the road; I didn't have all that much experience of driving civilian vehicles.

"What if there really are secret Russian ammo dumps?"

She waved at a vicar, standing outside a mediaeval church smoking a cigarette. "Honey, if things ever get to the stage where such a question becomes important, then believe me we're all dead anyway."

For the picnic, I found a humpy field, empty but for butterflies and dried-up cowpats. There was no rug in the car, but she didn't seem to mind. I sat with my back against a tree stump, and she lay with her head on my legs. Just above the knees.

I told her that this was what we did in this country, in the summertime. Pull off the road and picnic in empty fields, looking out at the view. Everyone – mums and kids, grannies and kids, old married couples.

"Young lovers?"

"I suppose so. Some families come back to the same spot year after year, for generations."

"It's nice," she said. "Thank you."

"Ideally, we should have brought a bat and ball – we could have played French cricket."

She was puzzled. She twisted her head to look up at me. The friction of her movement gave me vertigo. "Not English cricket?"

"I think French cricket *is* English."

"So is this bread, Jesus," she said, reaching into the supermarket bag.

"It is a bit hard, I suppose."

The cheese was soft, but entirely tasteless. The pickled onions, Sondra informed me, after biting one in half, were "disgusting". She took the uneaten half from her lips and popped it into my mouth. "Here, you finish it. You're used to this stuff."

I could hardly swallow. The onion was wet along its bitten edge, with vinegar and with her saliva. "You're really not all that keen on British food, are you?"

"If I ever get to try any, I'll let you know."

"OK," I said. "Tonight we'll eat haggis."

We did. It was very tasty. Halfway through the meal – in an Edinburgh hotel so smart it made me nervous – I told Sondra what haggis was, hoping to see her spit it onto her plate.

She chewed slowly, ran her tongue around her lips in a show of bliss, and said, "Listen, honey, I'm a New Yorker – I was weaned on deli food. You want to freak me out, you're going to have to do better than a sheep's stomach."

"Is that a challenge? All right, tomorrow we'll head for the coast. We'll see how you do with winkles."

Now she choked. "Winkles? Are you *sure* you pronounced that right?"

Our rooms were next to each other. I don't know how it happened, precisely – I can't seem to see Joe as a character during this bit, only as my younger self – but somehow, at the moment when we should have separated in the corridor, we didn't. We both went into her room, she put her arms around me and I kissed her mouth.

When she broke away – I don't think I ever would have – she said, "I'd been thinking we wouldn't do this until the final night. To make it special."

"It will be special for me," I said, because I wasn't embarrassed by the significance of what was about to happen. "As long as you don't say anything about nephews."

"Call me Miss," she said, when we were naked and on the bed. "Call me Miss, right in my ear. Say it right in my ear and hard and again."

"OK, this is the deal," said Sondra, at breakfast. "We just have a good time, and I'll leave the pendulum in its sacred sack."

"All right."

"It'll mean visiting a few more newsagents, that's all."

"OK."

"You don't have a problem with that?"

"What, with giving the funny boys a list of communists they already know about?"

She shook her head. "Not that. I mean taking a vacation on the firm's time?"

"I was told to consider myself under your command."

"Ooh!" She reached beneath the drape of the linen tablecloth and squeezed my thigh.

I smiled, but I was embarrassed; the hotel thought she was my aunt.

"What about lying in the debrief?" she asked.

In my naivety, I laughed then at her naivety. I'd joined the army because I didn't want to be a local government officer like my dad, or a farmworker like both my granddads. And so far, it was looking like a pretty bloody good decision: they served *seven* different types of marmalade at this hotel. You didn't have to ask for them, they were just there on the table! "They said I was to take your orders. So, if you order me to tell them only what you tell me I can tell them . . ."

"Orders is orders, right?" Her smile was wry, though I couldn't think why it should be.

"Right."

"OK, Friday night we'll go through the script. Today – Edinburgh."

"The castle."

"A big one, I believe you said?"

After a morning sightseeing, and an afternoon in bed (because it was a big castle, but it wasn't *that* big), we had our evening meal at the hotel, and then checked out. Sondra had decided she wanted to experience a night drive. "On those little twisty roads, the stars above and the rabbits in the headlights – wouldn't that be something?"

At dusk, we set course for Wales. I told her she couldn't do a tour of Britain, visit England and Scotland and miss out Wales. "It would be a diplomatic faux pas."

"They're easily upset, the Welch?"

"They are if you call them Welch."

She loved Wales. She'd loved England and Scotland, but today she really loved Wales best of all. "I think maybe I am Welch, way back. What do you think?"

"I don't know," I said. "Maybe you're part Welch, part Scotch, and part Englitch."

"Oh, stop teasing." She took her hand from mine for a moment, to slap my bottom. "Or don't stop. I don't care which."

We couldn't find any winkles, but I did buy her a Kiss Me Quick hat, which she wore with pride and dignity – but only after telling the man selling them that she'd prefer one that said "Kiss Me Slowly". With the kind of straight face that couldn't possibly have been faked, he replied that he didn't have any. "No demand, love."

Llandudno's delights swallowed most of our day, though we did make time to psychically divine and physically photograph a couple of communist saboteurs near Welshpool. This being our last afternoon, we enjoyed a cream tea in Gloucestershire and gradually drifted back east. We ended up in a modest, comfortable hotel an hour's drive from my base.

Along the way, I asked her what the point of her Parapsychological Surveillance Programme was, if even she didn't believe it actually worked. (I wasn't terribly interested, to be quite honest, but I was keen to avoid any conversation which might involve the word "tomorrow".)

"The point, honey, is the same as the point of all Cold War expenditure – if *we* spend a couple of billion on spooky science, that means the Russians have to spend a couple of billion too. In fact, they have to spend more, because they're playing catch-up. They have to act on the assumption, however unlikely it sounds, that we're making progress. Same reason we keep building more missiles than we could ever possibly use. Or sending people to the moon, or whatever. So they have to do it too."

"But won't that just prolong the Cold War?"

"God, I should hope so!"

That was the first thing she'd said that really shook me. "You don't *want* disarmament?"

"Listen, honey. World War Two was fought in Russia. It wasn't fought in America. OK? That simple fact is the history of the last quarter century in a nutshell. The war made the Russians poor, and us rich. The US can carry on spending billions on all this crap for as long as it takes. But the Soviets can't. Sooner or later, communism will go bust, and we'll have won." I said nothing, so she nudged me, and added, "Which is a *happy* thing, right?"

"What will we have won?"

"Territory, nephew! Land. What the hell else is there?"

"There's always tonight," I said, something I'd read in an American novel, and having said it I blushed so hard I went blind and almost crashed the car. We almost didn't have sex that night, because Sondra was still laughing so hard she couldn't keep still enough for me to hold onto her until well after midnight.

It's only looking back now, remote viewing my childhood, that I realize my Uncle Raymond was fairly mad. I always knew he was eccentric, but at this distance I can clearly see that he was also mentally ill to a pretty advanced degree. Whenever we returned from running away, my mother used to cry and squeeze her knuckles against her teeth, and cuddle me and slap me at the same time. I see now that she was, in fact, relieved beyond endurance; and not, as I thought at the time, simply overacting.

Uncle Raymond gave me my love of the unplanned journey when I was young, but I think his early death also, in a way, took it away from me. Joe, the child and the youth, wanted to be

Raymond; Joe the grown man feared, for a while, that he might become Raymond.

After she'd climbed out of the Cortina, at the base on that Saturday morning, Sondra and I never met again. I can hardly believe we ever met at all. I left the army in my mid-twenties, and joined the civil service. I did useful work for twenty-five years, and retired early without regrets.

The CIA's dabblings with parascience are well known today, the subject of many books, magazine articles and television shows. The Agency apparently got nowhere with such work, and abandoned it after a few years and a few billion dollars. No-one named "Sondra" appears in any of the books or articles or programmes, so far as I can discover. It probably wasn't her real name. And anyway, as she said, people like her never got the choicest jobs.

To me, now, the most extraordinary aspect of it all is the realization that she enjoyed me as much as I enjoyed her. To young Joe that idea was – and remains – inconceivable.

Almost awake, on Saturday at the dawn with my chin on her neck, I asked her if what she did worked.

She half sat up and shook her head. "Does it *work*? Joe, honey, how could something like that *work*?"

"I don't know. I don't know how computers work, but I know they do. They took us round one, in training."

"Computers are *science*, Joe. You're talking about a crystal on the end of a string, for Christ sake. Listen – have you ever prayed?"

I had prayed once. I prayed I'd pass my eleven-plus, so my mother wouldn't be upset.

"And did it work?"

"I didn't pass the exam. My dad went crazy."

"Well, there you go. The world is less mysterious than we think. Sensible things work and crazy things don't work. Missiles work, pyramid-power doesn't work. It's a dull old world, honey, which is why you got to keep moving."

We managed another hour's sleep, and then another hour's not sleeping, proving – to me, at least – that crazy things do work. We didn't have breakfast. That was the first time in my life I had ever missed breakfast, other than through severe illness.

As we approached the perimeter of the base, seconds away from returning to the province of the sensible, of the missiles and their sacerdotal keepers, Sondra squeezed my leg hard enough to hurt. She kept looking straight ahead, in case anyone was watching, and after a moment she took her hand away and shifted on her seat as far towards her door as possible.

Just before she reclaimed her hand, she said, "It *does* work, Joe. But don't you tell anyone, OK?"

I didn't look at her. I kept driving at a steady roll. "It does?"

She smiled. "Sure, honey. How else do you think I found you?"

Migrant People

John Steinbeck

The cars of the migrant people crawled out of the side roads onto the great cross-country highway, and they took the migrant way to the West. In the daylight they scuttled like bugs to the westward; and as the dark caught them, they clustered like bugs near to shelter and to water. And because they were lonely and perplexed, because they had all come from a place of sadness and worry and defeat, and because they were all going to a new mysterious place, they huddled together; they talked together; they shared their lives, their food, and the things they hoped for in the new country. Thus it might be that one family camped near a spring, and another camped for the spring and for company, and a third because two families had pioneered the place and found it good. And when the sun went down, perhaps twenty families and twenty cars were there.

In the evening a strange thing happened: the twenty families became one family, the children were the children of all. The loss of home became one loss, and the golden time in the West was one dream. And it might be that a sick child threw despair into the hearts of twenty families, of a hundred people; that a birth there in a tent kept a hundred people quiet and awestruck through the night and filled a hundred people with the birth-joy in the morning. A family which the night before had been lost and fearful might search its goods to find a present for a new baby. In the evening, sitting about the fires, the twenty were one. They grew to be units of the camps, units of the evenings and the nights. A guitar unwrapped from a blanket and tuned – and the songs, which were all of the people, were sung in the nights. Men sang the words, and women hummed the tunes.

Every night a world created, complete with furniture – friends made and enemies established; a world complete with braggarts and with cowards, with quiet men, with humble men, with kindly men. Every night relationships that make a world, established; and every morning the world torn down like a circus.

At first the families were timid in the building and tumbling worlds, but gradually the technique of building worlds became their technique. Then leaders emerged, then laws were made, then codes came into being. And as the worlds moved westward they were more complete and better furnished, for their builders were more experienced in building them.

The families learned what rights must be observed – the right of privacy in the tent; the right to keep the past black hidden in the heart; the right to talk and to listen; the right to refuse help or to accept, to offer help or to decline it; the right of son to court and daughter to be courted; the right of the hungry to be fed; the rights of the pregnant and the sick to transcend all other rights.

And the families learned, although no one told them, what rights are monstrous and must be destroyed: the right to intrude upon privacy, the right to be noisy while the camp slept, the right of seduction or rape, the right of adultery and theft and murder. These rights were crushed, because the little worlds could not exist for even a night with such rights alive.

And as the worlds moved westward, rules became laws, although no one told the families. It is unlawful to foul near the camp; it is unlawful in any way to foul the drinking water; it is unlawful to eat good rich food near one who is hungry, unless he is asked to share.

And with the laws, the punishments – and there were only two – a quick and murderous fight or ostracism; and ostracism was the worst. For if one broke the laws his name and face went with him, and he had no place in any world, no matter where created.

In the worlds, social conduct became fixed and rigid, so that a man must say "Good morning" when asked for it, so that a man might have a willing girl if he stayed with her, if he fathered her children and protected them. But a man might not have one girl one night and another the next, for this would endanger the worlds.

The families moved westward, and the technique of building the worlds improved so that the people could be safe in their worlds; and the form was so fixed that a family acting in the rules knew it was safe in the rules.

There grew up government in the worlds, with leaders, with elders. A man who was wise found that his wisdom was needed in every camp; a man who was a fool could not change his folly with his world. And a kind of insurance developed in these nights. A man with food fed a hungry man, and thus insured himself against hunger. And when a baby died a pile of silver coins grew at the door flap, for a baby must be well buried, since it has had nothing else of life. An old man may be left in a potter's field, but not a baby.

A certain physical pattern is needed for the building of a world – water, a river bank, a stream, a spring, or even a faucet unguarded. And there is needed enough flat land to pitch the tents, a little brush or wood to build the fires. If there is a garbage dump not too far off, all the better; for there can be found equipment – stove tops, a curved fender to shelter the fire, and cans to cook in and to eat from.

And the worlds were built in the evening. The people, moving in from the highways, made them with their tents and their hearts and their brains.

In the morning the tents came down, the canvas was folded, the tent poles tied along the running board, the beds put in place on the cars, the pots in their places. And as the families moved westward, the technique of building up a home in the evening and tearing it down with the morning light became fixed; so that the folded tent was packed in one place, the cooking pots counted in their box. And as the cars moved westward, each member of the family grew into his proper place, grew into his duties; so that each member, old and young, had his place in the car; so that in the weary, hot evenings, when the cars piled into the camping places, each member had his duty and went to it without instruction: children to gather wood, to carry water; men to pitch the tents and bring down the beds; women to cook the supper and to watch while the family fed. And this was done without command. The families, which had been units of which the boundaries were a house at night, a farm by day, changed their boundaries. In the long hot light, they were silent in the cars moving slowly westward; but at night they integrated with any group they found.

Thus they changed their social life – changed as in the whole universe only man can change. They were not farm men any more, but migrant men. And the thought, the planning, the long staring silence that had gone out to the fields, went now to the roads, to the distance, to the West. That man whose mind had been bound with acres lived with narrow concrete miles. And his thought and his worry were not any more with rainfall, with wind and dust, with the thrust of the crops. Eyes watched the tyres, ears listened to the clattering motors, and minds struggled with oil, with gasoline, with the thinning rubber between air and road. Then a broken gear was tragedy. Then water in the evening was the yearning, and food over the fire. Then health to go on was the need and strength to go on, and spirit to go on. The wills thrust westward ahead of them, and fears that had once apprehended drought or flood now lingered with anything that might stop the westward crawling.

The camps became fixed – each a short day's journey from the last.

And on the road the panic overcame some of the families, so that they drove night and day, stopped to sleep in the cars, and drove on to the West, flying from the road, flying from movement. And these lusted so greatly to be settled that they set their faces into the West and drove toward it, forcing the clashing engines over the roads.

But most of the families changed and grew quickly into the new life. And when the sun went down . . .

Time to look out for a place to stop.

And – there's some tents ahead.

The car pulled off the road and stopped, and because others were there first, certain courtesies were necessary. And the man, the leader of the family, leaned from the car.

Can we pull up here an' sleep?

Why, sure, be proud to have you. What State you from?

Come all the way from Arkansas.

They's Arkansas people down that fourth tent.

That so?

And the great question, How's the water?

Well, she don't taste so good, but they's plenty.

Well, thank ya.

No thanks to me.

But the courtesies had to be. The car lumbered over the ground to the end tent, and stopped. Then down from the car the weary people climbed, and stretched stiff bodies. Then the new tent sprang up; the children went for water and the older boys cut brush or wood. The fires started and supper was put on to boil or to fry. Early comers moved over, and States were exchanged, and friends and sometimes relatives discovered.

Oklahoma, huh? What county?

Cherokee.

Why, I got folks there. Know the Allens? They's Allens all over Cherokee. Know the Willises?

Why, sure.

And a new unit was formed. The dusk came, but before the dark was down the new family was of the camp. A word had been passed with every family. They were known people – good people.

I knowed the Allens all my life. Simon Allen, ol' Simon, had trouble with his first wife. She was part Cherokee. Purty as – as a black colt.

Sure, an' young Simon, he married a Rudolph, didn' he? That's what I thought. They went to live in Enid an' done well – real well.

Only Allen that ever done well. Got a garage.

When the water was carried and the wood cut, the children walked shyly, cautiously among the tents. And they made elaborate acquaintanceship gestures. A boy stopped near another boy and studied a stone, picked it up, examined it closely, spat on it, and rubbed it clean and inspected it until he forced the other to demand, What you got there?

And casually, Nothin'. Jus' a rock.

Well, what you lookin' at it like that for?

Thought I seen gold in it.

How'd you know? Gold ain't gold, it's black in a rock.

Sure, ever'body knows that.

I bet it's fool's gold, an' you figgered it was gold.

That ain't so, 'cause Pa, he's foun' lots a gold an' he tol' me how to look.

How'd you like to pick up a big ol' piece a gold?

Sa-a-ay! I'd git the bigges' old son-a-bitchin' piece a candy you ever seen.

I ain't let to swear, but I do, anyways.

Me too. Let's go to the spring.

And young girls found each other and boasted shyly of their popularity and their prospects. The women worked over the fire, hurrying to get food to the stomachs of the family – pork if there was money in plenty, pork and potatoes and onions. Dutch-oven biscuits or cornbread, and plenty of gravy to go over it. Side-meat or chops and a can of boiled tea, black and bitter. Fried dough in drippings if money was slim, dough fried crisp and brown and the drippings poured over it.

Those families which were very rich or very foolish with their money ate canned beans and canned peaches and packaged bread and bakery cake; but they ate secretly, in their tents, for it would not have been good to eat such fine things openly. Even so, children eating their fried dough smelled the warming beans and were unhappy about it

When supper was over and the dishes dipped and wiped, the dark had come, and then the men squatted down to talk.

And they talked of the land behind them. I don' know what it's coming to, they said. The country's spoilt.

It'll come back though, on'y we won't be there.

Maybe, they thought, maybe we sinned some way we didn't know about.

Fella says to me, gov'ment fella, an' he says, she's gullied up on ya. Gov'ment fella. He says, if ya ploughed 'cross the contour, she won't gully. Never did have no chance to try her. An' the new super' ain't ploughin' 'cross the contour. Runnin' a furrow four miles long that ain't stoppin' or goin' aroun' Jesus Christ Hisself.

And they spoke softly of their homes: They was a little cool-house under the win'mill. Use' ta keep milk in there ta cream up, an' watermelons. Go in there midday when she was hotter'n a heifer, an' she'd be jus' as cool, as cool as you'd want. Cut open a melon in there an' she'd hurt your mouth, she was so cool. Water drippin' down from the tank.

They spoke of their tragedies: Had a brother Charley, hair as yella as corn, an' him a growed man. Played the 'cordeen nice too. He was harrowin' one day an' he went up to clear his lines. Well, a rattlesnake buzzed an' them horses bolted an' the harrow went over Charley, an' the points dug into his guts an' his stomach, an' they pulled his face off an' – God Almighty!

They spoke of the future: Wonder what it's like out there?

Well, the pitchers sure do look nice. I seen one where it's hot an' fine, an' walnut trees an' berries; an' right behind, close as a mule's ass to his withers, they's a tall up mountain covered with snow. That was a pretty thing to see.

If we can get work it'll be fine. Won't have no cold in the winter. Kids won't freeze on the way to school. I'm gonna take care my kids don't miss no more school. I can read good, but it ain't no pleasure to me like with a fella that's used to it.

And perhaps a man brought out his guitar to the front of his tent And he sat on a box to play, and everyone in the camp moved slowly in toward him, drawn in toward him. Many men can chord a guitar, but perhaps this man was a picker. There you have something – the deep chords beating, beating, while the melody runs on the strings like little footsteps. Heavy hard fingers marching on the frets. The man played and the people moved slowly in on him until the circle was closed and tight, and then he sang "Ten-Cent Cotton and Forty-Cent Meat." And the circle sang softly with him. And he sang "Why Do You Cut Your Hair, Girls?" And the circle sang. He wailed the song, "I'm Leaving Old Texas," that eerie song that was sung before the Spaniards came, only the words were Indian then.

And now the group was welded to one thing, one unit, so that in the dark the eyes of the people were inward, and their minds played in other times, and their sadness was like rest, like sleep. He sang the "McAlester Blues" and then, to make up for it to the older people, he sang "Jesus Calls Me to His Side." The children drowsed with the music and went into the tents to sleep, and the singing came into their dreams.

And after a while the man with the guitar stood up and yawned. Good night, folks, he said.

And they murmured, Good night to you.

And each wished he could pick a guitar, because it is a gracious thing. Then the people went to their beds, and the camp was quiet. And the owls coasted overhead, and the coyotes gabbled in the distance, and into the camp skunks walked, looking for bits of food – waddling, arrogant skunks afraid of nothing.

The night passed, and with the first streak of dawn women came out of the tents, built up the fires, and put the coffee to boil. And the men came out and talked softly in the dawn.

When you cross the Colorado river, there's the desert, they say. Look out for the desert. See you don't get hung up. Take plenty water, case you get hung up.

I'm gonna take her at night.

Me too. She'll cut the living Jesus outa you.

The families ate quickly, and the dishes were dipped and wiped. The tents came down. There was a rush to go. And when the sun arose, the camping place was vacant, only a little litter left by the people. And the camping place was ready for a new world in a new light.

But along the highway the cars of the migrant people crawled out like bugs, and the narrow concrete miles stretched ahead.

Diversion

Elizabeth Counihan

On the morning the diversion occurred I was in a bad mood because of Mr Forbes.

He was one of my regulars and there was, as usual, nothing wrong with him – physically that is. He appeared at the surgery about every two weeks, opening with the line: "Doc, you know I never come to see you unless it's really necessary, but . . ." Then he would come out with his latest self-diagnosis.

I would look at his tall, rangy figure; the sticking-plaster holding his spectacles together; his knobbly knees protruding from khaki shorts; his wad of NHS notes, stacked on my desk and thicker than many a cancer patient's. I would listen impatiently to his droning voice. I wanted to see a real patient, one with gall stones, angina, bronchitis – someone I could cure – not nerdy Mr Forbes.

"I think I have Asperger's Syndrome," he said.

For once I agreed.

"Well," I said, "you could have the trait. Borderline of course . . ."

"It's in the autistic spectrum. High intellectual function, poor social skills . . ."

And sartorial style.

"A tendency to obsessive interests . . ."

Hill walking in all weathers and talking endlessly about it to people like me who wear high heels and tight skirts and obviously don't want to know.

"Many sufferers work in the IT industry . . ."

And look everything up on the internet so they know more than their doctors.

He continued at length. He knew his stuff, of course, as usual.

"Mr Forbes, as you will appreciate, the condition isn't reversible and is compatible with a normal life – a responsible job, like yours."

He looked so sad. I felt a stab of guilt. I told him I would refer him to a counsellor. I rummaged for a leaflet with a helpline.

"'Fraid I'm in a bit of a rush, Mr Forbes. Got a clinic in Tunbridge Wells at 1.30."

"Oh, then I mustn't keep you, Doc. There are roadworks on the A264 for six weeks from today with diversions through Cowden and that could extend your journey time by between ten and twenty-five minutes."

His eyes swam behind the bottle-glass spectacles. "You're always so kind, Doc. That's why I like a lady doctor." I smiled frigidly, hating myself.

In the pouring summer rain I could barely make out the scrawled diversion sign. Nevertheless the road was blocked across both carriageways – an amateurish confusion of trestles and logs. I fumed. Where was I supposed to turn off the road?

A scarecrow figure approached waving its hands. Alarmed, I locked the doors but opened the driver's window a crack.

"Where am I supposed to turn off?"

A scrawny arm pointed left. Down that muddy track?

"Down there, Missus. Sorry it's a bit narrer but it soon widens out." He ran ahead, his raincoat flapping. I registered that he was not dressed like a navvy, that there were no road drills or other equipment near the road block, that there were no vehicles other than mine. But I was angry. I was going to be late: would have no time for lunch before the clinic started. Ignoring all inner warnings I span off the road. My wheels churned up a muddy spray spattering the man as I passed. I saw him through the rear window waving, smiling.

The car lurched, the sides scored by bushes, the windscreen lashed by whippy, green-tipped branches as I squeezed through. I was in a green tunnel, a twitten as we call it in Sussex. The wheels skidded in mud and for a moment I was stuck. I heard a thump from behind and saw the scarecrow-man's grinning face in my rear mirror. The car rocked as he pushed at the rear bumper, then it jumped forward out of the rut, spraying more mud. I saw the man's face, indistinct now, camouflaged by smears of mud, then his figure receded and merged with the trees behind me, his arms waving like branches. I fought with the wheel, cursing at the rasping of wood on my paintwork but scared too, scared that I had been sent into some kind of ambush.

Suddenly the car broke free and I was in the open again. And I saw a road. My eyes stung with tears of relief. I rolled onto it and stopped at the verge, shaking but laughing at my fears.

Where was I?

I dug out a Sussex/Kent roadmap, followed the A264 to Tunbridge Wells, but searched the map in vain for a parallel road; a narrow, brown road winding into green hills under a sky so translucently blue I felt I should have seen through to the stars. There was no rain, no clouds, no puddles. There were no houses, no haze above the far hills. No people.

I flipped open my mobile phone. No signal.

I looked around carefully in every direction – no bushes nearby for robbers or rapists to hide behind. I opened the door and climbed out onto the springy wayside grass and found myself taking deep breaths, inhaling the faint perfume of grass, moss and earth. A bird was singing. I could see it, a tiny speck high in the clear air.

Still no signal from my phone. Still no one in sight.

I looked at the road surface; a bumpy, iron-coloured material – iron slag – where had I heard that term?

Well, the road must lead somewhere. Wherever it went I would certainly be late for the clinic but sooner or later I would find my way out of this communication blind spot, then I would telephone the hospital.

I started the engine and set off, the suspension bouncing and creaking on the strange surface; I supposed it to be suitable for tractors and suchlike, certainly not for my little Ford. Unable to go much above thirty, I wound down the windows and resigned myself to enjoying the trip. After five miles or so my worries returned. I had seen no turnings off the road, no other vehicles and not a single dwelling in any direction. I had seen birds, some brown long-eared rabbits and a couple of deer, but no domestic animals. The mobile still indicated "no service".

Then I discovered that the radio hissed and crackled but wouldn't broadcast in any frequency. I fumbled for a cassette and switched it on. Berlioz's Hungarian March blasted out at full volume. So if it wasn't mechanical failure why didn't the radio work?

Trembling, I stopped the car and turned the music off. I got out and checked the aerial was intact.

I listened to the stillness. My face was brushed by a gentle breeze. Then I heard a bird singing. There were no other sounds. In this busiest part of England there was no distant drone of traffic nor sound of aircraft on their way to London. I could have been in the far north of Scotland, but no, the countryside was warm and lush with grass and pale green trees in full leaf – Sussex not Scotland.

Had I strayed onto some hidden part of the countryside, some Government or military area, a secret area not shown on maps? Between two busy towns? Ridiculous! Then I must be asleep and had dreamed the whole thing.

But from when?

I went through the entire day in my mind – everything normal and rational until I reached that road block . . .

Should I go on or back? After at least five miles in this direction I must be nearing Tunbridge Wells. I insisted to myself that there had to be a turning very soon.

The land had been rising gradually for several minutes and I realized that I was almost at the brow of the hill. I started the car again and edged forwards to the top to look down into a valley, a green goblet full of sunlight. At the bottom a river flowed clean across the road. There was no bridge.

I was just about to make a U-turn when I saw movement near the river. A figure rose up from beside the road and I saw a blur of white face as it turned in my direction, then two arms waving. Was this someone who could tell me how to get onto the right road? I found myself driving slowly, bump, bump, down the side of the hill to the waterside.

It was a woman, now sitting on a roadside boulder. There was no one else. I made sure of that, and I had a clear view. I opened the door and got out but was careful to stay near enough to the car to get away quickly.

She raised her head and I saw a lined, middle-aged face surrounded by long brown hair. She was dressed in brown too – a long loose garment that reached to her feet. She smiled. "You got here quickly," she said. "I thought I would have to wait at least another hour."

"Perhaps you could tell me what's going on since you were expecting me," I said, "and there had better be a good reason or . . ."

She smiled again. "Or what? When it happened to me I said I would send for the police, or was it my solicitor? I can't remember it was so long ago. In fact there is not a thing you can do about it so the best thing would be if you sat down here and let me explain."

I stood belligerently and told her to go ahead.

"You've been chosen, you see. It's just down to luck. You happened to be passing on Midsummer Day – wrong place at the wrong time. You'll get used to it."

'What are you talking about? Will you just direct me to the next turnoff for Tunbridge Wells? I have a clinic in – " I glanced at my watch – "ten minutes."

She went on smiling benignly at me like some hippie earth-mother.

"Tunbridge Wells? I was trying to get to Midhurst. That was Midsummer seven years ago and my time is up. It's over to you now."

I tried to convince myself that the woman was a wandering client of Care in the Community. I reminded myself of the dictum of one of my teachers of psychiatry – if you can't decide who is nuts, you or the patient, then it's the patient. It didn't work. I looked around at the landscape, hushed, unpeopled, expectant.

If she was psychotic, so was I.

I dropped down beside her and sat uncomfortably on the tussocky grass, my skirt wrinkling halfway up my thighs, my heels digging into the turf.

"There are always nine of us," she began. "We walk the roads for an allotted time of seven years. Then a replacement is chosen and we can return to our own places."

"Look," I said, "this is nonsense . . ."

She sighed. "I can't explain it. I've been asking everyone I met through the years. They say it 'keeps the ways of Britain' and it's 'just the way it's always been'. It's quite nice once you get used to it. People respect you, feed you and shelter you. The wild creatures are your friends. The seasons follow you."

"Wildlife is great on TV but not in the flesh and I like seasons from indoors. I'm going to drive back now. If there is anyone I can call . . ." I waved my phone, averting my eyes from the flashing "no signal" icon.

"It must be hard for you," she said. "You are clearly someone of consequence." She gestured towards my Ford. "That's a wonderful-looking vehicle, the latest thing I suppose."

"It's an ordinary Ford," I retorted irritably. "They've been around for years." I was startled by the sudden fear in her face.

"I have not seen a car like that. Surely it cannot have been available seven years ago." I shrugged and said I was no expert on cars but that this model had been around for quite a long time. She was shaking and beginning to cry.

"I was taken in 1956. What . . . what is the year that you come from?" Hardly believing that I was colluding in her delusion, I told her. Then I got up and went towards the car. She ignored me; she was sobbing wildly. I turned the ignition. Nothing happened.

"It's no good, there's no way back for you," she muttered. "And it seems I won't really be going back either. It's as I feared, the trick, the old, old trick," she added in a choked whisper. As I looked her figure wavered. She lurched to her feet and suddenly she was changed. The brown robe had gone and for an instant I saw her in a tight costume with a mid-calf hemline – like someone in an old black and white movie. Then she vanished.

I felt unfamiliar clothes flapping about my legs and in the way of a dream found myself robed in brown, wearing sensible leather boots and holding a walking staff. But unlike in most dreams, where the weirdest happenings are accepted as matter of fact, I knew that this was all wrong.

At that moment I began to believe in magic.

I left my vehicle, already overgrown with grass like an ancient statue, and forded the river. It was fast-flowing but shallow and my boots behaved as sensibly as they looked. I reached the far side and marched slowly up the hill, leaving a trail of wet footprints. I had no idea where I was supposed to go or do but I kept walking. That seemed right.

Soon I felt hungry and remembered my missed lunch. Perhaps the magic that provided a dreary robe and clumpy boots would also supply something to eat. I sat down and made an inventory like people always do in stories about desert islands. Under my brown outfit my Marks and Sparks underwear had been transformed into something scratchy and ecologically sound – the term "homespun" came to mind, although I have never been quite sure what it means. More interestingly I had a leather belt with a satchel buckled to it, also a leather bottle attached by a leather string. The water in the bottle tasted stale but was at least wet and I was very thirsty. The satchel contained a change of homespun, together with my own comb, make up and purse, even the useless phone and yes – some bread and cheese. Recklessly I ate the lot – it was probably food poisoning now and starvation later – well, let the bloody fairies or whoever sort that one out.

I trudged on. The sun continued to beat down and I found the hood attached to my outfit quite useful. I had to admit that the clothes really were remarkably comfortable for walking, loose and somehow cooling. I reached the high point on the far side of the valley. Now I looked into more rugged terrain. The brown road wound into the depths of a tree-lined gorge which fell away in stark iron-coloured cliffs towards something that glinted white as snow.

The sun was still high – a relief to me as the woods on each side were dense and oppressive. But I was descending into shadow with the sun at my back until I dipped below it. There was a cool breeze now and I drew my robe more tightly around me. The utter solitude weighed on me and I began to think of who or what might hide in the forest.

When would people start looking for me? Fervently as I wished it, I knew that it was too soon to hope. When I failed to arrive for evening surgery maybe . . . Would someone have the sense to check with the hospital and so find out that I had never taken the clinic? Or perhaps no one would notice until the following morning. I remembered that Ian was in Holland this week and unlikely to telephone. I stopped for a moment to wipe my sweaty palms on the robe; my whole body throbbed with the beat of my heart.

Just then a troop of four or five deer wandered out of the trees. They were exactly like the Ashdown Forest deer I had so often cursed when they ambled across the road, delaying me as I speeded from one house call to another in the real world. But these were a welcome sight and they approached me fearlessly. The leading one – a doe I think – came right up to me and looked at me seriously. The others, one almost a baby, followed her. They kept to the verge but kept pace with me, so near that I could smell a faint animal smell. My eyes filled with tears at their comforting presence. Hadn't the brown woman said that the wild creatures would be my friends?

Like an escort of honour the deer followed me down onto the depths of the valley. In that clear air everything was vivid to my senses — the honey smell of clover by the roadside, the streak of a hawk falling out of the sky like a dark comet, the shriek of the invisible animal that fell to its talons. My eyes scanned constantly for signs of human life, for someone that might help me, but in vain. I was shivering a little and anxious to reach the bottom of the valley and start the ascent on the sunlit side. Soon I realized that the white and silver gleam I had seen far below was a swift-flowing river and I could hear

the roar of rapids. There was a hump-back bridge across it –
something man-made at last and an indication that I would
not have to ford the rushing stream. There was a long way to
go and the shadows were lengthening rapidly now.

Long before I reached the bottom I felt the chill of dusk. I
hurried downhill, loose chippings from the road rolling ahead
of me. The deer broke into a trot. Suddenly they stopped, ears
pricked. I heard a faint cry coming from the woods to my left.
The deer darted across the road in front of me and disappeared into the trees on the right. The cry was repeated –
something I recognized from wildlife programmes – the howl
of a wolf. I might be in some dream fairyland but this sounded
very real. I dashed forward towards the bridge. I saw to my
horror that the whole valley was now in shadow; the sun must
have set behind me. Dark shapes loped beside me. I found the
breath to scream. The wolves kept up their easy lolloping pace
but came no closer. I could hear their breathing, smell their
breath. Then the sound was overwhelmed by the noise of the
water, still gleaming white in the dusk. I reached the bridge
and leaned on its wall, completely spent. I shut my eyes,
expecting a heavy body to knock me down, for sharp fangs to
tear at me. After a moment I opened my eyes. The animals
had stopped in a line along the water's edge, dark shadows that
looked at me but came no nearer. They lifted their heads and
howled in unison. The world went black and I felt myself fall.

The next minute I was sitting on the hard stone of the
bridge and someone was putting my head between my knees.
The wolf howls became whimpers and then tailed off into
silence.

"You must be the new Walker," a voice said. "Didn't you know
that the wild creatures will never harm a Walker?" I muttered that
I had heard that animals would be friendly but hadn't taken it
literally.

I looked up, my head still swimming a little. My attendant was
a thin, oldish man with a goatee beard. It was nearly dark now and
I couldn't see much else.

"I don't think Nancy has tutored you properly. She was in such a hurry to get home, not that it will do her much good." He seemed pleased about that. "Come with me. I have food and shelter for you," he said.

A few minutes later I was sitting on a wooden bench in a small candle-lit room eating a meat and dumpling stew accompanied the some kind of rustic bread. I had entered the house or whatever it was (I couldn't be sure in the dark) through a round opening covered by a rough curtain. Inside a glowing stove as well as the candles flung crazy shadows at the rough walls. It was like the inside of a cave – or a hobbit hole. I kept looking at my host as he dished out the stew – no furry feet, but in the half-light I could not convince myself that his ears didn't stick up in points from his straggly grey hair.

After a couple of mugs of beer as well as the very welcome food I was too tired to argue any more, even to ask questions. The old man handed me a blanket and showed me a mattress over against the wall. I lay down without a murmur, my last thoughts being that I would surely wake back in my own bedroom, that the dream would be over.

I was wrong of course.

The dawn chorus woke me, not my alarm clock. The curtain had been pulled back to reveal the kind of half-light I only saw when reluctantly dragged out of bed to visit a sick patient. By its inadequate glow I perceived that I was still inside the strange hobbity dwelling. I sat up with a groan then disentangled myself from the blankets and went outside.

The doorway gave straight onto a grassy slope that ran down to the river. I could see the hump-backed bridge and hear the swish and rattle of the water. Unseen birds filled the air with their song. It was still night on the other side of the river and the stars glittered in more shades of blue, ruby and white than I had ever seen. I imagined that a cloak of indigo velvet strewn with precious jewels was being drawn westward across the sky to reveal an even more beautiful garment of gold and pink and faintest green and edged with grey cloud. I saw stern faces with glittering eyes and felt the presence of great and mysterious beings that knew nothing of me. Frozen in that moment of awe I could have fallen down like any of my most primitive ancestors and worshipped them as the Goddesses of Night and Day but when my host called to me the spell was broken.

Sitting over a bowl of a glutinous porridge I asked again where I was, what I was supposed to be doing and how I could get out of it. His answers were that we were in Britain, that I came "from the shadows" and that I had been chosen as one of the nine Walkers to replace Nancy who had done her time.

"Why me?" I wailed. "I'm a doctor, a useful kind of person back in 'the shadows', as you call it. I've got a boy-friend who will miss me. I've got parents. Who chose me for this anyway?"

He shrugged. "That would be the Hedge People. They cross over into the shadowlands." This, it appeared, was his idea of an explanation.

"How do I get out?" I demanded.

His goatee wagged. "It is an honour to serve and after seven years you are free," he said with a nasty grin.

I vaguely recalled some old folktales in which people disappeared off into Fairyland for a great all-night party only to go home in the morning and find that years had gone by. Is that what had happened to Nancy?

"Do you have to help me?" I asked suddenly. He looked shifty. I noticed that his eyes were yellow.

"Well?"

"All must aid the Walkers when asked . . ."

"Then I'm asking," I said, leaning towards him in what I hoped was an intimidating manner. "Has a Walker ever got away before seven years were up?"

He scratched his chin and muttered. I told him to speak up and his muttering became an admission that there was a tale . . . that it was said that . . . maybe one mortal had bucked the system but he didn't know how or who. Finally he admitted that Robin might know. Robin was "wise in such matters". I could find Robin if I followed the road down into the next valley until I came to a crossroads; there I should call for him.

I thanked him for his hospitality and set off at once continuing eastwards up the hill. An owl accompanied me to the top, then flew off to roost somewhere for the day.

I completed the walk to the crossroads by noon. Two red squirrels shared the remains of my bread and cheese. "You're welcome to it," I said, remembering hot black coffee and rolls. The thought of seven years eating traditional country food filled me with horror.

The ritual was not too difficult – an arrangement of twigs and feathers placed at the intersection of the road with a rough track that ran across it from the dense encroaching woodland; then calling a name three times. And there he was sitting on a tree stump. It was as if he had sat there all the time but that I had failed to notice him, or he had not allowed me to. He waved to me and jumped down. He was quite short, the size of a boy of twelve or so, but certainly no child.

"How can I help you, Walker?" he said.

"There's been a mistake. I shouldn't have been chosen. I'm just not the type."

"There is no type," he replied gravely. "Anyone from any shadow-time can be a Walker. The Hedge People find someone when a replacement is needed. They do tend to be arbitrary. They probably liked the look of your horse or flybug – no – car. It would be a car, wouldn't it, in your time?" I didn't understand what he was talking about and I only wanted to know one thing.

"I heard that one person escaped. Is there a way? I think the rules force you to tell me."

His face crinkled in a mischievous smile but he nodded. "There was one. He was a . . . I think you would say Lord in your time. He persuaded his servant to take his place. I don't believe you have servants of that kind in your shadowland."

But I was beginning to see a gleam of hope. "Are you saying that if I can find someone willing to change places with me . . . ?"

He said, "The other must be truly willing. If you can find such a one then you can go back to your fogs and noise and crowds, if that is what you prefer. But is it not better to walk the true, unchanging land? To know that you are keeping the shape of the roads that join it together? To spend seven years seeing the rivers and forests, the birds and animals, the mysteries and legends that have shaped your country?"

"Not for me," I said. "I want my own time, my friends, my job. But I do know of someone. How can I call?"

Robin waved his hand airily. "You still have your shadow device," he said.

I fished the mobile phone from a pocket. "But it doesn't work here . . ." My words trailed off when I flipped it open and it bleeped into action . . . searching . . . Pooktel net.

I dialled directory enquiries, then a number.

It took him less than a day to reach me. I was sitting on the tree stump at the crossroads eating a wrinkled apple and some nuts brought to me by the squirrels. Robin had long since merged into the forest. Two hares sat at my feet. A thrush perched on my shoulder.

"I came as quickly as I could, Doc," he said.

"I'm amazed. I thought you would think I was crazy."

"You're no crazier than I am, Doc. Funny things are always happening in this world, you know, but most people just don't see them. You try reading the *Fortean Times* if you don't believe me." He looked around smiling. The sun flashed on his glasses.

"I can't thank you enough, Mr Forbes," I said.

"It's me that must thank you, Doc. This is my sort of place. Seven years eh?" He grinned from ear to ear like a kid.

I saw Mr Forbes suddenly enveloped in a brown robe. He bent down to stroke one of the hares. A bird flew to his shoulder. I felt myself *fading*.

I had been missing three days but far from sending out search parties everyone seemed to think that I had been on a course, that I had booked it months ago.

Perhaps I had some kind of breakdown. But I don't think so. I think Mr Forbes was right. People rationalize "funny things". I know this now because I subscribe to the *Fortean Times* in memory of my ex-patient, now on the hill-walking holiday of his life.

Just Drive, She Said

Richard Paul Russo

Night.

Ahead of us, the road ended at a washed-out bridge, but we were driving for it at eighty-five miles an hour. Moonlight lit the barricades, the ruins of the bridge dangling over muddy water below.

"Jesus!" I said, trying to look at her. She pressed the gun harder into my temple.

"Just drive," she said.

I drove.

It wasn't even my car.

It was my sister's, an ugly brown Mazda RX-7 that drove fast and smooth. I'd borrowed it for a few days, and Friday night I drove to a nearby liquor store to pick up some wine – something to get me through another empty weekend.

I was inside for fifteen or twenty minutes. With three bottles of wine in hand, I walked back to the car. I unlocked the door, opened it, and the overhead light went on.

A woman sat in the passenger seat pointing a gun at me. She didn't move, silent and intense, and I thought she was trying to decide whether or not to shoot me.

"Get inside and close the door," she finally said.

I wasn't going to do anything stupid. I got in, closed the door, and the light went off.

The woman took the wine from me with one hand, and with the other jabbed the gun into my ribs.

"Start the engine," she said.

As I did, strange lights went on in the middle of the dash. The tape deck was gone, replaced by a larger, glistening piece of electronics with dozens of buttons, dials, and readouts. Amber and green lights flickered across the thing, the displays showing figures that were probably letters or numbers, though nothing I recognized.

"What the hell is that?" I asked.

"A probability wave console. Generator, tuner, and amplifier."

Jesus, hijacked by a lunatic.

She jabbed me again with the gun, and said, "Let's go."

"This isn't my car," I told her.

"You think I give a shit?"

No, guess not. "My sister's waiting for me," I said, without much hope.

"Want me to repeat what I just said?"

I shook my head. "Where to?"

"Just go right and drive a while," she said.

The gun was still in my ribs, so I did what she asked.

Her hair was short and dark, and she was wearing blue jeans, a grey sweatshirt, and dark boots. Slim, but strong-looking. She didn't look crazy, I thought, but then what did crazy look like?

As I drove along, she fiddled with the console, and a stream of figures moved across the largest display. She glanced up, nodded toward a wrecked Toyota ahead of us on the side of the road, and said, "That used to be my car." We passed the wreck, and she returned her attention to the console.

A blue light began to blink frantically on the side of the console.

"God dammit," the woman said. "How the hell did she find me so soon?" She pushed another button and a small screen emerged from the top of the console. A glowing map appeared on the screen, with two different blinking lights a few inches apart.

"Turn right at the next corner," she said, "and hit the gas. Move this crate."

I turned and accelerated. Traffic was light, but I still had to pay attention to other cars.

"Faster," the woman said.

"What about the police?" I asked. Which was a stupid question. I *wanted* the police.

"Fuck 'em," she said. "Just move it."

So I stepped on the gas. I was weaving in and out of traffic now, getting nervous. But whenever I started to slow down she jabbed the gun into my ribs and said, "Keep moving."

She had me make a series of turns, wheels squealing with each one, then we were on a long, open road with hardly any traffic. I was pretty sure the river was ahead of us somewhere.

"Now floor it," she said. I hesitated, and she moved the gun from my ribs to my head. "Floor it, god damn you!"

I floored it.

Which was how, a few moments later, we were headed straight for barricades and a ruined bridge at eighty-five miles an hour.

I should have hit the brakes. What was she going to do, shoot me? But I kept my foot on the gas, the steering wheel straight.

The woman punched a few more buttons. Green lights flashed, bright patterned circles.

Just before we reached the barricades, she jammed a switch on the front of the console.

Everything lurched sideways. At least, that's how it felt, lurched so hard I felt sick. But we were still on the road, still moving straight ahead at eighty-five. Except now the barricades were gone, and stretching out ahead of us, spanning the river and glistening with bright lights, was a whole, undamaged bridge.

We shot across it over the river, came down on the other side, and kept going. I braked through a long, sweeping turn, barely keeping the car on the road, then we were driving along the river road.

I couldn't see much in the dark. It wasn't a part of the city I knew well, but I had been through it a few times, and something seemed out of place.

"Just keep going," the woman said. She was watching a display on the console, a rolling series of figures that made me think of a time counter.

I drove along the river road, trying to figure out what seemed different, but unable to pinpoint anything. About fifteen minutes after we'd crossed the bridge, the console display stopped changing, and flashed a single figure.

"All right," the woman said. "Bring the speed back up."

The gun was gone from my head, but I wasn't about to argue. I accelerated until we were back up near eighty. The woman punched buttons, then again jammed the big switch on the front of the console.

We lurched sideways without moving again, and this time I thought I was really going to be sick. Everything in my vision began to tilt, and I had a hell of a time keeping the car on the road. I hit the brakes and brought the car to a stop, no longer caring what she would do to me.

I left the engine running, put my head on the steering wheel, and breathed slowly, deeply, until the spinning stopped. I straightened and looked at the woman. She now held the gun in her lap.

"Are you all right?" she asked.

"Sure," I said. "Terrific."

"We won't have to go so hard now," she said. "Just coast along at twenty, twenty-five miles an hour."

"Does that mean I start driving again?"

She nodded.

I looked down at the gun in her lap, and nodded back. "Give me another minute or two, will you?" I held up my hand, which was shaking. "I can't drive like this."

"All right."

I sat there, trying to relax, trying to cut down the shakes. The street was nearly deserted; only a few cars drove by, and there were no pedestrians. The cars looked odd, but there wasn't enough light for me to figure out why. Then I leaned forward over the steering wheel and looked at the front end of the Mazda. It was still an ugly brown, but the nose had become more elongated, sharper. The retractable headlights were gone, replaced by conventional stationary lights.

"What the hell is going on?" I asked.

"If it was daylight, you'd see even stranger things," she said.

Which made me look more closely at our surroundings. The nearby streetlight was mounted on an unusually thick metal pole, and gave off a sharp, emerald glow I'd never seen before. The lights in the buildings were brighter, harsher than I would have expected.

"Let's go," the woman said.

I breathed deeply a few more times. Then I put the car into gear, let out the clutch, and swung back onto the road.

We drove slowly, and I kept searching for changes in my surroundings, but it was too dark to see much. The woman directed me through several turns, then onto a freeway.

On the freeway there *were* differences I could identify. The overhead signs were blue rather than green, lit from below by rose-tinted lights. And the street and city names were completely unfamiliar – definitely not English. I didn't think I could pronounce half of them.

"You going to tell me what the *hell* is happening here?"

"Just look for a motel," she said.

"And how am I supposed to recognize one?"

She smiled. "Spelled just the same here as where you're from. It's practically a trans-universal word."

We drove on, and I wanted something to break the silence, to ground me. "Will that thing play music?"

The woman just laughed and shook her head, and I wondered what was so funny. She was right, though, about a motel. From a mile away I saw a bright glowing sign:

MOTEL

As we got closer, I could make out other words, but none of them made sense. There were numbers as well, but there were too many digits, and a strange hooked symbol instead of a dollar sign.

"Hope you can pay for this," I said. "My money's not going to be much good here."

She smiled. "You'd be surprised."

I pulled off the freeway, drove into the motel parking lot, and the woman pointed out the office at the end of the building. She made me go in with her. At the desk, she talked to a crusty old man who wore a black helmet, face covered by a smoky visor. What they spoke sounded like a mix of foreign languages – a few words close to English, others like German, a few like French.

The woman paid with large, brightly coloured bills, and the man gave her a narrow cylinder that hung by a chain from a plastic ball. We walked back to the car in silence, then she directed me to drive around the back of the building, where we parked in front of a tan door. The woman handed the wine bottles to me, took two duffel bags out from behind the seats, then made sure I locked the car. She inserted the cylinder into a narrow opening where it hummed, then clicked; the door swung open, and we stepped inside.

There was a table with two padded chairs, a television set, a radio, and a double bed. The woman set the duffel bags on the floor, and I put the wine bottles on the table; the labels had changed, and were now unreadable. I looked at her.

"There's only one bed."

"We'll manage," she said. "Let's go get something to eat, I'm hungry."

We went to a coffee shop next to the motel, where the woman ordered for both of us. I ended up with something that looked and tasted a lot like a Denny's chicken fried steak and mashed potatoes.

After we ate, the woman said she needed a drink. I figured I could use one too, so we went to the attached lounge and sat at a table in the back corner, empty tables all around us. She asked me what I liked to drink, and I told her Scotch. She ordered from the waiter, and when my drink came it did taste an awful lot like Scotch – cheap Scotch, but Scotch nevertheless. The woman was drinking something clear over ice.

"A trans-universal," the woman said. "Alcohol, coffee, and tobacco. Hotels and motels are close, along with guns and cars, but alcohol, coffee, and tobacco are almost everywhere."

Right. We drank. One drink, two drinks. Then a third. I was feeling it. We didn't talk, but we had another drink. I didn't know about her, but I was getting smashed.

"What's your name?" I asked. Drunk, I was feeling reckless, and it seemed like a reckless question.

"It would sound like garbage." She paused. "Call me Victoria." Another pause. "What's *your* name?"

"Robert."

"Robert." She nodded. "Robert, do you have any idea what's been happening to you?"

I shook my head.

"Of course not. Ever heard of parallel universes?"

"Sure. As an idea, not something that actually exists."

"They exist. We've been moving from one to another." She signalled for two more drinks, then looked at me for a minute before going on. "The console in the car? It generates probability waves that slip us from one universe to another."

The drinks came, and she drank half of hers immediately. It was a crazy idea, but how *else* had I come to this place? We sat for a while in silence, drinking. Actually, I kind of *liked* the idea of travelling between universes. It beat hell out of sitting alone in an empty apartment all weekend.

"Wait a second," I said. "How the hell do you know how to speak from one place to another? You can't *know* all these languages."

She shook her head. "I don't." She tapped at the base of her skull. "But *this* does. Batch of microchips planted in my head." Then she stretched out her arms. "Robert, I'm wired. I've got a built-in receiver running through my whole body. Every time I shift universes, my body pulls in all the radio and television signals, whatever's out there, and the batch in my head does the rest. In ten or fifteen minutes, I've got enough of the language to get by. That's how I picked up your slang. And each time I shift places, I shift languages. Or I can lock onto one, like I have with yours." She paused. "I like being able to talk to you."

I looked at her for a minute.

"Why? Why are you travelling between universes? And who the hell is after you?"

She didn't answer. She returned my gaze for a while, stood, then said, "Let's get back to the room."

Without thinking, I opened my wallet to leave a tip. My paper money had changed from green to the brightly coloured bills I'd seen Victoria use.

"Just like the car," Victoria said. "Anything that's not alive." She took two small bills from my wallet, left them on the table.

I felt a lot drunker as we walked back to the motel. Or maybe it was just overload. I felt I was moving through water. Or mud. It seemed like a long trip across the parking lot, but we finally reached our room and went inside.

I dropped into one of the chairs. Victoria sat on the bed with her back against the wall. Someone in the room above us kept dropping things onto the floor.

"When I first opened the car door and saw you," I said, "it looked like you were trying to decide whether or not to shoot me."

Victoria shook her head slightly and smiled. "I would never have shot you."

"Maybe you shouldn't tell me that. Maybe I'll just take off."

"Yeah? Where the hell are you going to go?"

I shrugged.

"No," she said. "I was trying to decide whether or not to take you with me."

"Why did you? Hostage?"

She shook her head again, the smile gone. "I've been lonely," she said. "I just wanted the company."

I didn't say anything. She pushed up from the bed. "I'm going to take a shower." She turned away from me and walked into the bathroom, closed the door.

Find the gun, I thought. But only for a moment. I didn't really care where the gun was, I didn't want to have anything to do with it. What I did instead was undress and get into bed. I was beat, still half drunk, and I needed the sleep.

But I *couldn't* sleep. I lay wide awake, waiting for her to return. It had been a long time since I'd been involved with anyone, and that had been a woman who spent all her time on speed of one kind or another; I'd begun to feel like I was moving in slow motion whenever I was with her. Now I felt as if *I* had been on speed most of the evening. I closed my eyes, but that didn't help. I waited.

I opened my eyes to the covers being pulled away, and Victoria standing over me, naked and wet from the shower. She was a completely normal woman, whatever universe she'd come from.

She crawled across the bed on all fours, dripping onto my skin as she leaned over me. She blew air across my belly, through the hair between my legs. She moved down toward my thighs, and straddled me.

"I'm too drunk," I said.

She looked down at my crotch. "No you're not," she said.

"I'm too tired."

"No you're not."

"I don't even know what you are," I said.

"What do you think I am?" She moved forward, lifted slightly, then lowered herself onto me, warm and moist. She smiled. "Just drive," she said.

I drove.

She wouldn't talk about where we were going, or why. I had the feeling she didn't have any particular destination in mind, that she was just shifting from one universe to another at random, trying to lose her pursuer. For a few days, it seemed to work.

I got used to the changes. Or rather, to the *idea* of change. Each day we made at least one shift, usually two. Once we made three, which was a mistake – I got sick all over the front seat and nearly ran the car into a concrete channel on the side of the road used by people on cable-powered skateboards. After that, we shared the driving, and stuck to two shifts a day.

Everything changed – the car, our clothes, money. Language changed, occasionally becoming so close to English that I could understand it again, but usually becoming completely unintelligible. And the world around us changed.

Once we emerged into a domed city, buildings reaching to the dome itself and through it, jutting into the open sky above. Another city was a maze of narrow roadways with hundreds of footbridges above the streets, connecting the stone buildings in a vast, chaotic network of bent and twisted metal. And once we came out onto a cracked and potholed concrete road in the middle of a dry, gutted wasteland, flat ruins for miles in all directions, no signs at all of life. We shifted out of there as soon as we could.

We spent several hours a day on the road. Sometimes we shifted at lower speeds, which was easier on me, but which, she said, made for smaller jumps that were easier to track. And though she could make a second shift as soon as fifteen or twenty minutes after the first, Victoria liked to put as much actual distance between shifts as possible. Left a tougher trail to follow, she said.

We spent much of the time driving in silence, but we did talk a little. I talked about my own world, my universe, my life – which wasn't much. I was in charge of the Documents Department of a large corporate law firm. I liked the job itself but working for asshole attorneys all day long had become almost unbearable. And my personal life was hardly fulfilling. But I talked about it all, and once in a while Victoria would talk about what it was like travelling between universes.

"Do you ever stop running?" I asked once. "I mean, how long can you keep it up? Don't you ever get a chance to just stop for a while?"

Victoria nodded. "When I've made enough shifts over a long period of time, it gives me distance. I get a few days, a couple of weeks. I'll just stay in one place for a while, relax, or maybe do something to pick up some money. But eventually I have to leave, start shifting again."

"You can't lose them?"

She shook her head and tapped the console. "These damn things leave a trail in the wake of the probability waves. Make enough shifts and you can make the trail faint, but a good hunter will always be able to pick it up eventually."

Hunter. And I was travelling with the hunted.

Victoria did talk about bringing me back to my own universe. First couple of times she mentioned it I didn't say anything. I was thinking about it. But I liked the idea of staying with her.

"I don't want to go back," I finally said to her.

It was dusk. Victoria was driving through the outskirts of a haze-filled city, blue flashes of light bursting silently and sporadically high above us. The streets were nearly deserted.

"You don't know what the hell you're talking about," she said. "You can't just stick around for a while and then change your mind, get a plane flight home."

"I realize that."

"You realize shit." She turned onto a busier street. Lights were coming on in buildings, and the blue flashes were increasing in frequency. "Just look for a goddamn motel, all right?"

Neither of us said anything for a while. The street seemed to be headed for the city centre, and it got busier and more crowded, brighter and louder. A couple of miles along, Victoria pulled into the parking lot of a run-down motel set back in the concrete pilings of an overpass. She drove into a slot, switched off the engine, and turned to me.

"Look," she said. "The farther we get away from your universe, the harder it'll be to get back. We get far enough away, it'll be impossible. You'll be stuck out here somewhere, no way back. And travelling with me isn't the safest thing you can do. I've had people hunting me for two years. Some day they're going to catch up with me. You aren't going to want to be around when they do." She paused. "I've been on my own for years, and that's the way I want it. I like your company, but I'm not about to make this permanent. You're holding me up, for Christ's sake. You can't handle more than two shifts a day. On my own, I can do five or six before it hits me that hard." She paused again. "You understand what I'm saying?"

"I'll get used to it," I said.

"Not soon enough for me."

"I don't want to go back."

"Christ." She turned away from me, opened the door, and went to check in.

Three more days. Travelling, shifting, no resolution, no final decision. Then, one morning, driving slowly through the heart of a city, we shifted, and dropped into the middle of a war.

We went from bright afternoon sunshine to grey skies darkened by clouds of ash. From laughter and shouts and purring traffic to screams and sirens and gunfire. From busy but orderly streets filled with calm pedestrians and cyclists to chaos, people running from shelter to shelter, and vehicles burning on the roads.

I saw the crater in front of us just in time, swerved, and jolted up a kerb, knocking over a metal canister that spilled fuming liquid across the sidewalk. I got the car back on the road, but half a block ahead of us was a barricade manned by armed soldiers. Huge guns were aimed directly at us.

I hit the brakes and made a half-accidental U-turn, downshifted and punched the gas. Gunshots exploded, something hit the car, but we were still going.

"Shift us the hell out of here!" I screamed at her.

"I can't, you fucking moron! It's too damn soon!"

I turned down the first side street, nearly losing control of the car, then, seeing more barricades up ahead, swung into an alley that dead-ended in a heap of trash.

Victoria was out of the car before it stopped, shoving aside the trash – blocks of foam rubber, huge wads of paper, and other light-weight bundles. I drove the car into the opening she'd made, half burying the car in the mound. I got out, locked the doors, and helped her finish hiding the car with the foam blocks and wadded paper.

No one seemed to have followed us. I wondered if we should have just stayed in the car, but Victoria was already crawling through a broken window into one of the buildings lining the alley. I followed her inside.

The building was dark, and nearly silent; the only sounds came from outside, muffled by the brick walls. There was enough light coming in through the grimy, cracked windows for us to make our way. I followed Victoria through jumbles of complex machinery.

"Where are we going?" I whispered.

"I want to get above ground level. I'll feel safer. Then we can find a window where we can keep an eye on the car."

She found a stairway, and we went up. The doorway to the second floor was scarred and warped, the door blown off its hinges. We went through it, and came out in a maze of clear-walled cubicles filled with cracked glass cylinders.

We made our way through the maze, the floor covered with

huge chunks of broken glass and twisted coils of wire. Every step made loud crunching sounds. Eventually we reached a window looking down on the alley, only to see half a dozen people dressed in fatigues and carrying weapons. At first I thought they were searching the alley, but it soon became clear that they were actually making camp for the night. The car looked to be safe, but we had no way to get to it.

The soldiers erected a structure that was half tent, half lean-to against the brick building across the way, and started a fire inside a squat metal cylinder.

We watched the soldiers and the fire for a while, but it was obvious they weren't going to leave, so we set up for the night ourselves. We cleared a space to sleep in, scrounged some scraps of cloth and some torn cushions to make a bed. Then we tried to sleep.

I didn't sleep much. Sporadic gunfire sounded throughout the night, and bursts of bright colour regularly lit up the window, reflecting shards of light from the broken glass and the cubicle walls.

I was glad when dawn came. The sky outside was overcast, a gradually brightening grey. I went to the window. Below, the soldiers were breaking camp. One of them extinguished the cylinder fire while the others broke down the lean-to and packed it away.

"It looks like they're leaving," I said.

Victoria joined me at the window. We watched the soldiers pack, and about a half-hour later they gathered together, talked for a few minutes, then marched half-heartedly out of the alley. They turned left onto the main street, and were soon gone from sight.

"Let's wait a while," Victoria said. "Make sure they don't come back for anything."

The soldiers didn't come back, but a few minutes later a woman appeared at the mouth of the alley. She was quite tall, with long, light hair tied into a double tail, and wearing a dark green, form-fitting coverall. She hesitated, looking down the alley, glancing in all directions.

"Jesus H. Christ," Victoria said, her voice hardly more than a whisper.

I realized then that this had to be her pursuer.

The woman started into the alley, walking slowly, looking up and down the walls of the buildings.

"What happens if she finds the car?"

"She'll find it," Victoria said.

The woman was two-thirds of the way down the alley, almost directly beneath us, when a shout brought her to a halt. She turned. At the mouth of the alley was a group of soldiers; maybe the same group that had camped overnight.

One of the soldiers called out something, and the woman responded. I couldn't make out what they were saying, it wasn't loud enough, but I wouldn't have understood a word anyway. Victoria just shrugged when I asked her.

The woman took a few steps toward the soldiers, then stopped. The soldiers came into the alley, marched down it, and surrounded her. She gestured at the street, then at one of the buildings. I could see her smiling. One of the soldiers jabbed at her shoulder. The woman kept smiling. Another soldier shrugged, pointed up at the sky.

Suddenly one of the soldiers raised a handgun, put it against the woman's temple, and fired.

The woman's head jerked – I jerked – and she crumpled to the ground, blood running onto the gravel and pavement. Victoria made a sharp, quiet sound and gripped my arm. My own hands gripped the windowsill, nails digging into wood.

The soldiers didn't touch the woman. They looked down at her, but they didn't search her, didn't move her, nothing. They stood around for a few minutes, smoking cigarettes, then walked out of the alley.

Victoria and I stood at the window in silence, looking down at the woman's body, the dark spreading pool of blood.

"Did you want her dead?" I finally asked. Hoping the answer would be no.

Victoria shook her head.

"Would you have killed her if she'd caught up to you?"

She hesitated, then shrugged. She was pale, the first time I'd ever seen her when she didn't seem completely self-assured. I didn't feel too good myself.

"That's it," she said eventually. "You're going back."

I didn't say a word. I still didn't plan to go back, but I didn't think it was the time to argue.

We waited a long time. Two hours, maybe three. The soldiers never returned. The dead woman lay undisturbed, her feet in the shafts of sunlight that broke through the clouds and the jagged building roofs.

Eventually we went downstairs and crawled back out through the broken window. We crossed the alley to the dead woman. Victoria knelt beside her, went through the coverall pockets and removed a block of keys and a wad of money. She murmured a few words in a language I'd never heard, touched the woman on her chest, shoulders, and throat, then gently closed the woman's eyes. She stood.

"Let's go," she said. "You drive."

We dug out the car, got in. I started the engine and backed slowly down the alley while Victoria played around with the console.

"That way." She pointed down the street as we emerged from the alley. "Go slow."

The street was a mess, but now there were people out on the sidewalks who didn't look like soldiers, and a few other vehicles drove slowly in either direction. We'd gone a couple of blocks when Victoria pointed to a driveway leading through a hedge. I pulled into the driveway, drove through the opening in the hedge, and stopped just behind another car.

"Get this thing turned around so we can pull out in a hurry if we have to."

I did, and left the engine idling.

"Wait here." Victoria got out, walked up to the other car, produced the block of keys she'd taken from the dead woman, and opened the front door. She ducked inside, seemed to do something at the dashboard – another console, I figured.

While she was in the other car, I dug through her bags until I found the gun. I checked to make sure I could work the damn thing, then tucked it between my seat and door.

Victoria left the other car, walked back, and got in beside me. She didn't say anything at first. Instead, she did things with the Mazda's console, working intently for several minutes. Finally she finished and turned to me.

"You're going back," she said. "I am *not* going to be responsible for you being killed."

"No – " I started, but she cut me off, sharp and quick.

"No, nothing," she said. "This isn't the end of it. There'll be someone else after me before long." She paused. "You're going back. I've programmed this thing to make all the shifts, reverse the route we took here."

"It'll take me back?" I asked. "To *my* universe?"

"Close enough so you won't know the difference. Two shifts a day until you're home." She gave me a wad of money. "This should be plenty to get you back. Pretend to be deaf and dumb and illiterate, for Christ's sake, and you'll probably be fine."

"What about you?"

"I'll be taking that," she said, pointing to the car in front of us. "The console in it looks to be working just fine." She turned back to me. "You pull out, and get up to speed as fast as you can. It'll make the first shift as soon as you hit thirty."

"I'd just as soon stay with you," I said.

She got out of the car without answering, shut the door, and came around to the driver's side. I rolled down the window.

"I mean it," I said.

She sighed. "You want me to threaten you with the gun again?"

I gave her a half smile. She leaned through the window and kissed me. Then she pulled back, stepped away from the car. "Go," she said.

I nodded. I put the car in reverse and backed up a few feet. Victoria walked over to the other car, and I stopped. I took the gun, picked what looked to be the most vulnerable spot of the console, and jammed the gun barrel against it. I closed my eyes and pulled the trigger.

I got off six or seven shots, metal flying everywhere, before

Victoria grabbed my arm. She screamed something at me that sounded a lot like, "Asshole!"

I opened my eyes. The console was a mess. I looked at Victoria, who stared at me through the open window. I held out the gun, and she took it.

"You're fucking crazy," she said.

I got out of the car, stood beside her. "Want me to drive?"

She didn't answer. We walked to the other car, and I got in behind the wheel, Victoria beside me. I started the engine, put it in gear, and backed around the Mazda. I shifted gears, moved through the hedge, then stopped at the edge of the street. I looked at Victoria, who was shaking her head, but smiling now.

"Do I have to say it?" she asked.

I shook my head. I let out the clutch, swung the car out onto the street, and drove.

The Road to Cedar Rapids

Greg Beatty

Allan stood on the Dubuque Street overpass. The day was clear. He could see all forty-six cars on I-80. When it was raining or snowing, he could only see the nearer thirty or thirty-one; he could tell how hard it was raining by whether or not he could see the grey Nissan.

But not today. Today he could see all the cars that stood on I-80 westbound, right up to where the road curved. He took a deep breath of the clean summer air, heavy with humidity and town smells. Allan could smell that the Niemeyers were cooking stew, down near Happy Hollow park, and the corn was almost ripe in the fields beyond the trees. The day was especially quiet; Allan could hear the family of raccoons that lived in the nearest Volkswagen arguing in the trunk.

"Allan! You gotta come with me! They say somebody's going to try the road to Cedar Rapids today."

Allan turned to watch his cousin Ray carefully run along the sidewalk towards him, the rope bridge from his uncle's family's property still swinging from his passage on the far side of the street. When Ray got close enough, Allan said, "Yeah. I'll believe that when I see it."

But he let his cousin pull him along the sidewalk, down to the sky bridge across to the Wilsons' back mound. They nodded to Old Man Wilson as they stepped down into his yard, trying to stay mostly on the worn footpath. Wilson was old enough that he still believed in property rights, sometimes, and he had a shotgun.

And Allan didn't bother running through the rest of his side of the argument. He knew his cousin would say that it was true, today was the day a guy was going to make it to West Liberty or Cedar Rapids or, in one ridiculous instance, Joliet. Joliet! Like the roads were ever going to clear that far, Allan thought. They waited for back draught from the phantom cruiser that had hit the abutment back in 1983 to clear, the screams to quiet down before they risked quickstepping across the street itself. Usually they were safe for as much as two to three minutes after the cruiser, though the kirillian flames had cost Ray more than one pair of socks.

Joliet. It was just like Ray to get caught up in the exotic allure of distant cities. If you were going to believe that a man could go from Iowa City to Joliet, why not say he was going to take the road to El Dorado, or Salt Lake City! But Allan didn't say anything. It wasn't like there was anything else going on in his home town of Iowa City today.

An immense brown shape pulled to a nearly silent halt in front of them. The driver, dressed in matching brown, descended most of the way down the gleaming metal ladder that stretched down from the passenger side before leaping to the kerb. His face was drawn. He stepped away from the road, set his package down, and stood there for a moment, shaking.

"Grady," Ray called, nodding. The driver of the UPS van nodded, wiping the sweat away with a handkerchief that looked like it was already pretty moist.

"Raymond. Allan."

"How are the roads today?" Allan asked.

Grady shook his head. "Ugly. A Model T I'd never seen before got crushed by a train out by the Hendersons' place. I think it was the first return for the poor folks inside. You could see the flames in the daylight, and the fender rocked the van when it blew loose."

Grady reached up to pat the underside of his UPS van, his voice calming. "I guess I should just trust the armour plating on this baby. I mean, it keeps me alive when the Big One comes back. But

I just hate the screaming. They've tried to build soundproofing into the insulation, but it's not just sound, so the armour can't keep that out. So I hear 'em."

Allan nodded, ready to walk on, but Ray inched forward. "You mean, you were on, well, above the road when the Big One came back? Is it true? Can you really feel the heat from – "

"Ray," Allan said. "Didn't you want to show me something?" He knew that Ray would bother Grady all day, and from the look of it, Grady still had a bunch of deliveries to haul across the corn. He'd probably have to cross the road proper a bunch of times, and he didn't need to be rattled by remembering all the ghosts that he'd survived. Think on them too much, and that would bring them back anyway, angry and shrieking, and maybe trapped looping near the city, like the old bus that had flipped, always flickering around the same corner, forever.

Ray got the hint, and led him on to the pedestrian mall near the Old Capital Building on the Pentacrest. It was a joke now, to call it the pedestrian mall, since the whole world had been turned into a pedestrian mall, since the cars stopped running, but people get used to calling things by a specific name, and it sticks even when the sense is gone.

The cousins walked down Dubuque and past the gleaming dome of the old Capital. Beyond the building, they could hear the distant call of the polemen guiding barges down the Iowa River, their electric burros humming in the sun, gyros stabilizing the massive barges against the current.

Ray cocked his head. "Sounds like a passenger barge. That means they'll have to get off to switch barges at the dam . . ."

"Well, you decide," Allan said. "I thought you wanted to watch the fool leave for Cedar Rapids. Do you want to do that, or do you want to look the strangers over?"

Ray shifted from foot to foot for a while, kicked a loose stone at one of the town squirrels, and said, "Maybe they'll hear about the guy and come over to watch."

Allan didn't think that was very likely, but he agreed anyway, just to get Ray moving again. For all that he was always mooning about the good old days, when people could drive on the roads,

Ray didn't move very fast, or very far. He was always getting stuck in an idea, and ended up standing under trees looking off at a blimp, or putting down an acorn to see what happened when the footpad of one of the town spiders landed on it. The thing that got Allan was, Ray was happy to do the same things over and over. It was like, for all that he dreamed of leaving town, he was content to dream. Why, if the roads were open, Ray might live right here in Iowa anyway, and be content to know that he could drive or walk anywhere he wanted to.

Allan didn't understand that. He wanted to travel so badly that he had apprenticed on the barges, walking cargo barges round the muddy bends in the slow-moving Iowa River. And he had an application in to crew blimps. But the waiting list was so long, and what he really wanted to do was drive. He was just born in the wrong era, he decided. He was a twentieth-century man sentenced to suffer through the twenty-first.

"There he is! Look, Al, he's got goggles."

"I see, Ray," Allan said, but it was barely true. The worn red brick of the town's pedestrian mall was so crowded that Allan could hardly see the stranger. And he really was a stranger, not one of the Iowans he'd known his whole life or one of the greatly reduced number of students who still came to the university via train or barge. Had he blimped into town? It didn't matter.

But he looked so ordinary. Only the goggles, and the crowd around him, laughing and buying fried snacks and sweets from vending stands that had been thrown up since this morning, marked the stranger as anything special.

"Maybe that's why he wears the goggles," Allan said. Ray looked a question at him, but Allan just shook his head. "C'mon."

Allan led the way, snaking through the crowd until they reached the Vukaviches, whose bulk blocked the way as effectively as if they'd been a road, instead of just being people who insisted they were big-boned. But that was far enough. They could hear.

". . . do it because I have to. It has to be done. Is there a man out there who hasn't wanted to take to the open road once upon a time? Is there a man, a real man anywhere, who hasn't wondered what was around the next bend in the road, who isn't tired of seeing the same cars, the same faces, the same town – nice though these faces are, and wonderful though Iowa City clearly is."

The stranger paused to let an appreciative rumble of laughter and some applause move through the crowd. From the back one of the Tullus brothers called, "Yeah, but you don't have to live here!" The laughter got louder.

"No I don't," the stranger said. "But you do. And you know what? If I can open the roads, you won't have to. And I am going to open the roads, today. But I need your help. That's why I'm asking . . ."

Allan turned and pushed his way from the crowd, muttering, "Excuse me. 'Scuse me." He made it all the way to the fountain down near the public library before he fell to his knees and threw up.

It was another one, he retched. Another one. It seemed like every couple of years some fast-talking huckster slipped into town with a solution for the roads. Last August it had been the guy with the ponytail selling "real Native American dream catchers", that he promised would trap the ghosts and let the people take back the roads. Two years before that, in the spring, there had been the "professor" who said he was from Northwestern University who had used his five dollar vocabulary to convince the people from Iowa City that he had figured out why the roads had closed in the first place, that it had been a mix of the hole in the ozone letting in more energy that had pumped power into the ghosts, making them visible, and the greenhouse effect, which had trapped them.

Maybe that part was even right, in theory, but his solution seemed to be the same as the exorcist from when Allan was five, the medium who came down river in a motorboat when he was eight, and so on. Their solution was to come to town, raise everybody's hopes, take all their money, and leave, with the roads still dead and deadly. And after they were gone – always by the river or the sky, never by the road – someone had to try their solutions. And whoever it was always got hurt, or worse, trapped by the ghosts of old accidents, reliving pain that they knew was there, but wanted to believe could be escaped. They'd pull themselves off the road like a possum, leaving a trail of blood leading from the flames of a spirit cab into rows of corn. For a few weeks, more people would go to church, and more people would visit the bars. And then everything would go back to normal, and they'd start growing hope again. Iowans were good at growing hope, the same way they grew corn. It grew tall, regular, and stupid, for other people to mow down.

Allan felt someone standing nearby. "Go 'way, Ray," he said.

Ray didn't say anything. "Go away!" Allan screamed.

"Allan," Ray said softly. "This one didn't ask for money."

"What!"

"Seriously, Al, seriously. No money."

"Then what does he want?"

Ray told him. Allan listened, idly wiping his tears. What Ray described scared him as bad as anything he'd seen on the road, including the 'cycle accident left over from the fifties that crippled his uncle. But at least it was new, and long before Ray finished talking, Allan was nodding. Ray held out his hand to help Allan to his feet, and the cousins headed home to get their phones and pennants and the rest of the stuff they'd need, and to change to mud shoes for a long trek through the corn.

By the time they left the house, it was clear that word had spread through the town, far beyond the number who could fit on the pedestrian mall. The sidewalks and lawns were all full of people heading west, and some of the braver boys dodged into the street for a minute, standing there with big fake smiles on their faces, counting down the seconds of vulnerability until they had fulfilled their bets.

"Afternoon Allan, Raymond," Mr Milton said. "You boys going to watch the man try the road?"

"Yes, Mr Milton. Do you know where he's leaving from?"

"Well, he walked around the parking lot behind the community theatre a few times, to kinda show off, then walked clear round the Pentacrest, on the road itself, to show that he could have left from the heart of town itself. But I think he said he was leaving from City Park, just to be safe."

"What's his secret?"

"Well, Allan, that's a tough one. He says there isn't any secret. He just wants the road open bad enough to face all the ghosts."

"And none of the rest of us did?" Allan demanded.

Mr Milton just shrugged, and gestured with his cane for them to step aside, so Mrs Anderson could sway past in her civic spider. She waved as she passed, but since she was going to be high enough to pass over the top of all the old carnage, she was really too high for more conversation than a distant call of "Boys. Milty."

The boys waved, then followed Mr Milton up and over the busiest street they had to pass to get to the park, occasional kirillian flames leaping to soften the soles of their shoes and gum them to the support grid of the bridge. They ignored the cries for help. One of the first things they'd learned once they were old enough to cross the streets on their own was how to tell the cries of the living from the cries of the dead.

And then they were there, on the outskirts of the park, joining the hundreds of fellow citizens who were already there. Fragments of the festive air remained, but the news that the stranger was not just going to walk to Cedar Rapids, but was going to leave in the sight of God and everyone had sobered most of the townspeople. Fun was fun, and strangers were fair game, but nobody wanted to see another death. The roads had taken too many; their very hauntings testified to the truth of that.

Somebody helped the stranger up onto the crossbars of the football goalposts. Everyone got mostly quiet, like they were expecting some sort of speech, but after grabbing hold of one upright to steady himself, he looked out at the crowd, then turned to look at the road. He stretched out one hand to point at it; most of the crowd turned to follow his finger as it traced the road to the corner, along the river, then up the hill where trees hid the closest ramp to I-80. "That's where I'm going. And when I'm done that's where you're going to go too, if you want to."

A few people tried a ragged sort of cheer, but Allan didn't think they were all that enthusiastic. This guy wasn't exactly the sort to inspire confidence. As he slid down the pole by himself, Allan could see that his arms were pretty skinny, and that above the goggles, his sandy hair was starting to thin out. Not a hero. Just a guy.

But when he made it down to solid ground again, he walked confidently across the field. The Iowans parted for him; an impressed murmur arose when he walked right out into the street. A bunch of boys and three dogs ran back and forth on the sidewalk, getting ahead of him easily, then looping back to follow every step as he moved down the centre of the street, following the distant traces of paint that marked forgotten lanes.

The first intersection was a T. The traffic light was dead, of course, but by some quirk of the winds, it was one of the few that hadn't fallen in a storm. The stranger gave it a vague salute as he angled across the intersection. Then the first accident hit him.

It was a familiar one. Two fraternity boys who had gone looking for women and beer, or maybe just more beer after too much beer, careened down the hill in a van that was so visible you could see the rust near the fender. Flickering into existence behind the stranger (and why didn't they know his name? Allan wondered), was a sedan that looked like it may have been green, back in the twentieth century when people drove cars.

The stranger sort of hitched a step when the sedan went through him, and everyone held their breath when the two cars collided right in front of him, and the flames erupted to engulf him and the surrounding area. The screams from the dead drivers were so loud that Allan couldn't tell for a moment if the stranger was screaming too, but he could see his mouth moving, and his hands waving urgently in the flames.

Then he emerged, shaking but still standing, and walked on, patting out the small fire that had caught on one sleeve, and walked on. A more unified cheer went up, and one dog actually ran out into the street to sniff his leg. People laughed at that, but a few older folks started to cry. The dogs had been the first ones to really figure out what was going on, back when it happened. Dogs never went into the street, ever.

Then the stranger went on. He went up the hill and out onto the ramp without further incident. Then he was on I-80 itself, weaving his way through the forty-six stopped cars that had defined the highway Allan's entire life. Each time he passed a car he'd pause, just briefly, and touch a hand to the hood.

About a dozen cars out the stranger reached the red Fiero. This time when he touched it, he stood there. The Iowans on the crowded sidewalks shifted from side to side, not sure what was going on.

"Oh shit, oh dear," Mr Milton said.

When Allan looked at him, Mr Milton swallowed twice. "That's my car. You know I'm from Ohio, right?"

Allan nodded. He wasn't ever sure how much of Mr Milton's stories to believe, but like all the other boys in town, he had listened to tales of Toledo and Cincinnati with awe. Did they really have a zoo in Toledo? And people there ate falafel sometimes? Nah.

"That's the car we were driving, my parents and my sister and me, the day that it happened. We were driving along, racing along about seventy, seventy-five, and then in front of us everything slowed down. We were used to it when it was crowded. Phantom accidents were common for years, but these were the open roads."

This was why Allan wasn't sure about Mr Milton's stories. Forty-six cars in a couple of miles seemed really crowded to him, and despite what the books said, he wasn't sure anything had ever moved across the ground faster than a horse.

Mr Milton went on. "Anyway, things usually slowed down, then sped up again after a while. This time, all the cars just kept getting slower. The engine was labouring, like it was fighting something, and the windshield got all cloudy. Dad started the wipers, but they didn't do nothing. Pale, gauzy things came at us in waves, and we didn't know what was going on. 'Course, we know now, but then we didn't have a clue."

Milton leaned on his cane, looking forward past the rusted red car, where the stranger still stood. "Then it happened," he went on. "The accident. It was like a picture suddenly coming clear. A semi tried to merge right, and a pick-up truck jogged left without signalling. Everything was pale, but we could see it, just barely. But we could feel it sharp and clear when they hit, we felt it. Dad's head snapped back against the seat, and he bit right through his lip. We were all screaming and didn't know where to go. Our screams mixed with the screams from the old accident, so we were all tangled up with them. My sister popped the back door open and ran, a few steps anyway. Then the ghost flames got her, and I watched her melt. And die.

"I sat there for three days, then eventually rolled down the window and ran for the woods, when I got tired of pissing myself. And what does he want from me now!" Mr Milton shouted this last line.

Allan shook his head, but Mr Milton wasn't watching. He was limping toward the stranger, carefully staying off the asphalt. "What do you want? What? Oh no. No."

Allan watched as distant shapes congealed around the stranger and Mr Milton, not the big accident he described, but a handful of pathetic shapes, including a little boy balled up in the back seat. As if he'd been waiting for this, the stranger motioned to Milton, who stood off to the side, shaking his head, until his father's head snapped back once, twice, three times. The faintest trickle of blood was visible on the ghost's chin, the only colour in the entire painful scene.

"Dad – " Mr Milton said, and then he was on the road, for the first time Allan could remember. He stumped over to the car, and helped his father out, arm around the translucent shoulders, murmuring the words he never got to say fifty years ago. The balled-up boy in the other seat floated after, and they all went to sit on the grass on the meridian. Someone unscrewed a Thermos and handed it to them.

The stranger nodded, patted the hood once, and turned to walk on. On both sides of the road, along the fences bordering rows of corn, phones flipped open, and the local cable news stringer set a camera hovering in the air and started muttering into his lapel mike. They'd known for a long time that road ghosts didn't show up on film, but footage of the stranger walking the length of the road should be picked up for global satellite feed, and if he got clips of townspeople like Milton on the road, folks who weren't the brave and agile boys that usually dared the roads, that wouldn't just be news. Or money. That would be a new day.

"Al?" Ray said. "How far is it to Cedar Rapids?"

Just then the stranger cupped his hands and started shouting to the crowd. "That's right, folks. These people are stranded on the road, just like you're stranded by it, and they may be dead, but they're still people. Help 'em get home, will you? You do that, and I'll walk the road."

After waiting to make sure the stranger was done, Allan answered, "Twenty-two miles. He's walking steady, but not fast. Just walking, it would be at least eight hours. Having to pass the roads too . . . better call ahead, and let the outlying farms know."

Ray did, and other people did too. They called their cousins, and the guy who walked the barges up river, and the guy with the industrial spider who came to town with those wonderful melons in the fall, and as the stranger walked on, sweating away under those heavy goggles as the August sun built on itself, driving moisture from the soil up and out, to hang around them in familiar, aromatic clouds and make them sweat. Except that the stranger took a deep breath every time the wind changed, like he'd never smelled dead skunk and soy beans before.

And after they called, as the stranger laboured on, the people on the other end of the calls answered, by coming out to see someone on the road to Cedar Rapids. They walked between the rows of corn, shouldering them aside and setting them moving like a storm was building. But it was a peculiar storm. It blew from both sides towards the road, and along the road on both sides it blew north, to Cedar Rapids, with both sides of the human storm collecting behind the spearhead of a ratty little man who was sending the ghosts home.

Things settled into a rhythm. The stranger would walk on, dodging the lesser ghosts and weaving around the dead cars that had been spawned by them, tapping each on the hood. Then he'd reach one and he'd stop and wait. Eventually the corn would part, and reluctantly a senior would walk out to greet his road ghosts, and welcome them home. Sometimes there was singing. Often there were tears.

Then, sixteen miles into the walk, long after everyone had gotten tired and started to slump in the heat and fan themselves with their hats, it happened. The stranger stopped in front of a Volvo and waited. Nobody came. A whisper moved through the corn. Ray looked at Allan. Allan shrugged. "Maybe the person's dead. Or afraid. Or busy. Or just not from around here."

On the road, the presence of a living being standing still on the highway was acting like a catalyst. Revenants raced back and forth, accelerating out of the patterns that had trapped them for generations, with more and more of them flickering into the visible the longer the stranger stood in the road.

He turned to face in the same direction that the car was and spread his arms. Along the road, people grew quiet. Those still coming through the corn grew quiet.

They saw it coming a long ways off. A sports car from a century ago was using the open road to see just how fast it could go. It was speeding up, it was flickering, it hit the divider, and it launched up into the air and at the dead car. And the crucified stranger.

It landed in a horrific crunch, one ghostly wheel breaking loose to bound off into the corn, where it landed with a squish. But no one looked at it, even those who were near enough to have to duck when it came past. Everyone was looking at the stranger.

If the sports car had been physical, it would have crushed him right away. Instead, it seemed to have pinned him against the dead Volvo by smashing into his spirit. It was upside down. Three wheels were spinning, and flames licked in and out of this plane of existence. But no matter whether they were visible or not, they clearly burned. And the stranger screamed, a high-pitched wail that went on and on as the tears welled up inside his goggles and leaked out the lower edges.

Everyone waited, but Allan could tell. It was clear. He didn't have an answer for this one. The stranger was going to die, just like everyone else who had tried the roads. Just like all the people who used to drive the roads, who were still stuck there.

He turned away, trying to pretend the screams he heard were from the long dead, rather than from the near dead. Sixteen miles was a long way to walk home. No way he'd be back by dark, and it wasn't always easy to find his way through the corn at night.

Maybe he could hitch a ride part way on the leg of a spider, at least to the river's edge, where he could wait for a barge.

"Al! You can't just leave him."

That was Ray. Ray was a dreamer. Always would be. Allan turned to snap at Ray, and saw that he wasn't behind him. Ray wasn't following. He had sprinted over to a place where a family had sat to have a picnic, and grabbed a Thermos.

Ray mumbled something that might have been an apology, then ran along the road. He hesitated before he stepped onto the road, but in the end, he walked out onto it, stepping funny but fast. He ran to the stranger and poured the litre or so of iced tea onto the flames.

It seemed to help, just the tiniest bit, and then the flames came back, and the screams, of course. But the crowd didn't move until Ray bent over to push at the spirit car. Ray was twelve, but small for his age, and it's hard to push a ghost anyway.

Allan could see Ray's hands reddening on the ghost bumper, and he couldn't take that. He came back to help, and set his hands into the semi-solid mass of the car. They were joined by people they knew, and people they didn't. The old ones dumped lemonade and more tea and soda on the flames. The younger ones pushed.

As they slid it to the edge of the road, the ghostly wreck slowly vanished. The crowd didn't even notice it was gone until they started to stumble forward and bump into one another in a warm, moist crowd. And then it was gone, and there were only people on the road, and no phantom accident.

A few cheered, but most were serious. They helped the stranger up. The lower half of his leggings were scorched, and he looked to be in pain, but after nodding his thanks, all he said was, "Anyone up for a walk? I hear Cedar Rapids is nice today."

The crowd walked on slowly, at a pace everyone could handle. When the little children who had come out from the farms and hadn't expected to walk that far got tired, they were given seats on the spiders, perched eight and ten feet above the road, or on shoulders. As they walked, Allan quizzed Ray about why he'd run out, how he'd known it would work, and how he was suddenly brave enough to face the road.

Allan was angry and jealous, but Ray just shrugged and said, "I don't know, Allan. I think everybody wants the open road." Allan had to be content with that.

And as Allan realized he was part of a growing crowd of ordinary people, not adventurers any more, and not risk-takers, who were taking back the roads as they vanquished a series of increasingly ethereal and harmless ghosts, he saw that Ray was right.

By the time they crossed the Cedar River and marched into downtown Cedar Rapids, it had turned into a parade.

One of the West Branch Boys was good enough to pick a banjo as he walked, and when they got close enough, they could hear the faint sounds of a hastily assembled brass band welcoming them to town.

Suddenly a girl rode out onto the bridge on an old bicycle. Allan didn't think it was supposed to wobble like that, and she eventually scraped her knee on an abutment, but she still got a cheer. Then the crowd from Cedar Rapids was all mixed together with the parade from Iowa City, and except for when Allan caught a glimpse of someone who looked especially sweaty, or whose clothes or hands were scorched, you couldn't tell them apart. And the stranger was gone. He could have been anybody in the crowd, anybody at all.

Allan turned and looked back at I-80 from the bridge over the Cedar River. He felt Ray come and stand beside him. He put his hand on Ray's shoulder and said, "Thank you."

Ray sort of shrugged like he was embarrassed, and said, "Al, what happens now that the road to Cedar Rapids is open?"

Allan looked out at the strange cars still dead on I-80. He tried to count them, but he couldn't see well enough to be sure. People were gathered around two or three of the nearest cars, opening the doors and welcoming the passengers home. And besides, Allan was crying, great wet tracks that ran down his face as he looked at the road. That must be from all the strange smells here in Cedar Rapids, a mix of industry and something like warm oatmeal.

Anyway, Allan wasn't sure exactly what would happen next, but he was very sure what would happen in general.

"If the road to Cedar Rapids is open, Ray, then the road to Des Moines can be opened. And the road to the Quad-Cities. And that means the Mississippi, and yes, even the road to Joliet. It means we stop floating, or skittering across our own roads like frightened bugs, and drive. It means that we'll get to see if Mr Milton's stories about what happens when you lean out of a car window and open your mouth are true.

"If the road to Cedar Rapids is open, it means we can get into cars and drive and drive and drive, and never see Iowa City again. Or maybe have an adventure and come home.

"If the road to Cedar Rapids is open, Ray," Allan said, "it means we can drive again, everywhere and nowhere. It means we own the world."

Kicks on Route 66

Sylvia Rose

"Kick – her name was Kick which is weird enough, but do you know what I really can't help thinking about?" she told the little wheat-haired hitchhiker. "Her eyes – isn't that silly?"

The girl, not more than seventeen, not under fifteen, nodded, looking shy and nervous – expecting, or maybe disappointed, that Julia wasn't asking for gas, ass, or grass and that, yeah, really, the ride was free.

"I mean, shouldn't it be like the colour of her hair – romantic shit and all – or the sound of her voice? Eyes . . . it's just too damned obvious, you know? But that's what I think about the most. She has these eyes, like marbles: blue and grey mixed together with a little bit of gold."

The girl, chin resting on the top of her thin, bony chest, smiled. Not a deep smile, just the hint of one: a few muscles, not a lot. She wanted to giggle at the tension dropping away from her, the free ride sinking in.

"But it isn't just her eyes – though they're really special and all – but what she does with them. She can see the most wonderful things: stuff that's there, but not, you know? Like, look out there – those birds . . . crows I think, I don't know birds . . . on those wires. She'd look at them and start to whistle . . . get it? Notes, music notes: that's what she'd see when she looks at birds on a wire. She'll call a wheat field at sunset 'burning' and you know that's all I'd think of when I saw one like that: sun going down behind it, the wheat all brown and glowing – "

The girl looked out the window, not wanting the nice young woman giving her the ride to see the snickering grin on her tiny face. Out the window, the fields were raw copper, the sun nowhere near setting – but then they started to burn in her mind, to glow like embers at a nice summer BBQ weenie roast.

"Or like the road – this road – with the dotted line down the centre, she'd talk about how it looked like a place where some giant would write its name, or cut the county in two with big-ass scissors. You know what I mean?"

The girl scooted down in her seat, mumbling something like "Yeah, I know." Low, she looked up and saw the wires, then the birds, and began to plink out a stupid little tune in her head: a crow or blackbird a low or a high note, depending on the bird or the wire.

"She'd see stuff – stuff you never would have thought of in a million years. She's great – oh, man, she's terrific. There's a lot of great things about her, but what she sees, that's really something."

The girl got off at Bark's Lake, a little down a rock's toss from absolutely nowhere, waving good-bye as Julia drove away. Walking down the dusty road towards the cheap jewellery neon of MOM'S DINER, she couldn't help but look down the road and wondering if she'd recognize God's name, scrawled on the asphalt, if she saw it.

A long day later: Julia was driving mostly by night, the hard Arizona sun too damned hot, burning her hands on the wheel. Long stretches of dark highway, only the stars and the quarter, then almost full; moon for company and light. Driving, she dreamed, trying to put herself at the end of the road: Boston, with its baked beans and "Boid on the wattah" accents (she'd never been before). Finding the little bookstore, walking in, smiling, having Kick smile back, offering coffee and a place to talk, Kick smiling more and suggesting a great little place nearby. The kiss, then more kisses, then that night, then the morning: back to the way things had been between them, but better.

Kick's absence was an ache, high and to the left – that part of her body that broke so badly and too damned easily.

"You got too much bad crap," Kick would have said about an ache like that. "Got to get it out, got to pour it out, babe."

Julia, behind the wheel, sighed deep and long, feeling tears making her eyes heavy, the stars and the partial moon a blur in the sky.

Got to ask someone to take it away, get it out of you. Can't ask your mom for that. Can't ask anyone else for that. Too much to heap on someone you love, too much for a stranger. You got to offer it up, you see? Got to give it to the Big Sky, the Universe Up There. It's a big place, more than enough room for all your hurt.

She pulled over and took a few deep, quavering breaths. Ahead, the road was long and dark, vanishing instantly behind the reach of her headlights. Behind, the soft black was even closer. She was alone in the middle of the desert.

At first she didn't think about taking her clothes off, stripping down, but then Kick was again in her mind and she knew that she wouldn't have had it any other way – can't make a sacrifice with your clothes on, right? She didn't go far into the desert, just a dozen or so steps. With her car behind her, the interior hovering in the night from the feeble dome light, and the stars high above – a billion, billion, billion bright, bright, bright stars – she spread her hands wide and cried until the tears wouldn't come any more.

When she was done she felt like Kick was standing next to her, a warm hand on Julia's now chilly shoulder. "Better?" she'd say, with a special, kindly smile on her face.

Even though she knew she was alone out there in the desert, she nodded, feeling warm, and walked back to the car. It was what Kick would have done, what Kick would have advised – and it felt good. In fact, it felt so good, she did it a lot as she drove – each time she felt the heaviness, giving it all to the night sky, which was big enough, and empty enough to take it all – with room enough for stars.

Four dollars for a cheese sandwich, a can of Pepsi, and a slice of gooey pecan pie. Except for Julia, a mysterious cook hidden behind steam in the kitchen, and a tiny bent old woman, the place was empty. Watching the old lady shuffle from one end of the tiny diner to the other, carefully tidying crusty and cracked sugar dispensers or swirling a once white, now yellow dishcloth over the red and white checked vinyl tablecloths, Julia could too easily imagine Kick saying something like "Be right back" and wordlessly adding her own elbows and grease, her own composition style with flatware and tiny steel pots full of warm cream.

Just like when they were together – even though they were apart – Julia got up and added her own hands. The road was very long that night, and very dark, and it felt good to be home – if only a kind of home, for just an hour or two. The old woman never spoke, and neither did Julia: they went from table to table, filling salt cellars, wiping away stains, straightening little jackets of jam, in warm silence.

Finally, when it was ten o'clock by the angrily buzzing beer sign behind the register, the old woman flipped OPEN to CLOSED. When it happened before, when Kick helped someone without asking, Julia had felt dragged along – pulled into Samaritanship by her lover's wake, but that night, the inertia wasn't there. It felt good, very good. She knew why Kick had done it.

When she went out into the cold dark, the old woman held the door for her, a sweet smile on her dried apple face – and Julia felt warm and good without having Kick to follow. She thanked Kick, though, as she stood by her car: under the stars and the gaze of the still smiling old woman in the tiny little diner.

"She's just so . . . impulsive – but that's not the right word. She isn't fickle; she just likes to do the unexpected, follow the twists of the world. Like when she got this offer to run a bookstore in Boston, she just went for it, you know? Just dove off and started swimming. I wish I could be like that – "

She said her name was Mary. Julia had spotted her standing on the side of the road, her sixteen wheeler now fifteen, one tyre now black curls scattered along the highway. Without thinking, Julia had pulled over: "Need a lift?"

"I just couldn't do it – I mean to just toss everything away and hit the road, without a guarantee of what would be on the other end. I just couldn't. I wish I could, you know? Just get behind the wheel, and head out for something like a job. Just not in me."

Mary was big, strong, broad: but her eyes, peeking out from under a gimmie cap, were surprisingly warm and soft. She wore grease like a heavenly mother wore butter and flour. As Julia drove, the truck driver calmly reached into a denim pocket and brought out a packet of tobacco and a sheaf of rolling papers. As Julia talked, Mary calmly rolled a cigarette, nodding and lowly answering when there was a pause long enough to do so. "Like you," she said when Julia was quiet for a moment, distracted by a particularly complex road sign.

"It isn't like she was rash or anything – just like, well . . . like she sees everyone like they could be a friend. She doesn't see serial killers everywhere, but rather strangers who could also be good pals. She isn't really scared of anything. Not foolish, just not so worried about people being bad."

The highway was a dark line pointing to where a too blue sky met bright green trees. It was a strong pull – so strong that Julia found it hard to tear her eyes away from the vanishing point, but when she did, she smiled at the big woman next to her, now leisurely smoking her hand-rolled cigarette. "Like with you, she'd just pull right over, open the door and say, 'Want a lift?' She's like that, you know – like the world's just full of friends she hadn't met yet."

"Like you," mumbled Mary around her cigarette, smiling so slight and sly that Julia didn't notice.

"She's like that everywhere – places to eat, movies to see, books to read: she'd just walk down the street till something just got her." Julia's laugh rolling and true in the small car's interior. "Got a lot of crap – oh, man, this place she found in Oakland, the roaches wouldn't even eat, you know? But sometimes . . . sometimes she'd touch something really special, something you'd never have noticed otherwise."

Signs flickered past their windows. Mary's side window was down, and each passing buffeted them – even with just a low roll of deep sound. Mary took a long drag on her cigarette and blew the smoke, carefully, out the side window – the grey instantly vanishing. "You can just let me off up there," she said, gesturing with the dry end at a sprawling truck stop, big machines swarming around islands of diesel.

Julia pulled over, the highway background moan fading as she slowed. Manoeuvring through the grazing trucks, she sedately cruised up to the frantic coffee shop.

"I miss her, I guess," Julia said, turning to smile at Mary. "I miss that sense of adventure she had. It just took me a while to figure that out, I guess. That's why I'm driving all this way out to be with her again."

Mary put her large hand on the door, popping it open but not swinging it out yet. "Thanks for the lift. You in San Antone, you come and look me – "

Julia leaned across and kissed her, quick (but not too quick) and hard (but not too hard). "Just miss that, you know – miss that kind of thing about her."

Mary got out, smiling, and carefully closed the door – feeling loose, lifted, and buoyant. She waved like a little kid as Julia pulled away, grin getting even wider as Julia waved back.

Before going in for a cup of coffee, before trying to track down a tow for her rig, she looked out at the highway and said to herself: "Just like you."

The cold bricks of Boston: grey sky above, hard looks from people on the street, people in other cars. Her heart should have been pounding, but instead she was cool and quiet. The city seemed held back, locked down by something: money, history, a faith packed with martyrs – she didn't know. The air was chilly, but Julia had the feeling that even if the sun had been out, the steel overcast gone, the people of the city would have put something up equally dull and oppressive.

She should have been light, flying with anticipation – or at least more of it. A tingling giddiness made her head feel light, her body shed pounds, but not as much as she had thought she would. On the road, between where she'd come from to where she – and Kick

– was, she dreamed of laughing, singing, cheering as she drove into the city. Instead, she smiled. She just smiled.

It wasn't hard to find the bookstore, surprisingly – for a big city; it felt like a brick-fortified neighbourhood. Tucked off a street of dull cement, cracked asphalt, and faded brick, a sign on a bright blue awning: She Space: Books for Women. Parking was easy, though she wished she had had more time to circle and get even more excited, wanting her fantasies to get close to matching reality. Getting out of the car, she looked down the street, seeing the looming dark sky like a great steel lid keeping the city cool and low.

A short distance down the street she saw a woman step out of her car, walk up to her house, one arm full of groceries, the other fumbling for keys. Without thinking, Julia stepped up, offered to help. The woman looked at her slightly askance, but as a plastic bottle of soda thumped onto the sidewalk and started to roll away, said, "Sure," with an embarrassed little smile.

After helping the woman with her bags – Susan, as she learned the woman's name was – Julia stepped towards the bookstore again, and again saw delightful, hidden things: the way the leaf-less trees made shadows like cracks on the sidewalk, the rust on an old car like metal acne, a headline cut to FALL LEAD by a newspaper rack, and then – completely on the spur of the moment, leapt up and grabbed a low-hanging branch. Hanging there she listened to the little noises of the tree, then let go – landing lightly, like a cat, on the balls of her feet. Taking a step forward, she noticed something tickling her hand. Looking down, she saw a chubby eyebrow of a caterpillar, working its way from one knuckle to the next. Laughing, she held her hand out to the tree, encouraging its slow progress with a gentle laugh in her voice.

Then she was in front of the store, and then her hand was on the knob. It was hot inside, like a sauna. It was full of mad colours, like a forest in autumn: too many bold titles, too many bright covers. She turned to the counter, spoke to the stern young woman meticulously writing in a ledger: "Excuse me, I'm looking for someone who works here. Her name is Kick."

The woman looked up, shock in her cloudy-grey eyes. "Julia?" Kick said.

Kick did know a place, not that far away. A hand-painted mural of a mermaid on one wall, with old Christmas glitter for seaweed-braided hair. The tables were roughly handled spools for heavy cable, no two chairs – or place settings – were alike. On a whim, Julia ordered the "sprout surprise" and Kick ordered "the usual".

As they'd walked, Julia had kept her eyes cast at her old lover – or, to be more precise, had looked for her old lover in this strange woman. The eyes were the same, the face was exact, the body – as far as she could tell under the brown wool suit – was similar, but nothing else was.

"How's your job?" was one of the first things Kick asked her.

Looking comically sideways at the "special" on her plate, Julia said, "Quit."

"'Quit'? Just like that?"

"Sure – I can always find another job." *But there's only one you* was left unsaid. "I've missed you," she finished in a low voice.

"That's nice," Kick said, looking for a long moment out the window.

"How's the job? You were so excited about it – is it everything you'd hoped it'd be?"

Kick looked down at her special blend tea. "I guess so . . . there's just a lot of emotions at play, you know. Like this girl, Alice, she's nice enough but sometimes she just sort of stands on process – like she has to make sure we don't turn into a dreaded patriarchy or something. Just the other day, in fact, I wanted to order this new book *Angel Falling* by Dorothea Lamont and she got all upset that the publisher also recently refused to publish this collection of Virginia Woolf essays because it wasn't 'commercially viable' and how this just proved that we shouldn't support this kind of 'machismo economics' and then Betty got involved, she works in our shipping and receiving department, but only part-time because she's also a massage therapist, and said that we shouldn't keep good work out of people's hands because the publisher was being a fascist . . ."

"Uh, huh," said Julia, noticing the way the mermaid's scaled tail reflected in the curve of her spoon, making the naiad appear to be swimming in a sea of mercury.

". . . which was definitely not the case, and besides, I've read those old essays – Virginia Woolf, I mean – and they are definitely not worth losing a publisher over, or even pissing off a distributor. I mean they're good, but there's some better stuff out there, and it was just too reactionary to cut off all these new people for something that's been in print before and probably will be again, but Alice is just like that . . ."

Julia smiled, holding up a hand. "Just a minute, hold that thought" – then she got up quickly and helped a delivery girl with her wobbly hand truck. When she'd given her a hand getting some boxes into the kitchen area she sat back down. "Just had to help out with that – please, go on."

"Anyway, then there's Diana – she's nice and all, but she really has issues about stripping books, so I have to make sure she's not around or she goes on this trip about 'destroying the trees of our mother' kind of thing, which I agree with of course, but if we don't strip the books then we have to pay for them and we just don't have that kind of income, not with the tax re-evaluation the city hit us with last quarter – "

Julia mumbled a fourth, or was it fifth . . . or more like a tenth "Uh, huh," and picked at her "special", deciding with a wry smile to herself that there was much that was special about it, taste not being one of them. Then there was a long silence, and she looked up, suddenly realizing that Kick had fallen silent.

"I said, 'What have you been up to?'" Kick said, a tiny burn of acid in her voice.

Julia looked at her, thinking: I've stood naked under the stars and offered my pain to the sky. I've seen birds write symphonies on telephone wires and driven down the dotted line of a highway contract with God. I've cleaned diners and cafés, hauled boxes up stairs and once helped paint a VFW hall. On a lark, a whim, I've driven hundreds of miles to see the World's Largest Nail, the

World's Smallest Church, and the World's Shortest Horse and then – sometimes they haven't been the world's best time, but sometimes it's come damned close. I've kissed a truck driver who had great motherly arms, I've cried with a young punk kid who wanted to go home but was also scared to. I've driven clear across the country to see you and . . .

"Not much," Julia said, after a long time, "just driving . . . just finding stuff out about myself, you know. That kinda thing – "

Kick asked if she had a place to stay, her tone hinting that if Julia didn't then Kick might, possibly, maybe have room for two, but Julia slowly shook her head. "Got to get going," she said.

"Where to?" Kick replied, sounding concerned – implying that any trip had to have a destination.

"No idea," Julia said, smiling. "Absolutely no idea. Maybe nowhere – I'll send you a postcard when I get there."

So Julia left, heading – with the flip of a coin – north, waving to Kick as she pulled into the light traffic, saying goodbye to what was behind her, and excited at what she'd find out next.

Not the end, not quite. Because for a long time – a cold winter and a very hot summer and then some – certain people . . . people like a hitchhiker not more than seventeen, not under fifteen; an old woman who cleaned a tiny café's tables each and every night, a trucker named Mary, and many others would look out onto the highway and think about the girl with the special eyes (and what she saw with them), the girl who helped people who needed it, who was wonderfully impulsive and caring, and smile, saying, "I think her name was Kick . . ."

24 Hours From Tulsa

Martin Edwards

Which way now?

Lomas is heading due west, but he hasn't a clue where he's going. It doesn't help that this is a route he knows well, far too well. He was up here a few weeks back, early in autumn, the low sun of evening half-blinding him, mile after mile. He was driving on auto-pilot. His eyes can't take the strain as easily as they did once upon a time. Today there's no sun, scarcely a glimmer of brightness to break up the clouds. Ten minutes ago the weather girl on Radio Leeds was warning about the threat of storms.

He ignores the turn-off, tells himself to keep straight on. His head is aching. Carter was right in one thing at least.

"You're not as young as you used to be."

Hills rise on either side of the road. A sign claims this is the highest motorway in the country. Lomas's instinct is never to believe what he's told; a lifetime of flogging ice to Eskimos has taught him that if nothing else. But if the sign had said it's the worst motorway in Britain, that he'd accept without a second thought. The landscape is lonely, but he thinks it drab, nothing like the Lakes beyond the Kendal exit. Over to the left, not so many miles beyond the brow of moorland, that's where Brady and Hindley buried their bodies. Were all of them ever found? Lomas can't recall. He's never kept up with the news and now it's too late to break the habit of a lifetime.

Traffic slows, the lanes narrow. Lorries are tailing back along the inside lane. A ribbon of cones stretches out in the distance, far as the eye can see. The next ten miles are sure to be a crawl. All those Mancunian commuters, making an early start. Lomas groans loudly, almost theatrically, even though there's nobody to hear, even though the delay shouldn't bother him a bit. He keeps reminding himself that time doesn't matter any more, but although it's true, he can't bite back the profanities when some pony-tailed kid with a death wish and a rust-bucket of an old Cavalier cuts in just ahead of him.

The day is fading and he switches on the lights. Time was when driving up and down the country was a pleasure, sheer bliss. Not this nose-to-tail grind, knowing that a cow with a laptop and a long face is checking on your every move. Once he could – digress. There are always opportunities, when you're out on the road. Bound to be. Lomas smiles to himself. He's been tempted and fallen, many a time. Only natural.

Selling has gone much the same way. Lomas blames the internet. He's a Luddite and proud of it. Tapping into a computer all day long is for kids, not a grown man who's been around the block a few times. But people don't buy the same way as they used to. They are busy, busy, busy, or so they say. Busy doing nothing, by and large. But that doesn't help when you have targets to meet.

The phone rings. The set is hands-free, a security measure the company insists on, though he's always had a sneaking preference for cradling a mobile against his neck. He grips the wheel tighter, doesn't press *Answer*. The trilling keeps on – bloody William Tell, he should have changed the tone years ago – so he ups the volume on the tape. *New York, New York*. He's always liked Sinatra, can't be doing with all this modern rap-crap.

At last they give up. *1 missed call*. He presses the arrow button and the office number flashes in silent reproach. Well, they can forget it. Tomorrow he'll be off the payroll. He's called in for the last time.

The tape's wound to an end. With practised ease, he slides another cassette out of its box and into the slot, keeping his left hand on the wheel. *Sixties Love Songs – Volume 14.* Never mind about love, it's melodic stuff he likes, even more now than when he was a youngster going out to the clubs. Tuneful, relaxing. Music to watch cones go by.

Trumpets cry out and a man's voice wails. Orbison, maybe? A song he's heard a thousand times, there in the background, part of the soundtrack of his life.

Something happened. To me.

This strikes a chord. Lomas has never listened to the words before. But what else is there to do, sitting on the outskirts of a dark wet conurbation, bumper-to-bumper in a three-mile queue?

Something's happened, all right. Talk about chickens coming home to roost.

"You should have seen it coming." Hayley, doing her more-in-sorrow-than-in-anger bit. Was she talking about the job or her new lover?

Funny, he thinks about her more now that she's going, now he knows that she's screwing someone else. All those years, the boot was on the other foot, and he found her so boring he could have screamed. Never mind, it's the kids he'll really miss. Or at least, the kids as they were. Tim in the days when they went to watch the match together, Tim before he started stashing dirty mags in the drawer under his bed. Sally-Ann when she wore pretty little party dresses and white cotton socks, when she didn't smoke and have a stud in her nose.

I won't be home any more.

You can say that again. So Lomas presses *Repeat.* The traffic's starting to pick up speed. The worst is over, at least in one way.

He presses the accelerator and the car leaps ahead. One time of day, his dearest wish was to drive a Lexus. He fought for it, stood on the shoulders of others to make his figures stack up. He deserved success and – leave aside the occasional weekend in Paris – this was his real prize.

The leather seats are rather grubby, sure. He's not paid for a valeting since the middle of summer. Not so long ago the company changed cars every three years. It made sense: saving on repairs and cashing in while there was still a good price to be had, but then the men in suits decreed otherwise and the garage bills have been coming in to the accounts department ever since. Typical finance mentality. No vision.

He's been behind this same wheel for five years, almost to the day, too long really, but it's still a super car. He's loved it as much as he's loved anything for as far back as he can remember. The engine doesn't roar, it purrs, the sat. nav. is terrific. A bit out of date, maybe; it doesn't know they've re-numbered the ring road, it's the 60 now, not the 62. Who cares? That's a detail.

Lomas remembers when he used to listen to the computer's voice, clipped and precise, and imagine that she was alive: a woman talking to him, a slave devoted to the task of making sure he headed in the right direction. He could forgive the occasional slip, when she said "Norwich" instead of "Northwich", that sort of thing, the kind of mistake that anyone could make. To err isn't only human. He's always liked listening to her; sometimes he'd keep pressing *Voice,* have her repeat the same phrases over and over again. Easy to picture a woman talking like that. Cool and elegant, someone who was sure to respond whenever he pressed her buttons.

Sad? Not at all, just a harmless fantasy. Carter is wrong as usual. He hasn't lost it.

Today, though, she's keeping quiet. He's finished with her. *Cancel Guidance.* Somehow he's taken the wrong route after all, and pressing *Detour* won't ever bring him back on the right road.

A madman in a Range Rover that has come from nowhere, maybe zipping down off the slip road, swerves right in front of him, heading off into the twilight in the outside lane. Lomas flashes his lights, then treats the bastard to full beam until he disappears out of sight. Hopefully there'll be a speed cop lurking under the bridge down past Burtonwood. Shit, Lomas thinks, if I hadn't touched my brake, I'd have been up his backside. People like that shouldn't be allowed on the roads. You hear a lot about road rage, but it's understandable. This country's full of people who deserve to be dead, yet all too often it's the innocent who get killed. How can anyone in their right mind believe in God?

"Answer me that," Lomas says. "Answer me that."

Roy Orbison doesn't offer any reply, he just keeps on singing about the day his life changed. Actually, it's not the Big O, is it? Silly mistake, no wonder the quiz team at the Waterman's Arms never makes it to the premier league. Gene Pitney, that's who it is, wailing away. Wallowing in self-Pitney.

Lomas chuckles. No way has he lost it, Carter's a fool.

Yes, yes, Gene Pitney. Wasn't this his greatest hit? The words aren't bad, they tell a story. People don't write songs like they used to; the garbage Tim and Sally-Ann fill their heads with, you can't even make out the words. Probably just as well.

Roadworks ahead. Just for a change. A 50 mile-an-hour limit coming up, speed cameras in action. You can't get away with anything in this day and age. We're living in a police state and we don't even realize it. A sign brags about the number of offences recorded. It's not the same as people convicted, though. Lomas has heard reps saying there is a get-out-of-jail-free card you can play. When the summons drops through the letterbox, tell them you don't know who was driving the car at the time. Some famous people have pulled that one to get off the hook. Lomas has never had the need, but he's always kept it in the back of his mind. How would it work, though? No chance he'd ever let Hayley loose with his pride and joy, never mind Tim or Sally-Ann.

Doesn't matter, anyway. The M6 junction is half a mile distant, it's time to peel off, see if things are any better over the Thelwall Viaduct. There's a first time for everything.

I'm just not the same any more.

Echoes of bloody Hayley. No, no, no. Hayley was wrong, he hasn't changed. It's the world that's changed. *No way* he's losing it. His temper, now, okay, that's a different matter. He's not superhuman, never claimed to be. Of course he gets angry now and then. Who wouldn't, these days?

Two bridges at Thelwall, one in each direction, eight lanes with generous margins and still it's a nightmare. Never anything different, it's notorious the length and breadth of England. A combination of circumstances: the rise of the viaduct slows the HGVs and the coming-together of traffic from all the intersecting motorways means that the slightest hiccup in the flow of vehicles slows everything down to a standstill. At least the place doesn't have a name for suicides. Runcorn Bridge, that's something else. Losers keep jumping off or threatening to. For some reason it gives them pleasure to do themselves in during the rush hour. Result: tail-backs full of fuming drivers, telling their passengers that some people have no bloody consideration.

Lomas thinks, if I wanted to end it all, that isn't how I'd do it. Not leaping down into a watery grave

On top of the viaduct, grinding along at ten miles an hour. Flecks of rain smear his windscreen. That's all he needs. Far below is the ship canal, but all he can see is the lights of the trucks and vans in front of him. He's hobbling along on the inside, because it's time to come off the motorway. Tiredness kills, so the signs always say. Time to take a break.

There's a truckstop with a McDonald's, straddling the junction of the 6 and the 56. He eases his way on to the roundabout: first left, first right and he's there. Parking isn't a problem. Switching off the tape, Lomas wonders for a moment about the drive-thru, but he can't face it. Maybe it isn't a good idea to drive on an empty stomach, but he's been short of good ideas lately. His eyelids were drooping on that last stretch; a black coffee wouldn't go amiss.

Outside the motel, a woman is checking her face in a compact mirror. Her thick red hair rings a bell. Wasn't she here a few weeks back? That time, he almost stopped to say hello, then thought better of it. He regrets it now. Maybe see if she's still around after he's freshened up? He throws her a glance on his way to the greasy spoon. Their eyes meet, but he carries on. A couple of blokes in jeans give him a furtive look as they sneak into the men's room. The shop's shut, so is the barber's, but the café lights are dazzling.

The prices are dirt cheap, although frankly money's no object tonight. He gives in to temptation and buys an all day breakfast. Why not? High cholesterol is the least of his worries.

The place is full of screens of one kind or another. Traffic info – nothing good's happening on the roads tonight, but what's new? CNN is covering some crisis in a foreign land. The President is talking about surgical strikes, but Lomas is hardly listening. Lights flash on the video game machines. A couple of truckers are talking soccer, another's pretending not to notice that the fat girl behind the counter's giving him the eye. It's a whole world, out on the road and here in the service areas. Most folk don't realize.

After he's finished, he goes for a pee and to wash his face. The men in jeans can't be seen, but he can hear whispering from the cubicles. Lomas sighs and shakes his head. He's never been one for prejudice, but he's never figured out why perverts have to congregate in places like this. Haven't they got homes of their own?

He's feeling better: the slap of caffeine has done him good. It's still early and he isn't in a hurry. His pace as he sets off back to the car park is deliberate, ponderous even. Two-to-one says she's slung her hook.

Good job he isn't a betting man: she's still there, sheltering under the covered walkway by the corner of the lodge. The rain is beating down much harder; he can see it bouncing off the tarmac.

"Horrible night, isn't it?"

He can still do it. Forget Hayley's complaining, forget Carter's judgmental shaking of the head. He can still sell. Best of all, he can still sell himself. Just look at her. The moment she heard his voice, smooth as treacle, she brightened. Four little words and she's putty in his hands. She'd been yearning for him to speak, he's sure of it. Walking past when he arrived was a good move. She's been waiting anxiously these last twenty minutes.

"Terrible."

Local accent. Late thirties, at a guess. The PVC coat is cheap, her legs are bare. What's unemployment like round here? Lomas has no idea, but it doesn't make any difference, we can all do with a bit of extra cash any time.

"Cigarette?"

"Thanks."

He lights it for her. They stand side by side, gazing out at the bright lights of the McDonald's. Companionable, almost.

He can feel her coat flapping against his legs. He moves closer to her, inhales her scent. Ladled on with a trowel, but that's what you expect at a place like this.

"That's a lovely perfume."

She turns to face him and smiles. Her teeth are yellow, but Lomas's motto is one he picked up years ago on the road. You don't stop to admire the mantelpiece, as long as you're poking the fire.

"You're a very generous man, Mr . . ."

"Call me Tom."

"Okay, Tom. I'm Melissa."

A likely story. All part of the game, of course. Lomas would put her down as a Dawn or a Tracey. Suddenly, he tires of the conversational waltz. After all, they are both aware of what this is all about. He tosses away his cigarette and nods at the motel.

"Come on, then."

She gives him a hard look. He thinks maybe there was a flicker of disappointment in her pale grey eyes, as if her preference is for men with a bit of class. Maybe she's spotted that his suit's a bit shinier than it ought to be. Well, beggars can't be choosers. He marches to the door, then looks back over his shoulder.

"Are you coming or aren't you?"

She hesitates, then shrugs agreement and trots along after him. As he pays the desk clerk in cash upfront, she loiters at the back of the lobby, running her finger along the leaves of the plastic rubber plant.

All these rooms in all these places are exactly the same. It's a strength of the motel brand. As a salesman, Lomas can see the point. People pretend to enjoy surprises, but the truth is that they fear the unexpected.

Her price is ludicrous in the circumstances, frankly, but Lomas hardly cares. He doesn't try to haggle. She's already seen the notes in his wallet when he paid for the room. He tosses the notes on to a bed and starts to unbutton his shirt. She stashes the money into her bag, then slips out of her skirt and blouse with a minimum, an absolute minimum, of finesse.

"Are you a rep?" she asks.

He pulls down his trousers. This isn't the moment for meaningless conversation. Meaningless sex, he thinks, that's what this is all about.

"Sales and marketing director, actually."

"I'm impressed," she says. Is there a hint of mockery there? Did he ask for it, was his tone pompous? He's never thought of himself as self-important. Never.

"For the time being."

She unhooks her bra. Her breasts are a disappointment: no better than bloody Hayley's.

Something in his expression catches her eye and she speaks more sharply.

"Got the push, have you?"

In the act of taking off his tie, he pauses. *Freezes*, to tell the truth.

"What makes you say that?"

His tone has roughened, but she isn't scared. It's not easy to be scared of a man in his socks and underpants.

"Lot of fellers in the same boat, that's all. I met this guy the other week. He was in computers, he was telling me he was going to get made redundant. Something about a downturn in the economy. Came from Tulse Hill, he did. Wherever that is. Somewhere down south, I suppose. Nowhere round here, that's for sure."

Twenty-Four Hours from Tulse Hill? Perhaps not. The heating is up in the room, he feels almost feverish. There's a pounding in his head. Why is England so much less glamorous than the States? You never hear crooners performing "By The Time I Get To Faversham" or "Do You Know The Way To Saffron Walden?." We always love most the things we can never get, the things and places that are out of reach. And now that bloody song is starting up in his head again.

I lost control.

"I have thirty men out in the field." The words are skidding into each other. He sounds as though he's been drinking. "Thirty, count them. Every single one reports to me."

"Keep your hair on, love." He sees alarm flickering in her eyes. "It's no disgrace, losing your job. Just like it's no disgrace, seeking a bit of comfort on a cold miserable night."

She's become ingratiating. God, he really doesn't like pleading women.

"Carter's a fool. They'll be sorry, I tell you straight." He's moving towards her.

She sits on the edge of the bed, pulling down her knickers. Breathing hard, she beckons him forward. She isn't excited, she's afraid.

"Come on, then. I'll help you forget all that."

"I don't need help."

"Look, love, all of us need help." Legs apart, hands on her knees. Not looking into his eyes.

"I don't need help." He's shouting now and as she cringes in front of him, he loops his tie around her neck, pulling it tight.

I hate to do this to you.

What happens in the next few moments isn't clean or pretty. It isn't what he'd expected. No, that isn't right, he has no expectations. All he can do is keep pulling tighter, yanking her hair to stop her struggling, until it is done. Over. Finished.

No need to look at what he's done. It doesn't excite him. Killing someone hasn't turned him on at all. Death disgusts him, it always has. He threw up at his grandfather's funeral. When it comes to his own victim, he's no different. He feels numb, wholly without sensation. Time to get dressed.

A girl is sitting at the desk. Shift change, presumably. The man who took his money is nowhere to be seen. Lomas gives her a curt nod and strides out into the car park.

Behind the wheel again, he revs up far too hard. Quite unnecessary in a Lexus, it isn't that sort of car. He jabs the audio button hard with his thumb. More music. He needs to fill his head with sound, blot out the roaring in his brain.

The rain's teeming down. The wipers work overtime as he heads south. This road isn't the busiest in Britain; in Lomas's book, the prize must go to the M25, Spaghetti Junction a close second. Even so, the stretch south of junction 20 is grim at the best of times.

Soon the weather will be even worse. Fog, snow, black ice. Lomas has driven all over England in all sorts of conditions, and he's never enjoyed it less. The motorways of Britain are falling apart, no wonder you hit roadworks every five minutes and the Highways Agency is constantly saying sorry for any delay. This country depends on transport, but the railways are a joke, the bus network in tatters, the roads a disgrace. Motorists are public enemy number one, taxed up to the ears and treated as criminals because it's easier for the police than catching the real villains. We've lost our pride, our self-belief.

As for me, Lomas thinks, I've lost everything. My job, my wife, my kids. My liberty.

I can never go home again.

Gene's dead right. There's nothing more that can be done. No healing, no absolution.

Even though it's getting late, traffic's still heavy. As juggernauts rumble by, the spray hits his screen and for a moment or two he can't see a thing. Perhaps that's the way it ought to be.

Never, never, never.

He moves into the outside lane. A sign anticipates a lane closure, but he no longer cares. In the distance, he can see lights flooding the night sky. Red stop lights and the flashing blue of the forces of law and order. He ought to slow down, but there is no longer any point.

He puts his foot down hard, hears the engine roar as if in approval and closes his eyes. Waiting for what will happen next.

Summer Cannibals

Maxim Jakubowski

The waitress came down from Tallahassee by Greyhound bus. She had a few remaining vacation days left, and she sure as hell wasn't planning to spend them on her own, inside the four close walls of that grey apartment she loathed so much. She knew she would never find a poet in Tallahassee. She was also aware that her own biological clock was ticking loudly. She wanted a baby. A blonde baby. It had to be a little girl. With blue eyes. Whose silken hair she could spend hours braiding into intricate, decorative patterns, with tiny coloured plastic beads at the extremities. She'd seen women do that on a travelogue on TV about Jamaica and its beaches.

She stuffed a change of underwear into an overnight bag, together with her toiletries, selected her shortest skirt, the blue cotton one with the white polka dots and wriggled herself into the red, ruffled tube top, then slipped on her leather sandals with the silver buckles.

The plane to the big city would only take an hour or so, she knew, but with the bus, she'd save at least sixty bucks. Which could go a long way, her gut feeling told her.

On the drive down, a couple of rude home boys – she thought she remembered them from high school days, or maybe not, they all did look much the same to her – kept on bothering her. Jokes, banter, but all too quickly the familiar lewd propositions, all part of a serving girl's burden, she realized. As the bus raced along, she had to keep pulling the tight skirt down to her knees for fear of showing her white panties to the guys. She blanked out their intrusion and imagined herself pushing a pram up and down Parisian streets. She found it difficult to picture this very precisely. Realized as an after-thought to the daydream that she couldn't even speak French. Of course, poets never did earn much money, she reckoned, so she would have to go to work. But she was confident that the diners in Paris would be busy and in need of her services. All she would have to do would be to memorize the names of the dishes and a few standard pleasantries, she guessed. Corned beef hash, juice and muffins must be much the same in every country. That wouldn't change. Of course, over there, they'd drink red wine with their meals.

The amorphous dreams inside her head came to an end as the bus approached the outskirts of Miami. Determined to ignore them, she hadn't even noticed that the black guys had already disembarked at the previous stop. She walked down to the narrow washroom at the rear of the coach and applied her make up with care. Powder, eye-liner, blusher, lipstick. Used the tweezers on a couple of recalcitrant eyebrows. Yesterday, she'd had her hair done at Lucy's Parlour and her dark hair shone with health. Yes, she thought to herself, this will do very nicely. Looked further into the patchy mirror, downward. The tits were a bit heavy, but still firm; the waistline could be thinner, but what could you do working all hours of the day with all that food around, and the smells of fat and cooking? You could put weight on just damn inhaling. Her thighs worried her, they were a bit lumpy. A few months ago, they were selling this exerciser for the stomach and thighs on the Shopping Channel and she'd impulsively sent off for one. Every morning before work, and at night before bed, she would spend a quarter of an hour bending and pulling, but it didn't seem to have made much difference so far.

Still, the men back at the Bordersnakes Café liked her; all the male customers did. They were always inviting her out, plying her with drinks, didn't mind screwing her when she allowed them to, when the itch was too strong and she had to accept second best, mostly out of boredom. They appreciated the way she looked, how she took care of her body. But she knew they were, one and all, simple men. Maybe a real poet would want more. Give something back. She'd once stolen a few skin mags from Joe Bob Wootton's mobile home after he'd boozily convinced her to spend the whole night there and quickly fallen asleep, spreadeagled over her, without even finding the energy to come inside her. Too much liquor. At least he hadn't been sick all over her while screwing; that had happened once to her friend Marie. She'd looked closely at the pictures of the women in the magazines, taken mental notes and, yesterday, in preparation for her Miami adventure, Sandra the waitress had, blushing deeply as she did the deed, carefully trimmed the shape of the hair around her pussy. Like the impossibly glamorous girls in the skin magazines. She knew that poets wouldn't like their women too hairy.

She left the toilet. Two other women standing right outside gave her dirty looks as she came out. They would have spent as long inside if they'd gotten there first, she knew, and breezed past them.

She returned to her seat. The tall Miami skyline was already visible in the distance. Sandra felt a dizzy knot in her stomach.

Maybe he'd fuck her on the top floor of a skyscraper?

It would be like heaven, she knew. She smiled. The old man along the aisle smiled back. Sandra squirmed in her seat as the bus began to slow down.

As Jacob swung the car into the rental space beneath the hotel, Anne's right hand alighted gently on his wrist. Her touch was warm.

"It was really nice, Jakey, thanks ever so much. I had a wonderful time. I really did," she said.

"Me too," he replied. "But don't call me Jakey. Jake, maybe. Not Jakey. Makes me sound like a kid."

She smiled back at him, mischief etched on her pink lips.

He pulled the key from the ignition.

"So," he said as they both sat silently in the penumbra, "this must be the moment of truth."

"Hey?" she questioned him.

"When I have to ask if I'll see you again?"

Her smile turned into a gentle laugh.

"Of course, Jake," she answered.

"I am a child, Anne, I'm greedy, I'm impatient, when?" he asked.

"Soon, very soon," she said. "There's this one job and then we can find time, a lot of time, I promise."

They left the car and took the elevator to the lobby.

The marble decor was flooded in fierce daylight. The clerk at the reception desk barely gave them a second glance. Jacob just stood there, dazzled by the brightness, waiting for her to make a move towards the door and Ocean Drive. She didn't.

Anne looked up to him.

Her ruffled red hair burnt like a sheer fire in the eyes of the sun.

Jacob swallowed once. Fear, again, lurking down in his stomach. I'm in love with her, I'm not falling in love because this way unhappiness lies, he whispered to himself.

"A last drink?" Anne suggested.

"A drink?" he repeated.

"In your room."

"Now?"

"Now. Or, if you prefer, a last fuck?"

He nervously looked around him, but apart from the clerk busy counting credit card slips at the desk, there was no one around.

"I'd rather call it making love."

"Is there a difference?" Anne asked him, already swivelling back towards the elevator.

"I hope so," he remarked, and followed her. "Yes," he said, "I'd like that very much."

The elevator doors opened as Anne pressed firmly on the lobby level button.

"It's hot in here," Anne said as the elevator moved up through the building.

"Yes," Jacob agreed. "We can take a nice long shower together to cool down."

"I'd prefer a bath," Anne answered.

Jacob mopped her sweating brow. "It's quite a large bathtub. We'll both fit, you'll see."

"Good."

It was already afternoon by the time Anne returned to her apartment. She'd insisted on taking a cab. She knew that if she'd allowed Jakey to drive her back, they would have just ended back in bed again. He was nice.

The red flashing light on the telephone indicated an avalanche of messages.

They were all from Teddy.

Urgent. Demanding. Angry. Pleading. Puzzled.

Fuck you, Anne thought.

Knowing she would probably have to again very soon, which made her flesh shiver.

She pulled her clothes off, showered, raided the refrigerator for the end of the orange juice and a few pieces of cheese, slipped an old T-shirt on and wandered across the two small rooms picking up discarded underwear and stuff, feeling the gentle breeze of the conditioning waft between her bare thighs. It made her randy, this insidious caress of the air against her genitals and her naked rump. Finally, she decided she couldn't put it off any longer and sprawled out on the rickety couch and dialled Teddy's number.

Another man picked up the phone.

A deep bass voice.

"Yeah?"

"Teddy, please."

"Who is this?"

She ignored the question. Something in his tone bothered her.

"Teddy, please," she repeated.

"Who the fuck are you?" the dark voice demanded.

"Anne Ryan," she finally said.

"Ah," the guy said. "We've been waiting to hear from you. You have been a busy lady."

"Can I speak to Teddy," she insisted.

"Where the hell have you been, Anne?" Teddy asked. "I tried your place. Nobody knew."

"I went away. Wanted a bit of sun."

"I needed you here," he insisted. "What were you up to?"

"Well, I'm sorry, Teddy, but you don't own me. Our relationship is a business one, whether it's the sex or the job. It doesn't give you any other rights to my life. And who is that other guy, anyway?"

"My business associate. He wants to meet you. Things are all set up. You have to leave in the morning. If you'd been in touch with us any later, the whole damn thing would have had to be called off."

"You mean, it's all on? As we agreed?"

"Yes. Get your sorry ass over here right now."

"I need to freshen up, Teddy," Anne said. "Let's make it tonight."

"No. Now. Right now."

She knew there was no point pleading otherwise.

"I'll slip something on and I'll be around."

The other man came on the phone again, must have been listening on another set, "Come as you are. I'm sure it would be fun," he said.

"Not as much as you think, you dirty bastard," Anne answered before slamming the phone down.

If she had known what he looked like, she wouldn't have used the parting shot. He was monstrous. Overgrown, pug ugly, like a tree trunk clumsily growing out of an elegant silk suit, at odds with every element surrounding him. His bald pate was severely scarred. Anne found him genuinely frightening as he gave her the once over at Teddy Caliban's penthouse apartment.

"I'm Evil," he introduced himself.

"I'm sure you are," she mumbled.

"He's part of the deal," Teddy added. "What he says goes, Anne. Don't forget that. Mr Evil means business." He held his arm limply against his side.

"Yeah, business," said Evil, waving them to the table.

His back was even more massive than his front, Anne observed. A veritable wardrobe.

"You've never been a courier before, have you?" Evil asked.

"No."

"Good. That's what Mr Caliban told us. We like people who are new to it. They look more innocent, more normal."

"I was told it wasn't drugs," Anne interjected.

"That's correct," the big man said.

"Are you sure?" Anne protested. "Really?"

"What do you want, woman, an official letter on embossed headed notepaper endorsed by a lawyer?" Teddy snickered.

"Well, I would like to know what I'm carrying; it would be nice to know," Anne insisted.

"We find it better for couriers to remain in ignorance. Better security that way," Evil said.

"Okay," Anne finally agreed. "So, tell me what needs doing?"

Teddy poured three glasses of bourbon. She hated the stuff. She gulped it down all the same, conscious of the burning gaze of Evil running up and down her body.

"Listen carefully, Anne, this is the way it's been planned. This is the gospel according to your good friend Teddy Caliban." He passed an envelope over to her across the table. "Tomorrow morning, you take the early flight to Caracas, the ticket and a thousand dollars in cash are in there. If they ask you why you're travelling to Venezuela, you say it's tourism, a bit of shopping, you've heard the stores there have nicer things than Miami. Remember: always act like a tourist. You take a cab from the airport. You have a room booked at the Tamanaco Inter-continental. Go straight there. You stay two nights. During the day, do some shopping, buy a few dresses, some shoes, some carvings in the Indian market, whatever takes your fancy. Don't make friends. Stay at all time on your own. Use the cash. Do not use your own credit cards. The room has been prepaid through a travel agent, so you'll only have to take care of the supplements, drinks and such. The flight back is on Thursday afternoon. You be on it. And go straight to your apartment. We will contact you there. Absolutely do not try and communicate with me here, whether when in Caracas or after you've returned. We'll be watching you to ensure there's no one on your tail. When the time is ripe, we'll meet up and pick up our merchandise."

"And I'll be paid when you get the stuff?" Anne enquired.

"Yes. Twenty-five thousand, as agreed. Is it all clear?"

"Absolutely."

"Good," Teddy Caliban said.

"The seafood's good in Caracas," Evil added. "Just stay in the city centre, have some nice meals, spend the cash. Keep away from others, keep your damn pants on. We can't afford for anything to go wrong, understood?"

"Yes," she sheepishly acquiesced.

Teddy poured another round of drinks, a satisfied look spreading across his face. As the two men on either side of her gulped down the bourbon, she set her own glass aside.

"I'd rather not," Anne said. "Haven't eaten since breakfast and my stomach is pretty empty; the booze won't agree with me much."

Teddy, pleased by the fact that the official part of the encounter was now over, solicitously asked: "Are you hungry? You should have said. I'll call for a takeaway, Chinese, Indian, Mexican? What do you fancy?"

"I'd rather go, Teddy," Anne protested. "I've got to get ready, pack . . ."

"Oh, come on, Anne, it's been a few days, you could stay a few more hours. We could celebrate the deal. I still have some of that great coke."

He looked up at Evil.

"And my business associate was about to leave, weren't you, Evil?"

"I'm too tired, really have to clean up, Teddy," Anne said. "You didn't give me a chance over the phone, you know."

"As a matter of fact, Mr Caliban," Evil slowly said, extending his hand across the table and placing it on Teddy's undamaged hand, "I wasn't thinking of leaving at all."

Both Anne and Caliban looked up at the man in dismay.

"We're in this business together," Evil added. "So why shouldn't we all celebrate together, hey?"

His other hand moved to Anne's bare shoulder. The skin on his fingertips was rough. She shuddered imperceptibly.

"No way," she exclaimed. "I'm not sleeping with either of you, let alone the two of you together. No way. You pigs. And if I hear another word, I'm backing out."

She stood up angrily.

Teddy tried to placate her.

"I was only thinking of you and me, honey. It wasn't my idea . . ."

Evil stood up in turn.

"Afterwards. When you get back from Caracas, then we'll celebrate properly with the little English lady, won't we, Teddy?"

Anne, feeling the onset of panic, began making her way to the door.

"Evil, let's talk about this later," Caliban said to the thug. "Let Anne go now. We'll talk."

Evil smiled. "Well, she'd better not forget the envelope."

Anne blushed and came back to the table to pick up the plane ticket and the cash.

Caliban was still sitting there, fuming. Red-headed little slut, he could guess from the colours in her face she'd spent screwing the weekend away with some other man, or men. He'd teach her a lesson, when the time came. A real lesson.

Evil moved up to Anne.

"I'll see you out to the elevator," he said.

As they waited for the lift to arrive from the lower floors of the apartment block, the thick-set man placed his palm against her butt and whispered in her ear.

"If anything goes wrong, Anne, I shall stick my fist inside your cunt and rip you apart from the inside." She remained silent. "And I shall greatly enjoy doing it, you know. I hurt people, you see, and I'm good at my job. So don't mess things up."

The elevator arrived. She felt she had been waiting for a century or more.

"See you in a few days, Anne; one way or the other I know it's going to be fun. I just hope it's good for you too."

The doors closed and she was alone at last.

She felt sick. Bile rising all the way up her throat.

She was beginning to regret the whole thing.

Oh shit. And shit again. London suddenly felt so far away.

"I'm going out," Evil said. "Need some fresh air. It's too stuffy in here."

Teddy nodded silently. They hadn't spoken a word to each other since the English woman had left, an hour earlier. The bottle of bourbon was long since emptied.

"Do you think I need my coat?" Evil asked. "Not sure if there's a storm about to break or not. Looks that way." He peered past the verandah.

Teddy glanced round at the windows.

"Just in case, take it," he muttered.

Evil left the apartment leaving him alone. At last. Not that there was anything he could do. He picked up the phone and dialled Anne's number. The damn answer machine intercepted the call. Yes, that's what he wanted to do, now he was rid of the bloody thug. Hell, why did the Venezuelans dispatch him over? They knew they could trust Teddy Caliban.

Eduardo Golightly y Robertson Caliban was not a complicated man.

He just had problems with women.

He required no psychotherapist to explain it. He could live with the problem.

Very early in his sentimental career, back when he was a teenager, and still an unimpressive wayward nerd, too many WASP would-be prom queens had messed him up, stood him up, let him down for others, for jocks, and the grudge inside him had festered like a dark flower of anger.

Even now that he had enough money and all the social graces to play the man-woman game with a modicum of manners, there remained a strong core of anger inside Teddy.

Making love to women was like making war. Something inside him sought vengeance even as he enjoyed the feel of their skin and the sweet taste of their kisses. So he had to push harder inside them, until they hurt. He had to make the thrusts ever more savage, and if the woman, often perversely, came to enjoy his brutality, Teddy would then lose all interest in her and quickly let her go. He wanted to see the pain in their eyes, the marks, the scratches on their flesh. Sometimes, he could almost come with his eyes closed, imagining images of savage devastation of torn female flesh, of pain.

In truth, he found most women deeply boring. Like all men, he was looking for something else, something different. He even eschewed pretty ones; too shallow, too loud.

He found it easier to screw hookers. If he paid over the odds, they even ignored the pain he inflicted on them. There was this agency in Coral Gables he used a lot. Reliable. Discreet. Most of their girls were unlike your average prostitute. Had more class. And innocence. Most of them were just housewives doing it out of boredom, seeking extra kicks, or part-time actresses or models in search of that extra cash to bridge gaps between real jobs. They worked harder at the sex, were less transparently uninvolved. This is where he'd come across Anne, the red-headed English woman.

The first time with her had been different. He'd needed an escort, a girl who'd look good and bright, and wouldn't embarrass him at the sit-down dinner at the Fontainebleau following the Motor Parts Suppliers' of Dade County Convention. He'd loved the idea she'd be British. A great touch, that was.

She'd been waiting for him at the hotel bar and behaved impeccably throughout the evening. Just a touch remote, but a good conversationalist with his suppliers, witty but not too much, pretty but not aggressively so. She had shown no irritation when some of the men pawed her while dancing. She seemed good at her job.

He'd offered her an extra five hundred to stay the night with him. She had agreed. He'd drunk too much, and could barely keep himself hard. She was small but had a great body. She didn't say much and it was all over in a few minutes. He asked her to stay longer, ready for more serious action when his energies returned, but she said she had this modelling gig in the morning.

He booked her again a week later.

Found out more about her. That she was game for a South American run, seemingly needed the money real bad. That she liked a nose full of the white Peruvian powder, but then all the whores did. But when she'd stripped and he'd entered her quickly, the damn woman was just too passive and once again he'd come too fast. There was the faint suggestion of a smile on her face as she lay there under him, silent – not even a moan or a fake sigh – as his come trickled weakly into her, as if she was telling him she was in control, that he would never own her totally.

Elusive, slippery, that's what Anne was, Teddy knew.

And the more she eluded him, the more he wanted her badly. He didn't just want to fuck her pale body, he wanted to hear her scream, beg, seek forgiveness, cry her pretty eyes out as he ravaged her, acknowledge his brute strength. Jesus, he almost frightened himself, the way he wanted to do bad things to this woman. She was just asking for it. Bitch!

Anne selected her clothes for the Caracas trip. The phone kept ringing every quarter of an hour or so. Either Teddy or Jakey, she knew. She ignored all the calls. Neither of them left messages on the machine.

She didn't have enough clean underwear and the washing machine in the basement was out of order. She'd have to buy some new stuff when she got to South America.

Didn't need that much, anyway, she'd only be staying in Caracas a couple of days.

She walked over to the fridge and picked a can of beer.

Remembered how her husband back in England always hated it when she drank beer, said he could smell it on her breath.

Well, that was yesterday, wasn't it, and she gulped the cold, refreshing liquid down.

She switched the radio on, surfed quickly through the wave band, seeking anything but Cuban or mariachi rhythms. Alighted on some unknown station right at the end of the dial.

". . . It's always 'The Wrong Time, The Wrong Place' innit?" said a distant DJ, out there in Radio Land.

Anne smiled.

The music exploded from the small transistor radio, washed across her untidy room, swirled around her tired but satisfied body and moved out of the apartment, threading its way into the Miami dusk. Anne closed her eyes. Relaxing at last.

But every time the darkness took over, the memories returned. The shards of her previous life.

"Damn," she muttered to herself, as the piercing chords of an electric guitar in full rock 'n' roll flow invisibly caressed the nape of her neck and she felt herself shivering as the melody captured her from head to toe.

No more memories.

This is why she was here. In Miami. No longer in London.

Running from yesterday.

"Yes," the voice on the radio said, as the tune faded away, "it's me, Mark of God, your unreliable host today. All the music you can handle, music for every day of your life, music as a soundtrack, music as a way of life, yeah! You've just heard Marshall Crenshaw and 'Twenty-Five-Forty-One'. Our man at the weather centre is still predicting dark storms, so cover up out there, y'all. And if rain makes you think of Europe, what do you say if we have some music from those watery climes? Here's one from the Pogues, folks. And if today's Tuesday . . ."

"No, not 'Tuesday Morning'," Anne blurted out. "No."

"The song's 'Tuesday Morning', folks, so sing along and think of rain . . ." the DJ continued.

Anne ragefully threw the radio to the floor and compulsively continued her packing.

Jacob couldn't sleep. He kept on tossing and turning.

The thin white sheet lay all crumpled up at the bottom of the bed.

Every so often, he'd look out for the LCD display on the alarm device and notice that barely ten minutes or even less had elapsed since his last glance. The night went on forever.

He was bone tired, following the weekend with Anne, but it didn't help. Sleep just wouldn't come. Storm clouds seemed to be gathering over the sea and Jacob struggled with the situation. Things were going too fast, he realized. It had the momentum of a car crash; you knew the vehicle was out of control, and your mind worked in slow motion, telling you to do something, anything, but your arms wouldn't respond, and the car careened further into an uncontrollable spin, and you braced yourself for the inevitable impact, idly wondering whether you would even survive it.

The glass of water on the bedside table was empty. Jacob rose to fill it again.

Decided on the spur of the moment not to go back to bed but to take a walk. Slipped on his jeans and a thick grey sweatshirt. Hunted under the settee for his battered brown loafers, and picked his wallet from the jacket hanging on the kitchen chair.

Walking directionless, wrestling with his unusual thoughts, Jacob was caught out by the storm an hour later. He had almost reached the causeway and took refuge in the nearest sheltered place, a bar called the Nighthawks Café near the coach station.

Cigarette smoke floated down from the celling like a bank of low clouds.

Jacob got himself a coffee from the counter and looked around for a table to sit down. The place was crowded. Refugees from the outside storm like him, regular vagrants, overflow from the coach station waiting for early morning transportation.

Few tables had space, or at any rate with anyone he'd wish to share it with. Jacob had never known how to communicate with tramps or drunks. Something in him rebelled when confronted too closely by them. Guilt or fear of becoming one of them? He was standing by the serving counter, nursing the hot coffee cup when he noticed a couple rising at the back of the room, leaving a solitary customer at the table they'd occupied.

Jacob zigzagged his way towards the free space.

Without even looking at whoever was still sitting there, Jacob asked them: "Do you mind if I sit?"

It was a woman. She looked up at him.

"Sure, honey."

"Thanks." He sat down. She was chewing on a doughnut, her other hand holding on for dear life to a small overnight bag she'd placed by the side of the chair.

He took a sip of the coffee. Tasteless but hot.

"You're not from here, are you?" the woman asked.

He smiled back. She was quite pretty, in a plain way, probably late twenties. Too much lipstick. Too many rings on her fingers.

"Yes," he agreed.

"I know," she ventured. "Australian?"

"No. English," Jacob answered.

"Oh," she said, visibly disappointed by her mistake. She extended her hand. "My name's Sandra," she revealed.

"I'm Jacob. You can call me Jake," he told her.

She took another bite of the doughnut.

"So what are you doing here in Florida?" she asked.

"Oh, you know, this and that. Bumming around, a long holiday of sorts."

"Really?"

"It's warmer than home, so it's a good place to be, I suppose."

Outside the rain kept on pelting down. They continued their conversation. Sandra was insatiably curious. Jacob felt comfortable with her, somehow. Oddly enough, he and Anne never did talk that much. The flesh had been stronger than the word. Coffee followed coffee.

She was a waitress in Tallahassee and had come down to see the bright lights of Miami Beach. She lived so close but had never been before. She'd spent the day walking around the Art Deco district like a tourist, and had come back here to get her bag, before the storm broke, to look for a hotel room for a few nights.

"I'm sure they have some free rooms at mine. It's not too expensive," he told her.

"Wow!" she reacted. "Really?"

Jacob indulgently smiled back at her. She was so genuine. Almost too naive for her age.

Underneath the transparent plastic mac, her chest was almost bursting out of the restraining confines of an impossibly tight red blouse.

"So how long have you been here already?" she inquired.

"Too long, I suppose," Jacob replied.

She was about to comment when they were distracted by the raised voices of an older couple at a table across the room. The woman, swearing loudly, had spilt the contents of her glass all over her lap and appeared to be blaming her companion.

"Night life, hey?" Jacob said.

"Yeah," Sandra sighed. And continued her questioning. "Have you ever been to Paris, Jacob? I hear it's very close to London, isn't it?" she asked him.

"Yes. Often," he replied.

"Tell me," she asked.

The night was drawing on and, now, Jacob felt all the tiredness surge over him like a mighty wave. The smoke in the bar was getting to him; the girl was nice but was beginning to get on his nerves. He needed the rest. He glanced at the windows. The rain outside had abated.

"Listen, Sandra," he told her. "I have to go, you know. Have to catch up with my beauty sleep. I've got a trip coming up soon, I think. Maybe New Orleans. With a friend. I really have to go back to my hotel. Sorry."

He laid out a few bills on the table top for the extra coffees, and stood up.

"Jacob?"

"Yes?'

"Your hotel . . . you mentioned they might have rooms. Do you think I could walk along with you?"

"I suppose so," Jacob said and she followed him silently from the Nighthawks Café to the Governor Hotel, cruising steadily through the Miami late night, avoiding puddles and sleeping drunks. All the while, Jacob's mind raced through crazy scenarios. Lynda. Anne. Sandra. How he could not invite her up when they reached the hotel, without offending her, hurting her feelings? But when they did, she resolutely approached the night porter's desk and booked herself a room for two days.

"See you tomorrow, maybe," Jacob said as they parted on her floor.

"Yeah," Sandra said.

Jacob began climbing the stairs to the next floor. She called him.

"Jacob?"

"Yes?"

"Have you ever written poems?" she asked.

He paused.

"No, I never have," he answered.

But they both knew he was lying.

And though Jacob was all too aware he once had penned maudlin lines, he also knew he would never write poems again.

Tina and Lucille

O. Z. Evangeline

The hunger

The Dixie Chicks blared from the jukebox as Lucille Sawyer covered her station at Pancake House.

Waitressing was not easy work and the tips could be lousy, but Lucille loved the hustle and bustle of hungry cranky patrons.

She loved to tease them. Mess with their orders. Mess with their heads. Make them wait. Wait until they ran out of breadsticks and water. Wait until their stomachs thumped with acid and need. Wait until they were on the brink of emotional and physical meltdown, arguing amongst themselves and slapping their children. By the time their food finally arrived they were begging. Grateful.

Then Lucille could play heroine. "Darn that new kitchen help. Always screwin' things up. I straightened *them* out, lemme tell ya'." She'd wink.

But even with job perks like this, Lucille still needed a break. She looked at the clock. It was time to call her friend Tina. She went into the back for a semblance of quiet and dialled the phone.

"HEeeeY little housewife. You packed yet?"

"No. I haven't asked Darryn yet!"

"*What?!* Well get crackin' and get packin', gal. I'll be over in a few . . ."

"Okaaaay." Tina pouted, displaying ample lipspace, which

would soon be enhanced by lip gloss, a tan, and amazing lighting.

Woman in a cage

Tina Dickenson puttered in the kitchen as husband Darryn slept. She couldn't seem to complete simple tasks. Talk show psychologists might describe her as having Domestic Dysfunctional Disorder. DDD. But she couldn't remember what they thought, or to care, or what channel Oprah was on, anyway.

"DARRYYYYYYYN! Better get *up*! Gonna be late for worrrrrK!"

Darryn propelled himself from bed and headed for the kitchen.

"Tina, I done told ya' a thousand times. I hate it when you yell like that. I'm going back to bed, until you can get your mind right!"

Tina took a softer tack.

"Pssssst! Darryyyyn . . . come on, hon, time to get up." She whispered.

"Well okay then. Now that's better."

"Whatcha want for dinner tonight, hon?"

"Tina, I might not be home for dinner tonight."

"Yeah . . . it's funny how many people want to buy nuclear warheads on a Friday night." Tina pouted.

"Well, Tina, that's how come I'm Regional Sales Manager . . . and you ain't."

The big stuff

Lucille pulled up in front of Tina's suburban home and blew the horn before hopping out. Lucille's 1953 Buick Roadmaster convertible sat in front of Tina's driveway. She was proud of her unique wheels. It was spotless. She was in fact smug. How many could boast of a Woody station wagon that happened to be a convertible?

Lucille met Tina in the driveway. Tina dragged massive suitcases behind her.

"Good lord, woman. We're just goin' away for a weekend. Do

you really need all this shit?! Certainly you must be aware of how *my* character packs. Learn from a *master*."

"Well geez, Lucille, I don't know what to take! Just play along. *My* character is childlike, disorganized, but lovable."

"What about precocious?"

"Um . . . no. Here, Lucille, take my gun. Take care of it. I don't know nuthin' bout handlin' no firearms!"

"Good *grief*, Tina, just hand it over here. Careful now. Now smile for the camera, girl, we're *off*!"

Highway women

Tina and Lucille relished the open road. Hair blowing in the wind, skin kissed by the sun, pink lip gloss glistening, braless, tank tops and nipples askew, they loved to tease truckers. But not just any trucker would do: only those with "Ass, Gas Or Grass . . . Nobody Rides For Free" mudflaps. As the adjacent trucker would leer down from his cab into their topless Woody, they would smile at him, lick their lips and stroke their breasts. Lucille got a thrill simply thinking of it.

Hey, man. What are YOU lookin' at? My breasts? Tits? Boobs? Hooters? Knockers? Betcha got some kinda goddamned goofy name for 'em too doncha, fella? Well, they're nice and soft and firm and high. And mine. Go ahead. Take a look. Sneak a peek. Imagine how they'd feel cupped in your hands or rubbing your naked chest. Imagine my hard bumpy erect nipples growing and throbbing in your slavering mouth. Go AHEAD . . .

Occasionally there were accidents.

But for the moment it was just Tina and Lucille, who were currently accident-free.

"So what did Darryn say when you told him you were goin' with me?"

"I didn't tell 'im."

"*What?!*"

"I didn't tell 'im. I just left a note in lipstick on the TV screen. He *hates* it when I do that." Tina giggled.

"Tina!"

Fuel and bullets

Tina and Lucille cruised west on 412 across the Arkansas/ Oklahoma line. The landscape would gradually change from a sparsely green West Arkansas to a flat brown Oklahoma plain.

Tina took in her environment. "Hey! I always thought that landscapes abruptly changed at state lines."

"Nooo, silly. Topographical variance can be a gradually changing delineation based upon plate tectonics, and not necessarily a sudden and abrupt physical change."

"Lucille! Sometimes you can be such a know-it-all!"

Blwah! BLWAAaaah! Blwah! BLWAAaaaaah!

Their conversation was cut short by the blast of an air horn. The forty-eight-foot big rig pulled up beside them and maintained position.

"Heeeeey, babies! What's a coupla chipmunks like y'all doing out in the middle of nowhere in a Woody?" The trucker looked down into their front seat. "And please excuse my crude simplistic character. I was simply written this way."

"Darnit, Lucille, I *hate* it when men call women chipmunks! God, it just makes me so *mad*. And how do we *know* he was simply written that way? We just met him . . .

"And Lucille, I know that we should wait until later to blow up Trucker Man, but why not simply wrap it up? Initially interact with him, express anger and disgust at his chauvinistic attitudes, then *ka boom!* Ignite his world with fuel and bullets . . ."

"You gals ready to *party?*"

"I think SOOooo. Follow us." Lucille smirked, putting the pedal to the metal.

"You crazy . . . *chipmunks* from *hell*!!" were the words uttered post-gunshot, pre-explosion, by an outraged trucker on a remote desert.

Joint

At a dusty crossroads, Tina spotted a bar.

"Lucille, can't we stop for one little bitty drink? Just one?! Darryn never lets me do *nuthin'*!"

"Well, okaaay, but just one. In and out. You hear me?"

"*Yes, ma'am!*"

It was close to nightfall as Tina and Lucille pulled into the crowded Arkansas Bar parking lot. Inside the club they at last found a table. They ordered beer and tequila and guzzled. The place reeked of beer, tobacco, burgers, chili, and pheromones.

Lucille sniffed. "Pabst. Marlboros. Cheap fatty ground beef. Three Alarm Chili. West Arkansas Male."

"Good call!" Tina observed.

A tall man swaggered from the bar to their table.

"Hey. I'm Harley. What's a coupla Barbie Dolls like y'all doin' alone in a place like this?" he asked.

"Well, technically we're not alone, are we?" Lucille observed.

"Whooooeeee, gal. You're a feisty one, ain't ya?"

"Hey, Harley. I'm Tina. Well, to answer your question, we just stopped in for a drink . . . I just had a fight with my husband, and my friend Lucille here, she hasn't had a good fuck in ages, and likely has legal problems . . ." Tina babbled, smiling.

"Tina! Shut the fuck up!"

"Wanna dance, Tina?" he asked.

"Sure!"

Disgruntled, Lucille headed for the ladies' room. Crammed elbow to elbow in a ten-by-fifteen-foot space with thirty women applying makeup and fighting for a two-by-three mirror, she took her life into her own hands.

"Bitch! Get out of my way!" one woman hissed, before going one-on-one with another. "Heifer! Cow!" the woman screamed. Lucille ran for the ladies' room door, not a long sprint.

On the dance floor, alcohol, heat and motion soon conspired to make Tina's head spin.

"I need some air, Harley. I think I'm gonna puke."

"Well come on, darlin'. Let's step outside. I wanted to show you my Ford Ranger anyways."

Tina and Harley wove through a tight crowd, towards the front exit. They staggered outside to the parking lot. His Ranger gleamed in the semi-dark, parked between a Blazer and a Ram. They stood beside it.

Tina leaned and hurled her guts. "Whoa . . . careful, darlin'. That stuff could peel paint. Okay now. Feelin' better?"

Tina leaned back against the Ranger's warm hood. "Yeah, thanks. I feel a little better now." Harley faced Tina and leaned into her. He stroked her face and lips. He held the back of her head as he stuck his right index finger into her mouth.

"Whaaa? . . . mmmph . . . gorf . . ." It was difficult to talk with her mouth full.

He ran his finger along the inside cheeks and over her tongue. Its soft wet warmness sent nervous vibrations to his cock. With a wet plop he pulled his finger from Tina's mouth.

"Tina, I'm not gonna hurt ya' . . . now do what I say . . . suck my cock . . . and wax my truck! . . . Come on now . . . come *on* now, you know you want it, you little tease."

"Harley, stop it! I have to go. Lucille's gonna be lookin' for me!"

"Hey, baby. You think you can just brush me off?" He unzipped his jeans fly, his spring-loaded cock popping out of denim.

Grabbing her shoulders, he pushed her to her knees. His cock danced in Tina's face. "Don't play dumb with me! Here. Open wide." He held Tina's head.

Click went the hammer of a .38 against the back of Harley's neck.

"Hey, *buddy*. When a woman says she's averse to waxin' a man's truck, she means it. Now let go of the lady's head and back away slowly . . ."

"You fuckin' bitch! Suck my cock."

"*What* did you say?!"

"I *said* . . . *wax* . . . my . . . *truck*." He sneered.

The sound of gunfire was partially muffled by the sound of a Country & Western band.

The getaway

In a daze, Tina and Lucille ran for the car and hopped in. Tina squealed out of the parking lot and in front of a big rig.

Blwah! BLWAAaaah!

His horn blasted. She pulled the car over onto the shoulder. Lucille quickly got out and doubled over, retching onto the ground. "Can you believe it? I'm hungry again."

Lucille took the wheel. "I need to get some coffee and think! Let's find someplace."

Tina was in a funk. "Okay. What*ever*."

Driving west on 412, they soon pulled into Oklahoma Truck Stop parking lot. Business was booming. They went inside and took in the ambiance. The decorative motif sported red vinyl, dark wooden panelling, and sports trophies mounted on the wall.

Lucille sniffed.

"Burnt white toast. Gravy past its prime. Recycled peas and carrots. Petrified instant mashed potatoes. Overcooked Salisbury Steak."

"Good call."

Tina and Lucille were seated in a booth. Lucille ordered coffee. Tina ordered the Chicken Fried Steak Dinner.

"Tina . . . we've got to get a plan! And how can you eat at a time like this?"

"Geez, Lucille, I don't know!" she whined/screamed.

"Tina. Keep your voice down. We can't afford to attract attention right now," Lucille whispered/spat in short bursts.

Coffee and food appeared. Lucille gripped and sipped.

Tina tore into her Chicken Fried Steak Dinner. "This shit has too much *salt*!"

"Tina. Be *quiet*," Lucille hissed.

"I'm goin' to the bathroom."

"Fine. Then we're *outta*, here." Lucille threw some money on the table.

As Tina and Lucille walked out of Oklahoma Truck Stop a spool rolled; toilet tissue trailed from Tina's right shoe.

Questionable

Officer Cal Holcomb interviewed waitress Linda in front of Arkansas Bar. It was not their first conversation. It would not be their last.

"Linda, we have reason to believe that Tina Dickenson and Lucille Sawyer were here at the time of the incident. We have reports of two women fitting their description, peelin' outta here in a Woody wagon. What can you remember about the night's events?"

"I talked to them gals. And they were great tippers. Cal, I know *people*. These two wouldn't a' done something like this!"

"Well, hon, see, now that's really more of an impression or a value judgement. I simply need to know the facts. Have coffee with me, Linda. Let's talk."

Wet

Ensconced in motel rooms in a dump off I-44, Tina and Lucille practised an ancient and sacred female ritual: bathing. They had been grimy. Filthy. And they would be so again. But for now hot water and expensive soaps, shampoos and cosmetics empowered them. Slipping into a shower or a bath, vigorously soaping their faces, necks . . . warm and soft and fragrant, they felt revived, as if they could conquer the world.

Lucille felt *dirty*. She'd been fantasizing about a hot shower for hours.

Mmmmm . . . Slip under the hot water, lather my hair, face, neck, shoulders . . . work down. Gently vigorously roughly soap my breasts and pinch my rosy erecting nipples between thumb and forefinger . . . slide my hand down Down DOWN my slippery belly and between my thighs . . . work Work WORK for the perfect balance of friction and pressure and lather . . . finger the soft warm cleft of lather and salt and sweat . . . stroke my swelling lips and clit . . . Slide in In IN OUT . . . deeper and faster until I'm . . .

clean . . . Clean . . . Oh God Oh God CLEAN!! Or I could
use the shower spray.

Jimmy

In the beginning stages of a plan, Lucille dialled the phone.
Jimmy's machine picked up. "Hey! I'm not home right now.
Please leave a message."

"Jimmy! It's *me*. Are you *there*?! Pick up the phone!"

"Hey, Lucille! What's up? Where are you?"

"Jimmy . . . I'm in trouble. I'm in deep shit. I can't explain things
right now. But I need money. Will you help me?"

"Kumquat, *what* is goin' on? Why can't you tell me?"

"Jimmy, please . . . just wire me some money and I'll be in
touch."

Jimmy took pause. Women were always giving him that line.

The hitcher

As they hit the road for Western Union, Tina first viewed TJ as he
leaned against a fence post on the North side of 60. His image
made her think of a combination of the Marlboro Man and a
Guess jeans model.

A highly cheekboned face moved above broad shoulders,
hard, flat belly, narrow hips, iron ass, and heavily muscled legs.
Tina had never been with a man like that. He appeared to be a
boy really. She had only been with her husband Darryn. *Been
with. Been with! What a vague term. Boring. I don't want to be
with. I want to have sex. Flail a fuck puppet. Bop and bounce a
boner. Fuck.*

"Oh puleeeeze, Lucille, can we pick 'im up, huh, can we, can
we?! I *never* get to have no fun."

"Well, okay, we can give him a ride . . . if you promise to keep
your propensity for blabbin' under control! I mean it. And if you
use a double negative one more time I'll scream!"

"Okay, *okay*."

TJ felt relief as the wood-panelled station wagon braked and pulled over to the side of the road. He grabbed his pack and hoofed it to the car.

"Well, heeeyy, ladies. Where y'all headed? I'm TJ and I'm goin' to Tempe."

Wired

Western Union was inconspicuously located in a small corner of an independent real estate office. It was harder to find than a small-town bus station: one that was located in the back of a doughnut shop, or in a bait and tackle store on a secondary highway. But Lucille found it. Tina and TJ stayed in the car as Lucille went inside.

The small room included an office of sorts, a desk/counter, and a battered sofa against the front wall. A large man sat upon it, partially obscured by his newspaper.

Lucille slapped her ID onto the counter. "Do you have a wire for Lucille Sawyer?"

The clerk rifled his work space. "No, ma'am. Sorry."

"How about for: codeword 'Kumquat'? Anything?"

"Hi there, Kumquat." The voice came from behind the newspaper.

"Jimmy!"

As a stunned Lucille and a cocky Jimmy walked outside and got into the car, Tina and TJ flirted in the back seat.

"Jimmy! What are *you* doin' here?! Um . . . this is TJ. We're givin' him a ride!"

Jimmy's and TJ's eyes met.

"I don't think that's such a good idea."

"Well, now, you're probably right. Thanks for the ride. I'll be goin' now. Y'all take care!" TJ stammered, gathering his stuff. Tina watched him walk away.

Tina pouted. *And they say* women *are competitive. Jimmy and TJ can't even share 90 cubic feet of interior car space without butting heads.*

Rooms

It was a rainy evening as Lucille and Jimmy shared postcoital conversation in her motel room.

"How come we aren't naked?" he asked.

"Silly. It's *later*. We *were* naked. Now we aren't."

"But how does the viewer/reader know that we had sex?"

"They just know! Don't worry about it. And hey, it's pretty neat how this film lacks gratuitous female nudity."

"Ahem . . . let's get back into character, shall we? Kumquat, come back to Arkansas Town with me . . . please . . ."

"Jimmy, what colour are my toenails?"

"Excuse me?"

"It's a question intended to determine if you really pay attention to me, and notice details. I said, Jimmy, what colour are my toenails?"

"Fuchsia." He sighed in relief.

"What shade of fuchsia?"

Jimmy began to sweat. It seemed that women were never satisfied.

Tina puttered in her room. Answering a knock at the door she was faced with . . . him. The delicious young hitchhiker with the hard bod and soft voice. He stood there, shirtless in the rain, raindrops loudly pinging off his hat.

"Tina, I don't mean to bother ya, but could I come in?"

"Oooh . . . Hi, TJ! I guess so. For a few minutes! At least come in and get dry."

"But what's the point of me comin' in and gettin' dry if ya' just gonna send me back out into the rain?!"

"Please, TJ. No more questions!"

They sat at the foot of the bed and watched TV. It was the WB Network.

"Shoot, can you believe some of these sitcom characters?!" TJ was more sophisticated than he let on. They laughed and lay back on the bed.

"It feels real good to be on a hard bed with a soft woman."

"I'll bet you say that to all the women . . ."

"Nah. No, ma'am. Some beds are soft. Some women are hard."

He stood and pulled her up against him. She felt a hardness. She desperately wanted to move upon it: up and down and around it.

She thumped with desire and enthusiasm.

"Come on now . . . I can tell that you *want* to . . . and Darryn should have his ass kicked for bein' insensitive to your needs, darlin' . . ."

Tina smiled. She would soon take a wild ride with a soft-voiced hard-bodied semi-stranger.

Squeals and cries were heard by motel patrons as Tina and TJ jumped up and down, up and down, on an extra firm mattress, their heads bouncing off the ceiling. "Weeeeeeeee! Higher! Higher! Harder! Yes! *Yes!*"

Tina and TJ were strong believers in foreplay.

Cash, stash, loot

The next morning Lucille sat in a booth sipping coffee as Tina strode into Motel Restaurant and plopped down across from her.

"Girrrl, you look beat! What on earth have you been up to?!"

"Lucille, TJ spent the night with me. I'm *exhausted*!"

"Awww, Tina. I'm so glad you finally got laid properly! But where is TJ now? And where is the money?"

"He's takin' a shower . . ."

They ran for Tina's room. TJ was gone. The money was gone.

Heading west on 60, Tina and Lucille pulled into the parking lot of Country Store. Tina went inside. Part convenience store, part snack bar, part Mom and Pop establishment, part firearms dealer, it had almost anything a person might need. Ten-day-old rotisserie chicken. Barbecued. Oklahoma Is For Lovers T-shirts. Turquoise jewellery. Liquor. Guns. Ammo. Notary service. Nightcrawlers. Crickets. Minnows.

Tina shopped for chocolate, tampons, liquor and ammo. At the counter, down to her last $20, she went for broke. She pulled her .38 from her purse and made an announcement: "Okay, people. This is a robbery. Down on the floor. Nobody lose their head, and nobody loses their head!"

"Do what she says. She's pre-menstrual!" hissed one terrified patron.

"Empty that register, buddy. Hurry up!" Tina groused. "And I'll be taking those mini-bottles of rum. The pink sunglasses. The fuzzy keychain. Put it all in a bag . . . yes, plastic!"

Tina ran for the car. "Gooooo! Drive, Lucille, drive!!"

"God, you're in a funny mood today."

Men together

Officer Cal Holcomb helped to set the trap. At the Dickenson residence, the surveillance was in place. Waiting.

"Okay, guys. We're set here. Darryn, now remember, if Tina calls, keep her on the line so we can get a trace. Pretend that you are happy to hear from her. Women *love* that shit."

It would be a while before the phone call came in. It would give the guys time to plan. Watch TV. Eat pizza. Talk.

"I don't understand why Tina went and run off. But I always said, 'that Lucille is a bad influence!'" Darryn shared.

"Women are funny. Moody. Don't I know it?! I've been in a relationship or two. Arrested a few gals in my time too. 'How can you *do* this to me?' they'd cry. 'I thought you *loved* me!' 'Well, hon, you broke the *law*. Not to mention, you pissed me off. In a general kinda way,' I'd explain. Women! Go figure!" Cal pondered.

The group shared a chuckle.

"Hello! Tina! Hon, it's so *good* to hear from you!" Darryn perked as the call came in.

A click and a dial tone followed. "They're on to us, Lucille."

Stuffed

Back roads became too taxing for Tina and Lucille. Boring. Not enough bathrooms. Not enough entertainment. They popped up to I-40. Where the food was bland and predictable. Where Denny's and Bob's Big Boy ruled. Where the shopping was good. Where major brand discount outlets abounded. Shopping would settle their jangled nerves. Afterward they could get off the main roads and head back for the boonies.

The shopping trip proved fruitful: they bought new underwear and jeans. Big bags of merchandise in their hands, they felt relaxed and fulfilled. It was almost as good as sex, and would suffice when no men were available. Walking into the store, cruising the aisles, looking for that perfect piece. Yearning. Searching. Finding. Touching. Stroking the softness and slickness of cotton and silk – wool if in the mood for something rough. Building to an explosive climax at the checkout stand, they would soon feel the inevitable Post Consumption Blues, part of the vicious cycle in the search for More. For Bigger. For Better.

New Mexico police officers Clint Ellsworth and Merle Franklin sat in their cruiser in the BigHugeSaveMart parking lot. From behind mirrored aviator shades, their eyes followed two women who strolled from the store. They wore tank tops, skintight jeans, and cowboy boots. Carrying large shopping bags, they slowly walked. Theirs was a fluid walk, languid, as if their nerves and joints and cunts were oily sticky wet. With WD4O. 3-IN-ONE. K-Y. Spit. Cum. To the men they exuded sexuality, as if the women had just tumbled from wrecked beds with respective spent lovers.

"Hey, is that a Buick Roadmaster? You don't see too many of them on the road anymore," Clint observed.

"Yup. Nope."

As Tina and Lucille pulled out of the parking lot, a police cruiser followed.

"Lucille, don't look now, but there's a police car behind us."

Lucille took a south left turn off an I-40 frontage road, cruising the gauntlet of low-rent apartments and duplexes. They viewed a perversion of nature: harsh desert turned lush by extensive watering systems. Some homeowners simply rolled out astroturf. Others landscaped with stone. The streets were named of various shades; they wound up in a subdivision: Pastels. Light pink, green, yellow and blue Ranch houses, rustic fencing, and swimming pools predominated on Cotton Candy Way. Butter Cream Court. Robin's Egg Lane. Easter Basket Circle. It was enough to induce nausea and dizziness.

"Hey. I wonder where these girls are headed? Maybe we should pull 'em over on a pretence. Feel 'em out. Ask 'em for their phone numbers! Ask 'em out for drinks! Our shift's almost over, you know."

"Yup."

WHOOOoooo Whooop! WHOOOoooo WHOOOP!

At the siren's sound Lucille hung a sudden sharp right onto Peach Blush Drive and another onto Pearl Pink Court.

"Lucille, I'm not really satisfied with the ending of this film. I realize that Hollywood dictates our characters be punished in the end . . . but suicide?! There must be a less extreme ending. A better way."

The station wagon barrelled over the kerb, across the sidewalk, across a lawn and through a wooden fence before going into a pool.

"Girl . . . hold your breath. And I assume that you can swim."

Two women in a Woody went under.

"Hey, Merle. Where did those girls *go*?!"

"Dunno!"

Endings, beginnings

Two cops in an Arkansas Denny's later ruminated.

"Too bad 'bout Tina and Lucille. They weren't really bad girls. First offence armed robbery is child's play for these parts. And destruction of property ain't that big a deal. But men are real picky 'bout their trucks. Harley went wild when Lucille pumped the Ranger full of lead. Insisted we press charges . . ." Cal sighed.

"Yup."

A small New Mexico town would gain two colourful new residents. Hair colour, glasses, sensible dresses, sensible shoes and food service would be their guise. Lucille was an old hand at waiting tables. But Tina would have to learn.

"Hon, sorry the food took so long. There was a problem in the kitchen. S'okay *now*, doll. Now y'all eat up!" winked the friendly new Steak House waitress.

The Flying Lady Diner

Debra Gray De Noux & O'Neil De Noux

Ominous clouds hover over Lake Borgne as I ease my new grey, two-door '48 Plymouth Business Coupe away from New Orleans along blacktopped Highway 90. The grey-brown lake water is curled into small white caps as a weather system moves in from the Gulf of Mexico. A typical summer rainstorm is moving in to drench the coast as I drive eastward toward the piney woods of Mississippi. I can smell the rain in the air, damp and salty like the marshes to my right.

I downshift as I approach the narrow bridge across the Rigolets pass separating Lake Borgne from Lake Pontchartrain. A woody station-wagon passes the other way. It's filled with kids, one who sticks his tongue out at me.

This should be an easy day's work. Breeze over to the coast, do a little snooping around, earn my forty bucks a day, plus mileage and expenses and report back how I couldn't find the missing son. I plan to put a move on the distraught mother and slip it to her. My kinda woman. Lonely widow with an oversize bustline and nice firm gams.

The marsh turns into swampland as I approach Pearl River, cypress trees dripping Spanish moss, towering oaks, also draped in moss. Snowy egrets dot the side of the road. I drive past the carcass of an armadillo and remember what a guy at the Audubon Zoo told me about the little suckers. Most drivers swerve to make sure they don't hit the critters, driving over them, instead of running over them with tyres. Only the stupid bastards jump when a car passes over them and get tumbled to death.

The storm gets to me before I reach the tiny town of Waveland. I get my windows up in time but the rain is fat and slams against the windshield, so much the wipers can't keep up.

Neon lights up ahead on the left slow me down and the rain seems to let up as I turn into a shell parking lot next to a diner in the middle of nowhere.

The diner is silver, looks like an oversized Airstream camper. The red and blue neon sign reads: Flying Lady Diner. Above its front door is an art deco painting of an airplane propeller ridden by a buxomy blonde wearing only a red bathing suit. She's winking.

I wait for a let up in the rain, which comes eventually. It's a momentary breath between waves of rain and I rush out, my Florsheims slipping on the shells before I reach the front door. Thankfully, I don't fall on my ass.

The only occupant of the diner, a chubby man standing next to the grill, waves a spatula at me.

"Come on in," he says. Nearly as round as he is tall, the man has snowy white hair and a full beard, rosy cheeks and rectangular, wire-rimmed glasses. That's right, Santa Claus wearing a cook's apron.

I sit at the turquoise Formica counter and Santa plops a menu in next to my car keys. The place smells faintly of pine oil and cooked eggs. I order a hamburger, fries and coffee, and look around the place. It looks new. No worn spots or even scratches on the counter or the booths. The vinyl seats look almost unused. There isn't even one dead fly inside the smoky glass domes of the light fixtures hanging from the low ceiling.

Turning around, I watch the rain wash against the windows.

"Quite a sight," I say as I catch the scent of my hamburger sizzling on the grill.

"What?" Santa says as he places a white mug of coffee in front of me.

"Like a damn hurricane."

He pulls off his glasses and blinks at me. His eyes are dark green and look far too young for his face. He shrugs and goes back to the grill.

A door opens at the rear of the diner and a woman steps out of a back room. My highly trained Private Eye eyes take her in: tall, red hair done up in a bun, Gibson-Girl style, slim yet heavy-chested, wearing a tight-fitting, white waitress dress, long slender legs.

Smiling as she approaches, she doesn't even seem to notice the rain slamming against the windows. She stares intently at me as she moves past. I catch a whiff of light perfume. She sits at the counter two stools away from me.

Up close, I see she's in her mid-twenties and *very* pretty, a face waiting to be discovered by some hot-shot Hollywood producer, if we were in southern California instead of southern Mississippi. Her eyes, even brighter green, give me a penetrating stare.

"You going to try your coffee?" Her voice is deep and sexy, a little like Lauren Bacall. No southern accent here. She sounded mid-western. So did the Santa look-a-like, now that I think it.

Santa slides an identical mug in front of her and we both take sips of the strong, fresh coffee. Nice. Both like it black.

She keeps staring and I almost start laughing. What's there to see? I'm your typical Spanish-American – olive complexion, dark brown hair, brown eyes. OK, I'm six-two and in pretty good shape for a thirty-year-old. My mother thinks I'm handsome, so have a few women, but only a few.

"Joe Torres," I tell her as I reach out my right hand. I don't tell her it's old New Orleans Spanish blood, Castilian to be exact, as my mother would point out.

She shakes my hand softly and says, "I'm Lily." She takes in a deep breath. "And that's Sam behind the counter."

I tell Sam hello as she finally lets go of my hand.

"Have you worked here long?" I ask Sam. Figuring I might as well start my search here, in the middle of nowhere.

"Couple weeks," he answers as he sprinkles onions on my simmering burger. He leans toward the deep fryer and swishes a metal spoon through my French fries.

"This is my first week," Lily says.

I reach into the inner pocket of my tan suit coat and pull out a black and white picture. I pass it to Lily.

"His name is Mike Stone and he's been missing three days."

She shakes her head and puts the picture on the counter.

"Ever see him in here?"

"Nope." She takes another sip of coffee.

Sam puts my plate down next to my coffee cup. I ask him to look at the picture. He lifts his glasses as he looks. "Never seen him before."

Lily picks up a bottle of ketchup and drips a thick glob on the plate with my fries.

I grab my hamburger. "His friends at work said he headed for Bay St Louis two nights back. Never realized Bay St Louis had much of a night life."

Lily just blinks at me.

The hamburger is delicious, the onions seared perfectly.

Lily continues to stare into my eyes, so I watch carefully as I tell her I'm a PI on a wandering son case. Mike's mother hired me.

"Strange thing is another accountant who works with Mike is also missing. His boss thinks he was heading this direction too, couple weeks ago."

Her eyes reveal nothing, just that penetrating, almost intrusive stare. Uncommon for a woman that pretty to stare so intently, especially as her eyes soften and I see something inside, something vulnerable.

I dip two fries in the ketchup and eat them.

Slowly, Lily lifts her mug and takes another sip. I watch her red lips touch the mug.

I force myself to look at Sam who is by the register at the end of the counter near the front door.

"Since you've been here a couple weeks, maybe you saw the other man who's missing?" I pull the second picture from my coat pocket and put it on the counter.

Sam flashes a warm, Santa-like smile as he climbs off his stool. He grabs the coffee pot on his way back to us. He lifts his glasses again as he looks at the second picture, shakes his head again, then refills my mug and Lily's before going back to the register.

I can't resist and eat more of the hamburger. Didn't realize I was so hungry. A sudden gust of wind slams against the windows and the diner rocks slightly. Lily finally looks at the windows. A wind-blown wave of rain washes over us and if we weren't five miles from the Gulf, I'd swear we were being inundated by salt water.

"Some rain," I say. (For a PI, I need to work on my lines with women.)

My ineptness has no effect on Lily. She turns those nearly hypnotic green eyes back to me and keeps staring. Then again, why women find any of us attractive is beyond me. I take another bite of hamburger.

Climbing off the stool, Lily takes in a deep breath as she moves up to me and puts her hands on my shoulders. She leans forward cautiously, turns her head and purses her lips.

I lean toward her lips and she hesitates.

"Kiss at your own risk." Again that deep, sexy voice.

I lean forward and we kiss, so softly I barely feel her lips. We kiss again and I feel them now, pressing against mine, parting slightly, her tongue flicking against mine. Our kiss continues as I turn on my stool, as she presses her body against me. Our kiss goes on and I feel my heart thundering in my chest, her arms wrap around my neck.

The kiss continues and we press against one another.

It ends as Lily pulls back slowly. Looking at my lips she says, breathlessly, "That was very nice. I think you'll do."

I'm about to agree when I spot Sam coming back in. So pre-occupied, I hadn't noticed him leave. He's drenched. He wrings the water from his hair and says my car's been taken care of. He tosses my keys to Lily who catches them and puts them back on the counter.

I hear the sound of a lock being set. Sam's hand moves from the front door lock. He's still smiling as he reaches for another switch. He flips it and stairs descend from the ceiling. Sam starts up the stairs.

Lily presses her lips against mine again and I start to resist, but can't. Our second kiss is longer than the first and I'm panting as we pull apart.

"What's with the stairs?" I point over to them.

Lily smiles. "Sam has to . . . drive."

As I open my mouth to ask – drive what – I feel the diner shake. Metal shutters roll down outside the windows and we're encased now, the rain a distant pinging against the metal.

I'm not sure but the diner seems to . . . rise.

Falling off my stool, I snatch my snub-nosed Smith and Wesson .38 from its holster along the small of my back. The diner is definitely rising, swaying slightly. I point my gun at the ceiling, as if it'll do any good. Lily crosses her arms.

"What are you going to do with that?"

She's got me.

The diner rises quicker and seems to take a slow turn to the north and west, I think. I put my gun back in its holster.

Lily reaches up and pulls the bobby pins from her hair. She shakes it out and her pretty face is surrounded by long strands of wavy red hair. Natural red hair, a little on the blondish side. No phoney dye job. She's ravishing as she stands there with her hands on her hips. She's so good looking. Is my heart still racing from our kissing, or the fact . . . *we're flying*!

"As you can surmise," Lily says. "We're not from these parts."

The diner seems to pick up speed. It's still rising.

"Where are you from?" My mouth is suddenly dry.

"Where do you suppose?"

"Mars?" The word sounds funny to me.

She laughs.

"Venus?"

"Oh no. Much further. It'll take us about a month to get there." She steps closer and puts her hands behind her back. "We'll be well acquainted by then."

A jolt and the diner accelerates. I sit back on my stool and hold on to the counter.

"Is that where Mike Stone ended up?"

"No." She sits on the stool next to me, crossing her legs.

"He didn't want to come, so we dropped him off."

"Where?"

"Idaho."

Lily leans forward and brushes her lips across mine and it's nice. Very nice.

"Idaho?"

"You've got ten minutes to decide. It's me . . . or Idaho."

She kisses me again, gently, lovingly. I'm so turned on, I can barely control myself from grabbing her and pulling her to the floor. It takes all my strength to stop kissing.

"You mean I have a choice?"

She nods and nibbles my lower lip.

"So do I," she says, her breath falling across my lips. "And I choose you, most definitely."

We kiss again, a long, deep, wet kiss.

Finally surfacing for breath, it takes nearly a minute for me to recover.

"I warned you." She smiles wickedly. "Kiss at your own risk."

I swallow hard, then say, "Idaho?"

"That's where we drop off rejects. You'll live in the backwoods. Won't remember any of this. Wind up a little paranoid. Vote Republican the rest of your life."

She drapes her arms across my shoulders again. "Or you can come with me. But you have to decide now."

"Where are we going?"

"You'll like it. You have to trust me. If you like me, you'll like it a lot."

My heart stammering and I have to decide now. No hesitating. No going back. It's her or Idaho. Not much of a choice.

Those penetrating green eyes seem to bore into mine as we stare at each other. In them I see such a warmth, I feel hot suddenly, feel sweat working down my back. I want her more than I've wanted anything.

Time is falling away. I have to think clearly. I have to ask.

"Why me?"

She lets out another deep breath. "There's one thing missing where we're going."

My stomach tightens. I feel a shiver deep inside.

"What's that?"

"Brown eyes."

The Road Calls Me Dear

Cory Doctorow

1. Realizing my potential on the banks of the river Junque

There's a knot of shame that twists my stomach when the kid talks to me. He calls me Mr Cornucopia, a name that won't turn up on any cop's computer, and when he speaks to me, he looks out into the river of highway and talks quietly into the traffic, like, I'm not really addressing you, I'm just thinking aloud, and if you don't want me to bother you, hell, that's okay.

I remember how cocky he was right at the start, and I am ashamed.

He was seventeen, and walked like he had at least six elbows and four knees. He looked so ridiculous, trying to strut in his oversized black leather pants, too-small vinyl biker-jacket and mirrorshades with tape across the bridge.

"I'm here to warn you off, fella," he'd said, his teeth brown and crooked, blowing a cloud of rotting sweet breath in my face. "I don't know what kind of hold you got on my Pa, but it won't work on me. These are my waters, and *I* fish 'em. If you know what's good for you, you'll get back into that shitheap and drive off."

"And if I don't know what's good for me?" I was still dressed for the road, instead of the cash-register, and I looked like some tough, I guess: hair long and ratty, three-day beard, big, scuffed stomping boots with steel shank and toe, and blue jeans gone black with grease and old lunches.

The kid pulled some steel on me then, an oiled switch with a matte-black handle. I'd seen one like it in Tokyotown for $250, but I don't think he knew what it was worth.

Anyway, I took it away from him, and we spent a little while on the guard rail up the road, his arms twisted behind his back, his greasy hair caught in my left fist.

"You son of a bitch, you just wait till I tell my Pa about this. He'll feed you your balls, old man, and stuff chopsticks in your eyes."

"Son, you ain't telling nothing to no one," I shouted into the wind of the traffic, my lips lover-close to his ear. Cars honked at us, seeing only an unexpected blur on a rail around a blind curve. "You are never going to get in my way, hear? I'm crazier than anyone you've ever met, and I'll kill you the next time you give me a problem."

I heard the truck gearing up on the grade as it neared the curve. Abruptly, I shoved my fist forward, pushing the kid's head into the path of that big grille. He shrieked, and piss ran out of his pants cuff – which must've felt nasty, what with the leather pants and all – but I held him there until the last possible second. Then I yanked as hard as I could, pulling him off his feet and tossing him into the ditch. It felt good and bad, a thrill down my spine and I felt the way the very first time I hit my wife; when her scream made me feel that shameful joy that later turned into a wolfish sense of *control*.

He lay on his back, stunned, and I took my time walking down to him. I picked him up by the collar of his jacket and dragged him back up to the roadside. He didn't struggle as I pinned his wrists behind his back with one hand, and grabbed his hair with the other.

"Do we understand each other?" I shouted into his ear.

The traffic whizzed by, fast, the winds blowing away the kid's tears.

"Yes!" he shouted back. "Yes, I understand you. I'm sorry. Lemme go!"

I did, and he looked surprised, but not as surprised as he did when I offered him my hand.

"No hard feelings, son, but I had to finish what you started. I hope you don't stay mad at me. I imagine I'll need a hand from time to time, bringing in the nets and so on."

He shook my hand, and we walked back to the car together, his steps all funny as the piss-soaked leather chafed.

On the morning of my last day at the old man's farm, I crouched before the cracked-up side-mirror of my cracked-up car. The roar of the eight-lane blacktop river was behind me. In my hand was a razor; my hand moved in sure swipes, taking off the night's whiskers with the slick bit of cheap plastic.

From the corner of the mirror I'd watched the kid slouch towards me along the gravel shoulder while I shaved and slid a comb slippery with Brylcreem through my hair until it gleamed like Army boots. I wiped the leftover lather and blood spots from my face with a black silk handkerchief and waited for the kid to get his balls up.

"Mr Cornucopia?" He faced the road, speaking meekly. Shame.

"Can I help you?" I asked in my professional cash-register voice, like the sound of the computer that says, "Thank you for using AT&T."

"Uh, I wanted to ask, did you find anything you don't need today? I just wondered, but it's okay if you haven't."

"Yeah, sure, I found some stuff this morning that I can let you have."

He turned back from watching the highway with a hopeful half-smile on his face. I picked up my jacket from the hood, dusted it off, and fished in one of the huge pockets until I found the CD case. I tossed it to him.

"Looks like a bootleg of the '91 Happy Mondays tour," I said. "You like them, don't you?"

I didn't have to ask. The kid had spent his whole life roadside, watching the pictures of the world that the chickenwire satellite dish pulled in for him, and hungering. He'd listen to anything that washed ashore from the cities, anything that he could fit into the jigsaw puzzle of a cool teenager that he was piecing together in his mind.

I had an impulse to jerk it back, to make the kid play monkey-in-the-middle for a while, but I stopped myself. He grabbed it from my hand and smiled as he turned it over and read the playlist.

"All right!" he said. He wore a discman on a strap across his chest like a bandoleer, and he popped the CD in and slipped the headphones on. A blissful smile spread across his face as the sound started. "Thanks a ton, Mr Cornucopia. This is great!" He looked about eight then, all his veneer of sullen acne and angst disappearing as he bobbed his head almost in time to the music. He reminded me of my kid for a second, and the little warmth I was feeling vanished, because thinking about my kid made me think about my ex, and what had happened, and that still stung.

"Yeah, sure, kid. I want you to cover the store for the afternoon, hear? I'm going into town. Be here at noon."

His mask of resentment slammed back and he stabbed the pause button on the discman. He barely nodded. "Okay."

That day had started when I sat up from the cracked black vinyl of the back seat of my crippled Ford, pissed into the ditch, and used the old bucket-and-stall shower next to the outhouse.

Then it was time to pull in my nets. In the night, piles of stuff that the alien had sucked in appeared in a rough circle around the old man's farmhouse, some of it spilling out onto the road. By then, traffic was starting to build, and if the alien had been a little more prolific, people would have been swerving to avoid the gleaming electronics and arty furniture.

The hardest part was staying brave. I've been around, and I've faced a lot of dooky, but you're lying to yourself if you think you can walk into the river of highway with its 60 mph sharks and not be shared. Even the kid, who hauled in nets from the river from the time he could walk until I took that privilege away from him, was always white and scared when he came back.

Working fast, darting in and out of the path of cars, I scooped, dragged and kicked the merchandise off the road and into the ditch. I sorted it quick and picked out the stuff that I could use, and something to keep the kid happy. It all got locked up in the store. I hadn't always done that, but I caught the kid hanging around the door a couple of times, and I didn't want to put temptation in his path.

Then I pumped a bowl of cold water, shaved and combed my hair, and dressed.

Within a month of my taking over, the river Junque had provided me with a whole new wardrobe. I sold off anything that didn't fit, and what was left might have been tailored for me. It was pretty mismatched, coming from all over the world, bright and shiny and with designer labels. If I wanted to, and I did, I could wear a new high-fashion outfit every day. The only thing that stayed constant was the big jacket; I'd pulled it out of the river thinking it was a joke or something. But no, it was an exquisitely tailored blue sharkskin sports coat that was made for a man at least seven foot tall, and as big around as a beer keg. I had to roll up the sleeves, and the tails hung down almost to my knees, but I liked it anyway. The pockets were big.

Then it was time to open up. I dragged the sandwich board out to the river-bank and propped it up so that it faced the road: MR CORNUCOPIA'S BAZAAR OF EXQUISITE JUNQUE IS OPEN FOR BUSINESS!!! TOYS! CLOTHES! ELECTRONICS! GIMCRACK AND GEWGAW SUPPLIER TO THE STARS! BY APPOINTMENT TO HIS EXALTED MAJESTY, THE KING OF ZAÏRE! I didn't know that Zaïre had a King, but it didn't matter; I liked the *sound* of it.

I kept the padlock keys with my money belt, and that money belt went where I did. I undid the three padlocks (the alien hadn't provided those, those I bought in town) and slid the metal doors up. I flicked on the cash register and pressed play on the CD player. It had a twelve-disc carousel; and I changed them from time to time, but usually I just forgot about it.

Opening up shop was a ritual for me. I did it all in the same order, every morning, and by the time I was finished, the methodical sameness had calmed me into a state that made it possible for me to face the day.

The first customers were type threes. The kid had started the classification system, and he kept a curling piece of paper taped to the wall behind the cash, with his illegible handwritten notes.

Some of the classifications were easy to understand: *White trash couple in a crappy Jap car, they buy stupid stuff*. Some of the others I hadn't understood the difference between until I'd actually met them: *Fat guy with little dog* and *Fat guy with big dog* seemed pretty arbitrary, but once you saw them you knew there was a real difference. Some of them I never will understand: *Guy who talks like the first Darren on Bewitched* and *Guy who talks like the second Darren on Bewitched.*

Type threes were *Old fart parents with pissed-off daughter (cute)*. Type fifty-eights were the same but *daughter (ugly)*. I guess he didn't think to add fifty-eights until much later.

These threes looked like they were from somewhere in the midwest, him with a genuine red neck and beety cheeks, her wiry and hard, with chapped hands and pursed lips. Their daughter looked like the poster girl for Hillbilly Hussy, with cornsilk hair in a long loose braid, jeans cinched tight by a wide leather belt between flaring hips and flaring bustline, all firm and pouty. Her lips were inexpertly smeared with Harlot Red #8 lipstick.

The man went to the rack of guns, knives and porn videos I kept closest the counter. The woman pawed through dusty shelves full of ugly designer kitchenware. The daughter went to the electronics rack, like the kids always do, marvelling at the compact sound-reproduction equipment that looked like racing cars. Her chewed fingernails brushed the eggshell finish of a top-of-the-line Sony Walkman, and she turned it over. Then she gasped at the price.

I love to watch their faces when they see the prices. They either look sly, figuring that the stuff is hot, or they look sly, figuring that I'm too stupid to know what I've got, or they look sly, figuring that they can screw their parents out of the money for whatever it is. I *always* look sly, because I know the truth: the stuff isn't hot, it's magicked here by an alien under torture by a crazy old man.

The threes left with the Walkman (half a c-note), a triangular chrome teapot (a fin), and a four-and-a-half-inch .22LR pocket pistol (a sawbuck). The money went into the till. *Ka-ching!*

I left for town at noon with over two hundred dollars in my pocket, and another hundred for a float back at the shop.

I didn't take the car, even though it was over four miles to town. It had been eight months since I took to the road, and I knew that the local fuzz had better things to do than to keep an eye out for a wife-beater, but you can't be too careful. Besides, the weather in this state was nice enough that the walk was invigorating, a nice warm-up for a nicer time.

The town was called Casket Junction, and it had once upon a time been a major nexus for European wine-sellers and American wine-buyers. The "Welcome to Casket Junction" sign at the town line sported a wine barrel that some local wit had spray-painted a crude coffin over. Casket, coffin; get it? Ha ha.

Casket Junction wasn't much anymore. A Circle-K, two gas stations, a second-hand store, a half-built misbegotten condo complex and a hotel by the train tracks. The Circle-K took fifty of my dollars and turned them into two white plastic shopping bags full of Pall-Malls, Wild Turkey and candy bars. Circle-K made a good first stop, because it meant that I bought essentials before heading over to the Lamplighter Inn.

Noontimes at the Lamplighter were pretty sparse. Nighttimes, too, I imagine, but I always left before dark to make the drunken stagger home easier. I ordered my Shepherd's Pie and my first beer of the day, and waited for Danielle, the sorriest whore I ever met, to come by and sit with me.

She teetered over on chipped spike heels, her hair big and teased, her face a clown's mask of blue eyeshadow and pink rouge laid over pancake makeup. Somewhere under there, Danielle had a brain, but she kept it hidden pretty well.

Over many lunches in the saloon and many afternoons upstairs in the inn's cheap rooms, we'd told each other all the lies that strangers exchange on the way to becoming friends. She laid one hand on my shoulder and leaned down over my neck, talking in a breathy voice into my ear.

"Buy me a drink, sailor?"

I turned and gave her a once over from toes to hair, and said, "Do I get change back?"

She burst out laughing, a little bit of Brooklyn and a little bit of the south, altogether sounding like bored wildness. She smacked the back of my head playfully.

"Paulie, you are *bad*!" She pushed my plate aside and slithered onto my lap. Her perfume was cheap and acidic, and it didn't hide anything; I could smell booze and a little armpit and sex.

I gave her ass a squeeze and pushed her off. "So they tell me. Sit on a chair like a normal person, Danielle. You want something to eat?"

"Naw. I eat enough as it is."

Truth be told, Danielle had a figure like a fencerail, but don't all women think they're fat? I ordered a plate of fries with gravy and cheese curds, something the chef had brought with him from Quebec, called *poutine*. I ordered the extra food because whenever Danielle turns down a meal, it means she eats half of mine. Sure enough, her long fingernails pincered up fries out of the gravy and slipped them into her mouth whenever she thought my attention was fixed elsewhere.

"I've missed you, Paulie. You ain't been visiting me as often as you used to. Are you getting bored of me? Or have you found some girl on your route with a thing for travelling salesmen?"

I'd told her that I was called Paul, and that I was a travelling novelty salesman, which wasn't exactly a lie. I sold novelties, and I had to travel to get to her. And Paul *was* one of my middle names. I've got four, which've provided me with enough aliases for a whole pack of ID cards.

"Danielle, honey, no one could take your place."

She simpered and pinched my cheek. "That's what I like to hear. You eat up now, and I'll get the room."

I don't know how Danielle made a living. Seemed like I was her only customer. Maybe she had a disability pension or something, and the whoring was just a side game.

I won't write about the sex. You want a stroke-book, you head down to your corner store and buy one. Suffice it to say that there was probably more talking than you'd think, and the sex was better than you'd think, and we held each other for longer afterwards than you'd think.

"Paul." She called me Paul, not Paulie, and that was the signal that she wanted to talk seriously.

"Mmm?" I was sitting naked on the edge of the rumpled bed, smoking a cigarette and staring off into space.

"You're married, aren't you?"

I swivelled to face her, but she was staring out the window.

"Not right at this second, no."

"You were married, though?"

"Yeah, I was married."

"I could tell. Want to know how?"

"Sure."

"When a man's been married to a woman, it, like, smooths him out. Makes him more understanding. A guy who's never been married, half the time when you say something he looks at you like you're nuts. Like you're an alien or something."

I must have jerked or something, because even with her back to me, she stopped.

"Oh, I don't care if you got a wife." I heard the lie in her voice. "I was just wondering. I've never been married."

"Uh huh."

"Yeah. Want to know why?"

"Sure."

"I don't need to! Women get married for a couple of reasons: we want to be sure that we won't be alone; we want to be sure that someone's going to take care of us; we want to be sure that we're attractive." Still facing the window, she held up one hand, ticking off the reasons by raising her fingers, one at a time. "I know I'm attractive: when there's a load of truckers here, I get all the business I can handle." She lowered one finger. "I got money, and I don't need no one to take care of me." She lowered a second finger. "I got my people: Tom behind the bar; my regulars . . ." She made a fist and leaned back into my chest.

She was shaking a little, her skin cool with dried sweat. I wrapped my arms around her, underneath her breasts and she leaned her face into me. I stroked her hair.

"You're set up pretty good, all right," I said, feeling a need to fill the silence.

"You damn betcha. I'm free and I like it that way."

I held her tighter, not sexual at all even though we were both naked. When I held her that way, I felt a little of the shame slip away. I never felt that way with anyone else: like I was protecting them without controlling them. It was like loosening a notch in the belt around my mind.

Danielle was about the closest thing I had to a friend those days, and she wasn't all business; I ran downstairs and bought a bottle and we shared it and sang old Buddy Holly tunes until it was time for me to go, and she never charged me extra.

2. *Self-actualizing on her respirator*

I knew that the kid would stay at the shop until I got back there to close up, but something made me want to get back and relieve him. I had a warm glow in my belly, supplies for a week, and I was chafed in all the right places.

I stuck to the ditch on the long walk home, the green velveteen pimp hat that I wore for a joke pulled low to shield my eyes from the setting sun.

About a mile from home, I stopped, as I always did, at the jagged smear of smashed vegetation and the spill of gravel that marked the spot where I went off the road, six months before.

I'd been cruising at sixty, my eyes red from too many hours behind the wheel, too much anger at my ex, and, truth be told, too much Grape Mad Dog 20/20. It was after midnight, nothing but potato fields as far as the eye could see, and I'd lost the last all-night radio station half a state back, so it was all silence except for the clunking transmission and the roar of wind through the open windows. I was badly spaced, but even if I had been wide awake and alert I don't think I could have done much better than I did. Here's what happened:

One second, I was driving along, smooth sailing and clear skies as far as the eye could see. The next second, there was a full-blown, high-end component stereo system in front of me. Whisper-thin speakers, flush buttons and quiet green LED displays. At least $8000. What would you have done? I swerved hard, and the rickety Ford went ass-over-teakettle into the ditch.

Any wreck you walk away from is a good one, and the Ford finished top-up and me still in my seat, a dull ache across my chest where the seatbelt'd caught me. The front end was toast: no headlights, no signals, no grille, and the Playboy bunny hood-ornament snapped off at the waist. The adrenaline made me oblivious to all of this as I jumped out off my car, kicking and kicking it, shouting, "Fuck fuck fuck fuck." My eyes took a moment to adjust to the sudden darkness that my shot-out headlights left behind. The moon was full and the sky clear, the light enough for me to see that damned stereo still sitting in the road.

Pissed and scared as I was, I still dragged the stereo off the road and locked it in the trunk of my car along with the duffel of dirty laundry before I set off walking down the road, looking for a farmhouse. The last one I'd passed had been more than a mile back, so I hoped that the next one couldn't be far.

The house was set back a piece from the road, and it had a halfwrecked flying saucer on the lawn. I knew it was a flying saucer because I'd seen the movies, but I figured it was some weird lawnornament. Driving cross-country, I'd seen stranger things on lawns: plaster dinosaurs, ten-foot Tweety birds, even a Stonehenge made out of junker cars. You live in the country long enough, something makes you want to put toilet-paper and paste statues out front of your house.

The lights were off in the house, but I could hear a steady machine noise coming from somewhere inside. I pounded on the front door of the sprawling bungalow. There was no answer at first, and I pounded again. I saw a light go on behind the drawn curtains of one of the prefab corrugated-metal additions, saw a shadow pass by, headed for the front. The door opened a crack, and I saw the crazy old man.

Understand, I did not see an old man and later find out that he was crazy; the door opened and a raw old guy with a steel-grey crewcut that went down to the bone was standing there in a threadbare bathrobe and worn slippers, crazy as crazy can be. I saw it in the way he held himself up, his head wobbling a little; in the way his eyes snapped from thing to thing, unable to concentrate; in the way his hands washed themselves over and over again, rubbing the rough scales of callous.

"Something I can do for you?" His voice was the least crazy thing about him. He just sounded tired and suspicious.

"Sorry to bother you. My car went into the ditch a piece back, and I was wondering if you had a phone I could use to call a tow." An hour before, calling a tow and paying for the repairs would have reduced my bankroll to the point where I would have to find work before I could go on. Now I was the proud owner of thousands of dollars worth of stereo equipment whose sale would keep me on the road for nearly a year.

"Went off the road, did you? We get a lot of that around here." He stepped back and I heard a clunk as he set something down and opened the door all the way. The hallway behind him was depressing and cramped, lined with dusty photos and peeling wallpaper. A heavy aluminium baseball bat rested by his leg. That was the clunk.

He sized me up, stomping boots and filthy jeans and stubble, but he seemed satisfied with what he saw, because he said, "Well, you ain't going to find a tow around here at this hour. I can bed you down on the chesterfield for the night, and in the morning we'll call the garage."

Was I nervous about sleeping in a crazy man's house? Hell yes. But the adrenaline had worn off, and I felt like someone had been working over my chest with a crowbar, and my head pounded and throbbed. The old man didn't turn on any lights as he led me into his living room, where a broken-spring sofa called to me. He took a ratty afghan out of a closet and wished me a good night. I barely had time to get my boots off before I fell asleep.

I woke in the morning to the sound of cartoons, loud. Loud. My head was still killing me, I had cricks up and down my neck and back, and a kid with a terrible hockey-player haircut – really long in back, short everywhere else – was eating Skippy out of a jar while he watched Tom clobber Jerry. The TV he was watching was a solid rock of electronics, modern and slick, and out of place in the crumbling living room.

Groaning, I sat up and rubbed my face. Sitting made me even more aware of the bruises on my chest, and I wondered if they had a tub I could take a long soak in before the tow got there. I also wondered if they had a coffee-pot perking.

The kid turned his head. "Oh. You're up. The guest shitter's out back, phone's in the kitchen."

Well, maybe I wouldn't get that soak and cuppa after all. I tried to start off right.

"Good morning, son. My name's Jack Kazzarets. I guess your father told you about my going off the road last night. Damnedest thing. I'm okay now, though. Wish I could say the same for my ride."

The kid nodded absently, then stabbed at the remote as a commercial came on. Now he was watching a badly animated Japanese cartoon show about killer robots and spaceships. His shoulders moved as he followed the battle onscreen, like a video-game player or a football fan. One of the bad guy's ships got hit and exploded in a fakey shower of sparks and noise.

"Aw, bull*shit*. Ships don't make no noise when they explode in space. The sound can't travel. And besides, my Ma could flay better than that guy. Who the hell ever let him behind the wheel?"

Like father, like son. Crazy as crazy can be. "Say, where are your mother and father? I'd like to thank them before I call the tow."

"Pa's in his workshop downstairs, and Ma's still in her room. She's sick." Something in the way he said it let me know that his Ma had been sick for a long, long time. That mechanical noise I'd heard last night came back to me: *crump-crump, crump-crump*. I listened for it, and it was still there. I placed the sound, from scary stories mothers told their kids when I was a boy to keep them from drinking from public water fountains and getting polio. An iron lung. *Crump-crump, crump-crump*.

"Well, if you could just point me to your Dad's workroom, I'll show myself down."

Tom and Jerry were back, and the kid was so glued to it, I figured he wouldn't hear me, but he shook his head violently. "Oh, I don't think you should do that; Pa don't like being disturbed. Go clean up and I'll get him when this show's over."

I slipped my feet back into my boots and went outside into the bright late-winter sun. There was a spider-infested outhouse with honest-to-God torn magazine pages for asswipe, and I used it quickly. I went in through a different door than I came out of – the house had a dozen extensions, each of them with their own entrance. This one led into a filthy kitchen. Every surface was stacked high with dishes, a huge garbage bag was wedged behind the door, overflowing.

I followed the smell to a coffee-maker, a silvery Kraut thing with one red on-button and a smudged half-full coffee pot beneath it. I found a mug that wasn't too scabby and ran it under the tap for a couple of minutes until the worst junk loosened and fell off. Then I poured myself a mug and tried a sip. It was surprisingly good, even though it had been standing for hours. I saw a half-empty bag of premium Jamaican coffee on the counter. I couldn't figure where they got that stuff way out here in the country.

(It was the alien, of course. All this stuff, the TV, the coffee-maker, the stereo equipment and designer plates, all of it was harvested out of the river, which was stocked by the alien as the old man tried to get his wife back, but I didn't know it yet.)

Back in the living room, I watched the last fifteen minutes of *Tom and Jerry*, interlaced with religious shows, MTV and a dirty-movie channel during the commercial breaks.

In short grunts, the kid introduced himself (Wayne), told me how old he was (sixteen and a half), whether or not he went to school (he didn't, his Pa was teaching him from correspondence kits), what he liked to do for fun (watch TV) and what he wanted to do when he grew up (anything but this) (I think he was going to say, "Be a rock star", but was afraid I'd laugh at him; still, he played air-guitar when he answered).

The show finally ended, and he turned the TV off. Before he went to get his Pa, he turned on the radio to a Top-40 station and left me there to listen to "Ooh Baby" music and the slippery FM DJ voices.

"Feeling better, are you?" Pa was still in his housecoat and slippers.

"I guess so. I just wanted to thank you before I left. Not many people would take in a stranger in the middle of night."

He smiled and was so all-over crazy at that moment that I wanted to run. "Oh, we get all kinds of visitors in the middle of the night. There's only one garage in Casket Junction that runs a tow. I'll call them and have 'em pick you up."

"I'd appreciate that. My name's Jack, by the way, Jack Kazzarets."

"Oh hell, haven't I introduced myself? My name's Len Donahue, like the fella on TV."

He went off to make the call, leaving me with the kid, who bobbed his head in time with the wailing electric guitars.

Len came back in the living room, shouted at the kid to turn it down, and took a seat on the sagging couch. He had a cup of coffee that he rested on the arm, not minding that some of it slopped over onto the upholstery.

I sat next to him, uncomfortable, not knowing what to say. "I sure hope they can get my car running again."

"You got a long way to go?"

"You could say that," I said. I wanted to change the subject. "How's the farming 'round here? Potatoes, right?"

He wasn't having any of it. "Where you headed?"

"Nowhere in particular. I'm just having myself a long drive, taking in the sights, getting some things straight in my head. Your boy told me about your wife. That's rough."

He jerked as if he'd been stung, and glared at the kid. The kid sneered back at him and turned the stereo up. "Yeah, but she's a tough old girl. She'll hang in. You married?"

"I was." I couldn't think of any way to change the subject again, and besides he had a knack for picking at your sorest scabs.

"Oh. Divorce?"

"She died. Cancer." She might as well have died. Left me, took my son away from me. The anger I'd been running away from for the last two months on the road started back in on me, and I dug my hands into the cushions.

The old man surprised me then. He put a hand on my shoulder and squeezed it. "I know how that feels. Cancer's a son of a bitch. Sometimes, I get so mad . . ."

He sounded genuinely sorry, sorry and angry and sad. His hand felt strange there on my shoulder; I realized that no one had touched me since I went on the road. I'd forgotten what it was like to have other people around. In a rush, all of my energy and anger flooded out, and I was so tired. So tired.

"Look, the tow'll be here in about half an hour. You want to come and meet the wife? She doesn't get much company 'cept me and the boy."

He was still crazy, but not so scary anymore. I let him lead me down more cramped, dusty hallways and into a bedroom.

The room was a stark contrast to the rest of the house; it was as sterile as a hospital. No, more sterile. Hospitals have a stink underneath the clean, left by a steady stream of people puking out their guts and bleeding and pissing themselves and worse, a stink that no amount of scrubbing can get rid of. This room was like a funeral parlour; every corner of it white and clean, the curtains open on a sparkling window, the sleek machine in the middle polished till it gleamed. *Crump-crump.*

She was frail and thin, and had the ashy skin of a dying person. A stack of worn paperbacks was on the bedside table: *Healing Through Meditation*; *The Way of the Serpent*; *The Way of the Lion*; *Secrets of Tibet*; *The Cancer Coverup* and *It's All in Your Head*. Self-help books, dog-eared and marked and re-re-read. Her eyes were closed when we came up on her, but they opened when I looked into her lined face.

"Who . . . ?" she said, weakly, her voice echoing in the breathing mask.

The old man stroked her brow. "Shh. It's me, and I've brought a visitor. Jack, meet my wife, Elaine. Jack's car went into the ditch a piece up the road. I put him up on the couch for the night."

She smiled and a faint glimmer came into her eyes. She slipped the transparent mask down. "I'm pleased to meet you. Have a seat."

I sat down on a high-backed kitchen chair, looking down and seeing the scuffmarks my boots left on the polished floor. I tucked my feet under the chair.

"Are you a Libra, Jack?"

I'd been expecting her to ask me about the accident or where I was going; this caught me out of left field. "No, ma'am, I'm a – "

"No, no, let me guess. A Virgo, then?"

I shook my head.

"A Leo?"

I shook my head.

"A Cancer." Her husband jerked at the word, and I nodded. "I knew it! I can always tell someone's sign. Want to know how I knew? Moon Children are always *so tragic*, like you with your long face; but at the same time, the Crab says *I feel*, like those little lights in your eyes. Our boy's Cancer, always moping around the house – " She was cut off by a coughing jag, the sound like splinters of glass clinking against each other, swimming in blood.

The old man waited out the jag with fists clenched, a vein showing his pulse at his temple. The look on his face was pure animal, lips skinned back from teeth, hatred and for a second I thought he was hating *her*, but no, he was staring at the wall like he could burn through it with his eyes.

"Wellness is my right; I claim it, I hold it to my chest; I banish the impurities from my body by the unquenchable fire of my will," she was chanting in a low, hoarse voice, and her lips had moved through the jag, in pain I thought, in this mantra I realized. "Wellness is my right, wellness is my right, wellness is my right."

The old man's crazy sick wife slipped her frail dry hands around one of mine and said, "It's in the mind, Jack. Sickness and health are in the mind, and all you need is the right attitude. Don't pay no heed to doctors and them, they're just looking to make a buck from what we could do for ourselves for free. Remember, the mind is mightier than the sword."

The mind is mightier than the sword? Plum loco, as they say in the grainy cowboy movies. That woman was plum loco and she wouldn't let go of my hand, staring up earnest from her deathbed and wouldn't let go of my eyes, either, until her husband, gentler than I had imagined him, loosened her grip and smoothed her arms down at her sides.

"You rest now, Elaine. There's no need to get yourself all

worked up about doctors again. You keep on thinking your wellness thoughts, and keep on taking your medicine, you'll be right
as rain soon enough, hear?" And her eyes already closed, that soft
soothe of his voice sliding her into sleep.

Twenty minutes till the tow, and already I'd seen the house, a
twisty, draughty maze of corrugated iron and Art Nouveau tables,
every door opened for inspection, every room looked over, dust
and the stink of old laundry in my nose, making me want to leave
and wait outside.

He'd opened every door except one, and that one he'd glared
at like he glared when his wife was having her coughing jag:
"That's just my workroom, it's a mess, no need to see it." About
as subtle as a road accident: whatever he kept down there was
more interesting than the whole place put together.

"What you got, a machine-shop?" I could pick at scabs, too.

"No, no. Just some hobby stuff. Model trains."

"My daddy used to build model trains. He'd spend hours
painting the scenery. He always said, 'The scenery is the key,
without the scenery, it's just a bread sandwich.'"

I watched the old man grab that line and make it his excuse.
"Yeah, I've been painting all morning, and the turp smell's pretty
bad. I've been meaning to put in an extractor fan, but it's just one
of those things I never seem to get around to. Maybe next time
you're by these parts, I'll show you around."

It was like a mad scientist horror movie: *Don't go into the lab if
you value your sanity*. Bullshit.

"Yeah, maybe next time." I'd be in town for a day at least,
longer if they couldn't get parts, and the front-door lock was the
same kind I used to slip with a credit-card. The back-door lock at
my place in Orangeville didn't have a key when me and the missus
moved in, never got around to having one made, and at three in
the morning, booze sweet on my breath and the little woman snug
in bed, awake in an instant if she heard the front-door deadbolt
shoot back, but never attuned to the snick of a credit-card in the
old wooden back door.

An air-horn blasted out front and I escaped with a firm handshake and hearty thanks; the tow driver and me were off to town, stopping to hitch up the battered Ford.

It was too cold, really, to walk all the way from Casket Junction to the old man's house, but that didn't stop me. I pulled my tractor cap down over the tips of my ears and stuck to the ditch, walking as fast as the dark would allow, until the pace started to warm me up, so that when I reached the house I was sticky with sweat underneath my jacket.

I reached into my wallet and pulled out my credit-card. The only sound was *crump-crump*, and then snick as the door swung wide, creaking a little. I left my boots on the doormat and padded in smelly socks down the dark halls.

Did I say mad scientist horror movie? The door leading down to the workroom was ajar, a sliver of light cast against the opposite wall, turning the yellowing wallpaper dried-blood brown.

Something was being beaten down there. There was a short whistling noise like a club being swung, then a wet smack and a sucky painful noise.

And the stairs gave me away (I should've paid more attention to the movies: the stairs *always* creak at the wrong moment), a squeal as I reached the third-from-bottom step, and the old man whirled around.

For a second, I believed he wasn't crazy. His housecoat was pulled tight over his skinny chest and his round little beer-belly, the aluminium baseball bat was loose in one hand like a cane, and he had this confused expression, like I'd interrupted him while he was thinking out a confusing problem.

"Kazzarets?"

I was in the shadow, and I might have turned and run. The baseball bat shifted in his grip so it was a weapon, not a cane, but I saw behind him.

The mad scientist's monster was strapped to his lab table, thrashing weakly like a preemie in an incubator. A monster that was seven foot long and as thin as a rail, and naked and knobbed, skin the matte eggshell-finish black of the stereo that forced me off the road, absorbing light. Its head was like a *Star Trek* bad guy, huge and pear-shaped, with insect-cluster eyes in a disc of teardrop-shaped wedges, centred in its face. Its mouth was open in a soundless howl, revealing row after row of blunt square teeth that seemed to extend all the way down its gullet.

Its arms were long as stretched taffy, like an orang-utan that's been distorted lengthwise, its knuckly hands shackled next to the huge ball-joints of its ankles.

Its limbs had too many joints, but the leg closest to me had more than the far one, and then with a lurch I saw that some of those joints were broken bones (Bones? Do monsters have bones? Broken something) and there was a slippery black slick coating the length of the bat.

"Kazzarets, that you, goddamnit?" The old man leaned the bat against the long table that I saw now was an old door on sawhorses, and he peeled off the disposable surgical gloves he was wearing, tossed them into a metal pail.

I stepped down the last three steps and stood with my hands at my sides, gaping at the monster. Then the old man was right in my face, angry, his hands nervously washing each other.

"What the *fuck* are you doing here?"

He hadn't cursed around me before, and the word made my stomach tighten. He was a little smaller than me, but I wasn't sure that he couldn't lift me up and drop me on my head. And if he couldn't, well, hitting a smaller person, that was bad, that was what got me into trouble in the first place. My old lady, pushing and whining, but I was already angry when I hit her, she just set me off, and it was so easy to smash her face, and while a little bit of me knew it was wrong, it felt *good*.

I spread my hands out and turned on my Smiling Jack voice. "Now, Len, I know you're angry, and what I did was wrong, but I'm only human. I guess curiosity got the best of me and I came back to sneak a peek. I didn't mean no harm, but damn, when you get all secrety, I just *got to* find out why; ain't you never felt like that?"

The monster on the table made the sucky noise I'd heard upstairs, and there was a hiss and I looked just in time to see one of the breaks in its leg go straight and heal up. I smelled a tang, like ozone, just a whiff and it was gone.

The old man didn't show any sign of hearing it, but he stepped back and picked up his bat, then swung it like a man chopping wood, smacking all the way across the monster's middle, and both arms snapped, its chest caved a little. There was no cruelty in the blow, and that made it all the worse; like the torture was some kind of chore and all the pain that twisted the monster's face was going to waste, with no one getting off on it.

I started to back up slowly, like maybe he wouldn't turn around and see me leaving until it was too late, but that never works in the horror movies, neither, and that third step gave me away, and he spun around like a top.

"Where you going, Kazzarets? Don't you want to know what this is all about?" Then he put down the bat and felt for his gloves, then slapped his hands together in anger. "Damn, I forgot the gloves! Look, come on upstairs with me, I'll tell you all about it."

When the mad scientist tells you all about it, it means that he's about to kill you, since it won't do to have all those mad scientist secrets running around. But then why was the old man inviting me upstairs, where it was easier to get away, where his wife and boy might hear my screams?

I let him lead me up the stairs, out the front door, and into the burned-out flying saucer, using a little step stool to climb up into the narrow hatchway.

Inside, there was a dim half-light that came from nowhere at all, and smooth featureless walls, and no banks of flashing instruments, and I wondered if I was right the first time, if this wasn't a spaceship but only a model the old man made, and who knows why crazy people make crazy things?

We sat crosslegged on the cool floor, facing each other, the old man's housecoat pulling up to reveal his pale, goose-pimpled thighs.

"The alien crash-landed here the week after our boy was born." I was off into *National Inquirer*-land, my head swimming. I wished I had a bottle of Grape Mad-Dog 20/20, that always made the tough stuff wash down easy, like unsticking a pill that's caught in your throat.

"It came down fast and woke the baby, which woke the wife,

and by the time it woke me, she was standing out on the lawn with the boy in her arms, watching the sheets of purple light that that thing spat out its backside as it tried to seat itself so it was level. I told her to go back into the house, to get my gun, but she just stood there, her face the colour of a grape from that light."

I was shaking my head a little, unconsciously, and the old man's eyes got angry.

"You don't have to believe it if you don't want to, Kazzarets. I gave you the hospitality of my house, and you come back and broke in, snuck into my workroom, and asked me to tell you what it's all about. Now I'm tellin' you, and you can either hear me through or get the hell away from me."

I apologized to the man, got myself a cigarette and lit it, noting that the smoke dissipated, sucked clean into the walls all around me. I put my palm flat on the curve of the wall above me, but I felt no suction.

"The wife came back out with my shotgun just as the hatch opened. I made sure it was loaded, then poked the barrel into the hatch, my head following it. The alien was lying in a pool of its black blood, all of it as dark as an oilslick inside the ship. It saw me and reached for me. I gave it both barrels in the chest, blew it back into the wall. It was still then, so I dragged it out onto the lawn by its arm, away from the pumping black blood.

"The wife, well, she's seen *Bambi* too many times, and she knelt by its side, took its hand. I *told* her not to touch it, but she had to try to help. My Elaine, she was so gentle, that's the first thing I ever noticed about her. Not her looks or her voice, but the way she was always careful with other people's feelings, the way she just gave and gave love until I couldn't hardly believe that she had any left." He stopped and reached for my cigarette. I gave him one of his own, and saw his hands shaking as he lifted it to his mouth.

"I didn't know what to do. I was halfway to phoning the sheriff, when Elaine called to me. 'Len, he's getting better.' *Getting better*? I ran back to her, and sure enough, his chest was uncaving, his skin was coming back to the middle and closing the wound. I watched the shot bubble to the surface of his skin and roll off his chest. Then Elaine gave a little shriek and showed me her hands, where they'd touched him. Her fingertips were black, not like his blood, but like she'd been playing with magic markers. I told her to go wash her hands in varsol, and got a pair of work-gloves from the shed and dragged the thing downstairs.

"I tied it up as best I could, and sat up all night, watching it heal. It made little noises while it was healing, I guess you heard that, a little pop every time something got better. I dozed off there, watching it, and I got woken by Elaine, all excited and talking a mile a minute.

"'Len, you won't believe it! Everything, it's all on the highway, everything!' Not only didn't I believe it, I didn't *understand* it, not until she dragged me upstairs and showed me.

"The boy was sickly when he was a baby, and there was all kinds of expensive things he needed that we just couldn't afford, not under that jackass Reagan: pills and warmers and formula and like that. Well, lying there around the house and on the road was all of that stuff and more: tools I'd been saving for, new knitting things, parts for the tractor. There was a hell of a mess, with cars swerving to avoid it and stuff getting smashed everywhere. I just ran out into the traffic and started grabbing things, throwing it to Elaine, both of us laughing like kids pulling salmon out of a stream during spawning season.

"We took it all back into the house and went through it, and I was looking out the window at the crashed ship when I heard another 'pop' from downstairs and I saw a new bassinet standing on the highway and I remembered the alien and all of a sudden, *it made sense.*

"I ran downstairs as fast as I could, talking to the alien. 'It's you, isn't it? You're doing all this stuff! Hell, that's great! How do you do that? Can you get me a car, a Ferrari? A new truck? A million dollars? Come on!' But the alien didn't even notice me. I jumped at it, waved my hands in its face, but it didn't flinch. Then another 'pop'; and all of a sudden its head jerked and for a second I know it could see me, don't ask me how, but I could tell. Then it was back in its mind again. I poked it with the end of a broom, shouting. 'Come on, I know you saw me, we can work out a deal, you want that, don't you?' But nothing. I was poking harder and harder, and finally I poked it right in the chest where it was hurt and the end of the broom slipped right in then I felt something give, and it *noticed* me!

"You know what happened next. I couldn't let the thing go, not unless I knew that I could get it to keep helping me out. Turning it over to the government was right out; you know what them boys're like. I'da never see the alien again. So I left it tied up, and kept up the farm during the day, and at night, I'd go down and try to get it to listen to me. I always ended saying to hell with it and giving it a good whack. I used to worry that if it could make things appear out of my mind, then why couldn't it make a big rock appear on my head? But after a while, I realized that it didn't even know where it was, what it was doing.

"It's like the old joke about the mule: this fella has a mule, and he's trying and trying to make it go, but it won't. So this other fella comes up, and watches for a while, then finally he takes a two-by-four and whacks the mule over the head, and it starts to move. The first fella says, 'How'd you do that?' And the second fella answers, 'It's real simple. The first thing you gotta do is get the mule's *attention*.'

"So I kept on getting the alien's attention, playing around with concentrating on different things while he was healing, and seeing if I could get that to appear. I'm not sure if this is the way his people talk to each other or if his brains got scrambled in the wreck, but either way, I was living pretty high off him.

"Things were great for more than a year, and the baby had all the clothes he ever needed, and what with harvesting the stuff in the morning before the traffic got too heavy and selling it in town, I pretty much gave up on the farm and concentrated on my experiment. Everything was fine until my wife took sick.

"Ever hear of Post-Polio Syndrome? You get polio as a kid, and make it through, and you're all healed up, and then all of a sudden, bam, you're sick to death. It started with some pain in her legs and I thought, well, maybe she's got arthritis, so we went to the doctor and he took us to the big hospital and they ran all kinds of machines through her, and next thing we knew, they were talking about six months to live. And cancer. Not just Post-Polio

Syndrome, but bone cancer too, and what with one thing and the other, she couldn't get therapy for one, 'cause that would set off the other. They wanted to keep her in the hospital to die, but I said no, I'd take care of her at home. In three months, she was on that machine, a *cuirasse respirator*" – he pronounced it *queer-ass* – "and we figured that was the end. They wanted to put a tube in her throat, one that wouldn't hardly let her talk, but the boy was starting to walk around now, and we didn't want his last memory of his Mamma's voice to be some croak coming out of a machine, so we told 'em no.

"Elaine's a tough old girl, and she's hung in now for fifteen years. Fifteen years, when those smartass doctors told her she wouldn't make six months! And all that time, she's been the only thing I've thought about. And at night, when I visit with the alien, that's what I think about, a cure for her sickness, and I hit him, hit him hard, and some day, my boy's going to go out in the morning, and he's going to find some pills, or a formula or something, and she'll be right as rain again. You watch.

"And I don't feel no guilt for it no more. Because I saw what colour her legs turned before she took sick, and it's the same damn colour her fingers were after she touched that thing. None of us got its blood on us, and we're all right, and she did, and she took sick, and so it only stands to reason that it's that *thing's* fault."

He choked and dropped his cigarette, and before I knew what I was doing, I was holding his head against my chest and he was crying, *whimpering*, like my wife when I went too far. I was embarrassed to see this hard old man – crazy or not – so weak and smashed. I wondered what I would have done.

He moaned, "Oh, Jesus," and pulled back. "Look, I'm sorry, it's just that sometimes it's so damn much to take and I lose it a little."

"I've been there," I lied, and it tasted like ashes, but I wanted to comfort him.

"That's right, you have, haven't you?" He eyed me strangely. "I expect you'll be leaving when they've got your car running?"

"I expect so."

"You said before you didn't have no place in particular to go."

He squirmed. "Look, what I'm getting at, it's not right, the boy having to take care of himself and his Ma besides, and I'm asleep by the time he gets up to harvest the stuff from the road, and he don't see no one 'cept his Ma, and it's not right, like I said, the boy needs some company, and . . ." He trailed off and reached for my cigarettes. "I promised Elaine I'd give these up when she took sick, but between one thing and another, I just never got around to it.

"Do you need a place to stay, Kazzarets? We've got plenty of room here, and you wouldn't need to do a whole lot, just help bring in the stuff and sell it, and keep the boy company, make sure he's on the right path. You don't need to answer right now, just think about it."

I had them do all the major work on my car, but left the trim and mirrors and such. Then I drove it to the old man's farm and parked it on the field side of the ditch.

I tried sleeping on their couch a few nights, but there was too much craziness for me, and the old Ford had been my home for a while anyway.

It wasn't a month before I decided to open the store. It was better than driving to the city and fencing the stuff. I figured we could cut out the middleman and all that travel, and not have to worry about receipts and taxes and nosy questions from pawn-brokers. When the sheriff came by, I told him that my brother-in-law was a damaged-goods wholesaler, and he seemed to believe me. The old man had gone into town and got a vendor's permit, and the sheriff had a boy Way's age, and he was always wanting a CD player, and of course, his wife wanted a microwave, but with a sheriff's salary . . . And besides, it was just one more crazy thing happening at that damn farm, first that old Len decides to build a model spaceship and now he's using his place to sell designer crap.

3. *Getting in touch with my inner child on the slippery slope to ruin*

Six months after I moved in, five months after I opened the store, four months after I met the sorriest whore I ever knew, three months after I stopped having nightmares about my wife, two months after the kid started his classification system for the customers, one month after the old man's wife took her bad turn, just a few hours after I got drunk and laid in Casket Junction, the shit hit the fan.

I'd just passed the place where I went off the road, and I was idling along with my legs all loose, stopping from time to time to piss, still broad daylight, when I saw the dinette set appear in the middle of the road.

And I broke into a run. Broad daylight, and the alien was doing his thing? Broad daylight, and the old man was down in his cellar, working that bat? I was so worked up about the dinette set that I was almost *through* the front door before I noticed that my Ford was gone.

Into the basement then, and grabbing the bat, not heeding the black blood that slimed it, stopping the old man in midswing. The alien was beaten down to ooze and pulp, thick oily green-black weeping from its orifices, its arms and legs like stockings full of broken asphalt. The old man was in his robe, covered, *covered* in the alien's blood, matted through his hair and beard, up to his shoulders like he'd been sticking his arm into an oil-well.

"Len!" I shouted. "Len! What are you doing, Len? What the hell are you doing?"

He tried to jerk the bat away from me, then pushed the blunt end into my chest so that I let go. He whipped it around and shoved the end into the open, soundless mouth of the alien. I heard a crunch, and Len moved around so that he could force half the length of the bat down the alien's throat.

I moved to stop him, to pull him back. The alien was making a choking noise now, a gagging sound and I could see the bat travel through its pipestem chest. Len screamed then, more animal than when Elaine was having her coughing jags, pure wild animal and I stepped back involuntarily.

Len jerked the bat free and swung it over his head, then down on the alien's chest. "*Sh-sh-she's dead, Kazzarets,*" he sobbed, "*this fucking thing and you and she's dead! And this thing and you, you and this thing and that boy, too, you distracted me, you kept me from concentrating on the things that would make her well! She's dead, and where the hell do you think all that shiny hi-fi shit came from? Not from my mind! And she's dead, and if it hadn't a been for you!"*

The blame washed over me like the hot blood that coursed from my boy's nose when I backhanded him across the room, and I bathed in it. I wanted to beg and plead for the old man's forgiveness, but instead I asked, "Where's my car, Len?"

"Your *car*? Who gives a shit?" He was screaming again, higher and higher, was he going to use the bat on me? I planted my feet a little harder, got ready for the blow. "Who gives a shit about your car? The boy took your car, Kazzarets. My wife died, and the boy took your car, and now it's just you me and this, this . . . *abomination*. Eighteen years worth of my family, and I got *nothing* to show for it! Nothing!"

He dropped the bat and hugged his arms across his chest, not crying, but shaking like he was ready to explode. He took a long, shuddery breath and said, "The boy took your car, said he was heading for Los Angeles. In California."

I saw the kid's face in my mind's eye, contorted in self-hate and hate of his father and the podunk-backneck he grew up in, saying, "Fuck you, Pa, and the horse you rode in on. I'm goin' out west where they appreciate me." Had he had his bags packed, waiting for this? He must've known where I kept my spare keys, under the register-drawer in the store. He'd seen me come home four sheets to the wind often enough and take the keys when I couldn't find my own set, let myself into the car and pass out.

The alien made a noise, not the "pop" and sucky sound, but a disgusting and deeply hurt grinding that came from somewhere deep inside its chest, and I believed that the old man had finally killed it, that I was hearing a death rattle.

The old man bent to retrieve his bat, but I stopped him by laying a hand on his arm and guided him upstairs, leaving a trail of black-bloody slipper prints on the wooden stairs.

I sat him on the unsprung couch in the living room.

"Len, I'm going to go fetch your boy, don't you worry about that. Elaine beat the odds for a hell of a long time, but her time had come, you got to know that. She was hurting awful bad, this last month. You know she's in a better place now, don't you?"

The old man didn't show any sign that he heard me, just kept hugging himself and shaking, but I thought he was listening.

"Len, this is important now, and I need you to listen to me. You hear me, Len? Listen to me." He slowly turned to face me, and I used one of the rotting end-cushions to wipe the black scum from his face. "Len, I'm going to get your boy now; I'll bring him back here for the funeral. But you're going to have to take care of the arrangements. You clean up downstairs, wash yourself, and call the sheriff, tell him that Elaine's passed on. He'll help you. You gotta get in touch with her folks in Calumet City, too. They deserve a chance to say goodbye. Call the editor of the town paper, get an obit in. Elaine's got people around here, you told me so yourself, folks who haven't seen her since she took sick. They'll want a chance to pay their respects."

The old man shook his head, like he was saying no, but I thought that maybe he was just clearing away the cobwebs. He sat silent while the time stretched, no more *crump-crump* and no more "pops" from below.

"You stay away from my boy," he said suddenly and crazy-mean. "You stay away from my boy, you stay away from my family, you son of a bitch. You get the hell out of my house and don't let me see your face again, or I'll tear it off. Elaine'd be alive today if it wasn't for you, butting in here where you weren't needed. I'd of been able to think straight, and the alien woulda come through for me, and the boy, well, he didn't get that urge to wander until you started telling him about the cities."

It was lies, all of it. He'd invited me to stay, and that alien didn't understand anything, least of all why the old man was torturing him, and I never, but never, fuelled that boy's desire to see the city. I've seen enough of city life and I wouldn't send a dog to it.

"Len, I'm real sorry you feel that way. I never meant no harm, not to your wife or your boy. I wish I could mind you, but you and I know that Elaine would've wanted her son at her funeral, and I owe her that much."

He went purple from the neck up. "Get the hell out of my house! Get out or so help me – "

I left then, knowing the old man wasn't in his head, and there was no telling what he would do. It was after six now, and the sun was still high. I went to the store, noticing the kid had left the locks undone. It was a sign of what was inside.

The kid had stripped the place. Everything that could be pawned had been taken, and I didn't imagine that there was much room in the Ford for him after he loaded up all that stuff. I ran my hand along the top of the doorframe, and the wad of twenties I'd stashed there was gone too.

The walk to Casket Junction sobered me up. I had maybe fifty bucks left in my pocket, my big blue jacket, and a triple-load of shame.

Danielle was still at the bar. She looked like she'd sobered up a little, too, and she was cracking jokes with Tom, the bartender. The restaurant was full of truckers catching dinner, but the bar was pretty empty. Danielle saw me coming in the bar mirror, and spun around on her stool.

"Paulie!" She teetered into my arms, hugging me with her whole body. "Back for seconds? People will say we're in love." She registered my expression and pulled away. "What's *wrong*?"

I thought about telling her the whole story, then decided against it. This was my load.

"I need to ask you a big favour, Danielle. And if you say no, I don't know where I'll go for help. You understand?"

She nodded solemnly.

"I need to borrow your car. And five hundred bucks. I can pay you back, maybe next week, the week after, but I *need this*."

She laughed loudly and smacked me playfully on the back of the head. "Paulie, you got it all backwards! *You* pay *me*, get it? I could get thrown out of the union for doing things the other way 'round!"

I didn't smile at her joke. "Danielle, I never asked you for no favours before. I don't feel so hot asking you for one now. But this is real important; something bad has happened, and I got to make it right."

She took me to the far corner of the bar, where Tom couldn't hear. She took my hand and stared into my eyes. "You in trouble, Paul?"

I blurted another lie without thinking. "Yes, yes, I am, but that's not it." Not a lie, then. There was still a warrant out on me for aggravated assault back in Orangeville. "It's something I can't talk about. I wouldn't ask you if there was any other way. You're my friend, Danielle, about the only friend I have these days. I don't know if I'm just a john to you, but I think of you as a friend."

Something cracked, and I thought I saw a flash of smarts beneath her lumpy mascara. "You mean that, Paul? You're not hustling me?"

I was, but not the way she thought. "No, no hustle. I wouldn't hustle you about something this important."

"Paul, will you marry me?"

I let go of her hand and my jaw dropped. "What?"

A slow tear crawled down the bridge of her nose. "I'm thirty-eight years old. I've been drifting for almost twenty years now, and I am tired." The way she said *tired* made me want to cry. "I don't want to hook no more. I thought it would be better in the country, but it's all the same thing. I want to settle down, eat breakfast with someone every morning, lie down with someone every night and have him tell me he loves me. I want to settle, Paul. And you're kind and decent and you ain't never done nothing but right by me."

She stood with her hands at her sides, not touching me, her eyes down, waiting for my answer. I thought carefully.

"I can't do that right now, Danielle." She didn't move a hair, but she seemed to slump all the same. I took her, stiff, into my arms, her perfume and hairspray strong and acrid. "I'm not playing around, Danielle. I don't ever want to hurt you. If I could say yes now, I would. But there's too much happening now, too much you don't know about me. When I get back, we'll talk about it, I don't know, we'll spend some time together, maybe go somewhere with a beach and spend a little while getting to know each other before we do anything drastic. You understand, don't you?"

Danielle took a step backwards, breaking my embrace. She was dry-eyed now, and her face was like stone. "Yeah, I understand." She rummaged through her purse. "Here're my keys; it's the brown Plymouth in the lot. Here's my ATM card, the number's on the back, I never could remember it. You go do what you got to."

I thanked her, tried to kiss her, but she turned her head.

Landsdown, Oregon, just across the state line, was where the kid used to fence the stuff he harvested. It had not one but two pawnshops, though neither of them gave him what he could've gotten if he'd gone as far as Portland.

If I was on the run, I would stop in Landsdown and sell off enough stuff to get me a trade-in on a different car, gas and eating money to LA, then wait until I hit the city to sell anything else. The kid would probably think that I'd report the car stolen, but that would mean giving my licence and registration to a cop, and that would be the end of me.

I had to catch up with him before he got to the city, preferably before he got as far as Portland. There was only one route to Landsdown, unless he wanted to try some dumb switchback dirt roads, but he'd want to unload the car as fast as he could.

I floored the Plymouth, dodging commuter traffic and sixteen-wheelers, looking out for my green Ford.

The first pawnbroker hadn't seen Wayne, but the second one had. He looked nervous when I asked, maybe because he thought I was trying to trace stolen goods.

He was a real Hollywood pawnbroker – green eyeshade balanced on a bald and sweaty forehead, face seamed and pale from long nights indoors. I'll lay two to five he had a piece of pipe within arm's reach, though a small town like Landsdown can't be holdup central.

"You just missed him," he said, after I made sure he knew I wasn't a cop. "Came in with a couple of super-VHS recorders. I gave him seven hundred even for the both of them. He running away?"

"Why do you ask?"

"He looked like he mighta been. Nervous."

"He say anything?"

"Say anything?" The pawn broker looked hard at me. "Yeah, he said 'Good afternoon,' and 'How much you give me for these?' and 'Goodbye.'"

"He didn't say anything about where he was going?"

"Nope." He didn't like questions, I could tell, probably still thought I was a cop.

"Did you get a look at his car?"

"No, I didn't. Look, you got something to sell? I got stuff to do in the back, you know?"

"No, that's it. Thanks."

On my way back to Danielle's car, I stopped and bought a quart of fortified wine.

I cruised every back street and farm road around Landsdown until it was true dark. I didn't see any sign of the green Ford, which he must've dumped if he bought a new car (not that he could've gotten much for seven bills, but then he had my wad of twenties, plus whatever he'd saved).

Not finding the car meant that he probably had kept going with it, to Portland, maybe halfway to LA. The empty quart of M/D 20/20 rolled around on the floor of the car. I rolled down the driver's-side window and let the breeze whip around me, cool off my sore, gritty eyes and peel the sweaty hair off the back of my neck.

I wondered if I should eat, and then pulled over at a Circle-K that was identical to the Circle-K in Casket Junction, in Orangeville and in all points in between. I grabbed a fistful of beef jerky sticks and another quart of wine. I paid for them, gassed up, and headed for Portland.

The kid wasn't on the road from Portland to Landsdown, wasn't on the cloverleaf that took me onto the I5, wasn't in the lot of the first five motels I pulled up alongside of.

He wasn't at the sixth one either, when I got there, and I was getting ready to leave when the Ford pulled into the lot, pulling off a little to the right the way it always had, with the New York

plates that had been on it when I bought it after I left Orangeville.
The kid was behind the wheel.

Somehow, with all my stopovers and searching, I managed to
overtake him. I scrunched down in my seat, watched him circle
the lot just the way I had, then pull up in front of the manager's
office. He left the engine running, and limped a little when he got
out.

I thought about sneaking into the car while the kid was inside,
surprising him, but I didn't want to piss him off, since that would
mean dragging him all the way home. I was hoping that I'd be able
to talk him into coming along peacefully, staying for the funeral
at least.

I smoked a Pall Mall while I waited, and stubbed it out in an
ashtray already brimming with Danielle's lipstick-smeared More
120s. The kid limped out, then drove slowly around the motel. I
noted what room he went into, waited ten minutes to make sure
he was settled in, then I parked and walked over to my Ford.

It had been through some rough treatment, I saw. There was a
big gouge in the passenger door, and the left rear wheel well had
been bent in so that it almost touched the tyre. The car was empty,
but I could see a slick of what looked like blood on the tan steering-
wheel cover. I got my keyring, opened the trunk. It was loaded
with stuff, but even so there should have been more – a lot more.
What had he done with it? Time to find out.

"Who is it?" the kid shouted through the door after I had pounded
on it for ten solid minutes.

"It's the manager. There's a problem with the plumbing in the
room next door. We need to get inside to get at the shutoff valve.
Sorry."

I stepped to one side of the fisheye in the door. There was a long
pause, then I heard the chain rattle, and the door opened.

I flashed back to his father, opening the door a crack, setting
down his bat. The kid wasn't crazy, though, just scared, and hurt.
His left eye was swollen almost shut, and he held himself painful.
I eeled past him and into the room before he could register the fact
that I wasn't the manager.

The room was cluttered with stuff, mostly clothes. Expensive items, representing a dozen different fashions, littered the floor: a Chicago Bulls toque; a shiny new biker jacket with cowboy fringe down the sleeves; chunky pump-up shoes; elephantine overalls; a *cholo* plaid shirt in Blood colours. The kid stood by the door in a towel, his hair dripping, but freshly cut and styled, angular shapes shaved into a mosaic over his head.

The kid snatched up the overalls and pulled them on while trying to keep the towel around his waist.

"What the hell do you want?" When he spoke, I saw that his lips were bruised, and one of his front teeth was gone.

"Jeez, kid, did you go through the windshield when you wrecked my car?"

He leaned nonchalantly against the door. "The way I figure it," he said coolly, "that car ain't rightfully yours, since you took all of that good stuff out of our road. The way I figure it, you owe my family at least that car and the stuff in the store."

I nodded. "You may be right, son. Tell you what: you keep that car, the stuff, too, and we'll call it even. Just come on back to the farm, help your Pa get through this funeral. He's in rough shape, you know."

"Let the bastard twist." He said it flatly, without emotion.

"Come on, Wayne, you know you don't mean that. You're shook up about your Ma, that's understandable, but your Pa loves you, and he needs you."

The kid barked a short laugh and spat thin blood on the carpet. "My Pa don't love nothing or nobody. He only hates. First he hated the alien for getting my Ma sick, then he hated me for distracting him from hating the alien, then he hated Ma for dying. He hate you yet, Kazzarets? He tell you to get the hell away from him? Did he give you a good whack with that bat?"

"Your Pa is just confused is all. We can talk about it on the way home. Then, if you still want, I'll help you get to LA, get you set up there, make sure no one rips you off."

"Mister, I need more of your helping like I need an asshole in the middle of my forehead. Why don't you get in whatever you rode down here in and drive away somewhere, find someone else to leech off. Or do I have to throw you out?"

For a second, I felt a little scared. The way he said it I knew that the kid wouldn't pause a second if it came to killing me. Then I felt angry: since when did I let little assholes push me around?

"You think you can do it, Wayne?"

He planted the sole of one foot on the wall behind him and looked me over. "Old man, I'll give you ten seconds to get the hell out of my room, and then I'm going to stomp a mudhole in your ass."

I settled back into my chair and matched stares with him.

"One. Two."

My wife, angry again about something, never did nothing right around her, always making one stupid mistake or another. She turns her back on me and walks around the little kitchen, transferring food from a saucepan to a serving-dish. I'm still half-drunk and the boss was on my back all day at work again.

"Three. Four. Five."

A loser, she calls me a loser, tells me that she rues the day she met me, tells me that I'm screwing up my son, turning him into the same kind of worthless jackass that I am. Tells me that I'm no catch, that she could find a better provider pumping gas at the Petro Can station. My son watches from the doorway, and I yell at her: not in front of the boy.

"Six. Seven."

She laughs at me. Not in front of the boy? Don't tell her son what a sack of shit his father is? Why not? Don't I think he's figured it out by himself already? Drunk. Wife-beater. Stupid.

"Eight. Nine."

What kind of moron do I take her for? If I don't want her to know about my girlfriends, I should take their love-notes out of my pockets before I put my jeans in the wash. I never cheated on you, I say, never. And it's the truth, isn't it? It doesn't count if you're drunk.

"Ten." The kid grabbed me by the lapels. Tried to haul me out of the chair. I kicked out violently, catching him in the right knee with my steel toe, the chair flipping over backwards. I leaped out of it and he got up again.

I grab the saucepan out of her hand, throw it through the kitchen window. Bitch! I scream as she runs from me. I sweep the food off the countertops and hear the glass shatter. I chase her into the living room, kicking over chairs, kicking the swinging door off its hinges.

The kid grabbed his belt off the bed, a studded leather belt with a heavy Harley Davidson buckle, and he started swinging it. I roared and caught it on my forearm, letting it wrap around and the buckle smashed against the back of my fist. I grabbed the leather strap and pulled it out of his grasp, and swarmed over him as he went down.

My wife is crying, but I can't stop slapping her. I hit her breasts, her belly, make a fist and smash her in the face. It feels good, it's shameful, I'm so angry I can feel it through my whole body. She's screaming but I can't hear any sound. Tiny hands catch my arm as I move to swing on her again: my son. He's crying too, and I can see how much he hates me. I pull my arm free and backhand him across the room, his nose pumping blood. I move after him, but somehow my wife grabs my leg and I kick down at her, feel something break.

The kid didn't make a sound as I worked him over, and he never stopped swinging back at me, never let me pin him. He spat blood as my knee connected with his kidney, then he twisted around fast and dug his fist into my crotch. I hardly felt it and I grabbed his shorn head and slammed it down into the cheap motel carpet.

Someone turns the volume on, and I hear the sounds my wife is making. "What are you doing? How can you do that? Don't hit him, he's your *son*! I'm your wife, God damn you. Stop it, you're killing him!" And over it, the sound of a siren, getting close. I shake my head, and I see her and my boy, blood and broken furniture and bones and he's screaming, *screaming* in absolute terror, looking at me with his eyes wide and horrified. I've got blood on me, and there's broken glass in my boot somehow, and food on my jeans. The sirens get louder and the room blurs with tears. I go through the back door and run.

The kid wasn't going to stop struggling, and my tears were flowing so hard I could barely see him. I leaped off him and retreated, bellowing. "That's enough, Wayne. Knock it off. Stop it, stop it, someone's going to call the cops, Wayne. Stop it!" I slapped his punch away.

"Wayne, look, stop it." I was sobbing the words now, and I didn't know why. I *hurt*. "Wayne!"

He looked into my eyes and saw the tears streaming down my face. That finally stopped him.

"What?" he shouted.

"Look, I don't want to fight with you. Come home. Go to your Pa, then do what you want to do. Do the right thing, Wayne." I was really crying now, sobbing like I hadn't done since I was a kid.

Wayne started to pick up his things and throw them into a frame backpack. He pulled on a shirt and shoes and the Bulls toque.

"What are you doing?" I asked him.

"I guess I'm going home. I can't stand to see a grown man bawl."

It didn't sting, but it was meant to, so I acted like it had. I wiped my nose on my sleeve and followed him out to the cars. "How'd you get busted up?"

"Gangbangers in Portland. I stopped to do some shopping, and when I came back, they were hanging out all over the car. There was a scrap. I ended up scraping the side against a lightpole."

"You okay?"

"I'll be fine."

"I'm sorry, Wayne."

"Just drive."

I got into Danielle's car, and Wayne got into the Ford, and I followed him back out onto the I5.

I only hit the alien once before. The old man had insisted.

"Go on, Kazzarets, swing! Just concentrate real hard on something and swing the damn bat. Not too hard though – don't break the skin."

The alien was immobile on its pallet, eye-disc empty of anything. The old man insisted, said I had to do it to see if the alien would mind me better than it did him. The real reason, though, the reason I saw in the way he dry-washed his hands, the way he stared intently at the bat, the real reason was that he wanted someone else to have some of the *blame*. Once I realized that, I knew that I would have to do it.

When the bat connected with its grapefruit-sized ankle-joint, I stared into its eyes and in that second, I saw the kind of uncomprehending terror that I had seen on my boy's face the time I nearly killed him.

I shouted something and dropped the bat, but I didn't hear what it was, because someone had turned the volume off again, and it didn't come back on until the old man peeled off my gloves and let me out of the room. We couldn't find anything outside the house, so the old man decided that as far as recovering treasure from the alien went, I was a dud.

I felt the alien's stare for days afterwards, piercing the ground and tracking me wherever I went.

While the kid and his old man were shouting in the living room, I snuck down into the basement. The alien was healing up, already less pulpy than it had been.

I looked around, found a hacksaw, and sawed its head off.

From the first time the saw bit into its neck, it looked at me with that huge disc eye, and I knew that it was grateful. I didn't see how it could heal such a wound. I paid no heed to the black blood that slicked my hands and arms.

The road outside was clear except for a silver money-clip full of hundreds. I drove Danielle's car back to Casket Junction.

My reflection on the bar mirror was haggard and filthy, caked with the alien's blood.

I peeled one hundred off the clip and stuck it down into my pocket. When Danielle saw me, her face went hard.

"I'm leaving here," I said. "I'm going home to stand trial for beating my wife. I don't expect they'll let me out any time soon. You deserve to know, Danielle. And I want you to know that I've changed. I wish to God it had never happened, and now I'm going to pay the consequences. I'll write to you once I know what pen they send me to."

I waited for her to say something. She just stared at me, her expression unchanged. I pressed the money-clip into her hand. "Here's some money. Settle down, go to school, maybe. Or go to a beach somewhere. Get out of the life."

She held the money lifelessly. I stared at my shoes and blinked back the tears. "Look, I've got to go now."

I waited again, my tongue thick. I forced myself to say the words "Thank you Danielle. I'm sorry. I lo . . ."

Her eyes narrowed to slits and her hand came up fast and caught me across the jaw. "Don't you fucking *dare* say 'I love you.'" She whirled and teetered into the ladies room.

It took two days on the Greyhound to get to the Peace Bridge in Windsor. The Canada Customs officer ordered us off the bus, then called us up to the desk one at a time to show ID. I handed him my passport.

"My name is Jack William Rudolph Paul Anthony Kazzarets. I am wanted for aggravated assault in Orangeville. I've come to turn myself in."

The RCMP cruiser pulled smoothly away from the border station. I looked down at my filthy handcuffed hands, still caked with the alien's blood.

I flexed my fingers, imagined that I felt cancer, degenerative arthritis, AIDS, festering beneath my skin, sinking in with the alien's blood.

I looked up, then, and out the front windshield. All the way back to the holding cells, I watched the car eat the kilometres of road, and wished that something would appear before us that would make everything right.

On the Road

Jack Kerouac

The greatest ride in my life was about to come up, a truck, with a flatboard at the back, with about six or seven boys sprawled out on it, and the drivers, two young blond farmers from Minnesota, were picking up every single soul they found on that road – the most smiling, cheerful couple of handsome bumpkins you could ever wish to see, both wearing cotton shirts and overalls, nothing else; both thick-wristed and earnest, with broad howareyou smiles for anybody and anything that came across their path. I ran up, said, "Is there room?" They said, "Sure, hop on, 'sroom for everybody."

I wasn't on the flatboard before the truck roared off; I lurched, a rider grabbed me, and I sat down. Somebody passed a bottle of rotgut, the bottom of it. I took a big swig in the wild, lyrical, drizzling air of Nebraska. "Whooee, here we go!" yelled a kid in a baseball cap, and they gunned up the truck to seventy and passed everybody on the road. "We been riding this sonofabitch since Des Moines. These guys never stop. Every now and then you have to yell for pisscall, otherwise you have to piss off the air, and hang on, brother, hang on."

I looked at the company. There were two young farmer boys from North Dakota in red baseball caps, which is the standard North Dakota farmer-boy hat, and they were headed for the harvests; their old men had given them leave to hit the road for a summer. There were two young city boys from Columbus, Ohio, high-school football players, chewing gum, winking, singing in the breeze, and they said they were hitchhiking around the United States for the summer. "We're going to LA!" they yelled.

"What are you going to do there?"

"Hell, we don't know. Who cares?"

Then there was a tall slim fellow who had a sneaky look. "Where you from?" I asked. I was lying next to him on the platform; you couldn't sit without bouncing off, it had no rails. And he turned slowly to me, opened his mouth, and said, "Mon-ta-na."

Finally there were Mississippi Gene and his charge. Mississippi Gene was a little dark guy who rode freight trains around the country, a thirty-year-old hobo but with a youthful look so you couldn't tell exactly what age he was. And he sat on the boards crosslegged, looking out over the fields without saying anything for hundreds of miles and finally at one point he turned to me and said, "Where *you* headed?"

I said Denver.

"I got a sister there but I ain't seed her for several couple years." His language was melodious and slow. He was patient. His charge was a sixteen-year-old tall blond kid, also in hobo rags; that is to say, they wore old clothes that had been turned black by the soot of railroads and the dirt of boxcars and sleeping on the ground. The blond kid was also quiet and he seemed to be running away from something, and it figured to be the law the way he looked straight ahead and wet his lips in worried thought. Montana Slim spoke to them occasionally with a sardonic and insinuating smile. They paid no attention to him. Slim was all insinuation. I was afraid of his long goofy grin that he opened up straight in your face and held there half-moronically.

"You got any money?" he said to me.

"Hell no, maybe enough for a pint of whisky till I get to Denver. What about you?"

"I know where I can get some."

"Where?"

"Anywhere. You can always folly a man down an alley, can't you?"

"Yeah, I guess you can."

"I ain't beyond doing it when I really need some dough. Headed up to Montana to see my father. I'll have to get off this rig at Cheyenne and move up some other way. These crazy boys are going to Los Angeles."

"Straight?"

"All the way – if you want to go to LA you got a ride."

I mulled this over; the thought of zooming all night across Nebraska, Wyoming, and the Utah desert in the morning, and then most likely the Nevada desert in the afternoon, and actually arriving in Los Angeles within a foreseeable space of time almost made me change my plans. But I had to go to Denver. I'd have to get off at Cheyenne too, and hitch south ninety miles to Denver.

I was glad when the two Minnesota farmboys who owned the truck decided to stop in North Platte and eat; I wanted to have a look at them. They came out of the cab and smiled at all of us. "Pisscall!" said one. "Time to eat!" said the other. But they were the only ones in the party who had money to buy food. We all shambled after them to a restaurant run by a bunch of women, and sat around over hamburgers and coffee while they wrapped away enormous meals just as if they were back in their mother's kitchen. They were brothers; they were transporting farm machinery from Los Angeles to Minnesota and making good money at it. So on their trip to the Coast empty they picked up everybody on the road. They'd done this about five times now; they were having a hell of a time. They liked everything. They never stopped smiling. I tried to talk to them – a kind of dumb attempt on my part to befriend the captains of our ship – and the only responses I got were two sunny smiles and large white cornfed teeth.

Everybody had joined them in the restaurant except the two hobo kids, Gene and his boy. When we all got back they were still sitting in the truck, forlorn and disconsolate. Now the darkness was falling. The drivers had a smoke; I jumped at the chance to go buy a bottle of whisky to keep warm in the rushing cold air of night. They smiled when I told them. "Go ahead, hurry up."

"You can have a couple shots!" I reassured them.

"Oh no, we never drink, go ahead."

Montana Slim and the two high-school boys wandered the streets of North Platte with me till I found a whisky store. They chipped in some, and Slim some, and I bought a fifth. Tall, sullen men watched us go by from false-front buildings; the main street was lined with square box-houses. There were immense vistas of the plains beyond every sad street. I felt something different in the air in North Platte, I didn't know what it was. In five minutes I did. We got back on the truck and roared off. It got dark quickly. We all had a shot, and suddenly I looked, and the verdant farm-fields of the Platte began to disappear and in their stead, so far you couldn't see to the end, appeared long flat wastelands of sand and sagebrush. I was astounded.

"What in the hell is this?" I cried out to Slim.

"This is the beginning of the rangelands, boy. Hand me another drink."

"Whoopee!" yelled the high-school boys. "Columbus, so long! What would Sparkie and the boys say if they was here. Yow!"

The drivers had switched up front; the fresh brother was gunning the truck to the limit. The road changed too: humpy in the middle, with soft shoulders and a ditch on both sides about four feet deep, so that the truck bounced and teetered from one side of the road to the other – miraculously only when there were no cars coming the opposite way – and I thought we'd all take a somersault. But they were tremendous drivers. How that truck disposed of the Nebraska nub – the nub that sticks out over Colorado! And soon I realized I was actually at last over Colorado, though not officially in it, but looking southwest toward Denver itself a few hundred miles away. I yelled for joy. We passed the bottle. The great blazing stars came out, the far-receding sand hills got dim. I felt like an arrow that could shoot out all the way.

And suddenly Mississippi Gene turned to me from his cross-legged, patient reverie, and opened his mouth, and leaned close, and said, "These plains put me in mind of Texas."

"Are you from Texas?"

"No sir, I'm from Green-vell Muzz-sippy." And that was the way he said it.

"Where's that kid from?"

"He got into some kind of trouble back in Mississippi, so I offered to help him out. Boy's never been out on his own. I take care of him best as I can, he's only a child." Although Gene was white there was something of the wise and tired old Negro in him, and something very much like Elmer Hassel, the New York dope addict, in him, but a railroad Hassel, a travelling epic Hassel, crossing and recrossing the country every year, south in the winter and north in the summer, and only because he had no place he could stay in without getting tired of it and because there was nowhere to go but everywhere, keep rolling under the stars, generally the Western stars.

"I been to Og-den a couple times. If you want to ride on to Ogden I got some friends there we could hole up with."

"I'm going to Denver from Cheyenne."

"Hell, go right straight thu, you don't get a ride like this every day."

This too was a tempting offer. What was in Ogden? "What's Ogden?" I said.

"It's the place where most of the boys pass thu and always meet there; you're liable to see anybody there."

In my earlier days I'd been to sea with a tall rawboned fellow from Louisiana called Big Slim Hazard, William Holmes Hazard, who was hobo by choice. As a little boy he'd seen a hobo come up to ask his mother for a piece of pie, and she had given it to him, and when the hobo went off down the road the little boy had said, "Ma, what is that fellow?" "Why, that's a ho-bo." "Ma, I want to be a ho-bo someday." "Shet your mouth, that's not for the like of the Hazards." But he never forgot that day, and when he grew up, after a short spell playing football at LSU, he did become a hobo. Big Slim and I spent many nights telling stories and spitting tobacco juice in paper containers. There was something so indubitably reminiscent of Big Slim Hazard in Mississippi Gene's demeanour that I said, "Do you happen to have met a fellow called Big Slim Hazard somewhere?"

And he said, "You mean the tall fellow with the big laugh?"

"Well, that sounds like him. He came from Ruston, Louisiana."

"That's right. Louisiana Slim he's sometimes called. Yessir, I shore have met Big Slim."

"And he used to work in the East Texas oil fields?"

"East Texas is right. And now he's punching cows."

And that was exactly right; and still I couldn't believe Gene could have really known Slim, whom I'd been looking for, more or less, for years. "And he used to work in tugboats in New York?"

"Well now, I don't know about that."

"I guess you only knew him in the West."

"I reckon. I ain't never been to New York."

"Well, damn me, I'm amazed you know him. This is a big country. Yet I knew you must have known him."

"Yessir, I know Big Slim pretty well. Always generous with his money when he's got some. Mean, tough fellow, too; I seen him flatten a policeman in the yards at Cheyenne, one punch." That sounded like Big Slim; he was always practising that one punch in the air; he looked like Jack Dempsey, but a young Jack Dempsey who drank.

"Damn!" I yelled into the wind, and I had another shot, and by now I was feeling pretty good. Every shot was wiped away by the rushing wind of the open truck, wiped away of its bad effects, and the good effect sank in my stomach. "Cheyenne, here I come!" I sang. "Denver, look out for your boy."

Montana Slim turned to me, pointed at my shoes, and commented, "You reckon if you put them things in the ground something'll grow up?" – without cracking a smile, of course, and the other boys heard him and laughed. And they were the silliest shoes in America; I brought them along specifically because I didn't want my feet to sweat in the hot road, and except for the rain in Bear Mountain they proved to be the best possible shoes for my journey. So I laughed with them. And the shoes were pretty ragged by now, the bits of coloured leather sticking up like pieces of a fresh pineapple and my toes showing through. Well, we had another shot and laughed. As in a dream we zoomed through small crossroads towns smack out of the darkness, and passed long lines of lounging harvest hands and cowboys in the night. They watched us pass in one motion of the head, and we saw them slap their thighs from the continuing dark the other side of town – we were a funny-looking crew.

A lot of men were in this country at that time of the year; it was harvest time. The Dakota boys were fidgeting. "I think we'll get off at the next pisscall; seems like there's a lot of work around here."

"All you got to do is move north when it's over here," counselled Montana Slim, "and jes follow the harvest till you get to Canada." The boys nodded vaguely; they didn't take much stock in his advice.

Meanwhile the blond young fugitive sat the same way; every now and then Gene leaned out of his Buddhistic trance over the rushing dark plains and said something tenderly in the boy's ear. The boy nodded. Gene was taking care of him, of his moods and his fears. I wondered where the hell they would go and what they would do. They had no cigarettes. I squandered my pack on them, I loved them so. They were grateful and gracious. They never asked, I kept offering. Montana Slim had his own but never passed the pack. We zoomed through another crossroads town, passed another line of tall lanky men in jeans clustered in the dim light like moths on the desert, and returned to the tremendous darkness, and the stars overhead were pure and bright because of the increasingly thin air as we mounted the high hill of the western plateau, about a foot a mile, so they say, and no trees obstructing any low-levelled stars anywhere. And once I saw a moody white-faced cow in the sage by the road as we flitted by. It was like riding a railroad train, just as steady and just as straight.

By and by we came to a town, slowed down, and Montana Slim said, "Ah, pisscall," but the Minnesotans didn't stop and went right on through. "Damn, I gotta go," said Slim.

"Go over the side," said somebody.

"Well, I *will*," he said, and slowly, as we all watched, he inched to the back of the platform on his haunch, holding on as best he could, till his legs dangled over. Somebody knocked on the window of the cab to bring this to the attention of the brothers. Their great smiles broke as they turned. And just as Slim was ready to proceed, precarious as it was already, they began zigzagging the truck at seventy miles an hour. He fell back a moment; we saw a whale's spout in the air; he struggled back to a sitting position. They swung the truck. Wham, over he went on his side, watering all over himself. In the roar we could hear him faintly cursing, like the whine of a man far across the hills. "Damn . . . damn . . ." He never knew we were doing this deliberately; he just struggled, as grim as Job. When he was finished, as such, he was wringing wet, and now he had to edge and shimmy his way back, and with a most woebegone look, and everybody laughing, except the sad blond boy, and the Minnesotans roaring in the cab. I handed him the bottle to make up for it.

"What the hail," he said, "was they doing that on purpose?"

"They sure were."

"Well, damn me, I didn't know that. I know I tried it back in Nebraska and didn't have half so much trouble."

We came suddenly into the town of Ogallala, and here the fellows in the cab called out, *"Pisscall!"* and with great good delight. Slim stood sullenly by the truck, rueing a lost opportunity. The two Dakota boys said good-bye to everybody and figured they'd start harvesting here. We watched them disappear in the night toward the shacks at the end of town where lights were burning, where a watcher of the night in jeans said the employment men would be. I had to buy more cigarettes. Gene and the blond boy followed me to stretch their legs. I walked into the least likely place in the world, a kind of lonely Plains soda fountain for the local teenage girls and boys. They were dancing, a few of them, to the music on the jukebox. There was a lull when we came in. Gene and Blondey just stood there, looking at nobody; all they wanted was cigarettes. There were some pretty girls, too. And one of them made eyes at Blondey and he never saw it, and if he had he wouldn't have cared, he was so sad and gone.

I bought a pack each for them; they thanked me. The truck was ready to go. It was getting on midnight now, and cold. Gene, who'd been around the country more times than he could count on his fingers and toes, said the best thing to do now was for all of us to bundle up under the big tarpaulin or we'd freeze. In this manner, and with the rest of the bottle, we kept warm as the air grew ice-cold and pinged our ears. The stars seemed to get brighter the more we climbed the High Plains. We were in Wyoming now. Flat on my back, I stared straight up at the magnificent firmament, glorying in the time I was making, in how far I had come from sad Bear Mountain after all, and tingling with kicks at the thought of what lay ahead of me in Denver – whatever, whatever it would be. And Mississippi Gene began to sing a song. He sang it in a melodious, quiet voice, with a river accent, and it was simple, just "I got a purty little girl, she's sweet six-teen, she's the purti-est thing you ever seen," repeating it with other lines thrown in, all concerning how far he'd been and how he wished he could go back to her but he done lost her.

I said, "Gene, that's the prettiest song."

"It's the sweetest I know," he said with a smile.

"I hope you get where you're going, and be happy when you do."

"I always make out and move along one way or the other."

Montana Slim was asleep. He woke up and said to me, "Hey, Blackie, how about you and me investigatin' Cheyenne together tonight before you go to Denver?"

"Sure thing." I was drunk enough to go for anything.

As the truck reached the outskirts of Cheyenne, we saw the high red lights of the local radio station, and suddenly we were bucking through a great crowd of people that poured along both sidewalks. "Hell's bells, it's Wild West Week," said Slim. Big crowds of businessmen, fat businessmen in boots and ten-gallon hats, with their hefty wives in cowgirl attire, bustled and whooped on the wooden sidewalks of old Cheyenne; farther down were the long stringy boulevard lights of new downtown Cheyenne, but the celebration was focusing on Oldtown. Blank guns went off. The saloons were crowded to the sidewalk. I was amazed, and at the same time I felt it was ridiculous: in my first shot at the West I was seeing to what absurd devices it had fallen to keep its proud tradition. We had to jump off the truck and say good-bye; the Minnesotans weren't interested in hanging around. It was sad to see them go, and I realized that I would never see any of them again, but that's the way it was. "You'll freeze your ass tonight," I warned. "Then you'll burn 'em in the desert tomorrow afternoon."

"That's all right with me long's as we get out of this cold night," said Gene. And the truck left, threading its way through the crowds, and nobody paying attention to the strangeness of the kids inside the tarpaulin, staring at the town like babes from a coverlet. I watched it disappear into the night.

Those Vanished I Recognize

Tom Piccirilli

Clay had heard about this sort of thing before, and he would have believed this was a sign of Obsessive-Compulsive Disorder if it had affected any area of his life but the driving.

But there was none of the repetitive hand washing or twisting of hair, no facial tics or other preoccupation. Only the impulse and need to ride. A sleek '68 Mustang Fastback, sky blue with one of the last 289 V-8 engines off the line, and the seat now perfectly adjusted, his legs finally long enough after all these years, so that he didn't even have to press down on the pedal, it all came naturally.

A steady 60 mph could take him anywhere if he could just get west of the Robert Moses Causeway. Hit the Long Island Expressway, cruise into Mid-town, squirm through the ice-slick streets and past the dying, pale whores waiting at the mouth of the Lincoln Tunnel. Hopefully get by them without incident, no dealings with the big poppa pimps and the wide-eyed stable of chicks that run the gamut from crackheads with the Herpes flair to ones that looked like Hedy Lamarr out of *Samson and Delilah*. Buzz beyond them and keep it going straight through Jersey, then slip out into the rest of the moist, flustered world.

Except he couldn't get west of the Robert Moses Causeway. That gave him a route heading two hours to the end of Long Island, only stopping when he came to a historical park called Montauk Point, where he'd pull into the lot at the base of the lighthouse, sit for a moment listening to the waves slash against the stone, and then head back again, right to the starting line.

Clay had been at it for fourteen hours straight, since noon yesterday. He felt wide awake and only a bit stiff. The six-packs and burgers held him over fine, and so long as it didn't take him more than two or three minutes to fuel up, he didn't get jittery at the gas stations. Still, he had begun to question himself over exactly why he had the urge and where it had come from. He had the uneasy notion this was starting to get a little unreasonable.

That was all right though. He drilled along on Sunrise Highway heading east, past the Pine Barrens and further until the island forked. For some reason he hadn't been able to take the North Fork yet and go out to Orient Point. Instead, every time he got to the end of Sunrise, with his hands growing sweaty, and his knuckles – even the pinkies – crackling, he swung south and continued to gun towards Montauk.

It had something to do with his father, Clay thought, and decided to let it come to him in its own time. That kept his pulse down as moonlight swept over the road, breeze hurling leaves against the grille and spinning across the hood. The burned remnants of the Pine Barrens came into view, his headlights illuminating the unnatural stance of scorched trees along the shadowed terrain. It had been five years since the largest fire in the island's history cut through this area, and still there had scarcely been any regrowth.

He kept heading towards Route 27 and on into the Hamptons, where the New York elite resided. His father used to point out celebrity homes whenever they came out here to fish and spend an afternoon at the beach: Joseph Heller, Kurt Vonnegut, Jackson Pollock, and dozens of others. Clay never understood where Dad got his information from.

A tightness seized him, maybe a touch of nausea. The heater softly hummed. This was where the pain would come. He waited and started the countdown, each car length left behind being another lost part of him. The rearview mirror had been removed for this reason. He couldn't stand to watch all that continued receding behind him. He watched the mileage gauge, knowing what would happen on the next tick of a tenth of a mile. There, almost there, almost –

The Hamptons, as always, invaded Clay as he entered town, mansions whirling by in a haze of jealousy, respect, love and wanting. The solidity of riches he would never own pressed him from all sides, dropping off his shoulders and into the back seat, where he could hear the vinyl groan beneath their weight. He gritted his teeth and fought not to let out a yelp. The Mustang slowed and he had to stamp his foot down in order to get past. There were hardly any street lights here, but the few he hit were already yellow and waiting for him, holding out the extra couple seconds, and just barely letting him slide by.

The road curved and kept coiling as if it would never finish going through this spiral. His odometer shot up insanely, engine squealing as the back end fishtailed on black ice. He struggled to regain control, letting the edges of his mouth hitch into a grin, fighting the wheel. At last he felt the smooth catch of the tyres on the pavement as he came out of the corkscrew stretch and manoeuvred past the saw grass of Southampton College.

That salty scent of the ocean clung to him, thriving everywhere in the car. He enjoyed watching the rising mounds and bluffs of the golf course on the other side, and he perked at the monolithic structures rising to the south. Jutting arcane shapes sloped against the rolling clouds. They might be homes or something more – trawlers dry-docked, or machinery to repair the damaged shoreline and bulldoze tons of sand back into place. Radio towers or high-voltage steeples, or maybe it was only his vision failing. No matter how many times he went past he could never be sure.

Twenty minutes later he wheeled through the fishing town of Montauk again, past the seafood restaurants where his parents would take him and his sister Jamie on the way to the park.

"The abstract expressionist Jackson Pollock painted in a barn, did you know that?" Dad had asked.

Jamie, beaming, twelve at the time, answered gleefully because she always had the answers. "Jack the Dripper! His studio was right there" – pointing, the index finger a little crooked, but knowing exactly where everything was as they drove – "in East

Hampton, back in the late forties and early fifties, after he and Lee Krasner got married and moved out of the city."

"Correct!"

Clay would keep silent, uncertain if these were particulars he was truly supposed to know or if this was a private diversion, a personal game between his father and sister. A series of meaningless questions and trivia, or maybe they were making it up as they went along. Dad had once claimed that three atomic bombs had been dropped on Japan: Nagasaki, Hiroshima, and *Tokyo*. Jamie, intent in either salving their father's conceit, or only wishing to be loved the best, curled lithely into the crook of Dad's arm and cooed, "Yes, I know."

Perhaps the rotten, weak son, the living disappointment, Clay had searched a dozen books and asked all three history teachers in school, searching for his father's fact.

The Mustang's engine had a nice thrum and rumble now, the oil beginning to break down after gunning a thousand frosty miles in fourteen hours. Clay didn't let the pressure of the night close in as he sped towards the park, headlights digging channels through the dark that let him cleanly pass through. He slowed until the sound of the splashing surf could be heard over the engine.

On the last circuit, four hours ago, there had been a dozen cars in the lot, mostly teenagers making out parked behind the storm fences or middle-aged couples bundled in sweaters taking a stroll up the beach. Now he was alone and wasn't sure how much he liked it. The lighthouse, which hadn't been lit in years, loomed above.

Clay pulled in and waited. He wondered if he could last longer than a couple of minutes this time. He hoped so, though he still wasn't afraid of this need for a bizarre, redundant journey. It would work itself out. He turned the key but wasn't convinced he'd broken the cycle yet. There was the strong impression that he hadn't been able to shut the car off the last time he was here – the time before, or the time before, or –

He sat back and let this interim carry him, with enough moonlight funnelling into the interior so that he could read his watch.

Five minutes passed, then ten. It wasn't until his breath fogged up the windshield that he realized he was cold. His brow furrowed until he remembered it was January.

"Do you know who ordered that the lighthouse be built over two hundred years ago?" Dad asked.

"The lighthouse was authorized by the Second Congress, under President George Washington," Jamie said. Clay thought it could be true.

"When?"

"In 1792."

When they got back home that day, sunburned and with the sea salt drying to a thick powder on their skin, Clay immediately noticed the stench. Jamie didn't, heading off to shower. Knowledgeable yet indifferent. The light in the living room was all wrong – dim, with a haze of smoke drifting past.

Dad leaned over the couch, peering. Mother's legs were folded behind her, one hand flat, palm-down on the throw pillows, the other fist positioned differently. Dark, and growing darker as Clay watched, not bloody but blistered and cracking, lying atop the exposed light bulb of the overturned reading lamp, skin charred and growing blacker. Her shoulders had slumped so far forward that her head hung over the far side of the couch where he couldn't see her face. Blue and yellow pills lay scattered across the carpet. Dad picked one up and tried studying it in the dim light. He had a rough time, squinting, holding the pill this way and that, and moved closer to the lamp with the fumes of frying meat rising from it. The billowing smoke broke against Dad's face. And Mother not moving her hand, and still not getting up.

By the time Clay walked the dirt path down to the water he realized somebody was watching him.

It took a while for his eyes to adjust, even with the vibrant moon and silver mercury clouds. The ocean splashed and churned, clawing up the beach. The other person's presence tugged at him like fishhooks, so that he let himself go and followed into darkness.

He found her within a hundred yards, sitting back in the sand surrounded by half-buried stones. She gestured but he couldn't make out what the motion might be. He picked his way carefully to her as the breakers clapped and roared around them.

From the midst of an enveloping blanket, with only the suggestion of something actually alive in there, she looked up. "Hello. Care for a swim?"

He let out a barking laugh, and the sound startled him. He could hardly make out her long hair swaying and flopping in the wind, murkiness braided into shadow. The white of her eyes came through. "I'll take a rain check until July."

"I suppose you're right." He saw the glow of her teeth. "This might sound crude, depending on what you do for relaxation, and seeing as how we've only just met, but I figured I'd ask anyway. Do you have any weed?"

"Some beer in my car."

There was an odd, lethargic trait to her voice. She spoke in sluggishly unwinding whispers. "I don't feel like walking back to the parking lot."

"Neither do I."

He got closer and really focused, staring until she took a more precise form. The eyes came and went as she blinked. He thought she was a couple of years younger than him, maybe seventeen or eighteen at the outside. She sat near enough the water that shards of moonlight swept up against her, illuminating her only in fragments.

Yet there was an extra quality to her that came through. She was at ease inside her body, even with him moving in now, cautiously taking another step, and one more, until he sat beside her. She contained the gentle sexuality of someone who lost her virginity long ago, and had never been burdened with any of the obsessions, fears and confusion that everyone else had to suffer through.

Dad had asked, "Are you a man yet?"

Clay, astounded and drawing away, grunted as if kidney-punched. His father had spoken with a kind of reverent tenderness, inquiring but embarrassed, yet desperately needing the truth. Clay remained silent, watching Dad gape and trying to say more, mouthing words or names, reaching to touch Clay on the shoulder but never quite getting there. Dad turned to Jamie, expecting an answer and, as always, getting one. She told him, "Clay's made it with that Felecia McAlester, down by the docks, in the front seat of your Mustang."

That got reality moving again. Clay didn't mind that his sister had told, or that she somehow knew what she couldn't have known. It made its own sense, which was a relief of sorts.

"Let's build a fire," the girl said so quietly that he almost didn't catch it. There was an odd clacking noise coming from nearby.

"There's not enough driftwood."

"You haven't even looked."

"I don't need to. There are folks who clear it out every day, not that there's ever much to begin with. The coast is too rocky."

"So what shows up gets turned into lamps and shit?"

"Pretty much."

They watched the foam dashing against the rocks, spattering and reforming into plumes. He thought he saw clothing floating out there, rising on the crests and retreating. The lighthouse stood silhouetted, perfectly centred before the blaze of the moon.

"My mother is out there," she said.

"Your mother?"

She started to yawn but didn't seem to have the energy for it. It took her a long time to talk, even with that intensity, everything coming out so languidly. "We lived in Queens. Forest Hills. She went out to buy fresh tomatoes and a week later they found her floating here."

"Yeah?"

"No marks on her." Slower still, her sentences almost solidifying in the air. "Everybody tried to believe she was kidnapped but I think she killed herself. It's the nicer thought, really, if you've got to dwell on it."

"And you do."

"Yes, of course."

She shrugged and the blanket slid off her shoulders, showing that she wore something too thin and pink beneath. He leaned forward and realized he was wrong, she was naked. Soft angles and outlines wove into one intimation. She must be turning to ice but didn't bother to pull the blanket back up into place.

Jamie had held tightly to their father's hand at Mom's funeral. It was allowed, even expected, though there remained a crass edge about it. She was fifteen then, dressed in black chiffon and appearing too adult, as if she had advanced into a new role. She never let Dad's hand go for a moment, not even while the priest droned on and the neighbours wept, and the roses were given out. They approached the grave together, his father and sister, pausing to pray as the seconds coagulated into a clot of unbearable time, until Clay, so miserably alone and lonely, joined them, and they moved away from him.

He stood there trying to say goodbye, but couldn't even recall what his mother had looked like. He wanted them to open the casket once more, so that he could see and remember. He must have asked this aloud, and repeatedly, because Jamie, from the far side of the grave, made excuses for him, smiling at the crowd and still not letting Dad go. "He was very close to her, and he's been running a high fever. You can't blame him his ways. None of us can blame him."

"The water has a draw," the girl said. The clacking continued until he realized it was her teeth chattering.

"I know," Jamie would have told them, "tidal forces. It's called the gravitational and centrifugal gradients theory of the Earth-Moon system."

He looked at her naked breasts, uncertain if he was feeling lust or not. Seashells prodded him, the rising wind slithering under his collar and swabbing his forehead, like his mother's compresses when the fevers got too high.

"I'm waiting," she said.

"For what?"

"The nerve to follow in after my mother. I thought it would be easy, but I'm too afraid. I don't want to die."

She tried getting to her feet but she was already hypothermic. She must have gone through the heavy shaking period before he got here, and was now experiencing the onset of serious cramping and muscle lock. She fell over and lay feebly trembling in the sand. He stood and took a step back.

"Will you take me home now?" she whimpered.

"To Forest Hills? No, I can only go so far."

"Home with you."

"I'm not going there."

Her lips barely moved. "I'll freeze to death. I threw my clothes away."

"I saw them. In the surf."

"Home." She tried gathering herself again, but could only turn over in the moonlight, revealing herself completely to him. A powerful gust caught the blanket and threw it at his feet – a deliberate action deserving another in response, where he kicked it into the waves. "Please, I want to go home."

"So do I."

"I was wrong. I don't want to die. Don't leave me here. Please."

Clay turned and walked back up the path to the parking lot, got in the car and started it.

He hoped the next time he got back he would see his father and sister well-defined in the foam, rearing and casually tumbling against the jagged rocks, hand in hand with each question and every answer. He could almost recall having watched them here in the tide before – perhaps swimming, laughing, begging or gasping. It would take hardly any effort to do what the girl had done, and roll among the whitecaps until his loneliness was at an end, when at last he joined them and the others like them.

As he came out of the park his mother was there, breaking from the darkness at the side of the road, awash in the headlights. With her one good hand held out before her, she urged him not to go on, to finally rest and find peace as she had, by the strength of one's own will, but he could only do what he had grown accomplished at, catching her sorrowful, black-rimmed gaze as he now, and forever, continued to drive by.

The Volcano Dances

J. G. Ballard

They lived in a house on the mountain Tlaxihuatl half a mile below the summit. The house was built on a lava flow like the hide of an elephant. In the afternoon and evening the man, Charles Vandervell, sat by the window in the lounge, watching the fire displays that came from the crater. The noise rolled down the mountain side like a series of avalanches. At intervals a falling cinder hissed as it extinguished itself in the water tank on the roof. The woman slept most of the time in the bedroom overlooking the valley or, when she wished to be close to Vandervell, on the settee in the lounge.

In the afternoon she woke briefly when the "devil-sticks", man performed his dance by the road a quarter of a mile from the house. This mendicant had come to the mountain for the benefit of the people in the village below the summit, but his dance had failed to subdue the volcano and prevent the villagers from leaving. As they passed him pushing their carts he would rattle his spears and dance, but they walked on without looking up. When he became discouraged and seemed likely to leave Vandervell sent the house-boy out to him with an American dollar. From then on the stick-dancer came every day.

"Is he still here?" the woman asked. She walked into the lounge, folding her robe around her waist. "What's he supposed to be doing?"

"He's fighting a duel with the spirit of the volcano," Vandervell said. "He's putting a lot of thought and energy into it, but he hasn't a chance."

"I thought you were on his side," the woman said. "Aren't you paying him a retainer?"

"That's only to formalize the relationship. To show him that I understand what's going on. Strictly speaking, I'm on the volcano's side."

A shower of cinders rose a hundred feet above the crater, illuminating the jumping stick-man.

"Are you sure it's safe here?"

Vandervell waved her away. "Of course. Go back to bed and rest. This thin air is bad for the complexion."

"I feel all right. I heard the ground move."

"It's been moving for weeks." He watched the stick-man conclude his performance with a series of hops, as if leap-frogging over a partner. "On his diet that's not bad."

"You should take him back to Mexico City and put him in one of the cabarets. He'd make more than a dollar."

"He wouldn't be interested. He's a serious artist, this Nijinsky of the mountain side. Can't you see that?"

The woman half-filled a tumbler from the decanter on the table. "How long are you going to keep him out there?"

"As long as he'll stay." He turned to face the woman. "Remember that. When he leaves it will be time to go."

The stick-man, a collection of tatters when not in motion, disappeared into his lair, one of the holes in the lava beside the road.

"I wonder if he met Springman?" Vandervell said. "On balance it's possible. Springman would have come up the south face. This is the only road to the village."

"Ask him. Offer him another dollar."

"Pointless – he'd say he had seen him just to keep me happy."

"What makes you so sure Springman is here?"

"He *was* here," Vandervell corrected. "He won't be here any longer. I was with Springman in Acapulco when he looked at the map. He came here."

The woman carried her tumbler into the bedroom.

"We'll have dinner at nine," Vandervell called to her. "I'll let you know if he dances again."

Left alone, Vandervell watched the fire displays. The glow shone through the windows of the houses in the village so that they seemed to glow like charcoal. At night the collection of hovels was deserted, but a few of the men returned during the day.

In the morning two men came from the garage in Ecuatan to reclaim the car which Vandervell had hired. He offered to pay a month's rent in advance, but they rejected this and pointed at the clinkers that had fallen on to the car from the sky. None of them was hot enough to burn the paint-work. Vandervell gave them each fifty dollars and promised to cover the car with a tarpaulin. Satisfied, the men drove away.

After breakfast Vandervell walked out across the lava seams to the road. The stick-dancer stood by his hole above the bank, resting his hands on the two spears. The cone of the volcano, partly hidden by the dust, trembled behind his back. He watched Vandervell when he shouted across the road. Vandervell took a dollar bill from his wallet and placed it under a stone. The stick-man began to hum and rock on the balls of his feet.

As Vandervell walked back along the road two of the villagers approached.

"Guide," he said to them. "Ten dollars. One hour." He pointed to the lip of the crater but the men ignored him and continued along the road.

The surface of the house had once been white, but was now covered with grey dust. Two hours later, when the manager of the estate below the house rode up on a grey horse Vandervell asked: "Is your horse white or black?"

"That's a good question, señor."

"I want to hire a guide," Vandervell said. "To take me into the volcano."

"There's nothing there, señor."

"I want to look around the crater. I need someone who knows the pathways."

"It's full of smoke, Señor Vandervell. Hot sulphur. Burns the eyes. You wouldn't like it."

"Do you remember seeing someone called Springman?" Vandervell said. "About three months ago."

"You asked me that before. I remember two Americans with a scientific truck. Then a Dutchman with white hair."

"That could be him."

"Or maybe black, eh? As you say."

A rattle of sticks sounded from the road. After warming up, the stick-dancer had begun his performance in earnest.

"You'd better get out of here, Señor Vandervell," the manager said. "The mountain could split one day."

Vandervell pointed to the stick-dancer. "He'll hold it off for a while."

The manager rode away. "My respects to Mrs Vandervell."

"*Miss* Winston."

Vandervell went into the lounge and stood by the window. During the day the activity of the volcano increased. The column of smoke rose half a mile into the sky, threaded by gleams of flame.

The rumbling woke the woman. In the kitchen she spoke to the house-boy.

"He wants to leave," she said to Vandervell afterwards.

"Offer him more money," he said without turning.

"He says everyone has left now. It's too dangerous to stay. The men in the village are leaving for good this afternoon."

Vandervell watched the stick-dancer twirling his devil-sticks like a drum-major. "Let him go if he wants to. I think the estate manager saw Springman."

"That's good. Then he was here."

"The manager sent his respects to you."

"I'm charmed."

Five minutes later, when the house-boy had gone, she returned to her bedroom. During the afternoon she came out to collect the film magazines in the bookcase.

Vandervell watched the smoke being pumped from the volcano. Now and then the devil-sticks man climbed out of his hole and danced on a mound of lava by the road. The men came down from the village for the last time. They looked at the stick-dancer as they walked on down the road.

At eight o'clock in the morning a police truck drove up to the village, reversed and came down again. Its roof and driving cabin were covered with ash. The policemen did not see the stick-dancer, but they saw Vandervell in the window of the house and stopped outside.

"Get out!" one of the policemen shouted. "You must go now! Take your car! What's the matter?"

Vandervell opened the window. "The car is all right. We're staying for a few days. Gracias, Sergeant."

"No! Get out!" The policeman climbed down from the cabin. "The mountain – pfft! Dust, burning!" He took off his cap and waved it. "You go now."

As he remonstrated Vandervell closed the window and took his jacket off the chair. Inside he felt for his wallet.

After he had paid the policemen they saluted and drove away. The woman came out of the bedroom.

"You're lucky your father is rich," she said. "What would you do if he was poor?"

"Springman was poor," Vandervell said. He took his handkerchief from his jacket. The dust was starting to seep into the house. "Money only postpones one's problems."

"How long are you going to stay? Your father told me to keep an eye on you."

"Relax. I won't come to any mischief here."

"Is that a joke? With this volcano over our heads?"

Vandervell pointed to the stick-dancer. "It doesn't worry him. This mountain has been active for fifty years."

"Then why do we have to come here now?"

"I'm looking for Springman. I think he came here three months ago."

"Where is he? Up in the village?"

"I doubt it. He's probably five thousand miles under our feet, sucked down by the back-pressure. A century from now he'll come up through Vesuvius."

"I hope not."

"Have you thought of that, though? It's a wonderful idea."

"No. Is that what you're planning for me?"

Cinders hissed in the roof tank, spitting faintly like boiling rain.

"Think of them, Gloria – Pompeiian matrons, Aztec virgins, bits of old Prometheus himself, they're raining down on the just and the unjust."

"What about your friend Springman?"

"Now that you remind me . . ." Vandervell raised a finger to the ceiling. "Let's listen. What's the matter?"

"Is that why you came here? To think of Springman being burnt to ashes?"

"Don't be a fool." Vandervell turned to the window.

"What are you worrying about, anyway?"

"Nothing," Vandervell said. "For once in a long time I'm not worrying about anything at all." He rubbed the pane with his sleeve. "Where's the old devil-boy? Don't tell me he's gone." He peered through the falling dust. "There he is."

The figure stood on the ridge above the road, illuminated by the flares from the crater. A pall of ash hung in the air around him.

"What's he waiting for?" the woman asked. "Another dollar?"

"A lot more than a dollar," Vandervell said. "He's waiting for me."

"Don't burn your fingers," she said, closing the door.

That afternoon, when she came into the lounge after waking up, she found that Vandervell had left. She went to the window and looked up towards the crater. The falls of ash and cinders obscured the village, and hundreds of embers glowed on the lava flows. Through the dust she could see the explosions inside the crater lighting up the rim.

Vandervell's jacket lay over a chair. She waited for three hours for him to return. By this time the noise from the crater was continuous. The lava flows dragged and heaved like chains, shaking the walls of the house.

At five o'clock Vandervell had not come back. A second crater had opened in the summit of the volcano, into which part of the village had fallen. When she was sure that the devil-sticks man had gone, the woman took the money from Vandervell's jacket and drove down the mountain.

Weasal and The Fish

Peter Turnbull

See me, I can't make relationships, so I can't. I didn't make a relationship with my mother so I can't make relationships with anyone. I know that 'cos I read my file, like I'm entitled to. See, one of the other lassies in here said you can read your file, Freedom of Information or some such. So I read my file. I managed to learn to read and write before I started to dog school, before I went to live in the drainage duct with the glue sniffers and the alckies and the smack heads. So I read that I can't make relationships because of my old woman, but see her, who *could* make a relationship with her. I mean who'd *want* to? See her lying drunk all the time, always getting hersen lifted by the polis, see her she'd start a fight in an empty house so she would. So that was what she wrote, the dark-haired woman that I saw once soon after I came here, and asked me all this daft, stupid questions like, what would I do if I saw a battleship going down the motorway? I said I'd get in my submarine and sink it. Daft cow. I mean, what would you do? But she wrote it down as my answer. Then she showed me these ink blots and asked me what I saw in them. So I told her what I saw. In one I seed a cave man battering a cave woman stupid with a club, a big club, giving her a real tanking, and in another I'd see a man getting burned at the stake, and in another there was this wee infant surrounded by wolves. Then she showed me drawings, real neat ink drawings full of detail and asked me what was going on in the picture. One was of this lad up a tree and this lassie running along a path beneath the tree. She showed me this picture and asked me what was happening. Obvious, I thought. So I said the lad's going to shin down the tree and run after the girl and murder her. Anyway, it was after that that she said I can't make relationships because I didn't make a relationship with my mother. So that's why they fixed me up with Cathy, my counsellor, big motherly type, big spectacles like a moth on her face. Want to crush the moth. Me and Cathy talk to each other twice a week, about me, about my feelings, but I go along with it, invent feelings. But see me, really I don't have no feelings. I don't have no feelings at all. I mean, what are feelings? And the dark-haired woman was wrong. I can make relationships. I can. I made a relationship with Weasal. We had a relationship. We were together for a week. So we were.

See Weasal. Some man. See the things I liked about Weasal. Still like. See him, he wanted me, seemed to, just me. He wasn't interested in the other stuff not like the other guys, not Weasal, he just wasn't interested. Not in that bit. I liked him for that, so I did. I mean, I would have let him if he had wanted to but he just didn't. Just didn't. So that was it. And he didn't drink. All the other guys just existed to get pure blitzed, so they did, but not Weasal. He didn't like the drink and I liked that. I don't like drink. I don't like the people who do it. Weasal didn't drink. I like that in a man. And the other thing I liked about Weasal is that he killed people. I like that in a man so I do. And Weasal was good at it. He was good at killing folk.

See, when I met Weasal I was with a group of lassies passing a bottle of 20/20 around. Except I didn't drink but I was sitting with them. We were in Bridgeton, down the east end, on a bench in a wee park when Weasal came along the road. One of the lassies says, "he's called Weasal, he's off his head. He's a pure headbanger, so he is." But he looked all right to me. He came up and stood in front of us and all the lassies went quiet like they were feared of him. So he just stood there, hot day, shirt sleeves, blue sky above the red tenements, they orange buses whirring up and down the road. And Weasal standing there, so he looked at me and he says, "you're not on the bevy then, hen?" So I said, "no", said I didn't take it. Then he smiled at me and said, "coming with me then, hen?" So I stood up and went with him and he said, "what's your name, hen?" So I said, "The Fish, they call me The Fish." He didn't say anything but he didn't call me The Fish. I liked him for that too. He just called me "hen", made me feel ordinary. I really liked that, feeling normal and ordinary. I liked being ordinary. So we walked on and he said, "where do you live?" I said, "the street, and the drainage duct when it's wet." Then he said, "want to earn some money?" I said, "All right."

We walked on, seemed to be just cruising round Bridgeton and Weasal said, "See that shop?" I said, "yes." It was a totty wee shop, a *Daily Record* sign above the window, a narrow door, the sort run by Asians. We walked past it and into the next close and stood at the turn of the stair just out of sight of the street and see Weasal, he pulled a plastic bag from his pocket. There was a wig in it, a long blond-haired wig, and a pair of spectacles and he put them on too, see the change in his looks, just they two bits. Then he pulled a length of metal from his trousers, shiny chrome-plated, I seen guys using them when they're working on their cars. It was about eighteen inches long and it had a fair weight to it, I could tell by the way Weasal slapped it in his palm. Weasal told me to go back to the shop and buy a copy of the *Record*. He gave me the money, told me to come back to where we were standing and tell him who's in the shop. So I did. Came back and told Weasal that the only guy in the shop was an Asian guy. Tall, but getting on. No other customers, least when I was there. Weasal said, "nice," and he said, "wait there," then he left the close with the bit of metal shoved in his trousers. Seemed to be gone a wee while but he came back and put the wig and spectacles and the length of metal into the plastic bag and gave them back to me. He told me to walk slowly, really calm like to the end of the street and wait for him. So I did. He also told me not to look at folk. So I didn't. Then Weasal joined me and we heard a klaxon and an ambulance passed us and stopped outside the shop. "Found him then," said Weasal. We walked into another close and went under the stair and Weasal emptied his pockets: paper money, stamps, envelopes, a ballpoint pen. "He went down easily," said Weasal. "I wasn't being fooled so I gave him a couple more until he started to groan. Can you write, hen?" I said I could. So he gave me the ballpoint and told me to write "Begg" that was his real name, "Begg", initial R. Never knew what "R" stood for. R. Begg. That was his real name. Then he told me to write 14, Caledonian Road, Calton, Glasgow. He said I had to write that name and address on each envelope and stick a stamp on each envelope. So I did what I was told, sitting there under the stair, addressing each envelope and sticking a stamp on each, first-class stamps I remember. Then he handed me the money and said, "Count it," so I did. One hundred and ten pounds. He kept the ten pounds back and put the rest in an envelope and sealed it. Then we went out into the sunshine and put the envelope into the first postbox we saw. "Don't want to get caught with it," he said. See Weasal, he's clever. I was learning from him. Then he said "You still with me, hen?" I said, "Aye" I was, I was still with him. So then all that day it was the same sketch. We found a wee shop, no customers, found a close nearby, Weasal changed into his disguise, went to the shop, came back with pockets full of paper money and blood on the end of the length of metal. I put the money in an envelope while Weasal got out of his disguise and we'd walk into the sunshine, it was August, and pop the envelope into a postbox. Then look for another shop. All round the east end we did that, Calton, Bridgeton, the air was full of klaxons, the polis were looking for a guy with glasses and blond hair. If they seed us they went past, because Weasal had short hair and no glasses and I was with him. They were looking for a guy alone, not a guy with a lassie. We got good at it. So good Weasal didn't have to tell me what to do. We went to the petrol station to look at magazines and Weasal said did I see the camera above the cashier's desk? I said I did. He said all petrol stations have them, so do all big shops and banks, so we can't do them. Just small corner shops. A little bit of cash from each bit it adds up so it does. Batter the shoppie over the head, take the paper money from the till and also from under the drawer of the till and walk out of the shop. Never run. Dive into the first convenient close and do a quick change. We did about ten shops that day, all the while the polis buzzing about like a nest of hornets. Then Weasal said we should skip because he was having to walk between the shop and the close in disguise and all it needed was a cop to come along the road in his car when Weasal was between the shop and the close. He said it was too much of a risk, so we had to stop while we were ahead. Weasal said the gaols are full of stupid criminals who keep going till they're huckled. Weasal said really clever criminals never even see the inside of a polis station, let alone gaol. I was beginning to learn from Weasal. I mean really learning.

So we walked to Calton, a lad with his lass, me and Weasal, and we passed a couple of cops and they didn't give us a second glance even though Weasal was walking with a stiff leg because he'd got his club shoved down his trousers. We got to Caledonian Road, got to number fourteen and went up the close. The door with "Begg" was one up. "Begg" was written on a bit of paper stuck to the door. The nameplate proper was "MacPherson".

Inside it was a tip so it was, but it was better than the drainage duct. Weasal gave me the ten pound note he'd kept back from the first shop he raided and sent me out for a pizza. That night we watched TV. It was an old black and white set and the aerial was a coat hanger stuck in the back. Weasal slept on a mattress in the bedroom and I curled up on the couch. See that's what I liked about Weasal, like I said, he just wasn't interested in that side of things. Before we went to sleep I asked him what sort of flat it was and he said it was a squat, so I said, "oh," like I knew what a squat was. Weasal said he heard the old woman who rented the flat was in hospital so he moved in. When the old guy across the landing asked him who he was Weasal said he was the old woman's nephew and was looking after the flat. After that they didn't bother him. Anyway we had to leave because the gas and electricity were going to be cut off. I liked the way he said "we". Made me sleep well that night so it did.

The next morning Weasal said we couldn't go to Edinburgh because he was known to the polis there. He said we couldn't stay in Glasgow because he'd done some things. He said what we did the day before was nothing, nothing. He said he'd got victims in this town and he'd left his fingerprints all over the tills he'd robbed. He said he'd done that deliberately, on purpose. So the police would know who he was. I didnae ken why he did that but I knew by then that Weasal knew what he was doing, but I thought he was like a wee child playing "catch", him and the police. And as we were talking the postie arrived and all these envelopes went "flop", "flop", "flop" on the hall carpet; it was all the money Weasal had stolen the day before, arriving for us. That was pure dead brilliant. Weasal asked me to count it. I did and it came to one thousand, two hundred and thirty pounds. Weasal said, "We can go a long way with that money, hen."

"Out of Glasgow?" I asked.

"A long way out of Glasgow," he said.

I told him I'd never been out of Glasgow. Then I made us both some coffee. We hadn't any milk so I went out and bought some. The nearest newsagents sold milk and there was the *Record*, with Weasal's E-fit on the front page and a write-up. Two of the shoppies Weasal had battered were still out cold and on the critical list. So I went back and told Weasal. I also told him his name was in the paper, Begg a.k.a. Weasal and a police photo of him without the wig and glasses – which it was. So he said, "We're going now."

There was this thrill. I've never felt it before. It was like I was somebody, life felt more real, the sky was bluer, the colours everywhere were stronger, I felt bigger. I knew then that Weasal was the best thing that had happened to me. I still think that. I always will.

We went by bus to Kilmarnock. Weasal carried a shoulder bag with him. It's a nice wee town. Weasal gave me some money to buy some clothes and a bag to carry them in. We went into a pub and while Weasal had an orange juice I went to the women's toilets and changed into my new clothes. I left the old ones shoved down the toilet, so I did. We walked out of the pub and Weasal said that we keep going, that's what we do, we keep going and if we want something, we take it. Just like that. I asked if we were going to sleep rough. He said, "No." He said we stay in folk's houses. He said he would show me how it's done. Then I asked him what was in the bag he carried.

"A gun," he said, "and some bullets. About fifty. I bought a lot from a guy in a pub in Possilpark. Didn't cost much. I bought sixty

bullets but shot ten off at a quiet place, getting to know the gun."
We walked on. Weasal said he was sorry it was summer. Too much
daylight, he said. Autumn's best for badness said Weasal. Dark
nights and it's dry. In the summer there's too much daylight, in
the winter it's too wet and slushy, but autumn, those few weeks
when it's dark and dry. See, that's my Weasal. I couldn't think like
that, I just couldn't, but I was learning fast.

Killing someone wasn't as bad as I thought it would be. Fact is,
it was fun. I got this power rush. I felt really . . . I don't know, really
someone.

The first thing we had to do was sight up a house. We walked
out of Killie under the railway bridge and got out into an area of
fancy bought houses. Weasal wanted a house with a motor in the
drive and one which looked like the owner was old in years. It's
not easy sighting up a house in the suburbs; you can't wander
about looking at houses, that gives the game away. You have to
walk looking dead ahead and sight up houses from a distance, then
a quick glance while you're passing. Weasal found three or four
which he reckoned were OK and out of them settled on one. I
mind it well, a white-painted bungalow, with neat gardens and a
wee white car in the drive. Weasal said that the car was a wee old
woman's motor and the garden was a pensioner's, too neat for a
working person and too professionally kept. It was a wee woman's
house who has a guy come and do the garden. I was tired. I hadn't
slept too well on Weasal's couch and I still felt tacky, despite the
new clothes. In my mind I was already in that woman's bath and
snoring fit to drive cattle home in her bed.

Then we had a stroke of luck. It's just the way it happened.
We were walking past the house when the old woman came out
of her house with a shopping bag. She got into her car and
drove out of the drive and down the road. Weasal said to keep
walking because she's got a rear-view mirror and we didn't
want her to see us loitering about her house. When she had
turned the corner, Weasal went back to the house crunching on
gravel as hard as he could and rang the front door bell. Later he
told me that if someone had answered he would have asked
them if "Joe" was at home and then kidded on he had mistak-

enly come to the wrong house. We went round the side of the
house to where the woman had come from. Weasal said if she
let herself out of the back door, she'd likely let herself in there.
So we waited in the back garden, squeezed between a garden
shed and a privet hedge. We made a bit of noise because a cat
appeared at the window and then went away again. We sat
there and waited. Weasal said she'd gone with a message bag,
so she was away to get her messages, so she'd be back soon. We
just had to sit and wait. So we did. I liked that really, the
garden, the silence, the flowers. She had trees round her
garden, keep her garden private I should think. Suited us,
meant we couldn't be seen. The woman came back after an
hour. We heard the car. Weasal said to keep quiet and he took
the metal bar from his bag. I kept still. I was surprised how
calm I was, sort of peaceful inside. We heard her walk round
the back of the house, just one set of footsteps, then we heard
keys rattle in a lock, then the woman said, "Hello, Pixie Puss."
Called her daft cat "Pixie Puss". Then Weasal struck. Moved
fast. I heard a dull thud, as he hit the woman with the iron bar.
Then he hit her again and again. Then he called me. "Come
on, hen." So I joined him. We were standing over the woman;
her blood was on the kitchen floor. We closed the back door.
Weasal said to look round the house, make sure it was empty. I
did and it was. Back in the kitchen I asked if the woman was
dead and Weasal said she was. She was the first dead person I'd
seen. Apart from the blood, she looked as if she was asleep. We
took some cans of food from her larder and then pushed her in
there. That was the last I saw of her.

We spent the rest of the day in her house. We both had a bath
and then a good sleep. When we woke it was dark. Weasal shut
the curtains and put on the lights. Weasal went about touching
things but told me to find a pair of gloves and wear them all the
time. He said they could have his prints but not mine. I made us
a meal, just stuff from cans, while Weasal searched the house for
cash. He found twenty pounds but it was better than nothing. And
we'd washed and rested. That was the main thing. Before we left
the house, Weasal made me do a weird thing. He made me take

the woman's lipstick and write a message on her dressing-table mirror. I had to write "Please stop me." So I did. "Please stop me." Funny, I thought. I mean funny weird. He seemed to do what he did with so much enthusiasm.

Later that night, near midnight, we shut off all the lights and opened the curtains so the house would look normal in the morning and took the woman's car and drove away. It was nearly out of petrol so Weasal said we had to stop and buy some. He said each time we stopped we had to fill up so that way we'd keep down the times the car was caught on the cameras the garages have. We saw a filling station and Weasal stopped the car and told me to get out and walk beyond the station and wait for him on the other side. That way it would look like he was alone. So I did. He put his wig and spectacles on and drove into the forecourt of this filling station which was all lit up like a spaceship, so it was. I waited for him like he told me to and he drove up and picked me up and we drove towards Ayr. Folk went to Ayr for their holidays and I'd heard it was a fun place but I never did see it, 'cos Weasal pulled up and stopped. He looked around the car and saw that the wee woman had a road atlas in the back seat and he picked it up and said, "Do you know how to read a map?" So I said, "I ken fine how to read a map." So he said right, which was north from here?

"Just follow the signs to Glasgow," I said.

"No." He was getting angry. "Tell me to go left or right or straight on. Understand?"

"Aye."

"And I don't want to go anywhere near Glasgow. All right!"

"Well, we're too late for the ferry across the Clyde," I told him. "So it'll have to be the tunnel." So he reckoned that that was fine. Told me to tell him the way to the tunnel. So I did, saying, "turn around and back to Killie." Then it was left or right, or straight on until we got to the tunnel and went through it. We got onto the Expressway and I took him out towards Crianlarich, up the side of Loch Lomond. See how it gleamed in the moonliglit.

We drove all night. Weasal was a good, steady driver, not too fast, not too slow. We drove to Fort William and stopped. It was about three in the morning, beginning to get light, but still. Weasal said we had to clear the pitch, get out of the town because a night cop might clock us. He said we looked suspicious and they could stop us for that. So he drove out of the town and turned left and asked me where the road went to. So I looked at the map and said Mallaig. I'd heard of Mallaig as a place for a holiday too, not as nice as Ayr, but folk went there, or they caught a ferry from there, or such like. I never got to Ayr and I never got to Mallaig. Weasal drove up a side road and stopped beside an old building. It looked eerie in the half light.

We sat there. Didn't feel tired. One or two cars went by as the morning went in, folk driving to Fort William for a day's work. At eight o'clock we went back to Fort William and split up for an hour. I ate in a breakfast joint. I met up with Weasal at the car. He'd got a can of spray paint and had fastened a Union Jack to the car aerial. He'd got the flag from a wee gift shop, the sort that sells daft wee plastic models of the Loch Ness Monster. Then we drove back to beside the old building which looked like it had been a school house. There was no reason why we should have gone there, it's just that we knew it was there, so we went.

Weasal spray-painted the car blue. Didn't look like the colour blue it was supposed to be but it wasn't white any more. Weasal said that soon the cops would be stopping every white VW Polo in Scotland on account of the wee woman's body would be found today, stuffed in her larder with her head battered in, and her car noticed missing, and him in disguise buying petrol for the wee woman's car at the filling station, that would be on film, that would. So we spent the day lying in the heather while the paint dried on the car. Weasal didn't try anything. But if he wanted to, I would have let him. When we were lying there Weasal said only one thing. He said the Union Jack was to make folk, particularly cops, think that we were bastard English. Only the bastard English would fly a Union Jack, the Scots would fly the St Andrew's Cross. So we had a blue Polo with a bastard English flag on the aerial. Weasal said that that might stop a cop being suspicious. See Weasal, he thought of everything. I was learning from him. I was really learning. When the paint was dry, we drove back into Fort William. "Same sketch as Killie," Weasal said.

"Find a likely house, batter our way in, rest up, then leave after dark."

The first time Weasal gave me a doing I deserved it, so I did. And it wasn't a proper doing, not like I remember my dad giving my mum before he left us for the last time. He just couldn't take the drink any more and when she came home with a good drink in her 'cos she'd spent all the "social" money on bevy. So he gave her a rare wee kickin'. I mean he put her blood everywhere. Then he picked me up and put me in a taxi and took me to the Welfare people and carried me into their office and sat me on the receptionist's desk and ran back out and went away in the taxi and I never saw him again. They put me in a foster home and I stayed for four days. It was on the fourth day that I lit a fire in the living room, anything I could find to burn, paper mostly; didn't get a proper hold 'cos the family dog started yapping and the foster mother came in and screamed then poured water over it. Then I was put in a children's home, then another, each one harder than the last 'cos I was a "behavioural problem". That's what they said. Anyway, Weasal didn't give me a doing like my dad gave my mum. Slapped my head a couple of times. That was all.

After we met up again in Fort William, we went to a café to get off the street. I sat opposite him and then I saw his eyes. Really beautiful eyes. I mean eyes I like, steely, cold, but not just that, it was like looking into two endless tunnels when you looked into his eyes, two bottomless wells, they just go deeper and deeper and deeper and you can't tell if there's any emotion in them at all. But it's there 'cos he could get angry so he could. But the other thing I liked about his eyes, one was blue and the other was green. So I said that. I said, "Weasal, one of your eyes is green and the other is blue," and he said, "Hey!" and grabbed my arm and pulled me out of the café. I knew folk were looking at us but that didn't bother Weasal, he slapped me around the head, right there in the café. He bundled me into the Polo and we drove off. I didn't know he was touchy about his eyes. So I never mentioned them again. But I sometimes wonder if me mentioning his eyes set him so he killed the woman. I don't mean the wee woman in Killie. I mean the other one, the one that was built like a Highland cow, the second one we did.

It happened like this. We'd been hanging around F.W. all day, meeting up and then separating for an hour and as it was getting dark Weasal said we needed to hide. He also said we needed to change the car. So we set off to cruise around the town. F.W. isn't a big place, smaller than a Glasgow scheme, so we got to know it well. Nothing for us in the council schemes, or the bought houses so we moved a wee bit out of the town and we found a house standing in its own ground, stone built with pushed-out windows. Weasal liked it because it had no gate and a grass driveway. Weasal said that they hadn't invented house breakers in F.W. so that's how folk could live with no gates and a grass drive. There was no car in the drive but Weasal said we couldn't have everything. I waited by the house trying to get the measure of it on the sly, while Weasal went into F.W. to get the Polo tanked up. He wanted to get his photo taken by the filling station camera but not in disguise. So he looked different than he looked when he got the car filled up in Killie and anyway the car was now blue. He reckoned that would fool the cops long enough for us to get out of the town. When he came back I told him a light had gone on in the house and I saw an old woman once or twice moving about. But she wasn't a wee wifie, she was built like a prison warder. I didn't see anyone else, I told him. Just her. I saw her when she was closing her curtains and she saw me, and see her, see the look she gave me, like I was a bit of dirt, see me, I've had that look all my life. I really wanted to be there when Weasal beat her head to pulp with his length of shiny metal.

"Just one person and the curtains drawn." Weasal smiled. "That makes it easier. But there could be more than one person, we'll have to take that chance. See her, the good thing about my situation is that I can't get any deeper. I am at rock bottom. Doesn't matter how many folk I kill, they can only throw the key away once."

"And me," I said, "I'm in deep too. I'm in with you, Weasal."

"No, hen," he said. "See, I need you, but you'll never be in deep. I'm going to make sure of that."

Made me feel warm inside that did. I've never been needed before. Not since either. But I was needed then.

When it was full dark, we went back to the house. Got close to it. No alarm. No dog. Heard music playing, fancy stuff, classical, violins and that. Weasal said the only thing we had to worry about was if the woman had a chain on the inside of her door but he said it was unlikely because no alarm and no dog meant she was unlikely to have a chain. Me, I knew she wouldn't have a chain, see that big old cow of a woman, glaring at folk with an "I'm the boss" attitude, I knew she'd swing her door open demanding to know who was chappin' her door at that time of night. Which is exactly what happened. It was then that Weasal pulled the trigger. Just once. But it was enough. I felt really good to see that little hole in her forehead. It felt good to see her fall backwards into her own hallway. That was sweet, when I thought of that dirty look she gave me, that was a sweet sight to see her dead. Weasal didn't hesitate, went straight to the phone in the hall and knocked it off its hook. "If there's anyone else in the house, they can't use an extension now," he said. Then he said, "Don't worry about the gunshot, it wasn't as loud as it sounded."

We pulled her away from the door and then shut it. She was too heavy to move so we left her in the hall. Weasal told me to go from room to room, make sure she was alone in the house. I did and she was. See Weasal, he knew how to sight up houses, he was right about that house in Killie and he was right about the house in F.W. Her house had five bedrooms. Five! But only one bed was made up. All the other beds were not. And the air in the other bedrooms was musty. So no-one would be coming home there that night and me and Weasal could relax. That's what I thought but when I went downstairs, I saw Weasal standing over the woman's body saying, "This is bad, bad, bad. This is wrong, shouldn't do this . . . wrong . . . bad . . . bad . . . bad boy. Very bad boy." I felt disappointed in him. It didn't seem wrong to me. Nothing wrong at all. The only thing I was sorry about is that she didn't see me, she didn't know I was a partner of Weasal's. I thought that next time Weasal drills a nasty who deserves to die, I'll make sure they see me standing there, smiling. I could fair fancy that.

We freshened up in her house. We ate her food. We watched her TV but when the news came on Weasal turned the TV off and said it was time we slept. We shared her bed, lying side by side. But Weasal didn't touch me. I loved him for that. And when he saw my body without clothes, because we'd both washed our clothes and left them drying on a radiator, he didn't bat an eyelid. I loved him for that as well.

So the next morning, when the clothes were dry, I crept out of the house, leaving Weasal snoring and I went to a newspaper shop and bought a copy of the *Record*. I was learning from Weasal and so I acted dead natural like and pretended I wasn't really interested in the headlines. I didn't react 'cos people always look at me and also I knew Weasal wouldn't want me to react. So I bought a *Record* and went back to the woman's house without looking left or right. I went into her kitchen and made a cup of tea and read the paper.

We'd made the headlines, me and Weasal. The wee widow woman in Killie had been found and her wee white VW Polo missing; the paper gave the reggie number, but then Weasal had repainted it and stuck a daft English flag on the aerial so I reckoned we'd be all right for a while yet. Anyway, I read about me and Weasal and what we'd done. The wee widow woman in Killie was called Bush, Sonia Bush, she was sixty-six years old and a retired school teacher. Her son was travelling up from London to sort things so that was all right. There was a street map of Killie showing where her house was and one or two folk were quoted as saying what a nice woman she was. See that helped no-one. Being nice wouldn't help you if you messed with me and Weasal when me and Weasal were travelling. Then I got onto the bit about Weasal. They knew it was him 'cos he'd left his prints everywhere. His real name was Rory Begg, twenty-eight years old, a.k.a. "Weasal" because of his small build and staring eyes between a pointed nose. He'd been in the State Hospital since he was sixteen until a year ago when he was discharged as "incurable". So they let him out. Just like that. Lucky me though, I mean, without Weasal where would I be? I'd be in the drainage duct with the rest of them so I would. Thanks be to Weasal. Then it said he had an accomplice because Weasal had left a message for the polis in lipstick on the wee woman's mirror, but Weasal was known not to be able to read or write or count.

That's when I knew why he needed me. He needed me to count the money, he needed me to read the road signs 'cos all he knew was his left from his right from straight on. And he needed me to write the messages for the polis. So he was a totty wee guy, so he had different coloured eyes, so he couldn't read or write or count numbers. But he never called me "Fish" and he could kill people. What more could a lassie want? What more?

When Weasal woke up and came down to the kitchen I told him I'd been out and that we'd made the headlines in the *Record*. He threw a blue one at that, a real wobbly and he gave me a right doing, right there in the kitchen, fist, boot, slap, stuck the head on me . . . when I went down he didn't stop. I was screaming . . . blood everywhere . . . me seeing double. When he'd calmed he said he didn't want to know. He didn't want to know what the polis knew. See me, I couldn't understand that, I may be big and stupid but I would want to know what the polis knew, see me, I would have thought the whole idea was to keep going for as long as we could. It would help if we knew what the polis knew, I would have thought. But Weasal knew best so I went along with what he wanted. I washed the blood from my mouth and nose and then we ate some food for breakfast. Before we left the old woman's house, Weasal took me upstairs and he made me write a message on the woman's dressing-table mirror, just like I'd done in Killie. This time I had to write "Catch me quickly. I'll be doing it again."

We drove from F.W. to Inverness along the banks of Loch Ness. I looked for the monster but I never saw anything, just a lot of water and a boat or two. I enjoyed the drive, I was learning about Scotland, the green and the blue, the hills and the valleys and the lochs. I grew up in Glasgow, I never left the city until I chummed up with Weasal. I never knew why guys in kilts came on the TV and sang songs about Bonnie Scotland until I took that drive with Weasal. Now I know. My eyes were fair opened, so they were. Towards the end of the journey we saw a polis motor at the side of the road. Weasal said to hold the road atlas up in front of my face so we'd look like bastard English tourists. See me, it was the first time I ever wanted to be a bastard English but it worked because the cop didn't pull us. But Weasal wasn't happy, he said that as we drove. We couldn't go on depending on a colour change of the car so we had to ditch it and steal another. See him, see Weasal, there were times I couldn't fathom him. First he acts like he wants to be caught, then he doesn't. See him.

We got to Inverness and Weasal parked up as close as he could get to the town centre without worrying about parking restrictions. We were sitting there as a cop drove past; he slowed to look at us and then speeded up. Weasal said, "That's it." We got out of the car and split up. We agreed to meet at the bus station an hour later. We did that and took a bus north. Weasal said he wanted out of Inverness fast. So we took the first bus north, into the Black Isle.

The end, when it came, came quickly. Very quickly. We were in the Black Isle, it was night. We were walking. We were tired and hungry. We saw a campsite but walked past. It was well turned midnight by the time Weasal saw what he wanted. It was a camper van, parked up a lane, a long way from anywhere. The light in the van was switched on. We crept closer and heard two people talking, a man and a woman. They were having an argument.

Weasal said we had to kill them. It's wrong, he said, but we had to do it. I asked him if I could do it. Weasal looked at me. It was the only time I ever saw emotion in his eyes. He looked worried, I mean worried for me. Then he said, "All right, hen, all right, you can do it. But I'll kill the guy, you can kill the girl." That suited me. I thought then that that would suit me fine, especially if she was a slim bitch, like they girls at school, like them, that day in the shower when I slipped and went on my back. I've always been big, I can't help it, I'd be slim if I could, but lying there, struggling to get up and all they slim girls standing round me giggling. One said, "She looks like a beached whale," and then they all started chanting, "whale, whale, whale . . ." Then that was my nickname for a few days until they hit on Fish instead and finally they settled for The Fish. See me, I hated they girls. I pure hated them. Hate, hate, hate to kill. I started dogging school then and went to live with the glue sniffers in the drainage duct. I was with them for a few days until Weasal came along and I went with him 'cos he called me "hen" like I was normal and I read the road signs for him, and I counted the money for him. Oh, yes, and I wrote messages with lipstick for him. So I did.

Anyway Weasal knocked on the door of the van, gun in hand. The couple stopped arguing and the guy opened the van door. The one thing he shouldn't have done and it was the one thing he did do. But my Weasal didn't hesitate. Up comes the gun and the guy's flung backwards into the camper with a bullet in his head. I took the gun from him, eager like, and I went into the van, and oh, it was lovely, this woman, slim and slender, just like the girls in the shower that time. She wasn't one of them, but she was close enough for me. She wasn't laughing, sort of whimpering, like a dog that wants something. All the while Weasal was saying, "Do it, do it, don't hesitate . . . no . . . this is wrong . . . this is wrong . . . stop me, stop me . . . stop me." But me, I thought, see me, this isn't wrong. It's so good, it can't be wrong . . . and I shot her in the chest. She slumped back and started to make gurgling sounds so I shot her again. And again. Weasal took the gun from me and wiped my prints off it. We stayed all night in the van, him in the driver's seat and me in the passenger seat, and the dead couple behind us. We sat there until well after dawn and all night Weasal kept saying, "No . . . no . . . no . . . wrong . . . wrong . . . this is wrong, wrong . . ." But he reloaded the gun anyway.

About nine in the morning Weasal started the camper and drove off, out of the lane. He struggled at first. He said it was a bitch to drive but eventually he seemed to get the hang of it. Then he laid a hand on my leg and said, "I shouldn't have got you into this . . . I shouldn't, but I've worked out a way to get you out." And I put my hand on his. We came to the main road, green fields all around, a wide blue sky. He said, "Will you do what I tell you to do?" I said I would. At the main road he stopped and put on the handbrake. He waited as a few cars passed us going south towards Inverness or north, deeper into the Black Isle. Then he saw a lorry moving slowly south. He said, "This will do." He told me to get out and pull the body of the guy out of the van and onto the grass verge. So I did. He got out too and went round the van and pointed the gun at me while I was doing what he told me to do. I saw the lorry driver's face as he passed, wide-eyed, open-mouthed. Then he looked straight ahead and speeded the lorry up.

We turned north then, towards Cromarty and drove through this lush green countryside. I'll never know why they called it the Black Isle. It's not black, it's green. And it's not an island. Weasal saw a house by the road and a guy sitting in the front garden on a bench. Weasal said, "Same sketch." He told me to pull the woman from the back of the camper and dump her body on the verge. I did so and all the while he held the gun on me. As we drove off I saw the guy stand up from the bench and run into his house. I glanced at Weasal and he was smiling. I knew he knew what he was doing. Weasal always did.

The Fatal Accident Inquiry was told that four bullets hit Weasal but I only heard three. I suppose two were . . . what's that word . . . simul something. Anyway I swear to God I only heard three.

Looking back the first indication of the end was when there was no traffic coming towards us. None behind us either. Next thing was a police helicopter flying above and behind us, shadowing us. Weasal saw it and smiled. From then on he never stopped smiling until he died. And he was relaxed. Totally relaxed. We cleared a crest of the road and in front of us was a polis road block. One car and one van. Blue lights revolving and headlights on. Polis with guns and body armour. Weasal slowed. I remember the green fields around us, the blue sky, no other roads leading off. Just a straight road to the polis road block and a helicopter above us. I knew, I just knew that the polis would be behind us as well. Weasal stopped short of the road block, about the length of two buses. Weasal got out and walked round the back of the van and round to my side and told me to get out. So I did. Then he pulled the gun and stood behind me and walked towards the polis road block. The polis kept yelling that they were armed police and he was to drop the gun but that didn't bother Weasal. They yelled at him to "let the girl go". Me a girl? Like I was slim and slender. Funny that. Then he stopped us from walking. He just said, "stop," so I did. He stood at the side of me, gun by his side. I remember a bird singing. He lifted the gun and pointed it at my head. At the inquiry they said he was shot four times, but like I said, I only heard three shots. I remember, someone had hold of me and was saying, "All right, hen, you're safe now." I didn't give anything away but inside I was all smiles.

They decided I had no case to answer about they murders. See, they had people who'd seen Weasal batter me in a café in F.W. And I still had bruises from where he'd given me a kicking for bringing a copy of the *Record* to the woman's house, and two folk had each seen me unloading a body at gun point, like two different times, one witness to each time, and the polis said I was being ordered about by Weasal who was holding a gun on me. But they did decide I was a danger to myself, couldn't let me go or else I'd be back in the drainage duct. So I got a one-year residential supervision order. So I'm in here, attending the Christian Union like a regular gaol house convert, and once I volunteered to unblock the toilets when it was the caretaker's day off – I did well for myself there. I'm really smoothing my way through here, talking to the dark-haired woman who asks me what I see in drawings and speaks to me about battleships and motorways. And I talk to my counsellor, with the big glasses like a moth that I want to squash, who says she's fond of me and that I have to like myself more. I think a lot about Weasal. I think what he taught me, about disguise and fingerprints. I learned all that. And I learned that I can kill, and I learned I like it, killing people. I like it. Anyway, I keep all that to myself, and I keep myself to myself. I do what I'm told when I'm told and I don't make waves. That way I'll slither out of here. Got my twelve-month review soon. I reckon I'll be out then. I'll be sixteen. Just turned.

Horizons

Colleen Anderson

Maria had been late again. In fact, if she made it in for work, there was a possibility she would lose her job. It had been boring for months, answering the phone and filing at the securities firm. That had been her fault really. After all, she'd always said, do the best you can and enjoy what you do. Maria hadn't been doing that for a while and as she ran off the subway train, weaving in between people and up the stairs, her purse flying behind her like an awkward bird, she felt guilty for the lie she told herself as well as others.

As she ran along the street, she straightened and retucked the cream blouse, hoping the sweat didn't show. Maria glanced at her watch and walked faster, pulling her fingers through tangled hair and then stopped. Her mind registered what her eyes took in before she consciously realized what was happening.

People were stopped like statues all over the street, staring up. Frozen. Others ran toward her away from the twin towers. But there was only one. Only one tower. Maria spun in a slow circle. Was this right? Was she on the right street? But horribly, Maria knew. She stared up at the last tower, and incredibly, slowly, like a deadly dance, the second tower fell.

Maria backed up, hands out before her, ridiculously wondering how she'd get to work now. The tower fell and fell, bodies and debris flew and spun out and smoke and fire flew up to fill the ghastly space left by the twin towers. Colour screamed about her; grey, orange-black fireballs, silvery knives of glass and metal, blue sky backtracking from the chaos. People around her cried and screamed, but most of all a great agonized groan emanated from everything, living, inanimate or dying. It was as if the colour fled before the leviathan that cloaked itself in ash. Maria could not move.

She was supposed to be there, to be part of the group working. The workers who were more diligent and harder working than she. Where were those who loved their jobs? Where were the co-workers who helped her when she slacked off?

"No." It came out quiet, barely audible. "No." It couldn't have been heard above the carnage. It would not have mattered for there was no one who mattered to hear it. No barista from the coffee bar who joked about her unruly hair. No aquiline-nosed man who smiled at her in the elevator. Not even recriminations from a tough boss who had given her a lot of leniency through her depression. No one. Nothing.

Maria would never know how long she stood there as the world fell and crumbled about her. She watched through the fall of the towers. She watched as people fled and wailed around her. She watched as the ensuing silence engulfed street after street. She watched as emergency teams came and went, as police started to cordon the area. It was only then that she turned and walked away, flowing in behind the crowds that walked like zombies out of Manhattan. She spoke to no one and few spoke back. The ash of destruction had blanketed the city and settled like a pall about her shoulders.

Somehow Maria found herself eventually in Brooklyn. Before she knew what she had done she had loaded a bag with clothing, thrown in some water and granola bars, and jumped into her old rusty car. No one really needed a car much in New York but she'd never quite got over her dependency on one. Now, like an automaton, she drove north.

She had told no one and had left no note. No one would know if she had lived or died. She could cease to exist. In anonymity she might join those who had been better than her and had not been rewarded for their duty and love.

Maria just drove, not caring where she went, not thinking about anything. All she could taste was gritty ash on her tongue, smell the char of unhealthy fires in the air. The colour of fall should have been vibrant but it was muddied, toned down, lifeless. She couldn't have said if it felt wrong or not because she felt nothing. All she knew was that she was part of the landscape, the horrid, deadly, carnage-laden landscape, and all she could do was remove herself from it.

Excised, pushed out through the bloodstream, an unthinking blindly moving organism. Maria never noticed if the air changed, or even how crowded the freeway was. It was as if the steering wheel turned her hands, as if the car itself drove her along, obediently following the grey tongue of the road. The yellow-brick road after the house had fallen and the witch had been crushed. After the munchkins with their tittering laughs built a bonfire of the witch's hair and clothing and danced while embers flew like frenzied sprites into the air, only to do kamikaze nosedives as ashes. The very same ashes that turned the road from golden bricks to muddy grey. Asphalt. The fault of ash.

Somehow Maria made it through the border into Ontario, though she would never remember what the customs people had said to her or she to them. Driving had once been a great pleasure of moving in and through the world, but that had died before she ended up in New York. Now she did not think, feeling numbed, yet as she drove memories came bright and clear to her.

It was stifling in the elevator as it dropped, letting people off, others walking on. A hot day in early September and it felt as if the air conditioning had quit in one of the world's tallest buildings. Some people managed to look crisp and professional in their suits and business attire. Maria's curly hair stuck to her neck. She reached up to pull it back and inadvertently caught the eye of one of the last passengers. The sea-green eyes of the tall man caught hers. He smiled.

She smiled back, aware how much more like a grimace of pain

it was. Had it become that hard to interact with people? Looking away, Maria pretended to search for something in her purse.

"It certainly is hot in here," the man replied lightly. "I'd find it preferable to be out in the sun before we lose it, walking or maybe drinking a martini somewhere."

Maria nodded dumbly, looking down. The elevator slowed and stopped and she started to get off, glancing up at the last minute and realizing it was too early. Blushing, she turned to get back on and nearly knocked over the man behind her. He steadied her by grasping her elbow, smiling as he moved by. As the brushed silver doors began to close he turned and said, "You have a great day."

Closed in, alone, Maria realized how small her world had become.

All Maria did was drive north, stopping long enough for gas and water. She didn't eat, she didn't think of much. When her eyes started to slide shut, she pulled over to the side of the road and slept, napping briefly before moving on, to keep outrunning the pall of grey.

If people talked to her, she didn't remember, if she spoke she had no idea of what. All she knew was that she too could drive into oblivion. No one would know who had survived and who had died in the fiery collapse. She could abandon her past, start again or disappear forever. Fade away to a pale silvery slip of ghost.

"Do you believe in ghosts?" Sal looked at Maria over the rim of her wine glass.

Maria gulped a mouthful of rich garnet-coloured wine and shook her head. "I don't want to talk about it." She stared out the window of her apartment to the night beyond. Streetlights shone like sentries, a car drove by, and somewhere a dog barked.

Maria heard the clink of Sal's glass being set down and a long sigh.

"Maria, I know it's hard. Jared's been dead over a year and you haven't moved on in your grieving. You *have* to talk about it. Or at least not drop any other conversation that might make you think of it. It's getting a little tiring talking about things only he never talked about. You can't seclude yourself like this."

She didn't even look at Sal as she replied, "So I should just forget about him, pretend like he wasn't a part of my life?"

She felt Sal's hand on her shoulder as she stared out at lights as bright as tears that she could no longer shed. "You know that's not what I mean. He'll always be a part of your life but that doesn't mean you should stop living because he died."

"I – " The hurt was so thick it stopped her throat. She shook her head, looking down into the burgundy sea of her glass. "It's just that he was so alive. We worked so well together and I feel like I've lost a limb, that it would have been better if I had gone too."

"Hey."

Maria looked up into Sal's sad smiling face. She pulled her straight blonde hair behind her ear. "We all miss him, but, sweetheart, it's not your fault that he died and you lived. No one could have foreseen the car losing a wheel. Be thankful that he never woke and experienced little pain. Yeah, we're stuck with the pain and you've got a big hole in you, but you need to move on."

Maria shook her head, staring into the night again. "I can't. I just can't see a future without him."

After Toronto, Maria drove northwest. Her memories were her only company. The radio stayed off; the invasion of the larger world never touched her. What was outside the car's windows was washed out and didn't catch Maria's interest. Only the grey tongue that might swallow her held her attention.

Four hours later, she made her first conscious decision. Georgian Bay, the great pewter plate of water stretched out with trees thick near part of its shore. Maria paid for a secluded cabin, primitive lighting, rustic, and in off-season totally deserted. She pulled her bag from her car, ignored the wild expanse about her and went into the cabin. Pulling off clothes, dumping them into a pile, she threw several blankets onto the bed and crawled under. She slept her first sleep since the towers fell.

Maria awoke in darkness and for a fleeting moment thought she had died. She lay staring into nothing, not knowing what day it was or what time. Eventually she got up, lit a fire in the stove and made some coffee.

The light gradually permeated the cabin, showing her details of morning. She sat drinking her coffee, no plans or even many thoughts moving her. It was as if her body's needs were all that moved her. Her mind had given up the controls.

When the light was as bright as it could be, Maria grabbed a piece of fruit and walked down to the beach. She sat on a rocky outcrop, eating, staring into the grey water. If she had had any emotion it might have soothed her. As it was, the water reflected her mind back at her and she just looked.

Night eventually pushed day away and only when cold or hunger penetrated her body did Maria move back to the cabin, to eat or sleep.

Days bled away and Maria repeated the movements of living. Her food supply was adequate and she ate only enough to stop the hunger. Each day she sat on the beach but explored no further. Each day, memories sifted back to her through the mist in her mind.

Some days, the water changed, rippling with the play of breezes, or lying flat and still and waiting. Maria barely noticed the change, only that it was water.

Crystals of water sprayed into the air as Jared flashed up out of the lake, imitating a dolphin in his breach. Maria laughed and dove into the chilly water. She surfaced near him, her hair sleek as an otter's.

Jared laughed and winked at her then was gone. She treaded water and looked under the surface, trying to find a shimmer of his passing. Turning, slowly moving her hands, she still could not see him even though the clear water showed depths of blue.

Then there was a splash behind her and Jared's long hands on her shoulder. She shrieked and turned toward him. His eyes were the richest umber, calming as the earth and showing depths. "Ah, look what I found on my shores. A mermaid far from her clan. I shall just have to keep her." He nibbled her neck as she mocked pushing away.

"I wonder if I should cook her up or keep her in a tank. She is sooo tasty."

"Neither, you scoundrel," and with that she leapt out of his arms, swimming fast to shore. Jared's sleek body swam closer to her toes and she felt a touch on her ankle. She pulled ahead and almost got out of the water before she felt his hands on her waist and they both lay beached half in water, laughing.

Maria stroked Jared's sun-lightened hair. He leaned down and kissed her. A warming tingle moved through her limbs.

"And what, lovely mermaid, would you like to do this evening?"

"You mean after you've tasted your mermaid?" Jared reached for her and she rolled slightly away, teasing. "I think we should find that nice flat spot, with a comfy blanket and see how many constellations we can count."

"And search for alien starships," Jared replied, wiggling his eyebrows. "But first, I must show you how to resist their brainwashing. Come with me."

He pulled her up out of the water and they made it back to the cabin but not inside before their suits were off and their hands running over wet, well-tanned bodies.

They spent two glorious weeks, boating, swimming, hiking, exploring the flora, the fauna, finding edible plants, fishing and getting to know each other on a deeper level. Nature healed and soothed here and let them drop the protocols and masks of the city.

Maria and Jared left finally, reluctantly, singing their way along the road in high summer. Everything from Eurythmics to Bare-Naked Ladies passed their lips as they pointed out to each other the animals along the road, the particularly verdant or full trees, the gentle roll of hills. They loved the lake but even more they both loved the changing scenery of driving along the road, the rolls and dips, the flashing as if the world ran past them.

Then, as they descended onto a long stretch, Maria driving, the wheel had spun off, forever changing Maria's world, forever ending Jared's.

Maria's heart pounded and she gasped for air. The water, the smooth lake was in front of her. How long had she sat here, how many days?

She stood up and unbuttoned her shirt. It dropped on the rocks, followed by her bra. Then her shorts, her socks, her shoes and her underwear. Shivering slightly in the cool fall air, Maria stepped away from her skins of every day. It was oblivion before her and she would be part of it.

Her foot hit the chilly water and she gritted her teeth, still walking, When it reached her crotch she was already partially numb and very cold. She continued to place one foot in front of the other, letting the grey envelop her, moving in. Her eyes closed as the water kissed her shoulders. She would be swallowed. Oblivion was at the end of the great tongue of road. The water closed over her head.

Like a tidal wave, it rolled through her, washing away the casing she built. A casing made of ashes and ruins. Against her will she surfaced, gasping, the pain so great she barely pulled herself from the water. Sharp blades of grief sliced into her abdomen, her heart, her eyes. And she was crying.

The hills echoed with the screams and Maria beat the water and the shore with her fists. She flung water away from her, salty tears mixing with the lake, her hair resembling Medusa's snakelike mane. She cried, shrieking, yelling, howling, "Why! Why! Why why why . . ."

She poured out all she could, all the sorrow that had been buried under layers of ash. Ash from Jared's funeral, from the cinders of her life after, from the consuming cloud of the two towers. The ash had covered her, buried her, and blanketed her from pain, until she had washed it all away.

Finally the ash that had held her heart was washed away with her hot tears. Exhausted, wrung out, Maria lay truly like a beached mermaid. She clawed her way up the beach then stood and stumbled back to the cabin. Crawling wet as a newborn babe into bed, she fell asleep, and dreamt for the first time in weeks.

She awoke nearly twenty-four hours later. The sun was just tingeing the sky to the lightest cerulean. Maria knew it was time to go.

Gathering up her goods, she stuffed them in the bag. There wasn't a lot to pack. One last mug of coffee in her hand, Maria walked down to the beach.

Emerald, pale green, golden yellow, sun-burnt orange, the autumn leaves slowly appeared in the light. The sky began to darken into the rich blue of day. Maria saluted the trees and then to Jared's memory. He would have been amazed at how her spirit had been tamped. She knew now that it wasn't time to die.

Maria's tower had collapsed when Jared died and she'd only been pretending to live from that time. When the towers went it had been the last of her pretensions at life.

The water had cleansed away the ash, like a cocoon it had let her renew herself. There wasn't much for her in New York now but still she would go amongst the grieving and help before she moved on. One thing she knew was how grief could leach the colour out of life.

Throwing her bag back into the car, Maria looked back at the lake one last time. Its beauty would never leave her, just like Jared and the co-workers she had known, even the people she had ridden elevators with but had never spoken to. They were all a part of her and she part of them. It was time to be involved.

Maria got behind the wheel and started the car. As she drove down the road the sun finally topped the trees. The colours burst into vibrant light, a quilt of life. Maria topped one hill, smelling the musky scent of pine and earth through the open window. Before her, the horizon stretched on and on, into vast possibilities of colour and depth. She sang as she drove.

Journey's End

Carol Anne Davis

I hitch to the Tampa truckstop and immediately recognize his truck. He's already in the diner. So I get me a beer and sit opposite him.

His smile is soft and he doesn't stare at my tits like the other truckers do.

"Been here long?" he asks.

"Five minutes."

"Yeah?" I'm about to ask where he's headed when he adds, "Where were you yesterday?"

I give him the version which doesn't include an overnighter in the cells where the cops offered bed but not breakfast. As we talk, I stare at his plate of bacon, fried eggs, muffins and French toast.

He follows my gaze, slides over ten dollars. "Help yourself."

I get myself to the service counter before he can change his mind. Not that he seems the moody type. I've seen him twice before at truckstops – probably in St Petersburg – and both times he's given me a bagel and some of his fries.

"Fried chicken and all the fixins," I say to the girl. She doesn't need telling twice. She's real agile. Me? I'm as clumsy as a racoon in a dustbin. No way could I do her job. And I couldn't stand getting decked up in that short waitress frock and having to do all that smiling. At least the johns can't see your face when you're sucking them so you can imagine biting their cocks right off.

"Thanks for this," I say when I sit back down.

He nods, seems keen to change the subject. "So, where you going next?"

What a lousy fucking question. I've never known the answer. But he's watching me, expecting a reply.

"Daytona," I say. Someone told me it's the party capital of the world and I could use me a party – the kind of party that brings in a good few bucks.

"Yeah?" He hesitates. "I'm passing through if you need a lift."

He doesn't seem to be a psycho and he's feeding me pretty good so I don't need a second invitation. "That'd be great."

It's got to be. I mean, surely there'll be punters of all ages in Daytona, the city of speed cars and bikers. There'll be elderly speed freaks who want to relive the past and ugly young bikers who don't care if a girl's had a few too many beers. Not that I look real bad – but it's a while since I saw thirty. And the girls are getting younger all the time. We had a twelve-year-old start work last month in Gainesville. The local rag reported on it, all shock horror. And after that, every second punter asked me, "Where's the twelve-year-old?"

I didn't ever see her so don't know if she still looks like a kid. But some of the college students were also working my patch and they were serious competition. Soon as I was busted for scaring the shit out of one of them, I moved on. And I'm still moving on.

"So, why Daytona?" the trucker asks. He leaves a long time between questions. He's slightly balding and slightly overweight and slightly too educated of voice to be driving a truck for a living. I reckon he might be shy.

I spear myself some collard greens as I try to think up an excuse. Truth is, I've got to go somewhere – and there's always a driver with a hard cock willing to do the taking.

"My mama tells me I've a half sister there." That second bit is true – I've more half brothers and sisters than I know what to do with but we sure as hell don't visit anymore.

I turn the questioning back on him but keep it real nice, real polite, not wanting to lose my ticket.

"You working?" Last two times I saw him he was working.

He pushes his plate away and blots the napkin against his morning stubble. "Half and half. I've to make a few deliveries ending with Ormond Beach and then I've got a few days off when I've to see someone down that way."

"And Daytona's on the way there?" Last time I got mugged, the bastards got my map. Not that I really miss it. Long as I'm on the road to somewhere, I feel okay.

He looks surprised. "Ormond's next to Daytona. I'll get you there, no problem. And if I like the place I'll stay awhile." There's a silence, then he adds, "I'm Paul, by the way."

I give him the name I most often give the punters. "Corrine."

It's sizzling hot when we leave the truckstop. My jeans are sticking to my legs, but I'm not complaining. I've had me a meal and a beer – and hopefully there'll be more where that came from.

I wait till he's about to start the engine before I ask.

"Paul, what say we have us a party? You got any beer?"

He stops and looks apologetically at me. "You're not allowed to drink on the roads. And anyway, I don't."

I look away, figuring he's been an alkie.

Suddenly he looks like a kid. "My wife was a real heavy drinker – well, ex-wife," he says.

Fuck it. The trick to making a few bucks is to make sure that they never mention their ill health, their work problems or their families. Sadness or guilt or anger can put a previously working stiff off its task. You got to give them a little beer – and give me a lot of beer – and get as relaxed as possible. That way it all happens quickly and I get the stash.

"I've got a flask of coffee and bottles of water," he says brightly.

Hoo fucking ray, I think, but bite it back. I take a weak coffee off him and make a note to get some beer next time we stop.

Then the road opens up before us, and it's just like every other road I've ever been on. All people in a hurry and me in no rush but still wanting to be somewhere else. Usually the company's less good than this guy – I got my ass from Alabama to Georgia recently, and the drivers cussed about the crackers the entire way.

"So, does your sister know you're coming?" Paul asks.

I'd better come partway clean. "Uh uh. I don't actually know where she is. My mama just said she'd heard tell she was waitressing in Daytona."

"She give you any more detail? Got to be five hundred bars out there."

"Is that right?" Way I see it, a city can never have too many bars. I'm craving beer like a tourist thirsts for water in the Sahara. I've never known a trucker that didn't have a coolbox on him before.

"So, you drive this route a lot?"

"All routes," he says with a smile. "I've never been able to work in a shop or a factory. This life suits me. You eat when you're hungry, take a kip when you're tired. And when I'm driving at first light it's like I own the world."

You have to put up with bad poetry – and a whole lot more – if you're going to hitch.

"You're not from around here, are you?" he continues softly.

Hell, do we have to do all the family stuff, go back thirty years? I'd like to squash that like a Palmetto bug.

"Uh uh – born in Arkansas."

"Yeah? Whereabouts?"

"West Memphis." A small city with small-minded attitudes.

"And your mama's still back there?"

I nod. Truth is, she could be dead or alive or in that place she was before, in the world yet not a part of it. That woman was so holy that she was no earthly use.

"I left a while back." Left when I was fifteen, made my way to the truckstop complex and got me a lift on the interstate. The guy took me to Nashville for the price of a blowjob – and I've been travelling the freeways with truckers and sucking cock ever since.

He tells me the places he's lived. I tell him a few of mine. I've never stayed more than six months in the one place. It's just not worth it. Soon as the cops know your face, you get hassled. And some of the younger girls work in twos and threes and can be total cunts. Thing is, when you're older you gotta charge less – and some guys won't fuck a young girl for fifty dollars if they can get me for twenty in the dark and sometimes get change.

So I keep getting on the highways and ending up somewhere

else. Doesn't matter where it is, as long as there's men without women. Men who aren't looking for a girl that's flash.

Paul – or whatever his name really is – isn't too flash. He keeps to the speed limit. He doesn't tailgate. He just takes us, nice and steady, through the Sunshine State.

We stop at a Denny's and he buys me coffee and pecan pie. Those of us who like a drink don't want to waste money on food unless we're really starving so I wrap it in my napkin for later. He doesn't mention beer and I try not to think about it.

He starts talking more now that he's used to me and his eyes aren't watching the road.

"I guess you've had a pretty rough time?" I finger comb my hair and he adds, I mean, hitching on your own."

I shrug. "Other people have had worse." I hate it when the johns act like fucking social workers. I look around the Denny's and see a couple arguing, which gives me an excuse to change the subject. "You said you had some problems with your ex-wife?"

He nods. "I was twenty-one when we got married but she was only seventeen and already pregnant. She . . . well, I was on the road a lot and she couldn't cope."

I nod and sip my coffee, still wishing it was a beer.

"We had twins." He smiles awkwardly. "Double trouble. She started drinking. We started fighting. She threw me out."

He's talking in short phrases now. I feel he's said all this before, maybe to another girl like me or to one of the other truckers.

"It's her loss," I mutter, scared to say too much in case I say the wrong thing and he leaves me here.

"My loss too. She's moved around a lot and the kids have had so many stepfathers that they don't know if they're coming or going." He pushes his pie away. "I send money and see them once a year or so and it breaks my heart."

He's a poor bastard. I feel for him. But talk like this isn't going to get me enough bucks to get tanked up in Daytona.

"You've been through it," I say softly. "You deserve a good time."

We walk back to the truck and climb in the cabin. I put my hand on his knee. He blushes and pretends not to notice, starts the engine. After a moment I take my hand away.

Life's a beach and then you die. At least, the first part's true as we near our journey's end late that afternoon. Ferdanina Beach . . . Atlantic Beach . . . He detours twice to make deliveries. Jacksonville Beach . . . St Augustine Beach . . . Flagler Beach . . . Ormond Beach where he delivers again. Then we truck on in to the mother of them all, Daytona Beach. The place where half the tourists want to get laid.

"I'm going to book a room here," he says after we've driven around.

I take a deep breath. "Want to make that a room for two?"

He reddens slightly then nods. "Most of my money goes to the kids so is it okay if we just lodge in the hostel?" Hell, to me that's Paradise. Most nights in summer I sleep in a doorway, in some john's truck or on the beach.

He unpacks his sports bag when we get to our room. Just a few shirts, some pants, a change of shoes and a softback book. Nothing fancy. I'm starting to feel real tired now and know I'll get a headache if I don't get me some beer.

"I'm going for a shower," he says.

He's gonna want sex after that but I need a drink first.

"Yeah? Okay if I go out and have a scout around?"

"You must want to see her real bad," he says softly and it takes me an age to realize it's my imaginary half sister he's talking about.

"Well, it's been a while . . ." Over twenty years but I sure as hell ain't counting.

"Go get her," he says and I take off into the bars. The bikers aren't going to waste a drop so I walk on till I see one of the classier bars for the tourists. Sure enough, there's a half inch of liquor left in every third glass.

I down five before the bar girl starts walking over with a mean look on her face. Then I leg it to the next bar. Twenty minutes later I'm fixed.

Time to get the fucking over with. I swagger back to the hostel and annoy half the sleepers till I find our room. He's already laying on the bed with just a towel on.

He sits up. "Sorry, Corrine. I didn't think you'd be back this soon."

I shrug. "I need to get me a plan of how to find her. This place is bigger than I thought." Then I sit down on the bed next to him. "So, how you been?"

"Clean again," he says. He smells of cheap soap but that's probably a hell of a lot better than I smell. Still, some punters like a bit of pussy acid to breathe in whilst they're doing the deed.

I peel away his towel. "You want to party now?"

He stares at me then nods uncertainly. I look at his prick and it's definitely saying yes.

He lifts his head up and I realize he's going to kiss me. Our lips land awkwardly together. Most punters don't kiss – hell, it isn't even on the menu – so I'm not used to this.

I take off my blouse and put his hands on my tits. Then I reach for his cock but he moves quickly to peel my fingers away. Seconds later he reaches for the button on my jeans then unzips them. He rears forward as he does so and I realize he wants to kiss me again.

For the next few minutes he strokes my arse and suckles on my right tit. Then he moves to my left tit and fingers the trimmed front of my cunt, palming the short and curlies but not touching the pink. I wonder what the fuck he's doing and try to guide him in.

"Not yet," he says with effort.

I'm baffled, 'cause he's well up for it. I can see him leaking away.

"You want something extra?"

"I just want you to enjoy it as much as me."

Then I get it. Oh fuck, he wants to make me come. What an optimist. I only come occasionally and then with girls.

Once we get it over with, I can have some kip. I start to breathe harder and he looks real pleased. I manage a little moan. The moan's for real, seeing as I'm shacked up with a teetotaller. I gasp like a landed fish as I guide him in. I went to the restroom moments before and put half a tube of jelly up there but he doesn't know that. He clearly thinks he's suddenly become a ladies man.

Afterwards we sleep. I think he sobs. Sometimes they think of their ex-wives afterwards, of how good it was in the first days. I don't mind the sobbing too much. Least when they're wailing for themselves they're not shouting at me.

When we wake, he takes us to a diner for roast ham and corn-bread. I've not eaten this much in weeks. It makes me feel a lot less spacey which is both bad and good.

"You ever had grits?" I ask. "Never could fathom out why some people like them."

"Had them salted as a side dish. Can't stand 'em sweet," he replies.

"You like Creole?" I talk about other foods I've had. He does the same. Neither of us are big on fancy sauces. He grew up poor so doesn't want to spend anything on a meal he might hate – and when you drink as much beer as I do, your guts want plain, hot food.

But there's more to do here than eat. We lay on the beach which is as white as the whitest thing, check out the car museum, taking a tour of the speedway and play the arcade machines. For three days we do this and I take him in my cunt each night. He seems absurdly grateful and holds on so tight afterwards that I wake up thinking I'm gonna suffocate. Then, on the third night he says that tomorrow he has business elsewhere.

"Want me to tag along?"

I already know what the answer will be.

He shakes his head. "No, I've to see someone – and I don't know exactly where I'm going to be staying. But I'll be driving back through here in two or three days. I'll pay for the room and you can stay on."

"You'll really come back?"

He looks surprised. "'Course I will. We make a good team."

After breakfast – coffee and cornballs and big sweet pastries – he presses a bundle of notes into my hand. "That should keep you in sodas and fried chicken dinners."

"Maybe I'll try me some alligator," I say and we both grin.

It's quiet after he leaves. I walk the room some, amazed that it's all mine. Then I go to the nearest leather bar and drink until I can't see straight. Who needs chicken? I go back to the room and sleep till midday then hit the bars again.

By the second day the money's gone and I finger-shuffle one of the oldies in the hostel for a few bucks. His circulation must be well fucked 'cause it's like touching a cold chicken skin. But it buys me a few more glasses of liquor to pour down my throat. That soon goes and I hang around the bars again, muttering about additional extras. And at last one guy bites. "If you want to party, love, I got some really good gear."

LSD. I haven't had me some of that for years. I stick it on my eyeball and loop the loop. I couldn't even tell you if he fucked me. One minute we're in the car park in his RV. The next, I'm flying. Some time later I wake up, giggling, on the beach.

Life's a beach. Paul doesn't come back on the third day, or the fourth. And I sure as fuck ain't tempting fate by asking reception if I've got any messages. The room's still mine but I'm long out of money for drink.

I hang around outside one of the clubs during happy hour. Hey, you can't say a date with me's too pricy. But I have to unbutton my shirt almost to the waist before anyone notices.

One shot of malt and one shot of vodka, then I suck him off in the gents restroom. Three streets later I pull off a similar trick and then make my way back towards the hostel.

I see Paul's truck and something lifts for a second in my chest. He wasn't lying after all – the man actually came back for me. Then I see the second head – the girl's head. And then I see him turning to her and kissing her.

I stagger over, pull open his cabin door. Fuck, she's a kid – maybe even the twelve-year-old who used to turn tricks in Gainesville. She has on so much makeup that she looks like one of those cheap Russian dolls.

And suddenly I'm back there in Arkansas, eleven or twelve, no tits to speak of but a stepfather that felt them up anyway. Twelve, and the bastard shoving his dick between my legs.

I stab him so hard that the knife goes all the way up to the hilt. His breath comes out real fast. I hear a scream and realize it's coming from her. She throws her arms around him, starts screaming, "Daddy! Dad!"

Fuck, it's Paul I've stabbed and she must be . . . I suddenly get my shit together. She's a twelve-year-old hooker who's suddenly become a witness to a violent death. She starts moaning, "Why you do that? Why you do that?" She's looking back and forward from my face to his real quickly and doesn't notice that I'm unstrapping my other knife from my leg.

She's harder to kill. Hell, she's young and she's just discovered what I'm capable of. I lunge over him and she goes for the lorry's door handle. My blade strikes when she's halfway out of the cabin. She falls the rest of the way out and I fall on top of her. Eleven stone on top of seven. There's no contest. I cut her throat then roll her under the truck.

I've got to act fast now. I push Paul so he's laying across the seats. Then I put my baseball cap over his face, like he's kipping. Should be a good few hours before anyone suspects it's the big sleep - and by then I'll be long gone.

If they catch me, I'll tell them he was fucking his kid. I'll say she was going to the cops so he stabbed her. Then he went for me but I got the knife off him and killed in self-defence.

It's not a good idea to catch a lift outside the hostel 'cause soon the cops'll be asking who was here that day. So I walk real fast for an hour then try to thumb a lift. I spend a long time walking and stopping with my thumb out. Then I get most of my tits out and try again.

At last a blue van stops.

"Where you headed for?" the man asks.

"Wherever you are."

He looks at me a lot more closely then he grins.

I'm looking him over too, of course, but not so's he'd notice. Not a tattoo in sight – the ones with the tattoos are usually the psychos. He's not packing a pistol and he doesn't drive so fast that we'll be flagged down.

"Thirsty?" he asks as I clamber into the front.

"As a cactus." I'm pretty shook up inside but I can still make them laugh.

He reaches down and hands me a beer. "We'll be in Miami by tonight."

"Yeah? You got work there?"

"No, lady, just pleasure," he says, the smarmy git.

I glance at him again. His shirt is cheap but his shoes are good and he's staring at my tits like he's never seen a cleavage. Maybe he'll just want a tit ride and still pay for a room downtown.

After an hour he pulls into a layby. "Suck it, bitch." Gee, where have I heard that before? I take him in real deep and lip him hard, keen to get it over with. He groans and comes thick and fast.

I finish sucking him and reach in my bag for my hanky. As my fingers roam, they brush against something heavy. It's the pecan pie Paul bought me days ago.

"What you got there?" the punter asks, all suspicious.

"It was nothing." I throw the pie out of the window and watch the napkin flutter away.

Orphans

M. Christian

Outside of Atlanta, after standing under the flickering fluorescent lights of a sprawling truck stop for almost an hour, he was picked up by a heavy-faced man driving a rattling sixteen wheeler. Red hair an angry mop on his head, brushy beard all wild and unkempt, the driver said, "Glad for the company," before they'd even pulled out onto the dark highway.

In a little town somewhere just beyond the Louisiana border, he was picked up by a middle-aged woman in a green station wagon, who seemed to delight in creating herself as the perfect housewife: housecoat, hair in curlers, kid's seat in the back. She spent the first few miles prattling nervously, obviously just wanting companionship but frightened with herself for choosing the young hitchhiker to try and sate it. He listened, hypnotized by the landscape blurring by. Finally she asked, "Been on the road long?"

"Not long," he said, wishing again that it had been someone else who'd picked him up, "just getting out. Meeting people."

"That's good," she said, innocently. "Nothin' worse than being alone."

To that he just nodded, still staring out the window.

He'd never heard of a nut log, and would be damned if he was going to try some. But the salesman, Lou Phillips, was so insistent that – before he was even aware of it – he had some on the end of his fork.

"Now me, son," Lou said, smiling broad and bright, "I ain't a flincher. You take that shit there on the end of your fork. What's the worst that could happen? It tastes like crap – but that ain't gonna kill you, is it? But maybe it's gonna be the best damned shit you ever tasted. Ain't gonna know till it's in your mouth, right?"

He didn't answer, and instead stared at the tip of his fork, at the brown sticky mass. Before he was aware of it he was categorizing diseases, vectors and transmission rates. Closing his eyes, he breathed in, out, in and out again, then put it into his mouth. The sweetness was almost alarming, and without conscious control he opened his eyes – and stared into Lou's sparkling brown eyes. "See, that ain't so bad! Fuck it, son – life's too short to be scared."

A cup of coffee later, Lou confessed that he was a widower his wife of twenty-six years having passed away that spring. "Some kind of virus got her. By the time she went to the damn doc she was thin as a rail. Didn't last more than a month."

Sipping hot, bitter – with a touch of slightly turned cream, he hung his head down, mumbling, "Sorry," like it was his fault.

"I mean we all got to go, right? When it's our turn. But what pisses me off is the shit those damned doctors put ya through. Pretend that they know it all when they don't know shit. Tell ya what, kid, if I ever get something I'm just gonna drive out to the desert somewhere and just lay out there in the sun. Damn sight better chance then letting them touch ya."

It seemed such a positive act that he smiled, despite himself – masking it by sipping the foul coffee again and saying, "Sometimes it isn't that they don't know – it's that it's just not worth knowing."

Another big truck – this time cleaner, almost polished. Like a fighter plane, sporting an elegant pin-up on the driver's side door. *Haulin' Ass*, scrolled under a cheesecake girl with golden-blonde hair. The driver was gaunt, a narrow sketch of a man. Peppered hair and the ghostly scar of a hair lip.

They didn't speak for many miles, then the driver said, unexpectedly, "What cha' runnin' from, man?"

His first reaction was to say, "Nothing," but the word didn't come. Was he running? When he thought about it, watching the double-yellow vanish under the windshield, the direction wasn't right. "Not from, towards."

"What cha' goin' to, then?"

He didn't know. He *did* know, though, that he couldn't stay in Atlanta. It was such a lonely place . . . no, not right. It was where he discovered loneliness. A dusty little room and files – at first just one or two then more. Some of them had faces, pictures charting their progress – images to match the declining graphs. Aside from the wasting, he'd seen something else in those faces, the sunken eyes, the fallen features – loneliness. In their worlds they'd been too few, not enough to matter . . . to save.

He'd managed a rough smile, trying to put a comedic face over tragedy. "Just makin' friends, " he said.

Texas was hot, ghostly heat hovering above the roadway. Sky too blue, too pure to be stared at for long. Sitting in a McDonald's, slowly sipping a shake to avoid going out into the hot, dry air, he struck up a brief conversation with a young couple. Too pressed, too clean. A few miles beyond, the air conditioner in their older car cranked up to full, they started to talk about Jesus.

He responded noncommittally, but soon their tone started to irritate him. Looking out at the hot land, he could too easily see the ghostly hopelessness, the abandonment he'd first seen in Atlanta overlaid on every face they passed. Maybe the harried father in the RV – stricken with something that struck one in ten thousand. Maybe that old woman, all blue hair and cautious hand on the wheel – catching something that would waste her, slowly, horribly but only affected one in a hundred thousand.

He listened, for a moment, about what they were saying – instantly realizing that they were following a well-hewn grove. Something like Parkinson's, a horrible in-law to the more popular disease: a gradual wasting of the mind – something affecting one in a million. He could too easily see them, parroting their beliefs till they had no more will, no more strength left to even move their lips.

At the next town he asked to be left off, dismissing their offer of finding him a shelter, a meal, but he did take the money they offered, more than anything to get them to leave.

Too many miles. Still in Texas but the weather had changed – high, turbulent clouds casting deep shadows onto the flat land. Too many miles. Maybe that was it. A pressure. They all saw him the way they wanted to, a young man travelling. A bum, a threat, a homeless person, an object of pity, something to hate and blame. The pick-up truck full of teenagers, throwing a half-empty can of beer as they passed, the too-helpful families that desperately wanted his absolution.

So he told some of it to the bald man, the man in the jeans and stained T-shirt. He knew he'd been picked up for rough trade, but didn't care. He avoided his inquiring eyes and, at first, answered with only a few words, but as they drove and the driver's interest became more and more obvious he found himself talking more, stringing together fact and fiction.

To "Where are you headed?" he said, "Los Angeles, my mom's in the hospital. Something wrong with her liver."

To "That sounds pretty serious. What does her doctor say?" he said, "They know what it is, some kind of hepatitis variant. Rare, though, like one in a hundred thousand get it."

To "At least they know what it is. They got all kinds of drugs and shit nowadays," he said, pausing. "They know what it is, but not enough people get it. So they don't make a cure, not cost-effective. They call them 'orphan diseases' – too rare to bother curing. She's going to die."

They rode in uncomfortable silence till the next town. This time he was asked to leave – and he did, stepping out into the darkness of a cloud's shadow. It had been the shortest trip he'd been on, but he felt lighter, less burdened. That it had only been part of the truth didn't matter; he'd spoken enough of it to get someone to understand, if maybe just a little.

A long time and New Mexico. He felt the fever start as he walked down dusty streets, passing stores selling fake Indian art, plastic tomahawks. In a narrow alley, an old man with heavy features slept out the hot afternoon, a bronze-coloured bottle by his hand.

He went into a dark bar and sat in the corner, feeling his core temperature rise, his skin shimmy with cold shakes. Taking deep breaths, he sipped a warm beer.

He remembered its pathology, its transmission rates, preferred vectors. He thought he'd have more time, and silently felt a heavy sadness at not being able to see the Pacific. It hadn't been a real goal, but had begun to be a kind of benchmark, a saccharin epitaph.

He'd met some good people as he'd travelled from Atlanta, and felt sorry for them. But he also remembered those faces on all those files. It wasn't virulent, but it did spread. Airborne was tough, but it could manage.

Too few to care about. Not enough to bother curing. It had almost been gone, at least to the Centre for Disease Control. Exiled to its refrigerator, the vault. A rarity that claimed maybe a hundred, maybe two each year, almost just a memory. So rare that they'd passed judgement on it: extinction. It had been his job to destroy the samples, to consign the virus to a few sad cases scattered around the world.

The faces on those folders. Too few to care about. As the shivers began in earnest, he tried to think about them, to hold each and every one of them in his mind. Coldly told there weren't enough of them to bother, to care about, to cure.

Sipping his beer, feeling his strength drain, he hoped that now – after all those miles he'd managed, those rides, those hands he'd shaken – they wouldn't be so alone.

Ice Bridge

Edo van Belkom

The continuous diesel-driven thrum of the loader was only occasionally drowned out by the crash of logs being dumped into place. The loud noise was followed by the faint groan of metal and the slight rumbling of frozen earth as the truck dutifully bowed to accept its load.

Rick Hartwick mixed his coffee with a plastic stir-stick and walked casually toward the far end of the office trailer. At the window, he blew across the top of his steaming cup and watched his breath freeze against the pane. Then he took a sip, wiped away the patch of ice that had formed on the glass, and watched his truck being loaded one last time.

As always, the loader, a Quebecois named Pierre Langlois, was making sure Rick's rig was piled heavy with spruce and pine logs, some of them more than three feet in diameter. Langlois liked Rick, and with good reason. Every other week throughout the season, Rick had provided Langlois with a bottle of Canadian Club. He'd been doing it for years now, ever since he'd called a loader an asshole during a card game and wound up driving trucks loaded with soft wood and air the rest of the winter.

He'd been lucky to hang on to his rig.

The next winter he began greasing Langlois' gears with the best eighty proof he could find and since then he'd never had a load under thirty tonnes and only a handful under thirty-five.

He owned his rig now, as well as a house in Prince George.

As he continued to watch the loading operation, Jerry Chetwynd, the oldtimer who manned the trailer for the company, came up behind Rick and looked out the window. "That's a good load you got going there."

"Not bad," said Rick, taking a sip.

"Are you gonna take it over the road, or take a chance on the bridge?"

Rick took another sip, then turned to look at the old man. They said Chetwynd had been a logger in the B.C. interior when they'd still used ripsaws and axes to clear the land. Rick believed it, although you wouldn't know it to look at him now, all thin and bony, and hunched over like he was still carrying post wood on his back. "Is the ice bridge open?"

Chetwynd smiled, showing Rick all four of the teeth he'd been able to keep from rotting out. "They cleared the road to MacKenzie last night and this morning," he said. "But the company decided to keep the bridge open one more day seeing as how cold it was overnight."

Rick nodded. Although the winter season usually ended the last two weeks of March, a cold snap late in the month had lingered long enough for them to keep the bridge operating a whole week into April. And while they'd been opening and closing the ice bridge across Williston Lake like a saloon door the past couple days, the few extra trips he'd been able to make had made a big difference to Rick's finances – the kind of difference that translated into a two-week stay at an all-inclusive singles resort on Maui.

"Anyone use the bridge today?"

Chetwynd scratched the side of his head with two gnarled fingers. "Not that I know of. Maybe an empty coming back from the mill. Harry Heskith left here about an hour ago . . . But he said he wasn't going to risk the ice. Said the road would get him there just the same . . ."

"Yeah, eventually," Rick muttered under his breath.

The ice bridge across Williston Lake was three kilometres long and took about four minutes to cross. If you took the road around the lake you added an extra fifty kilometres and about an hour's drive to the trip. That might have been all right for Harry Heskith with a wife, mortgage, two-point-three kids, and a dog, but Rick had a plane to catch.

Maui was waiting.

"Up to you," Chetwynd said, shrugging his shoulders as he handed Rick the yellow shipping form.

The loader's throaty roar suddenly died down and the inside of the trailer became very quiet.

Uncomfortably so.

Rick crushed his coffee cup in his hand and tossed it into the garbage. "See you 'round," he said, zipping up his parka and stepping outside.

"If you're smart you will," said Chetwynd to an empty trailer. "Smart or lucky."

The air outside was cold, but nothing like the –35 Celsius they got through January and February. Between –15 and –35 was best for winter logging – anything colder and the machinery froze up, anything warmer and the ground started getting soft. The weather report had said –15 today, but with the sun out and shining down on the back of his coat, it felt a lot warmer than that.

Rick slipped on his gloves and headed for his rig, the morning's light dusting of snow crunching noisily underfoot.

"You got her loaded pretty tight," he called out to Langlois, who had climbed up onto the trailer to secure the load.

"Filled the hempty spaces wit kindling," Langlois said with obvious pride in his voice.

"Gee, I don't know," chided Rick. "I still see some daylight in there."

"All dat fits in dare, my friend, is match sticks hand toot picks," Langlois said, his French-Canadian accent still lingering after a dozen years in the B.C. interior.

Rick laughed.

"You know, I uh, I haven't seen you in a while and I been getting a little tirsty . . . You know what I mean?"

Rick nodded. Of course he knew what Langlois meant. He was

trying to scam him for an extra bottle before he went on holidays, even though he'd given the man a bottle less than a week ago.

"I'll take care of you when I get back next week," Rick said, knowing full well he wouldn't be back for another two.

Langlois smiled. "Going somewhere?"

"Maui, man," said Rick, giving Langlois the Hawaiian "hang loose" sign with the thumb and little finger of his right hand.

"Lucky man . . . Make sure you get a lei when you land dare."

"When I land," Rick smiled. "And all week long."

The two men laughed heartily as they began walking around the truck doing a circle check on the rig and making sure the chains holding the logs in place were tight and secure.

"You load Heskith this morning?" Rick asked when they were almost done.

"Yeah."

"What do you figure you gave him?"

"Plenty of air," Langlois smiled. He had struggled to pronounce the word *air* so it didn't sound too much like *hair*.

"How much?"

"Twenty tonnes. Maybe twenty-two."

"He complain about it?"

"Not a word. In fact, he ask me to load him light. Said he was taking the road into MacKenzie."

Rick shook his head. "Dumb sonuvabitch is going to be driving a logging truck into his sixties with loads like that."

"Well, he's been doing it twenty years already."

"Yeah, and maybe he's just managed to pay off his truck by now, huh?"

"He seem to do okay," Langlois shrugged. "But it's none of my business anyway, eh?"

"Right," said Rick, shaking his head. The way he saw it, truck logging was a young man's game. Get in, make as much as you can carrying as much as you can, and get out. So he pushed it to the limit every once in a while. So what? If he worked it right he could retire early or finish out his years driving part-time, picking and choosing his loads on a sort of busman's holiday.

They finished checking the rig.

Everything was secure. "How much you figure I got there?" asked Rick, knowing Langlois could usually estimate a load to within a tonne.

"Tirty-six. Tirty-seven."

"You're beautiful, man."

Langlois nodded. "Just get it to the mill."

"Have I failed you yet?"

"No, but dare will always be a first time."

"Funny, very funny."

There was a moment of silence between them. Finally Langlois said, "So, you taking it over the ice?"

"The bridge is open isn't it."

"Yeah, it's *open*."

Rick looked at him. Something about the way he'd said the word *open* didn't sit right with him. It sounded too much like *hope* for his liking. "Did Heskith say why he wasn't taking the bridge?"

"Uh-huh," Langlois nodded. "He said he had no intention of floating his logs to the mill."

Rick laughed at that. "And I got no intention of missing my flight."

Langlois nodded. "Aloha."

For a moment, Rick didn't understand, then he smiled and said, "Oh, yeah right. Aloha."

The interior of the Peterbilt had been warmed by the sunlight beaming through the windshield. As Rick settled in he took off his hat and gloves and undid his coat, then he shifted it into neutral and started up the truck. The big engine rattled, the truck shivered, and a belch of black smoke escaped the rig's twin chrome pipes. And then the cab was filled with the strong and steady metallic rumble of 525 diesel-powered horses.

He let the engine warm up, making himself more comfortable for the long drive to the mill. He slipped in a Charlie Major tape, and waited for the opening chords of "For the Money" to begin playing. When the song started blaring, he shifted it into gear and slowly released the clutch.

His first thought was how slow the rig was to get moving as the cab rocked and the engine roared against the dead weight of the heavy load. It usually didn't take so long to get under way, Rick thought. Must be a bit heavier than Langlois had figured.

Inch by inch, the truck rolled forward. At last he was out of first and into second, gaining small amounts of momentum and speed as he worked his way up through the gears.

A light amount of snow had begun to fall, but it wasn't enough to worry about, certainly nothing that would slow him down.

The logging road into MacKenzie was wide and flat, following the southern bank of the Nation River for more than a hundred kilometres before coming upon the southern tip of Williston Lake There the road split in two, one fork continuing east over the ice bridge to MacKenzie, the other turning south and rounding the southern finger of Williston Lake before turning back north toward the mills.

Rick drove along the logging road at about sixty kilometres an hour, slowing only once when he came upon an empty rig headed in the opposite direction. Out of courtesy, he gave the driver a pull on the gas horn and a friendly wave, then it was back to the unbroken white strip of road cut neatly through the trees.

The snow continued to fall.

When he turned over the Major tape for the second time he knew he was nearing the bridge. He hated to admit it, but a slight tingle coursed through his body at the thought of taking his load over the ice.

When Rick first began driving logging trucks the idea of driving across lakes didn't sit all that well with him. To him, it was sort of like skydivers jumping out of perfectly good airplanes – it just wasn't right. Six-axle semi-trailers loaded with thirty-five tonnes of logs weren't meant to be driven over water – frozen or otherwise.

It was unnatural . . .

Dangerous.

But after his first few rides over the ice, he realized that it was the only way to go. Sure, sometimes you heard a crack or pop under your wheels, but that just made it all the more exciting. The only real danger about driving over the ice was losing your way.

Once you were off the bridge there were no guarantees that the ice beneath your rig would be thick enough to support you. And if you did fall through, or simply got stuck, there was a good chance you'd freeze to death while searching for help.

Even so, those instances were rare, and as far as Rick knew, no one had ever fallen through the ice while driving over an open bridge.

And he sure as hell didn't intend to be the first.

Up ahead the roadway opened up slightly as the snow-trimmed trees parted to reveal the lake and the ice bridge across it. In the distance, he could see the smoke rising up from the stacks of the three saw mills and two pulp mills of MacKenzie, a town of about 5,000 hardy souls.

He turned down the music, then shut it off completely as he slowed his rig to a stop at the fork in the road.

He took a deep breath and considered his options one last time.

Across the lake at less than three kilometres away, MacKenzie seemed close enough to touch. But between here and there, there was nothing more than frozen water to hold up over thirty-five tonnes of wood and steel.

He turned to look down the road as it curved to the south and pictured Harry Heskith's rig turning that way about an hour before, his tracks now obscured by the continuing snowfall.

The road.

It was Heskith's route all right . . .

The long way.

The safe way.

But even if Rick decided to go that route, there were no guarantees that the drive would be easy.

First of all he was really too heavy to chance it. With its sharp inclines and steep downgrades there was a real risk of sliding off the snow-covered road while rounding a curve. Also, although it hadn't happened to him yet, he'd heard of truckers coming across tourists out for Sunday drives, rubbernecking along their merry way at ten or fifteen kilometres an hour. When that happened, you had the choice of driving over top of them, or slamming on the brakes. And on these logging roads, hard braking usually meant ending up on your side or in the ditch, or both. And that might mean a month's worth of profits just to get back on the road.

But even if he *wanted* to take the road, it would mean spending another hour behind the wheel and that would make him late for his flight out of Prince George. Then he'd miss his connecting flight out of Vancouver which meant . . .

No Maui.

And he wasn't about to let that happen, especially when he'd been told that the resort he'd be staying at discreetly stocked rooms with complimentary condoms.

Man, he couldn't wait to get there.

He looked out across the lake again. The snow was still falling, but a light crosswind was keeping it from building up on the ice. He could still clearly see the thick black lines painted onto the ice surface on either side of the bridge. With those lines so visible, there was really no way he could lose his way.

He took one last look down the road, thought of Heskith heading down that way an hour ago and wondered if he'd catch up with good ole Harry on the other side.

If he did, maybe he could race him into MacKenzie.

The thought put a dark and devilish grin on Rick's face.

He slid the Charlie Major tape back into the deck, turned up the volume and shifted the truck into gear.

"Here goes nothing," he said.

The rig inched forward.

It took him a while to get up to speed, but by the time he got onto the bridge he was doing fifty, more than enough to see him safely to the other side.

The trick to driving over the ice was to keep moving. There were incredible amounts of pressure under the wheels of the rig, but as long as you kept moving, that pressure was constantly being relieved. If you slowed, or, heaven forbid, stalled out on the ice, then you were really shit-out-of-luck.

He shifted into sixth gear, missed the shift and had to try again. Finally, he got it into gear, but in the meantime he had slowed considerably and the engine had to struggle to recover the lost speed.

Slowly the speedometer's red needle clawed its way back up to sixty, sixty-one, sixty-two . . .

And then he heard something over the music.

It was a loud sound, like the splintering of wood or the cracking of bone. He immediately turned down the music and listened.

All he could hear was the steady thrum of his diesel engine.

For a moment he breathed easier.

But then he heard it again.

The unmistakable sound of cracking ice.

It was a difficult sound to describe. Some said it was like snow crunching underfoot, while others compared it to fresh celery stalks being snapped in two. Rick, however, had always described it as sounding like an ice cube dropped into a warm glass of Coke – only a hundred times louder.

He looked down at the ice on the bridge in front of him, realized he was straddling one of the black lines painted on the ice and gently eased the wheel to the left, bringing him back squarely between the lines.

That done, he breathed a sigh of relief, and felt the sweat begin to cool on his face and down his back.

"Eyes on the road," he said aloud. "You big dummy – "

Crack!

This one was louder than the others, so loud he could feel the shock waves in his chest.

Again he looked out in front of his truck and for the first time saw the pressure cracks shooting out in front of him, matching the progress of his truck metre for metre.

Finally Rick admitted what he'd known all along.

He was way too heavy.

And the ice was far too thin.

But 20/20 hindsight was useless to him now. All he could do was keep moving, keep relieving the pressure under his wheels and hope that both he and the pressure crack reached the other side.

He stepped hard on the gas pedal and the engine responded

with a louder, throatier growl. He considered shifting gears again but decided it might be better not to risk it.

He firmed up his foot on the gas pedal and stood on it with all his weight.

The engine began to strain as the speedometer inched past seventy . . . He remained on the pedal, knowing he'd be across in less than a minute.

The sound grew louder, changing from a crunching, cracking sound to something resembling a gunshot.

He looked down.

The crack in front of the truck had grown bigger, firing out in front of him in all directions like the scraggly branches of a December birch.

"C'mon, c'mon," he said, pressing his foot harder on the gas even though it was a wasted effort. The pedal was already down as far as it would go.

Then suddenly the cracking sound grew faint, as if it had been dampened by a splash of water.

A moment later, crunching again.

Cracking.

He looked up. The shoreline was a few hundred metres away. In a few seconds there would be solid ice under his wheels and then nothing but wonderful, glorious, hard-packed frozen ground.

But then the trailer suddenly lurched to the right, pulling the left-front corner of the tractor into the air.

"C'mon, c'mon," Rick screamed, jerking back and forth in his seat in a vain attempt to add some forward momentum to the rig.

Then the front end of the Peterbilt dipped as if it had come across a huge rent in the ice.

"Oh, shit!"

The tractor bounced over the rent, then the trailer followed, each axle dipping down, seemingly hesitant about coming back up the other side, and then reluctantly doing so.

And then, as if by some miracle . . .

He was through it.

Rolling smoothly over the ice.

Solid ice.

And the only sound he could hear was the throaty roar of his Peterbilt as he kept his foot hard on the gas.

He raced up the incline toward the road without slowing.

When he reached the road, he got off the gas, but still had plenty of momentum, not to mention weight, behind him.

Too much of both, it seemed.

He pulled gently on the rear brake lever, but found that his tyres had little grip on the snow-covered road. His rear wheels locked up and began sliding out from behind.

He turned the wheel, but it was no use.

He closed his eyes and braced himself for the rig to topple onto its side.

He waited and waited for the crash . . .

But it never came.

Suddenly all was quiet except for the calming rattle of the Peterbilt's diesel engine at idle.

Rick opened his eyes.

He breathed hard as he looked around to get his bearings.

He was horizontal across the highway, pointed in the direction he'd come.

He looked north out the passenger side window and saw the puffing smokestacks of MacKenzie, and smiled.

He'd made it.

Made it across the bridge.

The moment of celebration was sweet, but short-lived . . .

Cut off by the loud cry of a gas horn, splitting the air like a scream.

He turned to look south down the highway.

Harry Heskith's rig had just crested the hill and was heading straight for him.

Rick threw the Peterbilt into gear, stomped on the gas and popped the clutch.

The rig lurched forward, but he was too slow and too late.

All of Heskith's rear wheels were locked and sliding over the snow like skis. Heskith was turning his front wheels frantically left and right even though it was doing nothing to change the direction he was headed.

And then as he got closer, Rick could clearly see Heskith's face. What surprised Rick most was the realization that the old man was shaking his fist at him.

Shaking his fist, as if to say he was a crazy fool for taking the bridge.

But as the two trucks came together, all Rick could think of was how *he'd* been right all along.

The dangers of the ice bridge had been a cakewalk compared to –

Salvation

Stephen Dedman

The sign on the door read

MUSEUM
ADULTS ONLY
Mon.–Sat. 1 p.m. to 11 p.m.
Admission: $10.00

It was competently hand-lettered, but I guess in a place like Mercury you'd have plenty of time to practise calligraphy. I'd been surprised not to see any satellite dishes outside, until I saw the rack of videos – a third of them R-rated – in the roadhouse. I guess that answered any questions I might have had about what people did for entertainment around here.

Heidi had started making strange noises late that afternoon when I was heading back to the highway; I'd hastily grabbed a map to see if there was any place closer than Salvation, and discovered Mercury. The guy at the garage had promised to look at her and see if he could patch her up well enough to get me to a town where they might have some replacement parts for a '69 Kombi, but this threatened to take all night and he recommended I stay at the motel. The Mercury Motel proved to be an old mining company pre-fab hut behind the roadhouse, but I suspected that if I didn't hire a room, I'd find the $60 added to my bill at the garage.

Besides, the showers were free to hotel guests, against five bucks for transients, so I paid up. The room was spartan, its paint job reminiscent of a hospital, and the bed no better than the mattress in Heidi; no TV, no phone or phone jack (there was a solar-powered phone booth outside, but no-one was expecting me for at least a month and I couldn't think of anyone who'd be particularly happy to hear from me), no fridge, no bar, no plumbing, no towels or soap, but it had a noisy air-conditioner, cleanish sheets, a bolt on the door, a chair and table, and that courtesy common in English and Australian hotels and so often missing from their American counterparts, a kettle and the makings for tea and coffee. I plugged the laptop in to recharge, and looked through my haul of the last few days. Apart from an opalized ammonite, a beautiful *Dactylioceros* about 5 cm across, there was nothing to become excited about, and this showed in my notes for the article I was supposed to be writing. Wondering if there was anything interesting in the museum, I headed for the shower to make myself a little more presentable.

The water was so hard that I could barely even get the shampoo to lather, and it took me nearly half an hour to wash enough of the dust out of my hair and beard so that I looked like a blond instead of a redhead. Then I shaved and, wearing my cleanest jeans and T-shirt, walked back through the dust to the roadhouse.

There was a pretty blonde girl behind the counter, almost certainly the daughter of the woman who'd taken my money for the room. She looked to be about seventeen, with eyes of dark blue flecked with green, eyes that a jeweller would have paid a fortune for. She was nodding to the sound from the cassette player, a C&W version of "Green Green Grass of Home", probably someone's idea of a joke. The only green for miles was the paint on the roof, though maybe that changed in the rainy season. "Hi. Can I help you?"

"Museum open?"

"Sure. Ten bucks, and you get ten bucks off if you decide to buy anything."

"Okay." I fished two fives out of my wallet. She rang it up on the old cash register, then handed me a key she took from the drawer. I unlocked the door, hit the light switch, and then stared around the small, windowless room.

It was furnished like a bedroom, and once I'd gotten past the shock of the pictures on the wall, I guessed it'd been a girl's bedroom. Most of the pictures, however, were stills and covers from blue movies. I was reading one of the covers when the television behind me came on, showing a conventionally pretty redhead with augmented breasts performing a hasty striptease. I stared at this for a few seconds, then turned my attention back to the video cover. *Red Scorpio*, it screamed in imitation Cyrillic. *A Heavenly Body with a Stinger in her Tail*, starring Natalia, Cinnabar, Tianna, Ona Zee, Tony Tedeschi, T. T. Boy. The redhead on the cover might have been the redhead on the TV screen, but I wouldn't have sworn to it. The next title, *The Gods Must Be Horny*, boasted Dominique Simone, Janet Jacme, Nina Hartley, Cinnabar, Marc Wallice, and Julian St Jox. Cinnabar was the only common element (pun unintended) in *Bust in Space*, *Deep Down Under* and *Night of the Loving Redhead*. If I'd been left in any doubt, the two covers furthest from the door were for *The Sins of Cinnabar* and *A Taste of Cinnabar*.

Interspersed among the porn were amateur shots of the same girl pre-surgery – in a ballgown; in a leotard; in a bikini; in a gymslip; in the uniform of a popular fast-food chain; in a T-shirt and broad-brimmed hat accessorized with a bolt-action rifle; topless behind a bar; between another two pretty girls outside a King's Cross strip joint. I glanced around the room, and saw a bolt-action rifle – the same model, if not the same gun – and ballgown on display in a locked glass case amid an exhibition of bras, panties, corsets, suspender belts, high-heeled pumps and boots. The TV screen now showed the top half of Cinnabar's face; the video had been cut down for an R rating. I leaned against the door, and shook my head.

I've seen a lot of tourist traps, from Graceland to the London Dungeon, and I'm not easily appalled, but Mercury was starting to make my flesh creep. I kept glancing over my shoulder, half-expecting to see the *Candid Camera* team. Why a monument to a porno starlet here, in the middle of the outback? Even the probability that she'd been born here and named herself after the place (Cinnabar is a sulphide of mercury, approximately the same colour as her hair) didn't justify it.

Or maybe it did; maybe this reflected glory was Mercury's greatest claim to fame. Local girl makes it into movies, even if you can't see the bottom half of her face.

I took one last look, then walked back out. Before I could speak, the girl behind the counter handed me a catalogue. I looked at her, noticing the family resemblance for the first time; she looked almost nothing like the Cinnabar of the videos, but a lot like the girl in the ballgown and the bikini. The catalogue gave prices for different videos, magazines, and underwear. "The videos are uncut," she said, quietly.

"No, thanks," I said, and smiled weakly. "I don't have a VCR."

She looked at me more closely. "Is that where you're from? California?"

"Huh?" I looked down at my T-shirt; it showed a dinosaur eating a city, with the caption "Let's Do Lunch in California". "No, the shirt's from San Francisco; I'm from Sydney."

"What's it like?"

"Sydney? A lot like San Francisco, but warmer. They're my two favourite cities, but don't ask me to choose between them."

"Don't they scare you?"

"What? No. Why?"

"They'd scare me," she said, a little wistfully, and then looked me in the eye. "You're staying the night, aren't you?"

"Looks that way."

"Will you want dinner?"

"So, what brings you out this way?"

By eight o'clock, I was fairly sure I'd met the entire human population of Mercury. Sharon cooked and cleaned and worked in the shop, the mechanic was her brother, and her mother managed the place and kept the bar when there were any customers. There were none that night, so she was sitting opposite me at my unsteady table while I chewed at my microwaved cheeseburger.

"I look for rocks," I said. "Fossils, meteorites, that sort of thing."

"Why?"

I laughed. "It's what I like doing. I'm a geologist by training, and a bum by nature."

"You can't get a job as a geologist?"

I considered telling her that I could, if I was willing to work for my father, but she didn't inspire that degree of trust. "I probably could, but picking fruit pays better."

She grunted. "Sharon says you've been to America."

"A few times; my mother has family there."

"You been to Santa Monica?"

"Yes."

"My daughter used to live there. Cindy."

"It's a big place," I said. "Los Angeles . . . nearly as many people there as there are in all of Australia."

"I didn't think you'd know her," she said. "Just she's the only person from Mercury ever became famous. Town started drying up ever since they shut down the railway, we're too far from the highway, nobody comes here any more, the roadhouse is all that's left – that, and some ruins around the place. Roo-shooters used to come here, but there hasn't been a cull in a couple of years. Even our regulars are moving out, or going to Salvation for a drink, or dying. Where's your home?"

"Parked in the garage next door."

She stared at me, obviously trying to decide whether I was joking. "That's all you've got? That old van? Seems to me you could do better than that. No job, no home . . . what does your family do?"

"Work for a mining company; that's how I became interested in geology." Actually, they *own* the company, but I don't like telling anyone that.

"Are they disappointed in you?"

"Dad is. Mum . . . I don't know. Her parents were beatniks, big Kerouac fans." She looked at me blankly. "I used to spend holidays with them, and they'd drive me around the country, didn't much matter where we went."

She shook her head. "Strange people." I don't think she meant it as a compliment, but I let it pass.

Sharon hammered on my door the next morning, waking me. "Sorry about this, but Tom says he can't fix your fuel pump without getting some parts flown in. He needs to know right away so he can get them put on the plane."

"Plane?"

"There's an airstrip at Salvation, and they can put it on a truck through to here, but it'll cost maybe more than the car is worth, according to Tom."

I nodded. "Can you give me five minutes to get dressed?"

Tom, the mechanic, was leaning in the shade of the verandah, half-way between the garage and the phone. The cost of having the parts flown to Salvation was steep but it wouldn't break me, and quite apart from Heidi's sentimental value, I didn't see any other way out of Mercury in a hurry. "They should be here by sunset," Tom muttered. "Have you out of here tomorrow."

"Thanks."

He grunted. "Look, we're having a party here tonight. As long as you're staying, you want to come?"

I glanced at Sharon, who was looking at me with something like hope. "Yeah. Sure. What's the party for?"

"It's a surprise. You'll see."

The truck arrived at quarter to six, and the driver was carrying two parcels; Tom took one, and wandered back to the garage, and his mother grabbed the other and disappeared into her room. I expected the truckie to leave, but after filling the tank and grabbing a Pepsi, he also wandered into the garage. Less than an hour later, an old Land Rover pulled up outside, and by seven thirty, there were eight vehicles in the car park, and another eleven men in the bar.

At quarter past eight, when everyone had a beer, our landlady looked around the tavern with mingled excitement and disappointment, obviously resigned to the fact that no-one else was turning up. "Okay," she bellowed, "the moment you've all been waiting for." There was a loud cheer from Tom and the truckie, quieter approval from the others. I looked at her nervously; she was standing beneath a blow-up of the picture of Cinnabar topless in the bar, and I wondered what was coming next. Was she about to strip, or would it be Sharon? Then I remembered the package, and relaxed slightly; it was probably just another video, Cinnabar's latest opus. "The newest additions to the museum have arrived," she announced. "For the next hour only, admission is free!"

The truckie led the procession out of the bar, past Sharon, and into the room next to the rack of videos. I didn't notice anything different at first, but I followed Tom to the display case. There, on a small table, were a small revolver and an urn full of ashes.

"Some people say she was murdered," trumpeted her mother from the doorway. "Some say she shot herself. Whichever story is true, the important thing is that she's finally home!"

"Took a lot of red tape," Tom muttered, "but they got here at last. Reckon this'll bring a lot more people in, huh?"

I don't know what I said, but I slipped out of the crowd as quickly as I could without drawing attention to myself, walked a few hundred metres into the desert, and threw up.

"Are you going to be coming back?" asked Sharon, as I hauled the backpack into Heidi.

"No, I don't think so." Tom emerged from the gloom of the garage to hand me my receipt, then disappeared again to nurse his hangover. "But let me know if you're ever coming to Sydney."

"I can't," she said. "Mum needs me here. She's tried getting other people in to cook since Cindy left, but they keep leaving; besides, we can't afford to pay them any more. And this is our place, this is where we've always lived."

I looked at her, wanting to drag her into the van and drive away with her, just drive; instead, I grabbed my collector's bag and removed a small partly pyritized ammonite, a *Clymenia*. "I found this near here," I said. "They lived here when this place was under the Inland Sea. This species died out about 400 million years ago. Keep it."

She looked puzzled, then brightened. "Thank you. Have a good trip."

"Sure. Can I have another look in the museum before I go?"

"Yeah, no worries." I reached for my wallet, but she put her hand on my arm. "It's okay, no charge."

"Thanks." I took the key, walked in, shut the door behind me, then took a deep breath. The TV came on, showing Cinnabar straddling a ponytailed man in the back seat of a Land Rover. Forcing the lock on the display case was easy, and I emptied the urn into a ziplock bag, which I sealed and stuffed back into my kit. Then I replaced the empty urn, closed the display case, walked back to Heidi, and headed for Salvation.

It was a bleak grey April day when I returned to Sydney, and the beach was all but empty when I poured Cinnabar's ashes into the ocean and stared out to sea as the sun set behind me. I didn't know you, girl, I thought, but I think I know how you feel. There are some places no-one should ever have to go home to.

The Rum Diaries

Hunter S. Thompson

One Saturday in late March, when the tourist season was almost over and the merchants were bracing themselves for the muggy low-profit summer, Sala had an assignment to go down to Fajardo, on the eastern tip of the island, and take some pictures of a new hotel that was going up on a hill overlooking the harbour. Lotterman thought the *News* could strike a cheerful note by pointing out that things were going to be even better next season.

I decided to go along for the ride. Ever since I'd come to San Juan I'd been meaning to get out on the island, but without a car it was impossible. My furthest penetration had been to Yeamon's, about twenty miles out, and Fajardo was twice as far in the same direction. We decided to get some rum and stop by his place on the way back, hoping to get there just as he paddled in from the reef with a bulging sack of lobsters. "He's probably damn good at it by now," I said. "God knows what he's living on – they must have a steady diet of lobster and chicken."

"Hell," Sala remarked, "chicken's expensive."

I laughed. "Not out there. He shoots them with a speargun."

"God almighty!" Sala exclaimed. "That's voodoo country – they'll murder him, sure as hell!"

I shrugged. I'd assumed from the very beginning that Yeamon would sooner or later be killed – by somebody or some faceless mob, for some reason or other, it seemed inevitable. There was a time I had been the same way. I wanted it all and I wanted it fast and no obstacle was big enough to put me off. Since then I had learned that some things were bigger than they looked from a distance, and now I was not so sure anymore just what I was going to get or even what I deserved. I was not proud of what I had learned but I never doubted it was worth knowing. Yeamon would either learn the same things, or he would certainly be croaked.

This is what I told myself on those hot afternoons in San Juan when I was thirty years old and my shirt stuck damply to my back and I felt myself on that big and lonely hump, with my hardnose years behind me and all the rest downhill. They were eerie days, and my fatalist view of Yeamon was not so much conviction as necessity, because if I granted him even the slightest optimism I would have to admit a lot of unhappy things about myself.

We came to Fajardo after an hour's drive in the hot sun and immediately stopped for a drink at the first bar. Then we drove up a hill on the outskirts of town, where Sala puttered around for almost an hour, setting up his camera angles. He was a grudging perfectionist, no matter how much contempt he had for his assignment. As "the only pro on the island", he felt he had a certain reputation to uphold.

When he finished we bought two bottles of rum and a bag of ice. Then we drove back to the turnoff that would take us to Yeamon's beach house. The road was paved all the way to the River at Loíza, where two natives operated a ferry. They charged us a dollar for the car, then poled us across to the other side, not saying a word the whole time. I felt like a pilgrim crossing the Ganges, standing there in the sun beside the car and staring down at the water while the ferrymen leaned on their poles and shoved us toward the palm grove on the other side. We bumped against the dock and they secured the barge to an upright log while Sala drove the car to solid ground.

We still had five miles of sand road before we got to Yeamon's place. Sala cursed the whole way, swearing he would turn back except that he'd be hit for another dollar to go back across the river. The little car thumped and bounced on the ruts and I thought it would come to pieces at any moment. Once we passed a pack of naked children stoning a dog beside the road. Sala stopped and took several pictures.

"Jesus," he muttered, "look at those vicious little bastards! We'll be lucky to get out of here alive."

When we finally got to Yeamon's we found him on the patio, wearing the same filthy black trunks and building a bookshelf out of driftwood. The place looked better now; part of the patio was covered with an awning made of palm fronds, and beneath it were two canvas deck chairs that looked like they belonged in one of the better beach clubs.

"Man," I said, "where did you get *those*?"

"Gypsies," he replied. "Five dollars apiece. I think they stole 'em in town."

"Where's Chenault?" Sala asked.

He pointed down at the beach. "Probably sunning herself down by that log. She puts on a show for the natives – they love her."

Sala brought the rum and the bag of ice from the car. Yeamon chuckled happily and poured the ice in a tub beside the door. "Thanks," he said. "This poverty is driving me nuts – we can't even afford ice."

"Man," I said. "You've bottomed out. You've got to get some work."

He laughed and filled three glasses with ice. "I'm still after Lotterman," he said. "It looks like I might get my money."

Just then Chenault came up from the beach, wearing the same white bikini and carrying a big beach towel. She smiled at Yeamon: "They came again. I heard them talking."

"Goddamnit," Yeamon snapped. "Why do you keep going down there? What the hell is wrong with you?"

She smiled and sat down on the towel. "It's my favourite place. Why should I leave just because of them?"

Yeamon turned to me. "She goes down to the beach and takes off her clothes – the natives hide back in the palms and watch her."

"Not always," Chenault said quickly. "Usually it's just on weekends."

Yeamon leaned forward and shouted at her. "Well goddamn

you! Don't go down there anymore! From now on you stay up here if you want to lie around naked! I'll be goddamned if I'll spend all my time worrying about you getting raped." He shook his head with disgust. "One of these days they'll get you and if you keep on teasing the poor bastards I'll damn well let them have you!"

She stared down at the concrete. I felt sorry for her and stood up to make her a drink. When I handed it to her she looked up gratefully and took a long swallow.

"Drink up," said Yeamon. "We'll invite some of your friends and have a real party!" Then he fell back in the chair. "Ah, the good life," he muttered.

We sat there drinking for a while, Chenault saying nothing, Yeamon doing most of the talking, and finally he got up and picked a coconut off the sand beside the patio. "Come on," he said, "let's have a little football."

I was glad for anything that would clear the air, so I put down my drink and ran awkwardly out for a pass. He spiralled it perfectly, but it smacked my fingers like lead and I dropped it.

"Let's get down on the beach," he called. "Plenty of room to run."

I nodded and waved to Sala. He shook his head. "Go play," he muttered. "Me and Chenault have serious things to discuss."

Chenault smiled halfheartedly and waved us down to the beach. "Go on," she said.

I slid down the bluff to the hard-packed sand on the beach. Yeamon threw up his arm and ran at an angle toward the surf. I tossed the nut high and long, watching it fall just beyond him in the water and make a quick splash. He fell on it and went under, bringing it up in his hands.

I turned and sprinted away, watching it float down at me out of the hot blue sky. It hurt my hands again, but this time I hung on. It was a good feeling to snag a long pass, even if it was a coconut. My hands grew red and tender, but it was a good clean feeling and I didn't mind. We ran short, over-the-middle passes and long floaters down the sidelines, and after a while I couldn't help but think we were engaged in some kind of holy ritual, the re-enactment of all our young Saturdays – expatriated now, lost and cut off from those games and those drunken stadiums, beyond the noise and blind to the false colour of those happy spectacles – after years of jeering at football and all that football means, here I was on an empty Caribbean beach, running these silly pass patterns with all the zeal of a regular sandlot fanatic.

As we raced back and forth, falling and plunging in the surf, I recalled my Saturdays at Vanderbilt and the precision beauty of a Georgia Tech backfield, pushing us back and back with that awful belly series, a lean figure in a gold jersey, slashing over a hole that should never have been there, now loose on the crisp grass of our secondary and an unholy shout from the stands across the way; and finally to bring the bastard down, escape those blockers coming at you like cannonballs, then line up again and face that terrible machinery. It was a torturous thing, but beautiful in its way; here were men who would never again function or even understand how they were supposed to function as well as they did today. They were dolts and thugs for the most part, huge pieces of meat, trained to a fine edge – but somehow they mastered those complex plays and patterns, and in rare moments they were artists.

Finally I got too tired to run anymore and we went back up to the patio, where Sala and Chenault were still talking. They both seemed a little drunk, and after a few minutes of conversation I realized that Chenault was fairly out of her head. She kept chuckling to herself and mocking Yeamon's southern accent.

We drank for another hour or so, laughing indulgently at Chenault and watching the sun slant off toward Jamaica and the Gulf of Mexico. It's still light in Mexico City, I thought. I had never been there and suddenly I was overcome by a tremendous curiosity about the place. Several hours of rum, combined with my mounting distaste for Puerto Rico, had me right on the verge of going into town, packing my clothes, and leaving on the first westbound plane. Why not? I thought. I hadn't cashed this week's paycheque yet; a few hundred in the bank, nothing to tie me down – why not, indeed? It was bound to be better than this place, where my only foothold was a cheap job that looked ready to collapse.

I turned to Sala. "How much is it from here to Mexico City?"

He shrugged and sipped his drink. "Too much," he replied. "Why? Are you moving on?"

I nodded. "I'm pondering it."

Chenault looked up at me, her face serious for a change. "You'd love Mexico City, Paul."

"What the hell do you know about it?" Yeamon snapped.

She glared up at him, then took a long drink from her glass.

"That's it," he said. "Keep sucking it down – you're not drunk enough yet."

"Shut up!" she screamed, jumping to her feet. "Leave me alone, you goddamn pompous fool!"

His arm shot out so quickly that I barely saw the movement; there was the sound of a smack as the back of his hand hit her cheek. It was almost a casual gesture, no anger, no effort, and by the time I realized what had happened he was leaning back in the chair again, watching impassively as she staggered back a few feet and burst into tears. No one spoke for a moment, then Yeamon told her to go inside. "Go on," he snapped. "Go to bed."

She stopped crying and took her hand away from her cheek. "Damn you," she sobbed.

"Get in there," he said.

She glared at him a moment longer, then turned and went inside. We could hear the squeak of springs as she fell on the bed, then the sobbing continued.

Yeamon stood up. "Well," he said quietly, "sorry to subject you people to that sort of thing." He nodded thoughtfully, glancing at the hut. "I think I'll go into town with you – anything happening tonight?"

Sala shrugged. I could tell he was upset. "Nothing," he said. "All I want is food, anyway."

Yeamon turned toward the door. "Hang on," he said. "I'll get dressed."

After he went inside, Sala turned to me and shook his head sadly. "He treats her like a slave," he whispered. "She'll crack up pretty soon."

I stared out to sea, watching the sun disappear.

We could hear him moving around inside, but there was no talk.

When he came out he was dressed in his tan suit, with a tie flung loosely around his neck. He pulled the door shut and locked it from the outside. "Keep her from wandering around," he explained. "She'll probably pass out pretty soon, anyway."

There was a sudden burst of sobbing from inside the hut. Yeamon gave a hopeless shrug and tossed his coat in Sala's car. "I'll take the scooter," he said, "so I won't have to stay in town."

We backed out to the road and let him go ahead. His scooter looked like one of those things they used to parachute behind the lines in World War Two – a skeleton chassis, showing signs of a red paint job far gone with rust, and beneath the seat was a little engine that made a sound like a Gatling gun. There was no muffler and the tyres were completely bald.

We followed him along the road, nearly hitting him several times when he slid in the sand. He set a fast pace and we were hard pressed to keep up without tearing the car to pieces. As we passed the native shacks, little children came running out to the road to wave to us. Yeamon waved back, grinning broadly and giving a tall, straight-armed salute as he sped along, trailing a cloud of dust and noise.

We stopped where the paved road began, and Yeamon suggested we go to a place just a mile or so further on. "Pretty good food and cheap drink," he said, "and, besides, they'll give me credit."

We followed him down the road until we came to a sign that said CASA CABRONES. An arrow pointed to a dirt road that branched off toward the beach. It went through a grove of palms and ended in a small parking lot, next to a ratty restaurant with tables on the patio and a jukebox beside the bar. Except for the palms and the Puerto Rican clientele, it reminded me of a third-rate tavern in the American Midwest. A string of blue bulbs hung from two poles on either side of the patio, and every thirty seconds or so the sky above us was sliced by a yellow beam from the airport tower, no more than a mile away.

As we sat down and ordered our drinks I realized we were the only gringos in the place. The others were locals. They made a great deal of noise, singing and shouting with the jukebox, but they all seemed tired and depressed. It was not the rhythmic sadness of Mexican music, but the howling emptiness of a sound I have never heard anywhere but in Puerto Rico – a combination of groaning and whining, backed up by a dreary thumping and the sound of voices bogged down in despair.

It was terribly sad – not the music itself, but the fact that it was the best they could do. Most of the tunes were translated versions of American rock-and-roll, with all the energy gone. I recognized one as "Maybellene". The original version had been a hit when I was in high school. I recalled it as a wild and racy tune, but the Puerto Ricans had made it a repetitious dirge, as hollow and hopeless as the faces of the men who sang it now in this lonely wreck of a roadhouse. They were not hired musicians, but I had a feeling they were putting on a performance, and any moment I expected them to fall silent and pass the hat. Then they would finish their drinks and file quietly into the night, like a troupe of clowns at the end of a laughless day.

Suddenly the music stopped and several men rushed for the jukebox. A quarrel broke out, a flurry of insults – and then, from somewhere far in the distance, like a national anthem played to calm a frenzied crowd, came the slow tinkling of Brahms' Lullaby. The quarrel ceased, there was a moment of silence, several coins fell into the bowels of the jukebox, and then it broke into a whimpering yell. The men returned to the bar, laughing and slapping each other on the back.

We ordered three more rums and the waiter brought them over. We'd decided to drink a while, putting off dinner till later, and by the time we got around to ordering food the waiter told us the kitchen was closed.

"Never in hell!" Yeamon exclaimed. "That sign says midnight." He pointed to a sign above the bar.

The waiter shook his head.

Sala looked up at him. "Please," he said, "you're my friend. I can't stand this anymore. I'm hungry."

The waiter shook his head again, staring at the green order pad in his hand.

Suddenly Yeamon banged his fist on the table. The waiter

looked fearful, then scurried behind the bar. Everyone in the place turned to look at us.

"Let's have some meat!" Yeamon shouted. "And more rum!"

A fat little man wearing a white short-sleeve shirt came running out of the kitchen. He patted Yeamon on the shoulder. "Good fellows," he said with a nervous smile. "Good customers – no trouble, okay?"

Yeamon looked at him. "All we want is meat," he said pleasantly, "and another round of drinks."

The little man shook his head. "No dinner after ten," he said. "See?" He jabbed his finger at the clock. It was ten-twenty.

"That sign says midnight," Yeamon replied.

The man shook his head.

"What's the problem?" Sala asked. "The steaks won't take five minutes. Hell, forget the potatoes."

Yeamon held up his glass. "Let's get three drinks," he said, waving three fingers at the bartender.

The bartender looked at our man, who seemed to be the manager. He nodded quickly, then walked away. I thought the crisis had passed.

In a moment he was back, bringing a little green check that said $11.50. He put it on the table in front of Yeamon.

"Don't worry about it," Yeamon told him.

The manager clapped his hands. "Okay," he said angrily. "You pay!' He held out his hand.

Yeamon brushed the check off the table. "I said don't worry about it."

The manager snatched the check off the floor. "You pay!" he screamed. "Pay now!"

Yeamon's face turned red and he rose half out of his chair. "I'll pay it like I paid the others," he yelled. "Now get the hell away from here and bring us our goddamn meat."

The manager hesitated, then leaped forward and slapped the check on the table. "Pay now!" he shouted. "Pay now and get out – or I call police."

He had barely got the words out of his mouth when Yeamon

grabbed him by the front of his shirt. "You cheap little bastard!" he snarled. "You keep yelling and you'll never get paid."

I watched the men at the bar. They were bug-eyed and tense as dogs. The bartender stood poised at the door, ready to either flee or run outside and get a machete – I wasn't sure.

The manager, out of control by this time, shook his fist at us and screeched, "Pay, you goddamn Yankees! Pay and get out!" He glared at us, then ran over to the bartender and whispered something in his ear.

Yeamon got up and put on his coat. "Let's go," he said. "I'll deal with this bastard later."

The manager seemed terrified at the prospect of welshers walking out on him. He followed us into the parking lot, cursing and pleading by turns. "Pay now!" he howled. "When will you pay? . . . you'll see, the police will come . . . no police, just pay!"

I thought the man was crazy and my only desire was to get him off our backs. "Christ," I said. "Let's pay it."

"Yeah," said Sala, bringing out his wallet. "This place is sick."

"Don't worry," said Yeamon. "He knows I'll pay." He tossed his coat in the car, then turned to the manager. "You rotten little creep, get a grip on yourself."

We got in the car. As soon as Yeamon started his scooter the manager ran back and began shouting to the men inside the bar. His screams filled the air as we pulled off, following Yeamon out the long driveway. He refused to hurry, idling along like a man intrigued with the scenery, and in a matter of seconds two carloads of screaming Puerto Ricans were right behind us. I thought they might run us down. They were driving big American cars and could have squashed the Fiat like a roach.

"Holy shit," Sala kept saying, "we're going to be killed."

When we came to the paved road, Yeamon pulled over and let us pass. We stopped a few yards ahead of him and I called back, "Come on, damnit! Let's get out of here."

The other cars came up beside him and I saw him throw up his hands as if he'd been hit. He jumped off the scooter, letting it fall, and grabbed a man whose head was outside the window. Almost at the same moment I saw the police drive up. Four of them leaped out of a little blue Volkswagen, waving their billy clubs. The Puerto Ricans cheered wildly and scrambled out of their cars. I was tempted to run, but we were instantly surrounded. One of the cops ran up to Yeamon and pushed him backward. "Thief!" he shouted. "You think gringos drink free in Puerto Rico?"

At the same time, both doors of the Fiat were jerked open and Sala and I were pulled out. I tried to break loose, but several people were holding my arms. Somewhere beside me I could hear Yeamon saying over and over: "Well, the man spit on me, the man spit on me . . ."

Suddenly everybody stopped shouting and the scene boiled down to an argument between Yeamon, the manager and a man who appeared to be the cop in charge. Nobody was holding me now, so I moved up to hear what was going on.

"Look," Yeamon was saying. "I paid the other bills – what makes him think I won't pay this one?"

The manager said something about drunk, arrogant Yankees.

Before Yeamon could reply, one of the cops stepped up behind him and slammed him on the shoulder with his billy. He shouted and lurched to one side, onto one of the men who had come after us in the cars. The man swung wildly with a beer bottle, hitting him in the ribs. The last thing I saw before I went down was Yeamon's savage rush on the man with the bottle. I heard several swacks of bone against bone, and then, out of the corner of my eye, I saw something come at my head. I ducked just in time to take the main force of the blow on my back. It buckled my spine and I fell to the ground.

Sala was screaming somewhere above me and I was thrashing around on my back, trying to avoid the feet that were pounding me like hammers. I covered my head with my arms and lashed out with my feet, but the awful hammering continued. There was not much pain, but even through the numbness I knew they were hurting me and I was suddenly sure I was going to die. I was still conscious, and the knowledge that I was being kicked to death in a Puerto Rican jungle for eleven dollars and fifty cents filled me with such terror that I began to scream like an animal. Finally, just as I thought I was passing out, I felt myself being shoved into a car.

A Wet One

Jack Ewing

I hate rain.

Sure, I know rain's good for farmers, because it helps things grow. Birds like rain, because it brings up worms. And fish like rain, because it knocks tasty bugs into the water.

But I hate rain because it makes hitching a bitch. Especially when I'm stuck in the boonies. Like the unpaved road wandering west and north above Great Falls, Montana, where I found myself in late spring, 1962.

Rain had followed me the whole time as I wound north from Cheyenne, through Casper and Billings and Bozeman and Helena, towards the Canadian border. It would probably be wet all the way to Banff, where I hoped to land a summer job – if I ever got there.

Should have stayed on the main highway out of Great Falls, but I wanted to hit Glacier Park for a little sightseeing. So I took what I thought would be a shortcut and wound up on a web of snaky, patchwork blacktop highways and gravel roads.

Now I was paying for straying.

In late afternoon, I walked by a cracker box house sitting by itself on a knoll west of a whistle-stop called Bynum. A white-haired, potbellied guy in coveralls was rocking on the porch and waved me over to chat. I sat on the top step under the roof's over-hang, since he had the only chair.

The old bird's name was Joe O'Connell, and he was starving for human contact and conversation.

I let him do most of the talking, since anything I said probably wouldn't be true. I'd started with a lie: "Name's Jim Thompson."

"Nice to meet you, Jim. Glad you come along." Joe's cloudy eyes searched the empty greyness all around. "Ain't seen a soul in a week." His gaze found mine. "Don't get much company out this way."

The percolator was on the boil inside, so I stayed put while he fetched us steaming mugs of weak, watery coffee.

He rambled on for an hour, his scratchy voice a violin solo played with crippled fingers, backed by the soft, steady patter of rain. It was soothing, and I lazed, leaning back against the steps, head cradled by linked palms, eyes just slits. If I hadn't been required to grunt during pauses in the flow of words, to let him know I was still there, I'd have fallen asleep.

Joe had lots of stories to tell. Put them all together, and you had a pretty complete picture of the young man he'd been and the old man he'd become. He had lived in the area all his life, been a brakeman for forty years with Northern Pacific, been retired for twenty years.

His two boys, Joe Junior and Steve, were middle-aged now and had moved to the East Coast, where they had families and good jobs with big business. Neither had visited him in ages. They phoned only on holidays. Joe had never seen any of his grandkids, except for their pictures on homemade Christmas cards he received each year.

Joe's wife Norma had died a few years back. All his old friends – Sam, who he'd fished with for seventy years, Carl, his drinking buddy, Morris, his pal since grade school – were dead. With his bad eyes, Joe couldn't drive any more, even if he'd still owned a car, and had to depend on twice-a-month deliveries of groceries, medicines and other supplies vital for survival. There wasn't much to live for these days, but he hung on, anyway, because life, good, bad or indifferent, was better than the alternative.

When he'd run through his pent-up store of words and wound down, Joe offered to put me up for the night. Grateful to get in

out of the wet for awhile, I said, "Thanks," and we went inside.
Joe moved slowly, with a hitch in his giddy-up.

The house, divided into small rooms, was almost empty, as
though furniture had been sold off piece by piece. A single worn-
out easy chair sat on a threadbare Oriental-type rug beside a brass
lamp in the living room, and a wooden coat rack stood by the door,
draped with jackets, scarves, and hats.

The only decoration was the series of Christmas cards Joe had
talked about, tacked to a wall in two neat rows. If you started left
and worked your way right, you could watch two families grow.
This young dark-haired couple – Joe Junior and wife – became a
trio, then the babe in arms was old enough to stand and the
beaming mother held another diapered doll, then a third kid
showed up a couple cards farther along. That fair-haired duo
produced four children to show off over a dozen holiday seasons.
Last year's cards revealed that some of the little ones weren't so
little now, and a couple looked to be in their late teens.

The dining room was bare, except for a couple pots catching
raindrops leaking through holes in the roof.

There wasn't a stick of furniture in the parlour.

Everything was dusty and cobwebby. Dirty dishes clogged the
kitchen sink. A broken glass had been swept sloppily into a corner.

We shuffled past a narrow bathroom, an empty bedroom and
another bedroom with just a single twin-sized bed, a nightstand
and a chest of drawers. Thought for a minute I was expected to
bunk with the old man in his narrow rack, but he led me to the
rear door to point out a dinky ten-foot-long wooden trailer parked
back of the house. "You can sleep there," he said.

Joe made us dinner, heating what he called stew from a can
without a label, the size of a quart of paint. We ate whatever it was
over stale packaged biscuits, sitting in our usual seats on the porch.
If anything, it was raining harder. Cloud-filled skies darkened
from grey to the black of night.

"How do you get by these days, Joe?" I asked, munching. The
stew filled my empty spots but the meat in the thick gravy had a
peculiar, sweetish taste, as if it might have come from horse
instead of cow.

The wind picked up, spitting rain, as he answered. "Ain't easy, but I manage. Got a little pension from the railroad, a few other assets." Joe half-moaned as he got to his feet to go inside. "If I'm careful, it should last long enough. Don't figure I got more'n a few good years left."

He was probably right by the way he got winded and red-faced and had to rest for a moment every few steps.

After dinner, I washed and dried all the dishes and put them away in the lightly stocked cupboard, then swept the place out as payment for the hospitality. A little later we went off to sleep, since there was nothing for entertainment – no radio, no TV, no books, no games, no booze, hardly any lights – in the place.

The too-short bed in the closet-sized trailer had a lumpy, inch-thick mattress with a musty odour and I couldn't get comfortable. I thrashed around for a couple hours before deciding it was a waste of time and I'd be better off making miles north. I packed up and got out before dawn, leaving behind a $5 bill on Joe's porch rocker to help out the old man. Hoped I wouldn't regret my generosity and miss the money later.

I slogged for hours mostly by feel along a narrow gravel road that rose and fell with the rolling plains. The downpour continued, steady, thunder-sprinkled, lightning-lit. As sky faded to grey towards morning, I could see the Continental Divide, a dark and jagged promise twenty miles away to my left.

Around noon, I crossed over the swollen Depuyer River, which flowed fast and lapped at a rickety wooden bridge.

Nobody passed in either direction except a farmer hauling a hay baler behind a tractor, who turned onto a dirt road before he reached me, and a beat-up Ford stuffed with Indians travelling south.

Ten miles farther brought me to Birch Creek, overflowing its banks and running inch-deep across a one-lane concrete bridge.

I crossed into the Blackfeet reservation on worn-out Route 464 and tired of walking chose a low rise where I could spot a car – and be spotted – ten minutes before it drew level.

My last stand.

I pulled off my soggy knapsack, sat on it roadside, a canvas-covered can denting my butt. Liquid pellets fell to explode against my rubbery hooded poncho like buckshot while I lit up, protecting the cigarette coal in my cupped hand, and waited for a car to come along and take me for a ride.

A half-dozen waterlogged stubs of hand-rolled smokes lay scattered around my feet before the lane from the south was blemished by a dark dot that slowly grew in size.

When the car got as big as a pea, I went into my act.

Stood up, stuck my arm straight out, made a loose fist with my thumb cocked at the slate-coloured sky. When the car swelled to the size of a marble, I brushed my hood to the back of my neck so the driver could get a good look at the smile pasted on my mug.

The engine's high whine lowered in pitch as the approaching car, windshield wipers flapping, began to slow.

At a hundred yards, 30 miles an hour, I could see a dim face hunched over the steering wheel.

Fifty yards, 20 mph.

Looked like a man behind the wheel. I felt the driver's eyes following me, noting my plastered-down hair, raindrops falling from my nose and chin.

One hundred feet: down to a crawl.

Could almost hear thoughts rolling around the man's brain.

He'll dampen my upholstery.

He'll muddy my floor mat.

He might be dangerous.

I wondered about the driver, too. Had a pocketknife with two well-honed, razor-sharp blades in case of trouble – if the trouble was slow enough to give me time to snake the weapon out of my tight jeans, get a thumbnail into the slot on the back of a blade and flip it open. I'd never been threatened by anyone who'd picked me up so far, but you never could tell with the way of the world. The next guy to come along might be one who'd end up killing you.

The two-tone blue car pulled even and slid to a stop.

In silent gratitude I grabbed my knapsack, opened the door, slipped out of the poncho, and stepped into the car, a ten-year-old Pontiac with blanket-covered seats.

The driver was about my age, a scrawny guy with clear plastic-framed glasses, a burr cut and a pointed chin dotted with pimples. He gunned the car as soon as I'd closed the door.

"Thanks, buddy," I said, wiping my damp face with a damp hand. "It's slightly wet out there."

"I don't doubt it." He talked through his nose. "Where are you headed?"

"Up into Canada."

"I'm only going to Browning."

"Where's that?"

"East of Glacier, about an hour's drive from here."

"How far from the border?"

"Fifty miles, perhaps."

"Well, every little bit helps." To make conversation, I asked, "You live in Browning?"

"Part of the year. I work summers in the park."

"Doing what?"

"I'm a spotter for the US Forest Service."

"Come again?"

"A spotter. I live in a tower and watch for forest fires."

"Sounds interesting." Actually, it sounded like a yawner of a job, a good chance to catch up on your sleep.

He showed me crooked teeth in a smile. "Not really. It gets deadly dull sometimes. I read a lot."

I returned his smile. "Me, too. It's a little slow waiting for rides sometimes."

That perked him up. "What do you like to read?"

"Crime novels, mostly. You?"

His interest died as soon as it had been born. "I prefer non-fiction myself."

There was something snooty in the way he said it, as if my reading material was too lowbrow to be called literature, so I changed subjects. "You said you work at the park in the summer. What do you do the rest of the year?"

"I teach mathematics at the high school in Browning."

"No kidding. Is that on the reservation?"

"Yes. Most of my students are Blackfeet Indians." He gave me a quick, sad smile. "Unfortunately, they don't have much aptitude for learning."

Could be. Or could be this guy had no aptitude for teaching. Or maybe the Indians simply didn't have use for formal education. I could relate to that.

"Sounds like a tough job, teaching there."

He sighed. "I feel like I'm not accomplishing anything. This past semester I had to flunk half the students. So I'll just have to teach them all over again next year, those who return." His eyes darted at me. "There's a terrific dropout rate among Indians, you know."

I went, "Uh-huh," but it didn't slow him down.

"And the teaching job doesn't pay much either. I make more, proportionately, working for the Forest Service."

"Say," I said, "are there any openings for jobs in the park? I was shooting for Banff, but Glacier would suit me just as well for summer work."

"I don't know." His voice dripped with doubt. "What kind of experience do you have?"

"All kinds. I've worked farms, ranches, cafés, marinas, and service stations. I've done lots of different things." Some jobs I couldn't talk about.

"Well, you could complete an application at the lodge in St Mary," he said. "But I think most positions are already filled. You'd have had a better chance a month ago."

"Story of my life: day late and a dollar short." I settled myself more comfortably into the seat. "Even if I can't land a job there, at least I can scope out the park before I head into Canada."

"No, you can't. The park won't be open to the public for another week or two. Maybe longer, with the heavy snow pack they had this winter." He swiped at mist on the side window so he could see out. "Of course, much of the snow would have melted with all this rain. It's poured for the last two weeks."

"I noticed. Streams are running high."

"Flash flood warnings are out. Some area dams are earthen and may not hold." Vertical worry lines appeared between his thin eyebrows. "That's why I took this road. I heard on the radio the bridge over the Two Medicine on Route 89 is out. If the bridge ahead is closed, I'll have to backtrack, try the long way around, through Conrad, Shelby and Cut Bank. It's a good 150 extra miles."

The road got worse, turning into a rutted, muddy nightmare. We crawled through Heart Butte, a tiny town plunked in the middle of bluff-studded plains, with tumbledown houses surrounding a grocery store, a gas station, and a school made up of a pair of house trailers parked side by side.

A couple dark-haired, bronze-skinned, shirtless boys were shooting hoops on a puddle-covered, dirt-floored court in the rain, heaving a half-inflated volleyball at a basket with no net. They stopped the game and stood wide-eyed, skin glistening, clothes soaked, to stare as the car crept past.

Beyond the town was nothing but rumpled prairie for miles.

We didn't talk much, because the man behind the wheel wanted to concentrate on his driving.

He introduced himself at one point as Ted Perry.

I told him I was Casey Lynch, borrowing the names of a couple Wyoming towns I'd passed through between Casper and Buffalo: a new day, a new name for me. It didn't matter – once we split up, we'd never see each other again. In hours I'd forget his name and he'd soon forget the one I'd given.

The car slipped and slid at 20 miles per hour along non-banked curves of a slimy, shit-brown road pocked with mud holes.

When we reached the Two Medicine River, the water was charging at breakneck speed, slopping over both banks, ready to bust loose. Between the car and the opposite bank, a hundred feet away, the bridge spanning the river was completely buried – or gone. It was impossible to tell which.

"I was afraid of this." Ted pulled up a couple car lengths short of the water.

We both got out and walked closer to look over the situation. The rain fell in sheets. Fat drops dented the rushing water.

I grabbed a dead branch washed up along the bank and used it to probe where the bridge should be. It was still there, all right, three, four inches deep. Either there had been no rails or they'd been carried away already.

"You can make it." I shuffled farther out, poking ahead at the hidden bridge surface as ice-cold water the colour of day-old coffee-and-cream foamed around my ankles and seeped into my boots. I turned, waving him forward. "Come on, I'll guide you across."

"I don't think so." Ted stared at the water. "I'd rather play it safe and drive around to the other road."

I squished back, feet numb, to where he stood. He was short, about five feet six inches, probably weighed all of 120 pounds.

"It's really not as bad as it looks."

"Still, I'd hate to think what would happen if the car got swept off the road into all that." Ted's eyes were bothered. He made up his mind and turned towards the car. "I'm going back. You're welcome to ride with me."

I shrugged. It was his vehicle, his life. I wasn't that crazy about sharing either for another 150 miles. "Thanks for the offer, Ted, but I think I'll go the short way."

"You sure?" He seemed disappointed not to have company on the ride.

"Hell, I'm not sure about anything these days." I reached into the car for my gear, strapped on the clammy pack, pulled the poncho over my head. "I just know I'd rather see new territory than travel the same road twice."

We shook hands. His was a dead fish.

Ted climbed behind the wheel, rolled the window down an inch, stuck his face close to the gap. "Well, good luck, Casey." He put the car in reverse.

"Same to you," I said.

I watched while he got turned around and started back the way we'd come. We waved at one another like old friends.

He was almost out of sight when I started out on the sunken bridge again, tapping ahead with the stick like a blind man with a white cane.

The water had risen a little while I'd gabbed with Ted. It was tough sledding now: the swollen river battered my calves, trying to knock me off my feet. The hidden wooden surface beneath my soles seemed to sway in the surge.

The footing was so uncertain it took me ten minutes to travel a distance I'd have skipped across in ten seconds in dry weather. I had to finish the last ten yards on hands and knees, the poncho hindering me. I clung with a death grip to the upstream edge of the bridge to keep from being swept away.

Made it to the other side, soaked and shivering, wondering if I should've accepted Ted's offer of a ride after all. I was emptying water out of my boots when an uprooted tree long as a bus and a yard thick barrelled down the river roots-first and slammed into the bridge. There was a soggy groan of splintering wood and dark, wet pieces of plank popped up into the swift flow and rushed off, chased by the log.

That took care of the possibility of more northbound traffic travelling along this cruddy road.

I walked into the shelter of a close-set grove of birch trees, strung up the poncho like an umbrella. Beneath it, I stripped naked, dried myself with a rough towel monogrammed HOTEL ARMSTRONG. Then, dressed in dry clothes, I exchanged dripping boots for high-topped black sneakers, climbed into the poncho again.

The plastic-bagged wet clothes in my pack weighed a ton, and if I'd had a third set to wear I'd have ditched them.

Rain kept coming down as I sloshed along through wet weeds and grass at the edge of the swampy road. Little dips and gullies were now full of water, and tiny creeks had become raging rivers, with an occasional dead sheep or cow sailing belly-up downstream. Had to make lots of detours to skirt shallow lakes born of the rain.

An hour of walking brought me to the fringe of a town.

Off the road, halfway up a fifty-foot bluff, was what I took to be a mound of trash. As I got closer, I saw it was actually a crude building, made of scrap lumber, pieces of corrugated metal, cardboard boxes, old doors. In passing, I noticed a thin stream of smoke creeping out of a handmade tin chimney.

A hundred yards farther, a loose cluster of four rusting cars sat in the middle of a hubcap-high sea. From behind cracked windshields, dark-skinned children watched me pass.

I trudged by occupied log houses, the cracked chinking plugged with rags and newspapers, the sagging roofs patched with plastic sheeting. Way off, an honest-to-God teepee pointed at the blackboard-coloured sky. Next were scattered groups of haphazard heaps made from what others had thrown away, and another dozen derelict autos, all now called home by somebody.

Twenty minutes after I crossed some railroad tracks, I was suddenly in downtown Browning. There wasn't much to see.

On the main drag, Highway 89, was a gas station with a half-dozen trailers lined up behind it.

BULL DOZING was painted on the side of a farm implement store's badly patched stucco walls, and damned if there wasn't a live steer with its eyes closed, hunkered in the shelter of the eaves right under the sign. Wished I had a camera – I'd send in a snapshot for *Life* magazine's back page.

The rundown, lived-in houses were all in need of paint jobs.

A fleabag hotel offered rooms at $2 a night.

Sunday's sermon at the Methodist church was "The Wages of Sin". What does it pay? Even at only a dime a crime, I'd be rich.

A twenty-year-old ten-unit motor court advertised NO VACANCY, though only two cars were parked in the lot.

I passed three sad bars and a tired café – thought of stopping in one or the other for a bite or a warm-up nip, but I wanted to make miles. Didn't have but $25 or so left on me, either, and needed to make it last.

More houses and trailers slipped behind me.

Down a side street were two brick buildings, the first two storeys high and old, the other one-storey and new. By swings and teeter-totters on playgrounds out back and US flags snapping at the ends of poles out front, they were schools. Ted probably taught there. I wondered if I'd beaten him to town: no sign of the little guy's Pontiac.

Off an intersection, the rest of the town's business district dribbled away into scrub land.

At the far edge of town sat a new-looking low brick building with metal letters on its front: MUSEUM OF THE PLAINS INDIAN. The place wasn't doing much business today.

The town ended and empty road curved west across flats towards the piled-up mountains of Glacier Park.

Walked about six miles, halfway to Kiowa, the next town on Route 89, before a car came along.

Lucky for me, the people in the '57 Chevy – two dressed-up - teenage couples from Cut Bank heading for a dance at the Lodge in St Mary's – took pity and picked me up.

I stashed my gear in the trunk and sat in front alongside a pretty brunette who wore a red dress under a black raincoat. She was drenched in a perfume that made me gag.

The driver, a burly, moon-faced kid with a blond flattop cut so short his white scalp showed, yakked the whole way, mostly about sports and drinking and hunting and cars.

The young boy and girl in the back seat were too busy making out to bother talking.

At 75 mph in a hard downpour, skidding all over the narrow, wet road, we made it to St Mary's in fifteen minutes.

The driver parked in a crowded lot and I followed the two couples to the lodge, a big, sharp-peaked building made of wood and glass, that sat fifty feet from a narrow creek running high and fast alongside the highway.

When the front doors opened, I heard the muted sound of a saxophone carrying an upbeat version of "Red Sails in the Sunset".

The kids made for the music while I veered across a lobby teeming with dressed-up teens and tourists in casual clothes towards the front desk. Behind the counter, a peppy blonde girl informed me the lodge was full – at their prices, I couldn't afford to stay there anyway – but told me there were cabins for rent right next door, for just $3 a night. That I could manage.

I bought a couple sandwiches, bag of chips, some cookies and a pint of milk in the lodge cafeteria, and went back out to rent a bed.

In exchange for three singles I got a windowless 10′ by 12′ plank-floored log cabin sitting a yard off the ground on a concrete foundation. Inside was nothing but a steel-framed double bed with plenty of blankets, a straight-backed chair, a wood stove and a stack of split pine logs.

"Men's and women's showers and toilets are out back," said Dennis Smith, the man from the rental office. He waved towards a concrete-block building behind the staggered cabins, where under a string of lamps in cone-shaped metal shades I could see women in bathrobes hurrying in and out of one end through steady rain.

Standing under a big, black umbrella, Dennis pencilled in wrong information on a card as I gave it to him. He was a short, stocky guy old enough to be my father, with rimless glasses, a little toothbrush moustache, and a calm face.

Dennis pocketed my cash and handed me a worn towel to use.

Night had fallen and the temperature, which hadn't climbed above sixty all day, started to drop. I built a fire in the cabin's wood stove, tacked a string across one corner of the room to hang up the wet clothes in my pack, and sat on the bed to eat. When dinner was over, I burned trash and went, in just sneakers, underwear and poncho, to clean up.

Washrooms were nothing special, just a large, concrete-floored area: urinals and sinks under mirrors on one side, toilet stalls without doors on the other, showers at the back. A half-dozen men and boys were using the facilities: a young father and two small sons, two grey-haired guys – one fat, one lean – and a pudgy red-haired kid about fifteen.

After taking a long, hot shower, shaving, and brushing my teeth, I was ready for bed.

The mattress was too soft, and the tired springs sagged in the middle, so no matter which way I turned, I always ended up at the bottom of a trough. It was only a shade better than sleeping on cold, hard ground, but comfy enough to coax me into a few hours of deep, if restless, sleep.

I dreamed I was running. No surprise there – I'd been on the move since the summer of 1958. That's when I'd had a final knockdown, drag-out with my parents. I'd taken off to keep them from killing me or me from killing them.

I'd lived hand-to-mouth for four years, travelling from one end of the continent to the other, looking for a haven that didn't seem to exist. Did grunt work for slave wages to eat. Between jobs, I survived like a stray cat: sometimes digging through garbage for food, sometimes begging for a handout, sometimes boldly snatching a prize and running, pursued by angry cries and flung bricks. I always hoped for something better.

Tonight's dream was different than most.

Usually, in my brain-pictures the sky was dark and threatening like it had been all through Montana, the air filled with fog so thick I couldn't see my own feet, couldn't hear the slap of my shoes, as I ran without getting anywhere.

But tonight in my dream bright sunshine streamed from a cloudless sky as I zipped like a jet across green landscape bathed gold by the sun.

I wasn't running without purpose this time, either, I had a destination. There it was, in the distance: a huge glass triangle like a prism that fractured sunlight into a rainbow of colours. If I could just get to it, I'd be okay.

But I never did.

A sudden loud pounding at the cabin door shut off the dream as if the bulb in my projector had burned out.

I sat bolt upright in bed, getting my bearings. Held my breath.

The knock came again, more demanding. The door shook and the flimsy hook-and-eye latch rattled. I heard a voice calling, couldn't make out words.

I eased off the mattress, slipped into my clothes, fumbled for the latch.

Dennis the rental man stood at the foot of three steep wooden steps leading up to the cabin, holding a flashlight in one hand, umbrella in the other.

It was pitch-dark, felt like early morning. In a backwash of light, I saw he wore black rubber chest waders under his open rain jacket. He needed them: water flowed around him above knee level and two of the three steps were already buried. Raindrops fell like bullets, driven sideways by a stiff wind, and the night was noisy.

"Got to get out," Dennis shouted at me in shorthand over the water's roar. "Creek's overflowed. Water's rising fast. Dams upstream won't hold. Cabins could wash away when it crests."

"Where to?" I yelled back, speaking his language.

"High ground, other side of the highway."

He waved the flashlight over a shoulder. All I could see in the beam was an endless carpet of smooth water flowing by, dark and cold looking. "Hurry, everybody else is already gone," he bellowed. "I'll wait for you."

Got my gear together in a jiffy. Threw things into the pack every which way, emptied my pockets into it. I wrapped pack in poncho, tied it tight with a hank of rope, leaving a loop to hang onto, and was back at the door inside two minutes.

I went down the steps. The water, like ice, splashed my thighs.

"Hang onto me," Dennis said, and turned to lead the way across the flood. I grabbed the back of his slicker collar, the bundle on my shoulder.

It was slow going, as we had to feel for footing and keep a sharp eye out for branches and other floating objects driven along by the current, which seemed to be picking up speed. The flashlight wasn't much help.

Within twenty feet, I couldn't feel my lower legs. But I kept plodding forward all the same.

The umbrella was suddenly ripped from Dennis's hand by a gust, and it went sailing downstream.

The rain shot like needles against my face.

We had to bend forward to make even slight progress against the tide. The water grew choppier, and pushed hard against our hips.

"Getting worse," Dennis shouted over a shoulder to me. "Don't know if we can make it."

"Keep going?" I screamed in his ear. "Or go back?"

"Can't go back. Lodge is on low ground."

He was a game fellow, but the water was too much for him.

The level kept rising as we struggled across. By the time we'd made fifty feet, with probably five times that far to go, it was over my belly button and inching upward.

Dennis was half a head shorter than my six feet and he had problems with leverage. He stumbled, only his head and shoulders and flailing hands showing above the rush, and was nearly swept away before I hauled him upright again. The water must have lapped over the top edge of his waders and flowed down inside, where it acted like an anchor.

We came to a standstill. Water boiled around our bodies.

Dennis turned his head and in flashlight glare his eyes behind the rimless glasses had a peculiar shine to them. His hair, like mine, was soaked and plastered in lank grey strands across his forehead. He opened his mouth as if to say something.

Don't know if he lost his balance, stepped into a hole or just gave out. One minute he was there. The next he'd slipped beneath the surface without a word.

I yanked on his collar with whatever strength I had left, thought I had him, but all I came away with was his empty rain jacket. The light was gone, too, and I couldn't see a damn thing. I called but got no answer.

Finally, I let the jacket go and it was swallowed right up.

Felt bad about Dennis. He'd helped me, but I hadn't been able to help him. Didn't worry about him long, though. Had my own neck to save.

Without the other man's bulk as a buffer, I couldn't make much headway against the flow. Something nudged me, and I felt for it: a bush, still clinging to earth beneath the water, its budding branches pointing downstream. I got a grip on it, hoping the thing had deep roots. It was all I could do to jam both feet under hidden rocks and simply brace myself against the water's pressure to keep from being knocked off my pins and carried off after Dennis.

Thought about swimming for it. If I did, I'd have to let go the bundle, and everything I owned would be lost. No guarantee anyway I'd make it to the other side.

The cold sapped me as I clung there. I felt my energy draining away, like a car battery when you leave headlights on all night. Standing or paddling, I knew I couldn't last long. But I was helpless to do anything. My frozen muscles wouldn't do what I told them, and shook beyond my control. I breathed like a racehorse after the Kentucky Derby, so cold I almost felt warm. I'd gotten all turned around in the current and I couldn't remember where I'd been headed or which way lay safety.

A single clear thought penetrated my numb brain: it didn't matter which way I went, or if I went nowhere at all, the outcome would be the same – end of the road for me.

Sounds corny, but realizing I was a dead man, I felt real peace inside for the first time in a long while.

Guess this is where it ends. It was a good run while it lasted, but it's done now. Why fight it? Just close your eyes, relax, let go, and it'll all be over before you know it. You won't feel a thing. Drowning is supposed to be an easy way to go, they say.

They? Who are they?

What the hell do they know?

Anger at myself and at the nameless, faceless people who claimed to have all the answers gave me a hot jolt of energy. I gritted my teeth and lurched forward, determined to go down fighting.

Managed to move my two-ton concrete feet ten herky-jerky steps before I had to stop, panting like I'd run a one-minute mile.

I hit an eddy where a pocket of slower-moving water wet my chin. Took in a gritty mouthful catching breath.

Then back into the rush, moving at an angle against the flow that swirled rib-high, the bundle held over my head. My body wanted to float and it took all I had just to keep my feet grounded, wedged between rocks.

Stalemate.

I couldn't move forward and I couldn't go back. If I lifted a leg, my foothold would be lost. The flood would grab me, give me a wild ride, eventually drown me and dump my battered body on a muddy bank miles from here. They wouldn't find Dennis or me for days after the waters receded. Maybe they'd never find us at all.

If I managed to keep my toe-grip on the rocks, I'd freeze first, then drown. Same result, in the end. Why not take the quick way out, just let go?

I was nerving myself to give up, to let the water have me and drift away to oblivion, when light suddenly scythed across the dark, foaming water, stopping raindrops in mid-air. I heard a rumbling noise behind me and turned my head.

Two bright spotlights topped by twinkling stars seemed to be floating on the water.

As I watched, dumb with cold and fatigue, the lights came nearer and I saw they belonged to a service-station wrecker with all its travelling lights lit up like a Christmas tree. It was on a course that would pass upstream from me.

I called out, but the vehicle kept going straight on without pause – probably couldn't hear me over the fluid roar of the river and the snarl of the wrecker's engine. I stuck wet, frozen fingers in my mouth, concentrated, and after a couple soundless false starts, let loose with a piercing whistle a fellow hitchhiker had taught me. It was loud enough to make my eardrums vibrate.

Somebody shouted, "Over there!"

The truck veered, ploughed towards me, making waves like a boat.

Light hit me. I braced the bundle on my shoulder and lifted a frozen, water-shrivelled hand to wave.

A bearded driver leaned out the open window and his raspy voice cut through the clatter of water and rain and engine noise. "Can't stop. Grab on."

I didn't have to be told twice.

The big wrecker drew alongside me, a few yards away, its bulk slowing the water's flow enough to let me move against the current. As I lurched towards the vehicle, legs like concrete, I saw more faces peering out at me from the crowded cab. Other people, just shapes in the dark, were perched like half-drowned rats on the back, hanging onto the towing machinery.

Hands reached down to haul my bundle and me to safety – good thing, because I couldn't do it myself. Out of the water and draped over solid metal, I clung to the frame with unfeeling fingers, dumb with cold.

Somehow, the truck managed to crawl across the water, though it was touch-and-go in places.

The part of my brain still working wondered why the engine didn't die and leave us all stranded at the mercy of the flood. Then we chugged dripping onto dry land, and I saw the jacked-up truck had giant, five-foot-high lugged tyres, the kind you find on earth-movers, that left deep gouges in the soggy soil.

The headlights swept across a low, wide log building.

"Everybody out," the driver growled. He switched off lights, killed the engine, and climbed down.

Feeling drained, but relieved, I piled off with everybody else, my bundle under an arm, my quivering legs barely able to support me. My body was one big goose pimple. I shook as if spastic and my teeth chattered like castanets. All around, waterlogged people mimicked me. Knees knocked everywhere.

The driver, a short, burly guy in a checkered wool jacket, talked to us as we gathered around, vibrating. Most of the others had suitcases. One young guy carried a duffel bag.

"We're gonna go into the general store there," the driver said. He pointed a flashlight at the darkened log building. "We'll take all the supplies we can carry and head up them stairs." The beam moved left of the building, lit up the lower steps of a wooden stair-case bolted to rock. The steps climbed beyond the range of the light.

"At the top, a hundred feet up or so, there's a cabin hunting parties use," the driver said. "It's empty now, and it's big enough for all of us. Let's get moving. We don't have much time."

The driver led the way to the store.

The rest of us, a dozen or so men, women and children, I vaguely noticed, tagged along behind.

At the front door of the store, the driver took a split log from a half-cord stacked on the porch – my kind of house key – and smashed out a pane of glass near the doorknob. He reached in and unlocked it, then lit a kerosene lantern hanging handy on a wall so we could see.

It was a good-sized shop, with a wide centre aisle from the door to the counter at back, and contained half-a-dozen aisles of loaded shelves running off in either direction. Three walls held more shelves full of stuff.

We trooped in, grabbing food and drink.

Trembling and fumbling, I untied the bundle, and slung on my pack and poncho to keep both hands free. I slapped myself to get the circulation going and worked by feel in the half-dark.

Found a new waterproof flashlight on a rack, dropped in fresh batteries from the next rack, clicked it on and hooked it to my belt so I'd have my own pocket of light.

Gave myself a new horn-handled hunting knife in a sheath, a carton of Camel studs, a fancy compass, a new chamois shirt in just my size, a three-pack of thick wool socks, and a pair of mittens. I thrust the goods into pockets on my pack, pulled a knit cap with GLACIER PARK woven into it over my wet hair and numb ears.

Happy Birthday and Merry Christmas to me!

Finally, I packed a wooden apple crate with loaves of bread, cold cuts and condiments, sweets and snacks, wrapped rolls of toilet paper. I hoisted the box onto a shoulder, scooped up a case of bottled beer from the cooler, and joined the rest with their bags and boxes toiling up the wooden steps like a line of ants bringing food to the nest.

It was a long, slow climb, straight up the rocky face of a cliff. The railed staircase went six steps one way to a little landing, then cut back the other way six steps to another landing, and so on, zigzagging to the top. I had to rest after twelve steps, until a man behind me grumbled, "Move on."

Out of breath, my legs turned to lead, I reached the top and staggered on. The person ahead of me was a guy in a yellow hooded slicker carrying a small suitcase in one hand, and in the other a bulging paper bag that had soaked through and was about to burst. My cardboard box of beer was sagging, too. I dropped my knapsack on the porch before stumbling inside.

The cabin was about fifty yards left of the steps, perched on the edge of the cliff so there'd be nice views from the covered deck surrounding the building. It was a big, square-timbered structure hidden among a thick strand of hundred-foot evergreens, with lots of windows and a steeply pitched roof. Lanterns flickered inside.

We tumbled in, one after the other, set down our goods, and flopped panting onto a bare plank floor.

My head reeled, but at least the climb had warmed me some. While regaining my breath, I let my gaze wander.

The cabin was one big room with a high, beamed ceiling, maybe fifty by twenty, with small, high-set windows spaced around the room to let in light. In the middle of a long wall squatted a stone fireplace with a yard-square opening.

One man built a fire from a bushel basket of twigs and a heap of split softwood logs. The rest lay about.

In the centre of the room, a man and woman, mid-thirties, huddled with a boy about ten and a little girl, five or six years of age. The adults were soaking, but except for wet hair, the kids looked dry. The boy was interested in all the sights and sounds, his bright, dark eyes darting everywhere. Now that immediate danger had passed, the girl was crying and whining so Mama could pat her and coo, "There, there," while drying the child's head with a towel.

A grey-haired couple slumped side by side against a wall. The old man had his arm about the old woman's shoulders and she leaned into him. Both had eyes closed and, except for the rise and fall of their chests, could have been dead.

In a corner, near a pile of foldout wood and canvas Army surplus cots, a young man and young woman sat a few feet apart. He hugged his wet knees and stared at nothing. She squeezed water from her blonde ponytail.

A well-built young fellow with an overgrown crewcut, late teens or early twenties, opened cabinets above a dry galvanized sink at one end of the room.

At the other end of the room, two women, one short with short dark hair, the other taller with long brown hair, stared out at the night. They stood at opposite ends of sliding glass doors that took up the centre half of the cliff-side wall and led out onto the railed deck.

The truck driver made fourteen of us in all. The burly, bearded man entered the cabin carrying a couple of huge plastic bags. He ripped one open to reveal a bunch of Indian-design blankets, all neatly folded.

People came at him from all directions, arms outstretched like late-show zombies hungry for warmth.

"Hold on," the truck driver said, keeping a tight grip on his load.

"I know you're all wet and cold and tired, but some of us need to go down again, right now, and get more stuff before the water reaches the store."

Somebody whined in protest, but the bearded man cut the sound off with a slash of a hand like a bear paw.

"We don't have enough to feed this crowd for more than a day, and we're going to be here a lot longer than that."

A babble of voices started up, but the bearded man was in charge. "Listen up," he said with authority, and the rest fell silent. "There's no time to argue. Kids and women stay here, get the fire going, and dry off. Pops, you stay, too."

He waved the grey-haired man back to his place beside the older woman. "The rest of you men come with me."

Six of us hustled off. I hung close by the bearded man. "Say," I asked him, "is there another road heading north? I don't want to get stuck here." I didn't feature being cooped up with a bunch of strangers for who knew how long. I'd sooner take my chances on the open road.

He shone his flashlight on my face and squinted at me through driving rain. "You got an appointment somewhere?"

"Supposed to be a good job waiting for me in Canada," I lied. "I'll lose it if I don't get there in a couple days."

He studied me a moment longer. "You might make it to Route 464, and hike to Babb, then catch either 2 to Cardston or 17 towards Watertown – if they're not under water by now."

"How would I get there?"

"Have to climb this here ridge and hoof it about twenty miles." He waved at the steep, tree-crowded hill towering darkly above us. "Ain't gonna be easy. Probably slick as snot with all this rain. But if you get to the top, at least you'll be on high ground, above the flood. There's jeep trails you can follow."

"I'll give it a whirl. Thanks."

"How about helping us bring up more food before you take off?"

"The least I can do."

It was easier going down the stairs than up, but it wasn't easy. My thighs and calves groused at the labour.

At the bottom, water had risen and spread. It lapped at the wrecker's fenders, sent liquid fingers onto the general store's front porch and crept towards the staircase leading up.

Inside the store, I found a pile of empty burlap gunnysacks and passed them out among the men.

We loaded up canned goods – Spam, tuna, chili, soup, fruits and vegetables – from the shelves.

I emptied countertop containers of beef and salmon jerky, beef sticks, packaged peanuts, candy, crackers. Raided the cooler, stuffing in my sack two five-pound smoked hams, a couple two-foot-long summer sausages, and a six-foot link of wieners. I added five-pound wheels of cheddar and Swiss cheese, a handful of one-pound packages of bacon.

"Hurry," the bearded man shouted. "Water's coming in!"

Busy, I hadn't noticed the other men had already taken off. I hustled towards the door, making splashes, my new flashlight showing me the way.

The water was knee-high and rising fast as we sloshed to the stairs, and felt even colder than before. I started to climb after the other men, just dark shapes far above me, halfway up the cliff.

At the fourth landing, well above the water, I paused for breath and noticed the bearded man, last in line, had left his sacks on the third landing. He was heading down, his light bobbing as he took the steps at speed.

"Come back," I called to him. "We've got enough food."

"Going for my truck."

He stepped into the water and waded towards the wrecker, his light pointing ahead. The big vehicle was hood-deep now, a metal island. I could just see the bearded man, a blacker shape against the flow, silhouetted against his flashlight's glow.

"Not worth it," I yelled.

"Is to me." The water was up to his wide waist. "Got my whole bankroll tied up in that truck."

"What are you going to do?"

"Pull her downstream of the store," he bellowed. "If the building holds, maybe the truck won't be washed away."

He made it to the truck, struggled against the current to get a door open, swam inside. The truck seemed to slide a couple feet in the water.

"Get out of there!" I screamed. "You're too late."

The interior light came on when he got behind the wheel so he could see to try the key. I heard the engine grinding, but it wouldn't catch.

"Come on, you can still make it back!" I waved him towards the staircase, and safety. I wanted to help him, but I was glued to the steps.

The bearded man was stubborn. He kept trying to get the truck to move, and it cost him.

The engine missed, then fired, sputtering, barely alive. Headlights and running lights snapped on, painting muddy water and raindrops in streaks of white and yellow, orange and red. Gears ground as the driver tried to find LOW.

The river surged, as if somewhere upstream a giant had released the plug on a huge new vat of dirty water. A wave broke over the cab and the truck finally moved – sideways.

By the truck's lights I saw the bearded man struggling to kick the door open. He got it open a few inches, and water slammed it shut. He pushed it open again, gained enough space to force his head and wide shoulders out of the cab.

"Jump!" I called. I dropped my bag of food and started running down the steps to lend him a hand.

Then, a second surge, bigger than the first, crashed against the truck and it rolled over with the driver's upper body still pinched between door and frame. Headlight beams whirled in the air, spotlighting a tree, the store, and me perched on the stairs with my mouth open.

I flinched for the bearded man.

The same powerful wave that got him ripped away the last ten feet of staircase below me with a crack like a rifle shot, and I hung on to keep from being thrown off. The section I was on, a couple yards higher than the break, swayed and shuddered like crazy above the dark foaming flood, but held, thanks to the support of steel braces and inch-thick bolts driven into the rock face.

Downstream, I could see the truck tumbling over and over,

lights still shining, pushed along by a wall of water. Then the lights went out and the vehicle disappeared.

The bearded man was gone. Didn't even know his name.

Walking on eggshells for fear of jarring the rest of the staircase loose from its moorings in the rock, I picked up the bearded man's fifty-pound load. I added it to my own stash and, bent under a hundred pounds of food, slowly and painfully made my way to the top.

As I neared the cabin I smelled wood smoke, and thought how good it would be to warm up, to change into dry duds. I paused on the porch and set my burden down to catch my wind. On the other side of the front door I heard the crackle of burning logs and the hum of chatter as people got acquainted.

A small, soft voice inside my head whispered, "Go on in. You know you want to."

I reached for the doorknob but paused.

What did I need with a whole new flock of temporary friends? Marooned here for days together, we'd be forced to get to know one another, to trade histories, to reveal ourselves. When you start to get acquainted, you leave yourself vulnerable. Dimes to doughnuts, they'd just disappoint me and I'd end up deceiving them, like always.

"Open the door," the small voice insisted. "Take a chance."

"I'll take my chances in the open," I murmured, drowning out the soothing words.

I strapped on the pack under my poncho, and turning away from the dim light and beguiling shelter and false companionship, began to pick a path up the steep slope climbing to the top of the ridge. Somewhere out there, a new road waited, ready to lead me into the open, comforting arms of the unknown.

The Two-Ton Turtle
of Tattler's Terrace

Michael Giorgio

It was the turtle that made the trip to bring Grandpa home to die more memorable than it had any right to be. I was curled up in the back seat of the DeSoto when it all started, thinking of how Mary Ellen Cardilucci's swimsuit jiggled when she hula-hooped. In my imagination, I was telling her how pretty she was and how much I hoped me and Mom would be back in Florida soon. Midway to my fantasy first kiss, the car screeched to a stop, throwing me and my daydreams into a tangled heap on the floor.

"Fannie, what in the name of Sam Hill was that?" Grandpa wheezed.

Mom shut off the ignition. "There's a turtle in the road. I think I hit it."

"Well, leave it and let's get movin'. I don't want to be late for my dyin'." Grandpa clutched his heart for emphasis, a manoeuvre that lately helped him get his way.

No soap this time. "I'm going to save that turtle. It might be a long-lost loved one reincarnated." Reincarnation was my mom's latest fad after waking up with indigestion one morning. Instead of going back to sleep, she watched a professor from Cornell lecture about the afterlife on *Sunrise Semester*. "How would you feel if Mother's tormented soul was in that turtle and you left her?" Mom slammed out of the car.

"Your mother and her foolish notion of the month. One silly idea after another," Grandpa grumbled at me. "Ain't no immortal souls trapped in turtles, Richard. Only immortals are them what does somethin' to make themselves immortal. Just you remember that, boy. Folks like Abe Lincoln and Babe Ruth and Charlie Derry from the livery stable back home that they named Derry's Alley after – after he got hit in the head with a horseshoe and died out there on Kickapit Island during the Shriners' picnic back in 1907. Same year that the general store switched to that brand of oatmeal that gave your Aunt Cordelia such terrible gas if she ate it after seven thirty in the a.m. Ended the picnic right then and there, that horseshoe did. We ate potato salad every meal until what was left up and went bad from old age. Potato salad day and night and we ain't even Irish! Anyways, damn fool like Charlie Derry gets himself immortalized in a high-class way like havin' an alley named after him because he leaned forward to get a better look up Minnie Hannigan's skirts just when Clem Femly lets fly with a sure ringer and a hard-workin' guy like me's gonna be forgot five minutes after I'm planted."

Thankfully, Grandpa's reminiscence was cut short by the opening of the back door on the other side of the car. "Shove over, Ricky. Give this poor thing plenty of room." Mom shoved the biggest turtle I'd ever seen onto the seat. "His feet are bleeding a little, so we'll take him into the next town we come across and find a vet for him."

"Sure don't look like your mother, Fannie," Grandpa snicker-wheezed as Mom shook her head and returned to the driver's seat. The turtle squinted at me through ugly turtle eyes, snapping at me when I dared to move toward him. I sat back and tried to conjure up images of Mary Ellen and her hula-hoop.

The engine sputtered to life and we were off again. Or at least we thought we were. After just a few feet it became apparent to all of us that our sudden stop for the turtle left our tyre flat. Mom slumped in her seat, staring straight ahead and saying nothing. I thought about the spare tyre Grandpa sold en route to pay for an "immortalize-your-profile-in-cement" slab from a street vendor while Mom bought gas. The mortar hardened as Mom cried and I had to chip it away so Grandpa could lift his head.

Not surprisingly, it was Grandpa who finally broke the awkward silence. "Dang fool car. Told you this piece of junk would conk out one day, Fannie. Ain't a long-lastin' car like my old Model T was. Forty years old and still ran like a champ. Man what sold me that car, Rufus Farlowe his name was, owned the biggest dealership in the county. He married that pretty Ellie Munschauzer from the five and dime and later died in that elk huntin' accident with Cy Polner. Anyways, even though old Rufe's been dead for twenty years or better, Farlowe's Automart is still standin' with his name on it in big electric lights. Back-slappin', money-grubbin', sell-an-old-widow-a-lemon crook like Rufe's got his name livin' on long after he's cold in his grave and I'll be lucky if mine don't wear off my headstone a'fore winter's done."

My mother sighed loudly. It had been a long trip from Florida to wherever we were stranded in Tennessee and there was still quite a way to go to get to Kansas. "I'm going to see if I can flag anybody down." Mom sounded tired. I knew she was upset over the news about Grandpa's cancer, even though she did her best not to show it. Even though we still missed Dad, I hoped she'd find a boyfriend to help her get through it.

"Ain't nobody gonna help us," Grandpa informed me after Mom was out of the car. "In my day, folks was always out, visitin' and whatnot. Plenty of people about, and all willin' to lend a hand to a stranger in need. Nowadays – "

"Look, Grandpa!" I interrupted, pointing out the window. "A tow truck!"

"Dumb luck," he muttered as the truck pulled over.

The tow-truck driver got out and talked to Mom for a moment, then hustled over and opened my door. "Hi! Ricky, right? I'm Bess. Bess Haltrough, though folks 'round these parts all call me Butch. Yer maw said ya had Zip in here."

"Zip?" I asked the massive woman.

"The turtle . . . Ah, there he is! I'll just go 'round to the other side and get him. You and the old man kin climb on up in the truck while I grab this here li'l runaway. Zip got away from us a couple days ago when we was preparin' for my brother Leander's big new scheme to get us some attention from tourists. Wouldn't work without Zip."

"How come?"

"You'll see soon enough, young'un. Big unveilin' of Lee's newest crackpot idea's gonna be in just a bit. I was on my way back from a final hunt fer Zip when I seen ya. Didn't 'spect to find Zip sittin' on yer back seat like he was." She breathed deeply, the mighty heave of her ample chest scaring Zip back into his shell. "Well, I'll have ya in Tattler's Terrace 'fore y'all know'd what hit ya. And, y'all are in luck. Yer stuck here just in time for the Black Beetle Harvest Festival. Biggest shindig in town all year. Ain't no hotel rooms available hereabouts, so y'all be bunkin' with my brother and me."

Butch rushed around to the passenger side for the turtle. Grandpa and I got out and headed for the truck. "Blamed fool idea stayin' with strangers," he griped. "Can't be too careful these days. I heard about a fella once who was on his way to somethin' or other, got stuck on the side of the road just like us, stayed with a farmer and his daughter, and never did make it back to his own wife." He wheezed hard, then pulled me toward him like he was going to share the secret of life. "I'm tellin' ya, Richard, don't ever trust strangers. They don't make 'em like they used to."

A two-lane country road off of the main highway brought us to Tattler's Terrace, Tennessee, where we were stuck until the car was fixed. "Ain't nobody workin' today," Butch told Mom as we pulled into Butch's Truck Stop and Wayside Bistro. "Festival's goin' on and folks is all hepped up over that. Cain't get none of my mechanics in durin' festival time. Tonight's the last night though, so we'll have y'all on yer way t'morra sure. Meantime, y'all enjoy the fun long as yer here."

Mom climbed out of the tow truck. "I think I'll pass. I'd rather just sit and relax. It's been a trying trip."

"She's never been the same since that husband of hers up and died," Grandpa said. "Thinks she's got to find a man who'll go along with her silly whims and whatnot, just like Pete did. He died without nobody even knowin' who he was. Not like Ezekial Follin back home. He landed on his head in the crick out on the edge of town when he was tryin' to sneak up on a possum he thought looked tasty for dinner. Why, that particular spot's been called Follin Point ever since! Idiot like – "

"Dad, please!" Mom pleaded with Grandpa. "No more stories about dead people in Grainville Center and how you're gonna die soon! I can't take it anymore!"

"Where you goin'?" Grandpa demanded as Mom stalked off.

"To this bug thing, whatever it is. Anything to clear my mind for a bit!"

"Hang on there, Fannie," Butch called out. "Zip and I'll show you the way."

Mom walked quickly, with Butch bustling to catch her. We finally caught up two blocks away, on the far end of the festival grounds. Here, on the edge of the bluff overlooking the highway we should have been travelling, was a mountain made of canvas, with ropes and pulleys rigged up to it. A banner waving between two stakes identified it as "A New Symbol of Progress in Tattler's Terrace. Grand Unveiling Today at Noon." I pulled Grandpa's watch from his pocket and checked the time. Eleven fifty. Bursting with sudden curiosity, I took a seat in front of Mom, Grandpa and Butch and waited.

People started filing in from other parts of the festival grounds. I watched without paying too much attention, killing time until the show began. Then I saw her, standing all alone holding a stuffed hippopotamus that she must have won at one of the booths. Sit by me, sit by me, sit by me, my mind screamed at her. She scanned the rapidly filling bleachers, then waved at someone. It was like a punch in the stomach. Until I noticed her walking in my direction.

"'bout time you showed," Butch scolded mildly. "Yer uncle's 'bout to start."

"Sorry, Aunt Butch. Had to help my parents in the church booth and I almost didn't get away at all." She was Butch's niece? "Anyone sitting here?" she asked me.

"N-n-n-n-" I couldn't make my body stop quivering.

"Ya gotta forgive him," came Grandpa's voice from behind me. "Richard here don't know how to treat a lady yet. Ain't his fault though. Hard to know how when you ain't been introduced proper. You are?"

"Callandra Haltrough. Callie." Her perfect name matched her angelic voice.

"This here's Richard. Richard Mezner. I'm sure he'd be pleased if you joined us."

Callie settled in next to me, our bodies touching slightly on the cramped bench. My mind was swirling, my body whirling out of control. I could feel beads of sweat breaking out all over my skin. My throat dried, my palms sucking all of the moisture from it. I was scarcely aware of the drum roll starting the show.

"Welcome, citizens of Tattler's Terrace," the man on the platform intoned. "Most of y'all know me, but I hear tell that we got some visitors t'town, so let me introduce myself. I'm Leander Haltrough, Tattler's Terrace mayor and leading real estate agent."

"Only agent," I heard Butch whisper. "My brother is prone t'ward exaggeration."

"As y'all know, Tattler's Terrace was an important part of Tennessee's proud heritage durin' the War 'tween the States. This very bluff was used by our brave confederate boys as a prime place to watch for the onrushing Yankee bas – soldiers under command of General Sherman coming to march through our fair town."

"That isn't true," Callie whispered to me. "Moonshiners used this bluff to watch for revenue agents coming from Memphis to smoke them out."

"This here" – Leander Haltrough indicated the tarp mountain – "is a symbol of the progress Tattler's Terrace has made in the years 'tween then and now. Folks is gonna be able to see this monument from the highway and know we're here. Tourists will come in droves once they spot our new mascot. Now, just a few words before the unveilin'."

"You done already used up most of the air 'round here!" Butch yelled at him, to the delight of the crowd. "Get on with it!"

Leander ignored her. "This two-ton rock monument will stand on this bluff forever. Long after the rest of us have moved on to our next life, this memorial will remain on this very spot. Now, without any further ado, the grand unveiling." Leander reached for the rope. "Wait!" he cried as the crowd moaned. "Bess, bring Zip on up."

Butch brought the turtle onstage, carefully turning his bloodied feet from the crowd. "Folks," Leander said, "meet Zip, the inspiration behind this grand monument."

Leander pulled the ropes and the canvas fell to the ground, landing in a neat pile on "Auntie Minnola's Rhubarb Stand". A giant snapping turtle crafted in mortar glared at the highway below, looking like a low-budget monster from the Saturday afternoon matinee. A smattering of unenthusiastic applause ended the show.

"Damn idjits don't recognize art," Leander complained when it was just the Haltroughs and us remaining around the giant turtle.

"Don't worry, Unk," Callie reassured him. "Who cares what they think?"

"They'll see. When folks start showin' up and spendin' money in town cause they saw the turtle, then they'll know I was right."

Mom studied the giant turtle. "Maybe if you did something to personalize it somehow. A nickname maybe."

"Well, he cain't call it Zip," Butch complained. "What the hell kind of monument is named Zip? Tell you what might work, though. You found Zip. We'll name it after you and ignorant fools 'round here'll think you was somebody important in history."

"Hell, they ain't never asked about them statues in the park, the ones I bought at wholesale in Mississippi," Leander laughed. "I thought it gave the park some class to have statues. If you'd do us the honour, I'd be pleased to name the turtle after you."

"Well, if you want . . ." Mom's eyes widened. "But . . . I didn't find Zip. My father did. If he hadn't noticed the turtle in the road,

I would have hit Zip for sure. By all rights, it should be named for my father, Titus Tipton."

"If that's what the pretty lady wants. The town council gave me free rein to do as I please regardin' this here monument, so the Titus Tipton Memorial Monument it is." Leander tugged at his suspender straps. "The name Titus Tipton will live forever."

"I'm flabbergasted," Grandpa finally sputtered. "I mean, when a great man like Dr Percival Hawkshaw, who saved Grainville Center, Kansas from the terrible earwig fever epidemic of 1902 and was later turned into a statue in town square near Barney Belton's Bar and Beanery gets commemorated like this routinely. But a common man like me, well, I'm honoured."

Leander clapped Grandpa on the back, causing my grandfather to wheeze. "In Titus's honour, let's git over to the Bistro for some of Butch's special recipe sippin' brew."

"I made a fresh batch yestiddy mornin'," Butch grinned. Noticing the worried look on Mom's face, she added, "Don't worry, Sugar. Ain't got nothin' in that kids cain't handle. C'mon, kids, don't dawdle," she said to me and Callie.

"Wait!" Leander cried out suddenly, taking my mother's arm. Mom stopped in mid-stride. "What is it?"

"There's a worm on the ground, just there," Leander pointed. "You wouldn't want to step on him. He might be somebody you once cared about reincarnated."

Mom smiled for the first time. "Are you interested in reincarnation, Mr Haltrough?" They walked off together, leaving us with Grandpa and Butch.

"Go on ahead, Aunt Butch. We'll be right there," Callie said.

"See that you are. My special recipe will give some dimension to your bosoms, Callie," Butch cracked. "Give the young man some hair on his chest, too. Or where ever he needs it." As we blushed, Butch chortled and took off, pulling Grandpa in her wake.

When they were gone, Callie faced me. "Looks like your Mom likes my uncle."

"Yeah, looks like it."

"Maybe you'll be back here someday after your grandpa . . ." Her voice trailed off.

I remembered the look in Mom's eyes when Leander mentioned reincarnation. I had a good idea where we'd end up. "I'm pretty sure we will be."

"Good," Callie smiled. "Maybe you can stay longer next time and we can go swimming down at the spring. I got a new bathing suit I haven't used yet."

Without warning, she moved forward and gently kissed me on the lips. A quick, soft brush that held a promise of more. "I hope you and your mom stay a good long time when you come back," she whispered.

I pictured her in a swimsuit. "So do I." As we walked toward Butch's, I wondered if Callie owned a hula-hoop.

Mojave Nocturne

Thomas S. Roche

You really have to wonder what kind of parents name their daughter Electra. It's like naming your son Oedipus, and you really don't see that at all any more. But Electra, that crops up from time to time, affixed to girls who are destined either for a toxic overdose of Daddy's affection or, it appears, a life of crime.

I'd seen plenty of photos, but that never prepares you. Not when the girl's Electra Sinclair.

It was noon when she stepped out of her '66 Plymouth Baracuda with the stereo blaring Social Distortion, with its bumper sticker that said "How's My Driving? Dial 1-800-EAT-SHIT" and one that said "WHITE TRASH". Some vatos were drinking beer on the corner, and when they saw her get out of the car they turned and stared. I expected them to shout some sort of comment, either about her or the car, but they didn't say anything. Electra killed the engine, got out of the car and stood there leaning on the hood, looking at me without taking her sunglassess off.

"You Cooper?"

"That's me," I said. "You must be Electra Sinclair."

"There some other Electra floating around Berkeley in a muscle car?"

"Let me lock up."

"Need some help with your stuff?"

"I got it. It's just the one bag."

She was wearing a skintight leopard-print top that left her midriff exposed, her belly ring glinting in the sun. They weren't exactly hot pants, but they weren't exactly shorts, either, and they didn't match the fishnets very well – black on blood, a garish combination with the leopard print. But at least the red fishnets matched her shoulder-length hair, which she had braided into short pigtails. Her logging boots came up to her knees and looked as if she could stomp someone with them and never work up a sweat.

I opened the door and tossed my army-surplus duffel in the back with hers. "Hey, nice bag," I said.

"Twenty bucks at Stockard's Army Surplus. Everybody in town's got one."

"Never noticed," I lied.

"Well," she said with a smirk, "everybody cool."

I got in.

"Nice to meet you," she said. "Cooper your first or last name?"

I tried really hard not to stare at her cleavage or at the way her nipples gently tented the leopard print through the red satin bra whose straps I could see at her shoulders. "Cooper's my nickname. I used to work at Cooper tyres."

She started the car, turned down Social D so we could talk, started driving. "Hey," she said. "That's pretty cool. I got my wheel alignment done there."

"Beautiful ride, by the way," I said.

"Yeah, that's what they tell me, nice ride," she said with a smirk. Then, "The passenger window doesn't roll up. Hope you don't mind the wind."

"Love it. How'd you get a car like this, anyway?"

"I inherited it from my brother."

"He upgrade to a GTO or something?"

"He got killed."

"Oh," I said. "Sorry."

"That was TMI two minutes after I met you, but you asked." She took the on ramp to 80, driving too fast. "Buckle up."

I did.

"You got the money?"

"Yeah," I said. "Fresh from the ATM." I took out my wallet and counted out ten Jacksons, handed them to her. She counted them while she drove with one hand and changed lanes every five seconds, going around tanker trucks and commuter BMWs. "Great. You care what route we go?"

"I hear Mexico's nice this time of year."

She smiled. "That's what I hear, but I got a schedule to keep. You got family in Phoenix?"

"Just an ex-girlfriend."

"Shady," she said. "Going back for a quick throw before classes start?"

"Wedding," I said.

"Hers or yours?"

"Hers."

"Bummer."

"If you knew her you wouldn't say that."

"And yet you're driving to Phoenix with a stranger to be there."

"You might say it's the last relationship obligation."

"Just tell me you're not giving her away."

"I'm not."

The softly playing Social D reached the end of the disc. "There's a CD wallet under your seat. You want to pick something out to listen to?"

"Sure." I looked through the fat leather wallet stuffed with CDs, some in the sleeves, others just shoved in there between the pages. I recognized every one of them, which freaked me out a little bit. I picked out the most obscure industrial disc I could find and put it in. Fast, grinding rhythm started to pulse through the car.

"You got a 329 in this thing?"

She nodded, her eyes studying me from behind their death-black shades.

"What kind of carb?"

"Holly haystack," she said suspiciously.

"I knew it. Those four barrels are overrated. Fast as a motherfucker, huh?"

"Zero to sixty faster than the space shuttle."

* * *

There's a certain necessary distance that occurs between besieger and besieged, con artist and mark, stage magician and bedazzled audience member. There's a certain frozen manipulation of the emotions controlled by the killer, the one who seeks out naiveté and innocence wherever it sits in order to corrupt, use, and destroy it. I ruin people. It's my job.

Still, there's a certain symbiosis between pursuer and pursued, for neither one exists without the other. Neither luster or lustee can afford to let go entirely, but hunt too avidly and your prey will scamper away like a bird on the wind. Back off, though, and you might lose the scent. You must stay close, always – almost closer than you dare, but not quite. That shadow band of safety grows ever narrower the more dangerous your prey: a doe, frightened, will run away leaving your family hungry for the night, but a lioness – a lioness will tear you limb from limb and enjoy it more than you ever could, because she feels no shame at killing.

You must never feel sympathy for your quarry, nor dehumanize it to the extent that you forget it is a living thing with its own unpredictable and possibly illogical wants, needs, impulses, desires. You must never want something from it, other than the opportunity to kill rather than be killed.

And you must never – not for a second, not for an instant – you must never want to fuck it. Because fucking is the same as killing – but they are mutually exclusive.

Miles of desert unravelled around us like an expansive vision of Georgia O'Keefe's mind, dust-devils dancing to a travelling soundtrack of Switchblade Symphony and the subterranean rumble of the Cuda's 329.

"How old are you, anyway, Cooper?" She took a swig of Michelob.

"Twenty-six, " I said, shaving off the four years I knew I could get away with. "How old are you?"

"That's rude."

I shot her a quizzical look. "You just asked me."

"That's different," she smiled. "A lady never tells. All right, since you insist. I'm twenty."

"How'd you buy the liquor?"

"Why do you think I'm not wearing a bra?"

"I hadn't noticed."

"Bullshit," she said.

"Did you grow up in California?"

"Los Altos Hills. Go ahead, say it."

"Say what?"

"Rich girl."

"I don't even know where the fuck Los Altos Hills is."

"It's a rich suburb for computer millionaires, down near Palo Alto. Where are you from?"

"Guess."

"Let's see. The most obvious choices are San Francisco and Phoenix?"

"Nevada," I said.

"You must be a Jack Mormon, then."

"How did you know?"

"I had a boyfriend who was one. He was from Nevada. I love lapsed Mormons. You're so into being bad."

"I'm a linguistics graduate student, how bad can I be?"

"Pretty goddamn bad," she said with a mischievous sidelong glance. "You like studying linguistics?"

"Sure."

"What languages do you know?"

I said something in Russian, something in German, something in Arabic.

She nodded appreciatively.

"Pretty cool. Anything else?"

"Chinga tu madre."

"Ah-hah. I see you're teaching useful life skills. Maybe I'll take one of your seminars next semester."

"Interested in the development of dative structures in Germanic languages?"

"No, but you seem like a nice enough guy."

"What do you study?" I asked her.

"Well, I'm still technically a literature student, but I'm taking some time off. Mostly I'm a stripper."

"You don't say."

"That always shocks guys, no matter how cool they are."

"It doesn't shock me."

"Bullshit. I saw your fucking eyebrows go up, Mr Spock. Why does it surprise you that I'm a stripper?"

"Oh, I just figured you were a nun or a Catholic schoolgirl or something."

"That costs extra. You think I'm too ugly to be a stripper."

"No, it's just that I haven't seen you in any of the strip clubs I hang out in."

She laughed and slapped my arm. "Bullshit! Graduate students can't afford to go to strip joints. Besides, I would recognize you."

"You remember all the guys you do lap dances for?"

"Who says I do lap dances?"

"Just a hunch. Where do you work?"

"A place in North Beach called Guys and Dolls right now."

"You've got to be fucking kidding."

She laughed. "No, that's really what it's called. Cheesy, isn't it? At least I'm not working at Boy's Toys any more. But I've worked like six clubs at various times."

"Been doing it long, I guess?"

"Almost three years. I started stripping when I was seventeen."

"You're joking."

"Nope. Walked into a strip club wearing a miniskirt and a G-string and demanded a job."

"What happened?"

"The owner took me into the back room and told me to come back when I was eighteen or had a better fake ID. But not until after he'd fucked me."

"What'd you do?"

"Got a better fake ID. I was still in high school. I made a lot of money that year."

"Where was this?"

"Place called Mickey's in San Jose. I was still living at home."

"I see, and I suppose your parents thought you were working at Bob's Big Boy?"

"Puh-leeze. Like they had any clue what I was doing. Mom's

too busy with her guru and Dad's either closing corporate dot-com mergers or off chasing tail."

"Weren't you afraid he'd walk into your strip club some day?"

"Oh, he usually skips the strip clubs and goes right for the brothels. Besides, he did."

"You've got to be kidding me."

"Nope. I was eighteen by then, so what could he say? He thought he was saving me from it by making me go to school in Berkeley. But it was out of the frying pan, into the fire. I've danced at like fifteen places since then."

"If your Dad's a dot-com merger millionaire, why do you need the money?"

"I dance because I like it," she snapped, sounding more than a little pissed off.

"I'm sorry," I said. "I didn't mean that to sound fucked up."

She was still glowering. "Besides, trying to get money out of a millionaire is like trying to get blood from a stone." Her words sounded bitter, loaded. "I should have fucking blackmailed him when I had the goods, but now Mom knows he fucks around, and she just pretends she doesn't see it."

I stared out at the blasted plains of the Mojave, a dirt-brown world swirling past us as fast as Electra could drive.

"Normally I wouldn't be telling this to a guy I just met."

"Why not?"

"Especially not a guy I was going to spend a night in adjoining hotel rooms with."

"Why not?"

"Guys always want to make it with strippers."

"Oh, is that what we want?"

"I'm sorry, maybe not always. I didn't mean to assume. But guys tend to think we're easy."

"And are you?"

She laughed a little and then acted offended. "That's hardly the point."

"Look," I said, pointing. "A lizard."

"Bug sucker," she said. "Lots of them out here. I guess the reason I told you is because road trips have special rules."

"What do you mean?"

"It's like, a break from your real life. You get out on the road, and you don't have to be the person you usually are. Out here I don't have to be a stripper, I don't have to be a rich girl, I don't have to pretend to be a college student. It's just you and me. We get to take a break from real life – no responsibilities, no obligations, no morality. So I can just tell you."

I took a deep breath and watched another medium-sized lizard skitter across the distant road a few hundred feet in front of us. It stopped in the middle of the highway, stared at the Cuda as it came barrelling on. It didn't move as we neared.

Electra pulled the Cuda into the oncoming lane. Both lanes were empty on the hard-baked plain for as far as the eye could see. The lizard stood there and watched us, then panicked as we passed it and darted in front of us. Electra didn't even have time to slam on the brakes before we heard the crunch and thump under our tyres.

"Fuck!" she screamed, hitting the brakes. The Cuda screamed to a halt in the middle of the double-yellow, turned edge-on to the long smear of lizard. Electra took off her sunglasses and pressed her forehead against the steering wheel.

"Nice brakes on this ride," I said. "It's just a lizard."

It took me a minute to realize she was crying. I put my hand on her shoulder, rubbed it.

"Electra. It's just a lizard."

She started sobbing, hysterically. I looked out at the remains of the lizard, centred between two fading lines of sunlight.

"It's not the lizard," she said. "It's everything. My life's fucking out of control. I guess I don't realize it most of the time. That's what I mean by road trips having special rules. Every time I go on one of these, everything changes."

I got out of the car and walked thirty feet over to the remains of the lizard. I closed my eyes as I walked, feeling my way through the ribbon of flat black asphalt. "Don't fuck up," I kept telling myself, over and over again. "Don't fuck up. Don't fuck up. Don't fuck up."

I bent down and looked at the lizard. Its head was mostly intact, its eyes staring blankly up at me, its forked tongue hanging halfway out. It twitched slightly.

"That's how I fucking feel," she said, standing ten feet behind me. "Smeared on the middle of the road."

I turned around. "It'll get better," I said. "You're young. It's a tough time. It'll get better."

"Yeah," she said. "I'll be able to fucking buy alcohol next year, that should improve things. Besides, you're only twenty-six," she said. "What the fuck do you know about anything other than being young?"

"Twenty's a lot younger than twenty-six."

She looked down and started crying again. "Don't fuck up," I whispered under my breath. I walked up to her and put my arms around her. She melted into them, sobbing.

"Come on, Electra. What's so bad?"

"I just fucking met you. I'm sorry I'm doing this."

"Don't be. What's the problem?"

"I can't tell you. I don't even know you."

"You've already told me a lot. Tell me."

"You're one of those sensitive new age type guys, aren't you?" she choked through rapid sobs.

"Yeah, me and John Tesh. I've got a pony tail in my duffel bag, let me go put it on."

"Don't . . . make . . . me . . . laugh," she pleaded, half laughing, half sobbing, all choked up and red-faced. She melted back into my arms and I held her there in the middle of the double-yellow, wishing a semi would come and smear us both on the road with the lizard.

I could feel her face against my neck, her hot tears tickling my five o'clock shadow. I could feel her body against mine, breasts swelling and full against my solar plexus, hips tight in her black leather shorts. I could smell her road-sweat, sharp and mingled with dust, mingled with my own. I could feel the dampness of her back, the leopard print crop-top soaked through with sweat. I could feel my crotch fighting to stir against the weight of willpower I heaped on it.

"Sorry," she said. "My life sucks."

"It's going to suck even more if a car comes along and kills us. Want me to drive?"

She thought about it for a minute, nodded, little sobs still punctuating her movements.

"Come on."

We walked back to the Cuda. The engine was still running. I leaned into the back seat and took a CD out of my duffel bag. I popped out something called *Recreational Dissection* and put in the new disc. Electra put her sunglasses on and curled up in a ball on the passenger's side without her seat belt on. I buckled mine, gunned the engine, and flipped a U. I shot one last glance in the rearview mirror: the lizard's corpse bizarrely dominated the centre of the highway. Objects in the mirror are larger than they appear. I stepped on the gas.

Chopin filled the car, given an odd percussive background track by the rhythmic purr of the 329.

"I love classical music," said Electra softly after about ten minutes. "I don't know anything about it. My Dad only listened to hippie shit from the seventies. My Mom only listened to Tibetan chants."

"This is all you need to know," I said. "Chopin's Nocturnes make everything better."

"Aren't you supposed to listen to a nocturne at night?"

"See, you know more than you thought you did. That's the point of a nocturne. It evokes a soothing night scene. When it's 110 in the fucking Mojave desert and some freaky punk rock stripper is wigging out on you, that's when you need a nocturne the most."

I thought she might get offended at that, but it broke the spell. She laughed hard and unravelled from her ball. She stretched and took deep breaths.

"You're an unusual guy, Cooper."

"That's what my therapist tells me."

She laughed again. Chopin, wind and the 329 filled the air for a while.

"I'm sorry I freaked out back there. I guess it's been building for a while. I always seem to lose it on road trips."

"No apology necessary," I said. "It's good to cry."

"It's just that I, like, just met you, and I feel like I know you better than I know my boyfriend."

"Uh-oh."

"No, I don't mean like that, it's just that he and I never talk about anything any more. I guess I forgot how much I miss it. Having a real conversation, I mean."

"Yeah," I said. "Conversation."

"Look, I'm not coming on to you, okay? I'm just saying, it's nice to talk, really talk. Not so that it means anything, it's just nice to talk. You seem like a really nice guy."

"Thanks."

"Antoine's not a nice guy at all. I never thought he was."

"Why'd you go out with him?"

"I thought he was cool. He's a bit of a gangster."

I felt that cold feeling down my spine. "Isn't that like being a little bit pregnant?"

"More like being a little bit of a stripper. I'm sorry I freaked out."

"Don't mention it again. Look, we've been on the road since noon, and we're almost to Barstow. You're probably just getting tired. The sun'll be down soon. You want to stop for the night?"

"I don't think I could bear to stop," she said. "It feels like if we stop we'll have to go back to the real world, and I don't want that." Her voice got quiet, rough, like it was closing up, trying to stop her from staying it. "It feels like if I stop I'll die. Can we keep going? I'm sorry, you're probably tired."

"No," I said. "I'd love to keep going."

"Forever?"

"Sure," I said, smiling softly. "Who cares. Fucking forever."

We passed a sign.

Carson 4
Needles 86

"Shit, it didn't look this far to Needles on the map," she said, her voice no longer dulled by tears.

"The desert has a way of doing that."

"You ready to hole up for the night? I don't know if I can make it to Needles."

"Let's hole up," I said. "We're almost out of gas, and look, that sign says Carson's the last gas for sixty miles."

"I am not pumping gas at this hour," she said. "Let's stop at a motel and we'll get gas in the morning."

Carson turned out to be a gas station with a twenty-four-hour convenience store and a motel with six rooms.

As soon as I was in the twenty-dollar room, I got out my cell phone and dialled. There was a Joy Division sticker where the door to the battery compartment used to be. I got a dull beeping busy signal. The small LCD screen said "DISCONNECTED".

I used the motel phone and one of the calling cards in my wallet. Bogan picked up on the first ring.

"How's it going with little miss wonderful?"

"We're in Carson."

"Where's that?"

"Eighty miles to Needles. We'll be in Phoenix tomorrow morning."

"You guys made good time. She tell you anything?"

"Not really," I lied.

"She make a pass at you?"

"Fuck you," I said.

"Come on, Coop. You know as well as I do this chick's the kind of whore who'll do anybody. Antoine Miraud is proof of that, dig? If you want to mix a little pleasure with business, I'd be happy to cover for you." He laughed. "Just make sure you use a Trojan. You've seen the tapes. Who knows where else that fucking skank's been in her twenty years on God's green earth."

"Put a cork in it, motherfucker."

"Come on! You've seen those photos. Is that an ass or is that an ass? This bitch'll fuck anything that moves. Besides, she'll probably be more likely to give up her loverboy if she gets a little of that lethal injection you've been hoarding – "

"One more word, motherfucker. One more word and I'll pop a cap in your ass."

Bogan laughed. "Electra Sinclair's the one who needs something popped in her ass," he said, and I hung up.

I rubbed my eyeballs, took deep breaths. I said, "Fuck," and put a hole in the cheap orange-striped plasterboard with my fist. I ignored the two cut knuckles and blood ran down my fingers as I stripped off my sweat-soaked black T-shirt, jeans, underwear. I put on a pair of shorts and a dingy wifebeater, looked at myself in the mirror and said, "You, motherfucker, are fucked." I sat down on the bed and stared at the clock: three minutes to midnight.

There was a knock at the door. I got up and opened it. Electra stood there holding a bottle of Jack Daniels and a six-pack of Budweiser, with her duffel bag over her shoulder. She had changed from her punk duds into a tight pair of gym shorts and a well-washed white undershirt with no bra. Her dyed red hair was out of pigtails and scattered around her shoulders. She was still wearing the knee-high logging boots.

I tried not to stare.

"If I drink Budweiser with you, will you respect me in the morning?"

"Did I respect you to begin with?"

"Jesus, I hope not," she said, coming in the room.

I shut the door. She tossed her duffel bag next to the bed. I looked at it. "I thought you wanted separate rooms."

"It does get boring in a motel room when they only have three stations, two are showing Jerry Fallwell and the third's showing Billy Graham. What happened to your hand?"

I jerked my head at the hole in the wall. She walked over and peered at it. There was a faintly translucent splinter of my flesh hanging from one of the jagged plasterboard edges.

I stood behind her, staring at the spider tattoo in the small of her back, hovering where the T-shirt rode high and the shorts rode low.

She turned and looked at me. "Am I responsible for that?" she asked, her eyes sparkling for the first time since this morning.

"Yes."

"I'm sorry."

"No, you're not."

She shrugged. "I am, kind of. But I do like making men crazy."

She put her arms around me and kissed me – once, lightly, a "just friends" sort of kiss, a "maybe if you play your cards right" sort of kiss, a "save me from my fucking self before I go too far" sort of kiss, the same kind I gave her.

"If we get drunk together we're going to end up in bed," she said.

"No, we're not."

"You've got a girlfriend, don't you?"

"Yes," I lied.

"She a linguistics student?"

"Women's studies."

"Nice. You love her?"

"Very much."

"And you're made out of willpower?"

"I am," I lied.

"Phew," she said. "That's a relief. You have to promise me you'll be the adult here," she said. "I can't be trusted once I get a few drinks in me. I'll throw myself at you."

I took a deep breath.

She sat down on the bed, her T-shirt riding up so I could see the jewelled ring and her shorts riding down so I could see the Middle Eastern-style tattoo work around her hips.

She looked me in the eyes, a winsome look on her face. Her lips were full and bee-stung and still had deep burgundy lipstick on. Even after all that pizza, beer, and lipstick-stained cigarettes. She'd fixed her lipstick before coming over, I realized. She looked away, closed her eyes, stretched on the bed, her arms over her head, her back arching as her breasts strained against the white cotton, nipples in evidence. She wriggled back and forth on the bed, stretching for a long time, well aware that I couldn't take my eyes off of her. She was a stripper performing onstage, a lioness hunting her prey.

"If we get drunk together we're going to end up in bed," she repeated.

"Yes," I breathed. "We are."

How to describe that moment of transgression when you go far, too far, way too far, further than you thought you could ever be goaded to go by circumstance or moral failing. When you pull across the double-yellow and into the wrong fucking lane, shutting your eyes tight and not even caring if it's a lizard or a Peterbilt you're about to collide with. You sit back, disconnected, watch yourself knocking on the door to hell. You re-evaluate yourself, understanding now that the face in the mirror is not the man you know, or think you know; you are not who you thought you were, or who you pretended to be. You have another beer, and perhaps another shot of cheap Kentucky whiskey, understanding now: no one ever is.

Her first kiss tasted of cocaine.

After we made love, if you prefer to call it that, she clutched me like a shipwreck victim in the North Atlantic desperately clinging to a floating chunk of ice: it burns her flesh, but she clings to it anyway.

"Would you mind if I did a little cocaine?" she asked softly.

"You didn't ask the first time," I said.

"How'd you know?"

"I know what coke tastes like," I said. "You licked the mirror."

"Do you mind?"

"Not really."

"Would you like some?"

"No thanks. One of us has to get some sleep."

"It's already three," she said. "I need to be in Phoenix tomorrow night. We're not going to be getting much sleep."

"Speak for yourself," I said.

"You've got a naked stripper in your bed offering you cocaine and you'd rather go to sleep?"

"Hm. Good point. On second thought . . ."

She kissed me, hard, climbed on top of me.

"Have some coke with me."

She reached over and got her duffel, leaning heavily on me as she picked it up and placed it on the bed amid the rumploc, sweaty sheets stained with spilled beer and whiskey.

She unzipped the duffel, took out a small mirror and a white-dusted razor blade. The duffel was stuffed with Ziploc bags of white powder.

"Where the fuck did you get that much coke?"

"I'm sorry," she said. "I should have told you."

She set the mirror on my belly, opened up one of the ziplock bags and measured out a small mound on the corner of the razor blade. She began to chop it up on the mirror.

"Electra, exactly how much cocaine is that?"

"Six kilos," she said. "Give or take a bag or two. To get me there and back."

"Holy fucking shit. Were you going to inform me of our cargo at some point?"

"I'm sorry. I know I shouldn't have brought along some innocent linguistics student."

"Linguistics student slash drug trafficker now, Electra. We crossed state lines. You made me a fucking accessory."

"I know, I know," she said miserably, methodically chopping up the coke. "I know I shouldn't have brought you along, but I didn't expect this to happen. It never has before."

"You've done this before?"

"It's easy to get rideshares at the university," she said. "I know it seems crazy, but it gets fucking lonely driving from Berkeley to Phoenix."

"So you just advertise for someone to share gas, motel, and federal felony convictions."

"I've never told anyone before."

"How did you get into something like this? I thought you were a stripper."

"Antoine owns the club I strip at. I mean, he doesn't really own it. He's what they call a 'silent partner'."

She had chopped up two neat lines on the mirror. She took a tightly rolled twenty dollar bill out of her duffel and put one end in her nose. She snorted up the two lines like they were nothing.

"Just call me Hoover," she said, and gave me a naughty smile.

She closed her eyes and bent down, licking the mirror and then continuing down.

"I'm sorry I didn't tell you," she said, her breath warm on my flesh. "Let me make it up to you."

"You think that'll make it up to me?" I growled.

"No," she said. "But it's hardly going to make things worse, is it?"

"What time is it?"

"Seven."

I sat up in bed, stretched. "I guess we won't be on the road by eight, like you wanted."

"Sure we will. There's still time to shower, and get breakfast."

"Don't you think it would be better to get some sleep?"

"I've got to be in Phoenix this afternoon."

"Then I hope you can drive hung over."

"You mean drunk. I'm still feeling it."

"How much?"

"Lots. I polished off the last of the Jack about an hour ago while you were in the bathroom."

"Then you're not driving."

"What are you, my father? I've still got plenty of coke."

"Yeah, more than plenty."

She sat up, put her arms around me, kissed me.

"Come on, Cooper, you're not mad, are you?"

"You have any idea what the penalty is for this shit?"

"We won't get caught. Kiss me."

"I'm taking the bus home."

"Good luck finding one. Come on, Cooper, I'll give you some of the money."

"You've got to be fucking kidding."

"Come on, don't be like that," she said. Then, in a whisper: "I only told you because I figure you've got experience."

"What the fuck makes you say that?"

She smiled fetchingly, ran her hand down my chest and let it rest in my lap. "Well, besides this . . . you just have that feel about you. Plus, you've got tears on your hand. You're a gangster."

I stared at her. I shrugged.

"I left that all behind," I lied.

"Then why do you still carry a gun?"

"You looked through my bag?"

"I knew it! I knew you were loaded! No, I didn't look through your bag, but you just told me. What kind is it? Revolver? Semi-automatic?"

"None of your business," I said.

"Can I see it?"

"No, you cannot see it."

"Fine, then. I'll be the brains and you can be the muscle. We'll be partners."

"What about your boyfriend? Anton, Antoine, whatever?"

"He doesn't care," she said. "I'm just a convenient stripper for him to have hanging off his arm, and to run stuff back and forth from SF to Phoenix."

I looked at her. "Why are you doing this to me?"

"It gets lonely driving back and forth across the country. I'm tired of nerdy computer geeks."

I reached out to the nightstand, got her pack of Marlboros. There was nothing left in the box but half-smoked butts with her lipstick smearing the filters. I hadn't smoked in two years. I took out one of the butts and lit it.

"I thought you didn't smoke."

"I make an exception whenever I commit felonies."

"So what do you say?"

"I'm not going to be your boyfriend," I said.

"Fine. Lover? Fiancé? Fuckbuddy?" She nuzzled her face into my neck and said, "Or maybe I can just be your whore. Except you pay me by protecting me."

"You're not driving drunk," I said.

"What are you, my father?"

There's a moment when you realize you're fucked that, if you have time to understand in the midst of said fucking, you are absolutely and totally, for one split-second, one micro-instant, altogether free, maybe for the first time in your life.

That's how it was when I stepped into the parking lot and saw the movement in my peripheral vision. Without even seeing the shiny silver .45 or the black ski mask in the August light, I knew I had been liberated, or was about to be liberated, from that which I hold most dear. I had that instant of clarity as the guy lifted the pistol, tried to place it against my ear, found only air.

Down on one knee, I hit his balls with my first blow. The .45 exploded and unburned powder singed my face as he doubled over. I got a good grip on his gun hand and brought my knee up into his face. Blood sprayed as his black mask came off, and he hit the ground screaming.

Electra stood in the door, gaping. I took the .45 away from the guy and shouted, "Go! Go! Get in the car!" because as I bent over to take the .45, I saw a black Dodge Challenger sitting at the far end of the parking lot, and someone was aiming a rifle.

She ran, but she didn't go to the car. She went to her room and fumbled with the key.

"What the fuck are you doing?"

"What does it look like I'm doing?"

There were three sharp pops and the rear window of the Cuda spiderwebbed in an instant. I hit the ground as the guy next to me started groaning.

"Get in the fucking car!" I screamed. I lifted the .45 and squeezed off two rounds as the Challenger started moving toward us. It was a Model 1911 – seven rounds and one in the chamber. I couldn't afford to rock and roll.

Electra came barrelling out of the motel room with her duffel bag and backpack. She jumped in the driver's seat and jammed the key home. The 329 roared like it was pumping adrenaline. She slammed it into gear and flipped it around, aiming it at the highway as rifle bullets scattered asphalt pieces all around me. I looked at the guy on the ground; he was starting to recover.

I kicked him hard in the head, grabbed my duffel and ran for the Cuda. He groaned and started to get up. I jumped in the open window Dukes of Hazard style and looked back at the guy as he pulled a piece from his ankle holster and aimed it at me. Glock,

9mm compact, and, like most guns, deadly accurate at a distance of a couple yards.

Still hanging half out of the window, I aimed the .45 and popped one off. Electra chose that moment to floor it, and the tyres squealed as we lurched forward. The Glock flashed and I didn't even have time to pray before I realized that mine had hit and his had missed. He went stumbling back and crashed into a bunch of garbage cans.

His face burned in my mind's eye even as he started to struggle to his feet. I knew him from somewhere. Somewhere. Probably a rap sheet or the case file, but I couldn't place it.

I twisted around as the rifleman aimed. I recognized the outline of an AK. "Get down!" I screamed.

She ducked down beneath the steering wheel as I hooked my feet under the dash and started firing at the rifleman. He was a lousy shot, or maybe the ski mask just made his face hot. I squeezed off two more rounds; he went down. Electra stayed under the dashboard, driving with one hand. It's a wonder she didn't hit anything. She hurtled past the Challenger as I watched the guy struggling to his feet. As we passed, I shot him one more time at point-blank range in the chest. We went shuddering onto the frontage road; I twisted around and looked back. Both of the men I'd shot were standing.

They started running for the Challenger.

"Fuck," I said. "Don't these people die?"

When we hit the street, Electra slammed on the brakes in front of the Texaco station and sat up to see where the fuck the on ramp was. She took it doing 60, shooting past the sign that said twenty-five.

I slipped into the passenger's seat, breathing hard. "Give me a fucking cigarette," I said.

"There's a pack in the glove compartment." She was starting to cry. "Light me one, too?"

I punched the dash lighter, found the pack of Marlboros, took out two cigarettes, lit them both. This was becoming a habit. I handed her one of the cigs and she accepted it with a violently shaking hand.

"Breathe slow and deep. Try not to cry."

"I'm still a little fucked up," she said.

"Oh, shit. How fucked up?"

"Okay, more than a little. Really, really fucked up. I figured you'd be driving so I opened another bottle of Jack while you were in the shower."

"Hair of the fucking dog?"

"I'll pull over and you can drive."

"They're following us."

"Oh, God. How do you know? How do you know, can you see them? Are they close?"

"Try not to get hysterical. Just drive fast. I'll call the cops." I took out my cell phone. The LCD screen said "DISCON-NECTED". I tried to dial 911. I got a rapid busy signal.

"Fucking free nationwide long distance my ass," I said. "Do you have a phone?"

She'd stopped crying and was barely weaving at all; she was doing pretty good for a 110-pound girl who'd spent last night slamming four beers and three-quarters of a bottle of Jack, not to mention God knows how many sips this morning.

"Electra. Listen to me. Do you have a cell phone?"

She shook her head. "Someone once told me it tips the cops off that you're a drug dealer."

"You've got to be fucking kidding me."

"It doesn't?"

"No," I said, resisting the urge to add "and I should know."

"I have a two-way pager."

"Give it to me."

"It's in my lunchbox."

"Jesus fucking Christ," I growled, and popped open the Partridge Family lunchbox next to her on the seat. It was stuffed full: a bag of grass, a pack of Zig Zags, a butane lighter, two unmarked prescription bottles, four kinds of lipstick, a black Motorola pager and three clips for the Sig-Sauer .380 that sat glinting and silver in the Mojave August.

"Why didn't you tell me you were loaded?"

"Same reason I didn't tell you I was carrying cocaine. Oh, God,

Cooper, I think I'm going to be sick. I think I'm going to fucking puke."

"Don't puke. Breathe slow and deep. You're *not* going to puke."

"Oh, God, I think I am."

"You're not. Breathe slowly." I punched up Bogan's number on the pager and sent a message, adding 911 to the end of it.

"Oh, God, Cooper."

"Don't puke. You're not going to puke."

"No, no, it's not that. We didn't get gas last night. We're on empty. That sign said 'Last gas, 80 miles.' Oh, God, Cooper, what the fuck are we going to do?"

I looked at her, tearstained and beautiful. She had gotten dolled up for the drive like she was going to spend the evening in a punk club. Skintight see-through mesh black top, crop sleeves, black lace bra plainly evident underneath, belly bared under the shirt's hem. Black skirt with skulls all over, and fishnets visible between the skirt and the top of the logging boots. Hair back in pigtails. Dog collar.

"When I was fifteen I would have died to sleep with you," I said.

I heard a gunshot behind us.

"Looks like I'm about to get the chance," I said, and thumbed the safety off Electra's Sig.

"Fuck, fuck, fuck, they're gaining," she said. "Why are they gaining?"

"440 Magnum. That your boyfriend back there?"

"Cooper, I don't fucking know! What the fuck should I do?"

"Can you pull a bootlegger's turn without rolling it?"

"Maybe, when I'm fucking sober," she said. "Now, no fucking way."

"You've got to. There ain't jack shit up here, there's no way we're going to get to a phone. We have to cut back and get to the motel again."

"Cooper, what if I fucking roll it?"

"Don't. Just turn. Like your fucking life depended on it."

She slammed the brakes, twisted the wheel, shut her eyes and gritted her teeth.

"Oh, God, I'm going to fucking puke," she said as the Cuda

went spinning around and came to a stop pointing straight at the Challenger.

"Floor it!" I shouted, and she did. The guys in the Dodge scrambled to get a shot off as we shot past them. I saw them in the side view doing a haphazard Y turn.

I got out my Beretta as Electra floored it, the car only swaying slightly as the Challenger grew in the side view.

I heard another shot. They were maybe a hundred feet behind us now. I leaned out the window and aimed.

I emptied the Sig, putting a neat row of spiderweb cracks in the windshield. The two ski masks in the front seat didn't even duck. One leaned halfway out the window and propped the muzzle of the AK on the side-view mirror.

I tossed the empty Sig on the front seat, aimed my Beretta.

He aimed too, and I saw puffs of smoke; I stood my ground, the top half of my body screaming with pain as I fought to hold still against the hundred-mile-an-hour wind at my back.

A spray of blood went up from his arm; he screamed and the AK went flying. I kept shooting until I saw the front tyre explode; the Challenger went skidding in a big circle but didn't roll. It screamed to a stop and disappeared in a cloud of dust far behind us.

"Floor it."

"We're almost out of gas," she said, her speech still slurred. "Cooper, what should I fucking do?"

"Just floor it." I loaded the Sig with one of Electra's extra clips.

A mile later the Cuda's gears grabbed, the 329 going suddenly silent. She put it in neutral and we coasted as far as we could, finally coming to a stop in the middle of the highway, its fat mags straddling the double-yellow.

I looked at my cell phone. SERVICE UNAVAILABLE.

"Bring the coke," I said.

Eight o'clock in the morning and it had to be 110 degrees already. We sweated across what felt like an endless plain of hard-packed earth. We reached an outcropping of rocks and I spotted a hollow near the base. Sweat soaked my T-shirt and the strap of the duffel bag bit into my shoulder. Electra sank to her knees, her spandex skirt riding up her thighs, her booted feet splayed at impossible angles. She doubled over and rocked back and forth, gripping her sweat-soaked fishnet crop-top with both fists as she shook violently.

I put down the duffel bag of cocaine and swept her burgundy hair out of the way as she vomited Jack Daniels and beef jerky. Tremors racked her body. Her hair was soaked with sweat. When she was finished, she coughed and spat. I lifted the hem of my shirt and wiped her face. Sweat streamed down my chest.

"I'm sorry, I'm sorry, I'm sorry," she choked. "We're going to be okay, right?"

"Yes," I said. "Absolutely."

"Who are these guys?"

"I'm hoping it's not your boyfriend."

"That's his kind of car all right." Her voice was rough with her abraded throat.

"Maybe he didn't like our little coke party last night. But why would he have someone watching you in the first place?" I already knew the answer, but I wasn't ready to give it up just yet.

"He wouldn't."

"He the jealous type?"

"Cooper, I fuck around on him all the time. He knows and he doesn't care."

"You sure about that?"

"Positive."

"Fuck."

I unzipped the duffel bag and took out my Beretta and Electra's .380. I made sure they both had rounds chambered and handed the .380 to Electra. She looked at it like I'd just handed her an alien artifact.

"Cooper, I've never shot anyone. I've never even shot *at* anyone."

"Hopefully you won't get the chance."

She bent over and puked again. I held her hair back until she finished coughing and spitting.

Then I left her there weeping and picked up the duffel. I cleared away the hollow at the base of the rocks and crammed the duffel in there, then kicked chunks of rock and dirt over it.

I checked my cell phone: SERVICE UNAVAILABLE. Something was wrong: you were supposed to be able to make 911 calls from anywhere in the fucking globe, except maybe the middle of the ocean. Something was really fucked up.

I stood there smelling of her vomit and watching her cry on her knees in the heartless Mojave. "Electra, I'm going to tell you something, and if you pull out that .380 and shoot me, I swear I'll shoot you back."

She looked up at me, her lips slick with smeared lipstick, spittle, and vomit. "What?"

"I'm an undercover cop."

Her eyes were so dull with nausea and fear that she didn't even register what I was telling her for a minute.

"You're a cop?"

"Special task force of the SFPD. My specialty's Antoine Miraud."

"You're a fucking cop and you fucked me?"

"Yeah," I said. "I'm not supposed to do that. Look, things are totally different now. If we get out of this, I promise I will fucking make everything okay."

She took out her gun and waved it weakly in my direction. "You're saying if I get out of this alive I'm going to prison?"

"No, that's exactly what I'm not saying," I told her. "We have to keep moving. They'll fix that tyre fast and be waiting for us back at the motel."

"Can we make it, Cooper? Can we make it out of this alive?"

"If not," I said, "we're taking your boyfriend with us."

We found the motel. We crouched behind a pile of rocks and watched for a few minutes to make sure there was no sign of the black Challenger. There wasn't a single car parked in the parking lot, in fact; as far as I could tell, we'd been the only guests last night. I checked my cell phone one last time. Still not working.

"Wait here," I said. "I'll go in and call the sheriff."

"If they have one."

"Or whatever."

I came around the side of the building, edged up to the office. It was locked.

I rang the bell, my hand on my Beretta shrouded by the front of my puke-soaked T-shirt.

Through the glass door, I could see it all. The scared-looking clerk came out of the back room, wearing a filthy terrycloth bathrobe. He was about sixty and had seen better days, but he hadn't looked that scared last night.

As he went to unlock the door, his eyes locked with mine, and I knew.

I stepped back from the door and looked around for someplace to run. The clerk's terrycloth robe exploded in red and the glass door spidered in six places. One of the masked gunmen came around from behind the counter and started trying to get the door open as I turned to run. I saw the Challenger appear from where it'd been hidden behind the gas station across the street. I heard it laying down rubber as it headed toward me.

I stopped running, turned and shot the guy in the motel office. When the first bullet hit him he tried to get his AK up, but I followed the first with three more and he was down for good. He slumped against the glass door and it finally gave way, the glass peeling open as he fell onto the porch.

The Challenger barrelled across the parking lot. I stepped through the ruined door into the office and picked up the phone, dialled 911.

"Emergency services, can I help you?"

"I have an attempted robbery hostage situation at the motel in Carson," I said. "Two gunmen with automatic weapons."

"Sir, it'll be at least a half-hour before the sheriff can get there from – "

I dropped the phone and got down behind the counter, Beretta resting atop it. The Challenger was parked outside. The two riflemen took positions on either side of the door.

I shouted: "The sheriff's on his way, Bogan."

"You're not as stupid as you look," he shouted back. "When did you figure it out?"

"Just now, you dipshit," I said. "I was fucking kidding last night."

"Yeah, I should have known. But I couldn't take any chances."

"Who's with you, friends of Antoine's?"

"Just a couple of guys from Mission Station," Bogan called back.

"Stevenson and McCambridge," I said.

"You're really *not* as stupid as you look. You could have been in on it too, if you weren't such a boy scout. The three of us have been together since the beginning."

"And then there were two, motherfucker. Your fucking careers are over, whatever happens," I said.

"Oh, I don't think so. Seems I keep forgetting to file those weekly reports. Too bad I'm always so slow with the paperwork."

"You've still got to get me."

"Two of us, one of you," called Bogan. "When we come out, you can only take out one of us, maybe."

"Right, but which one of you shitbirds gets to die?"

"You've been reading too many detective novels."

I caught the movement out of my peripheral vision, through the side window. My heart pounded.

"Now!" I screamed, and I saw a spray of blood as Bogan's head broke into about half a dozen pieces. I took a guess, started shooting through the wall, praying that they didn't build with oak in the desert.

Two bodies went down on top of each other in the pile of shattered glass. One of the AKs chirped a single time.

I vaulted over the counter and put two more bullets in Bogan. I kicked his body over and wrenched the rifle out of his hands. I kicked the other AK out of Stevenson's limp grasp and ran down the stairs and around the motel porch. Electra was down, beneath the edge of the railing. Her face was bloody.

"Am I dead?" she asked as I knelt over her. She had a crease across the side of her head, and the dyed hair was soaked.

"No," I told her. "But your hair just got a shade darker."

"Oh fuck," she said. "Now my nail polish doesn't match."

*   *   *

She was waiting for me when I came out of Howard Street. She'd double-parked the Cuda and was sitting on the hood wearing a black spandex tank-top, a long black leather coat and a red miniskirt with knee-high cherry Doc laceups. She had a zebra-print pillbox hat cocked at a jaunty angle on her head, but I could still see the white bandage underneath. Her hair hadn't quite grown back where they'd had to shave it.

"I've got a bone to pick with you, Cooper. What the fuck is your real name, anyway?"

"Cooper'll do," I said.

"You look pretty good in a suit. I thought you cops were supposed to have crappy taste in clothes."

"What do you want?"

"When your boys put my Cuda back together, they lost my fuzzy dice."

"Sorry," I said. "There wasn't much I could do about that."

"You could have told them where you stashed the coke," she said. "That would have avoided everything, and I'd be in County."

I walked closer and spoke in a growl. "You want to keep your fucking voice down? We *are* in front of a fucking court-house."

She uncrossed her legs, crossed them, smiled at me. I got up on the hood of the Cuda and sat next to her. A Parking Control officer pulled up behind us and honked. I flashed my badge and she pulled around us.

"So what happens to you?"

"I'm on administrative leave," I said. "Pending my resigna-tion."

"Bummer."

"It was my choice. When your partner tries to kill you for six kilos of coke, it's a bit of a shock to the system."

"I bet," she said. "Like finding out the guy you just fucked is a cop."

"Yeah," I said. "A little like that."

"So it was those three cops who set you up?"

"Looks that way. My partner, Bogan, he killed my cell phone

service at the source so I couldn't call in. He even purged all your boyfriend's files."

"That means I'm off the hook?"

"You don't even have a rap sheet for jaywalking," I said. "Bogan planned this perfectly. He covered his tracks like a pro."

"I guess that's one good thing, if you don't mind my saying so."

"You can start wearing white again."

"I look lousy in white," she said. "What are your plans?"

"Visit my family, I guess."

"Nevada?"

"Yes," I said. "That part was true."

Electra looked at me.

"I was thinking of going on a road trip," she said.

"Electra, don't even start."

"Seems I left something in Carson last time I was there. You know the place? About eighty miles out of Needles?"

She smiled and licked her burgundy lips. I saw that she had a new tongue piercing.

"I mean, you're not a cop anymore, right? So what's keeping you?"

I thought about it.

"I get to drive the Cuda."

"Deal."

"And no more guns."

"Wouldn't dream of it."

She got in the passenger's seat, punched Social Distortion into the CD player. I got in and started the car. I could feel the 329's throaty rumble in my breastbone.

"You look cute in navy blue, Cooper, but you'll have to lose the suit," she said.

"Jesus. Can't you wait until we get to the motel."

She smiled. "Only if you insist."

I put her in gear and floored it, laying down rubber for half a block outside the courthouse.

The Romance of the Road

Daniel Kaysen

My mother cried at the news. A lot.

I was hoping for less. I was hoping for glistening eyes with a brave smile. I was hoping for stoically stiff upper lips. I was hoping for some reserve, dammit.

Instead we got howls.

"My baby!" she said, between ululations. "How can you *do* this to me?!" More howls.

Jacob, beside me, stared at his shoes. Sensible fella, Jacob. I felt like staring at his shoes too. But sometimes you have to grasp the bull by the horns.

"Mother, there's always the telephone. I'll call on the road. Lots of times. You'll get bored of hearing my voice."

I was being as calm as I could, but actually I was touched. She didn't normally call me her baby. It was maternal in a way that usually seemed repugnant to her.

"My baby!" she said again.

"Oh, Mother." I went forward to hug her. She took a step back, and put her arms in a position that lent itself to offence and defence. Not a good sign.

"My baby can't call me! She won't even be *talking* for a couple of years!"

Oh. Mother. I'd got the wrong baby. She meant *my* baby. Or our baby, as Jacob called it. The baby that was no more than a blue line on the pregnancy test. Well, when the going gets tough, the tough had better start bringing up things from ancient family history.

"Mother, you said you loved the road when you were my age. You loved the romance of it. You said I was even conceived on a road trip, dammit! You've always told me that."

The howling stopped and she got That Look, the look that Prosecutors and chess Grandmasters and mothers of three-year-olds get when the total and indisputable victory suddenly appears whole and complete before them.

"*Conceived* on the road is romantic, Barbara. Giving birth, on the other hand, is downright . . . uh – " She turned round, looking for my father, who had spent twenty-two years of marriage finishing her summing-up arguments for her when she got stuck.

Father had left her last year for a blonde in Editorial, but Mother kept forgetting, momentarily.

"Irresponsible?" said Jacob, still looking at his shoes.

"Thank you, Jacob. Yes." And then she turned to me as if I hadn't heard their exchange. "Giving birth on the road is downright irresp – "

"Mother, Jacob and me are doing this road trip, whatever you say. Okay? We'll phone you later in the day."

"But the baby! It was going to be the first baby I'd *loved*."

This was a signal to go, if ever there was one. "Keys," I said to Jacob, under my breath. There was a blur at my side and suddenly they appeared in my left hand. Clever hands, my Jacob. Which was most of the reason we were in this and-baby-makes-three pickle in the first place.

"*One* minute please, young lady," said Mother, holding her hand in the air like Canute turning back the tide. She marched back into the house.

"She getting a camera?" Jacob said.

"That or a gun."

We waited. Exactly one minute later she returned, carrying an overnight bag. She locked the front door and marched down the drive towards us.

"What's in the bag?" asked Jacob.

"You better start praying it's baby clothes, as a going away present," I hissed.

But Mother walked straight past to the car, got in the back seat, wound down the window and called happily: "Okay, let's go!"

I tell you, I learned a lot on that road trip. A lot about life, a lot more about family, a deal about love. I learned about faith, hope and depravity, and the greatest of these is – well, we'll get to that bit in a while. But the first thing I learned is that *nothing*, repeat nothing, seems romantic with your mother sat a couple of feet behind you.

You know that scene in *Titanic* when Kate Winslet and Leo diCaprio do it in that car? You can bet your house that Kate's mother was *not* in the back of the car at the time. Or if she was, she was offering pointed advice to her daughter.

Actually, that was the second thing I learned. The first thing I learned is that Jacob is one of nature's crumblers. When Mother stomped into the back seat of our car and smiled that stupid smile I was all for taking a few seconds to think up some tactical response.

Before I met Jacob I dated a lawyer a few times, and he was always quoting pithy little bits of *The Art of War* at me. To be honest, that's why I stopped dating him. That and his idea of kissing as re-enactment of the Normandy beach landings. But I bet *he* would have come up with something clever: "Enemy climb in back of your car, time to consider many benefits of public transport." Something pithy and neat like that. He certainly wouldn't have come up with the line that Jacob came up with, when Mother climbed into the car.

Nowhere, nowhere, in *The Art of War* does it say: "Bar, how bad can it be?"

To which the only possible response was: "Jacob: watch and learn."

Still, the first two hours weren't so bad. Okay, so she didn't like my music that much. Odd, that. And she said I drove too fast, or too slow, or just plain wrong. I've never figured out how you can drive *wrong*, but apparently I was a natural at it. And she wanted us to stop for a newspaper in the first town, because she'd left hers in the house, and a pen in the second town, because the pen I offered her was too pencilly, whatever that meant, for doing the crossword. And in the third town she wanted us to stop for postcards.

"Mother, we haven't actually *gone* anywhere yet. You come to this town once a week for poker, remember? Wait until we actually get somewhere, huh? Which we won't if we have to stop at every place so you can buy whatever's next on your shopping list. A pool table, maybe? A new porch? What about a dog? That'd be cool, wouldn't it. And we could . . ."

Mother moved over so I could see her face properly centred in the rear-view mirror and then she rolled her eyes.

That's the third thing I learned on the trip. There isn't any good answer to rolled eyes. There was no way I was going to fall into the trap of saying: "And don't you roll your eyes at *me*!" It's way too Mr Potato-Head in *Toy Story*.

Jacob murmured that perhaps he should drive and take some of the flak? I murmured to him that if he drove then he'd crumble again and we'd end up back home sooner than you could say Jack Robinson.

"Jack Robinson," said a childish voice from the back seat. And then, conspiratorially: "Never underestimate the hearing of a mother."

Now *there's* a line that should be in *The Art of War*.

"Say," I said, to the world in general, "that looks like a good place for lunch."

It was a diner, a roadside diner, the kind I always liked going to and never did. The kind that were romantic as long as you didn't work there, or have to eat there more than once in your lifetime.

"Over my dead body," said mother.

"That *can* be arranged," I said, with an over-bright smile. Mother kicked the back of my seat.

"Hey! Look, Mother – "

"Bar," said Jacob.

"What!!" I screamed back at him. "Have you got anything constructive to add to this? If you haven't then I suggest that – "

But actually, he did.

"Bar, look, if you want to eat here then maybe that means you're craving the kind of food they serve here. Maybe the baby *needs* something that's missing in your diet."

Clever mind, too, my Jacob. Clever mind.

"Funny you should say that," I said, gaily pulling into the parking lot. "It *does* feel a lot like a craving."

"Hogwash," whispered my mother to herself.

"And never underestimate the hearing of a mother-to-be," I said, in the sing-song voice that had worked as a major irritant on her for the past thirty of my thirty-three years.

"Come on then, let's get this over with," said Mother, opening her door.

Jacob flashed his winning smile at me.

Did you see *Erin Brockovich*? It was all about breasts, basically (like *Titanic* come to think of it. You think thirteen-year-old boys went back so many times to see Kate Winslet's *acting*?). But there was a sub-plot about Julia Roberts playing a gritty working-mom legal-assistant-type person. Well, when Julia takes her family to the diner in the film the waitress is played by, get this, the real Erin Brockovich.

So I studied our waitress in case she showed any signs of incipient multi-million legal victories, but she didn't even quote *The Art of War*. She just quoted the specials.

The baby decided on pie, so I had that. Mother decided she really wasn't hungry, and a few minutes later aired the opinion that perhaps her loss of appetite was down to travel sickness, given she was stuck in back and all. Perhaps after lunch she should sit up front with me?

"Or there's the roof," I said.

"Bar," said Jacob.

I resisted asking him whose side he was on, in case the judgement went against me.

"This is *much* better," said Mother, when we were on our way again. She turned round to Jacob in the back. "And thank you for sharing your meal with me. My appetite returned, just like that."

Imagine.

Jacob told her she was welcome, but I detected the first hint of strain in his voice.

She turned back to face forward again, and out of the corner of my eye I saw her hand move towards the car stereo and change the tape to radio.

"No!" I screeched the car to a halt.

"What?" she said, all injured innocence.

"That's it! I've had it up to here!"

"Ba – " started Jacob in the back.

"And don't 'Bar' me! I'm not a sheep! Rule one: driver always chooses the music. Rule two: I always drive. Rule three: next stop is the bus station and we'll see you off, Mother. We'll phone you later to check you get home safely. We'll phone you once a day, no more, plus two postcards a week. Rule Four: no crying."

But this was proper crying, hurt crying. I felt like a louse, worse than a louse.

"Dammit," I said.

A truck went by. I caught a brief glimpse of tattoos and mirror-shades in the cab. No glimpse of the driver's mother, anywhere.

We sat in silence for a few minutes. I patted Mother in a lousy kind of way, and she cried in a defeated kind of way, and Jacob thought with his clever mind of his.

"I'll drive," he said. "You two sit in back and sort it out between you."

It wasn't a great idea, but it was better than any idea I had, and Mother was too past it to think.

So, Mother and I got in the back, Jacob shifted over to the driver's seat, and pulled back onto the road. He reached into his pocket, pulled out a cassette, and put it in the stereo.

"Rule one," he said, as he waited for it to start. "Driver always chooses the music."

Then the music started.

"Not *country*!" Mother and I said in unison, and then we did double-takes as we realized we agreed on something. I waited for her to change tack and say actually she quite liked *this* country music, just to aggravate me. And she was obviously waiting for me to do the same, because she had that counterattacking posture she gets when she thinks her opponent's going to make a dumb move.

But neither of us said anything.

This was new.

Once I got past the shock of listening to real country music that wasn't about gee how sad it was that some guy's dog had run off with the sheriff, or whatever dumb stuff you normally hear, the music actually kind of grew on me.

It was a woman singing, but she didn't sound like she had outlandishly large hair and breasts. And it wasn't about horses or shacks or boys with girls' names. Oddly enough, there was lots about cars and roads.

"Kinda fitting," said my mother, at the end of side one.

"See?" said Jacob.

"Are you sure this is country?" I said.

"Of course it's country, young lady, you can tell by the pedal steel," said Mother, definitively.

Jacob turned the tape over.

"Mother, how do *you* know about pedal steels?"

"Hush. Later."

The music rolled by in time with the scenery.

I had that heartache and happiness feeling, and smiled to myself.

"What was that?" said my mother, noticing my smile.

"Just, heartache and happiness. I think it's the music, you know?"

"Nope. That's not the music. That's the road," she said. And we all went back to watching the scenery.

We listened to that tape three times right through. No one said much, we all just got into the passing land, and the feeling of forgetting there were ever such things as homes or rushing or time that wasn't on the road.

After the third play of the tape, Jacob didn't turn it over, and we all watched the sunset in silence, drawn together by the spectacle, lost in our thoughts. And when the sun had finally set and the sky had turned from pink to red to blue to black, Jacob pulled over to a motel and stopped the engine.

The motel looked homey and comfortable and ideal rest for those that had travelled long.

"Perfect!" Mother and I said, in unison.

That was scary, to be honest. I mean, this was me *agreeing* with my mother for the second time in a day, but too many miles of music and scenery can soften a girl's edge, so I just smiled at her and opened the door.

"Wow, stars!" I said, looking up.

"Yes, ma'am," said a warm deep voice from the motel porch, "free of charge."

I learned more things that night.

I learned that old habits die very very slowly. We freshened up and had a drink under the stars and talked about nothing much apart from what we'd seen and then went to eat supper.

I think we were all enjoying the new, improved, relaxed atmosphere, complete with absence of fights and bickering. But as soon as I was sat down at the table to eat then boom – I was back in Daughter Mode. Disagreeable Daughter Mode.

See, the thing is most family fights take place at the dinner table, maybe because it's one of the few reliable places that families actually share the same little slice of space-time.

So, like Pavlov's dogs, who learned to ring bells when they salivated, or whatever it is that they learned, I had long been conditioned to regard a table with family around it as a battlefield. And that old thing about getting your retaliation in first definitely applied.

"So, Mother, bus station tomorrow, right?"

"If you think that I'm going to – "

"Mrs Richardson!" said Jacob.

"What!" said my mother, bristling.

"How come you know about pedal steels?"

"Don't interrupt a fight, young man. Charming as you are, my daughter and I need to get one thing – "

"Mrs Richardson!

"What now!"

Jacob opened his mouth to speak before he had any words to say with it. So he faked it.

"It's . . . it's this thing!"

"You're talking gobbledegook," and she turned back to me. But by replying she'd given him enough time to catch up with himself. Quick tongue, my Jacob. Which is precisely *none* of your business, by the way.

"Listen, Mrs Richardson, the thing is I'm really sorry your husband left you. He made a big mistake doing that, because you're a clever and . . . and determined and strong woman and you're going to find a fine man for your second husband. I bet there'll be dancing and everything."

Silence reigned, I can tell you. No one had ever mentioned mother's newly single status. No one had mentioned Father leaving her, even though it was the cause of all her pain and cussedness and fear of separation from me.

I'd never seen my Jacob as a gambling man, but this was something else I learned. When the chips were down, he wasn't afraid to slide them all into the middle of the big green baize.

It sure was a gamble. Like putting your life savings on a single number in roulette. If it worked, we were all going to live happily ever after – or at least get through the meal without armed combat. And if it didn't work, as my free-falling heart told me it couldn't possibly, then we were all going to be looking a special kind of misery right in the face for the rest of our born days.

Mother's eyes widened. Then closed. Her breathing stopped, and for a second I thought she'd passed away. And wouldn't *that* be a fine and dandy story to tell the baby one day. And the homicide judge, too.

But before I could call for an ambulance she breathed again, in fact she took the biggest, deepest breath I ever saw a person take, before or since. And then she exhaled and opened her eyes.

"You're right in your assessment, Jacob," she said, looking at him with a calm I'd never seen. "In all but *one* factor."

It was our turn to hold our breaths, but she was playing her audience like she was top-billed and we were Las Vegas. I caved.

"What?" I said. I was terrified she was going to say she had cancer or something, and that she wouldn't last the year.

"My next husband will be my third husband, dear. Not my second," she said. "I wonder, shall we have some more wine?"

"What!" I said. "What!" I didn't have a clue what she was talking about, but it was making me dizzy.

"Wine," she said, simply. "You know, comes from grapes."

"Not the wine, the *husband*," I said. Forget Vegas, I was a two-year-old wanting to know the whole story, and *now*.

"Oh him," she said. And she sniffed, like Marcel Proust sniffing that stupid biscuit or whatever it was. "After the meal, perhaps."

"Per*haps*!?" I practically screamed.

"After the meal, I *promise*, then. Under the stars. Some stories should only be told under the stars."

"That's the truth," came a deep warm voice from the bar. "That's the truth."

So we talked of idle things. Jacob talked about his childhood, and Mother talked about her poker nights and I talked about how unbearable suspense could be and how I really thought it would be best for the baby if its grandmother spilled the beans, like, this instant. But Jacob and my mother carried on the idle chit-chat like old pros.

I wolfed my food and slammed down my cutlery. "Right, it's after the meal, now talk!"

I heard a *tsk* come from the bar.

Jacob reached over and held my hand.

Gee, that was a first. The way he acted when my mother was around, you would think we were both those boy-in-the-bubble people to whom human contact was fatal.

I looked at my hand in his, and squeezed it experimentally, to see if it fell off or something. He squeezed it back.

Sheesh. More uncharted territory.

"I feel like that guy in the boat, who discovered that new place. I feel like . . ." I stalled.

No one jumped in to help.

"Who?" said Jacob.

"Armstrong," I said. "I changed my mind, I feel like Neil Armstrong."

"I know a joke about Neil Armstrong," said my mother. "See, he had these neighbours growing up and the husband always wanted a – "

"Heard it!" said Jacob, brightly. "Very funny! Ha ha *ha*!"

"What is it?" I said. Jacob was acting way too enthusiastic.

"I'll tell you later," he said. "Ha ha *ha*!"

Mother looked at her empty wine glass. "I think I must be a little bit drunk," she said. "Let's have coffee outside, under the stars."

We sat watching the empty road, with our coffees and the stars and the occasional lonesome vehicle travelling on to a place in our future, which we'd get to when we got there. I don't think I ever felt such peace. Jacob came and sat next to me, real close. I felt warm and loved and like anything was possible, like anything was a good idea.

If I hadn't been pregnant, I'd have wanted to get a baby started right that night.

"That's exactly how I felt," said my mother, reading my mind. "That's how you came to get conceived. The road will get you every time. Makes you feel like doing all kinds of crazy things."

"Yeah, but – but with *who*?"

"Oh, anyone with a lazy smile and a smooth kind of walk and trousers that fit nice and – " Then she caught herself and apologized.

"I'm having trouble seeing Dad in that picture," I said quickly. "Are you saying that he isn't my real father?"

"No, he was your father all right. Oh yes," she said. And she looked sort of dreamy.

I looked away. I guess I hope my baby looks away too, when I get dreamy looks about nights with Jacob in three decades time.

"He was such a nice change from husband number one, who was called Donald, by the way. He, Donald, said he was going places, and he'd take me too. My parents saw him for the liar he was, and married me off to him quick, knowing that he wasn't going anywhere, ever. His idea of adventure was a night with his bank book.

"And the thing was, he hated cars. I had to fight tooth and nail to learn to drive, and when I passed my test he wouldn't buy a car, even though we had money enough, thanks to his habit of not spending anything, ever. His idea of a holiday was – well, actually, he had no idea of a holiday. He worked seven days a week, every week, with a half day at Christmas. He couldn't understand why I wanted a job, either. His job was his whole life, but he didn't want me to have any life, so he didn't want me having a job. But I'd have gone nuts – I was going nuts so I got a job in the department store."

She tailed off into silence, back in some dusty prison of wedded hell.

"So what happened, Mrs Richardson?"

"Well, there was a nice boy, Joe Richardson, worked across the road, and we smiled at each other whenever we saw each other, and then one Friday clear out of the blue he asked me if I wanted to go for a drive that Saturday. And we went for a drive that Saturday. We stopped for lunch at a diner and then we lost track of time, and there was this motel and, well, we sat under the stars and watched the road and drank wine and then yadda-yadda-yadda." I'd never heard it described like that before, but I got the gist.

"In the morning I told him I was married, and he excused himelf. I thought he was gone to the restroom but after ten or so minutes I got suspicious. His car had gone. He'd left me! I caught up with him of course, and he did the right thing and married me after my divorce, but twenty-two years later he pulled the exact same trick and left me again. I know you don't take in a word I ever say, but men never change, Barbara, remember that."

But I wasn't taking in a word she was saying. I was trying to get my head around the first husband, who didn't exist until now, for me.

"You know what I feel like?" I asked Jacob, in bed that night.

"Mmmmm," he said, snuggling very close. "Me too."

"Really?"

"Can't you tell?" he started doing something clever with his hands.

"I don't know. How do you tell if a man wants to get married?"

Jacob froze. Not a muscle moved.

"But you hate the idea of getting married," he said. "You said it's just a bit of paper and it's like manacles and it's hypocritical and it never lasts *and* it's eternal hell." He said it all a bit sadly.

"I'm sure I never said all of that. There's contradictions for a start. I could drive a truck through some of those contradictions."

Jacob jumped in. "And your mother wouldn't like it, you said. For a start, you'd have to invite your father to the wedding and you know how she feels about him."

"There's ways round that," I said.

"Like what? You're going to hire the mob to wipe him out?"

"Um, there must be better ideas than that."

We talked and argued for hours until we finally sort of agreed a plan. It wasn't a great plan, as it involved going home again, but we were both too tired to come up with a better one.

Thanks to the length of the discussion the night before we managed to oversleep in the morning. By the time we got down to breakfast Mother was dressed and scrubbed and on her second cup of coffee with a man halfway between her age and mine.

She introduced him as Al, and he smiled a lazy smile and we all shook hands, and she lightly commented on whether we'd had a nice night given the lateness of our appearance this morning and I blushed deep red to my roots.

Great. And Jacob and I hadn't even fooled around.

But, as I slowly worked out, someone in my family had had a good night, even if it hadn't been sleep-filled. And Al had had a good night too. He and my mother had matching twinkles in their eyes.

"We've got something to tell you!" I said quickly, before I thought too deeply about matching twinkles.

"So have we!" said my mother.

Oh, lord.

"What's yours?" asked my mother, not really listening.

"Well, the thing is we're ending our trip and going back home because we're going to start planning our . . . our wedd – "

"Oh Barbara, that's wonderful."

"You haven't even heard what's wonderful yet!"

"No, but it's wonderful that you're going back. See, I'm going to drive with Al, down the road a bit, and I didn't want to disappoint you by not being able to come with you two on your road trip. And now you've cancelled it, so I don't have to feel guilty about disappointing you. Isn't life grand!"

Al and she squeezed hands. No boy-in-the-bubble troubles *there*, then.

"But, listen, Jacob and I are going to get – "

"Al and I met outside, after you two went to bed. He likes crosswords too, isn't that amazing!"

"I sure do," said Al, with a lazy smile again, and a deep warm voice I recognized from the night before.

I couldn't see his trousers, but I bet they fit to perfection.

Jacob and I drove back home the next day and started planning the wedding. During the following week we didn't hear anything from Mother apart from a giggly call from two states away, and a scrawled postcard with *wish you were here* written insincerely as a ps.

My powers of imagination were badly strained when it came to telling my father where she was. I felt guilty, too, like she was my younger sister and I'd lost her.

"That's an interesting response," said Jacob.

"Oh shut up," I said. "Look, I'm not sure I want to get married after all."

His face fell a little.

"It's just – "

"Listen, Bar, do you want to go for a drive?"

"Jacob, look. You know what's going to happen. We're going to go on the road, I'm going to be overcome by the romance of it and want to marry you again, and then when we come back the romance will disappear again and I won't want to marry you, and then we'll go for a drive again. It's going to be like yo-yo dieting, except we'll spend more on gas."

"There's a way round that," he said.

"What?"

He told me.

Oh.

I asked him where on earth *that* idea came from.

"Well, Bar, you said there were holes in your arguments against marriage that you could drive a truck through. So, I suddenly thought, well, why don't we drive *actual* trucks? That way we'd be on the road most of the time. We could be like a driving team and – "

"And the baby?"

"The baby better like country music. Besides, this way we'll see more of your mother, what with her being on the road too."

"Are you sure that's a good thing?"

"Yes, Bar. After all, we never did find out about her and pedal steels.

We haven't, yet, caught up with my mother. I'm seven months pregnant now, and Jacob and I are two months married. We had a mechanic and a waitress as witnesses. A hitch-hiker gave me away. It was very romantic.

Neither of my parents could make the ceremony. That sure simplified things. But we've agreed we're going to meet up with Mother and Al in a few weeks, a few thousand miles down the road, to do the baby thing.

That's going to be weird. Meeting Mother and Al. Dodging the twinkles in their eyes. Giving birth.

Jacob and I being in the same place for more than a night is going to be weirdest, but I figure as long as the next journey's onward rather than backward, the romance won't run out till the roads do.

I bought a map.

You know what? The best thing I learned is there's enough roads to last a girl forever.

Cooper's Creek

Mike Lewis

The road stretched ahead in a long gleaming ribbon. Jerry glanced in the mirror. The same ribbon unwound behind him. He sighed and fiddled with the radio.

"Hey, I was listening to that!" Sue said, her high-pitched voice cutting through the static.

"And I wasn't," Jerry said. Sue's whining was starting to annoy him. He looked across at her. She sat with her arms folded and her face set in an ugly pout. She had been fun when they had been together in the Basin; they seemed to share the same outlook on life. After two days alone in this car, after two days without the buzz and noise of the Basin, he wasn't so sure.

The radio picked up another station and a familiar song filled the car.

"Hey, we sure showed that guy, didn't we, Jerry?" Sue said. She looked across at him. Jerry was forced to smile.

"We sure did," he said and let the beat pound in him as Sue sang along quietly.

"Whatever the road ahead,
That's where we're going
Whatever the life ahead
That's the seed we're sowing . . ."

"I'm thirsty," Sue said, breaking Jerry's concentration. He had been thinking about the Basin and his father's store. They were passing a faded sign, on which Jerry could just make out the words "Cooper's Creek". Sue pointed to a dusty-looking shop with a spinning OPEN/COKE sign and shouted something above the noise of the stereo. Jerry nodded and turned off the highway, the car's motor whining as it adjusted to the rough ground of the store parking lot. He stopped in front of the large store window and cut the power. The car settled with a last gentle gasp onto its parking shocks.

Sue turned off the stereo. The sudden silence was like a blow and Jerry felt disorientated. Other sounds drifted back in. He could hear the wind along the highway whipping up the tumbleweeds, the grains of sand hitting the polished sides of the car, the click-click of the cooling engine. He was suddenly aware of the swish of Sue's lipstick across her mouth as she redid her makeup. Then the moment of quietness collapsed.

"Wanna eat?" asked Sue. She threw her makeup bag on the back seat, then opened the car door and stepped out into the parking lot. She stood for a moment, wriggling to get the creases out of her dress and down over her hips. Jerry admired the wriggles and pushed open his own door. He slipped his shades on.

"Sure," he said, "sure." He slammed the car door shut and locked it with the dead guy's print. He slipped the severed finger back in his pocket.

The store was old, the letters spelling out Cooper's Creek just visible above the door. The window had faded yellow plastic across it and posters for long-gone concerts and garage sales. Jerry hadn't realized that there were still places like this around.

The door creaked as Jerry pushed it open, a bell jangling faintly above his head. The inside of the store matched the outside. A row of sparsely populated shelves at one end of the shop contained tins and packets of food, heaped in a seemingly random fashion. A long, high counter, lined with bar stools, ran across the back of the room. Bottles, with peeling labels, stood on the shelves behind the counter, either side of double doors. A faint glimmer of light came from the doorway.

Jerry went to the counter and pulled one of the stools away. He sat up on it. The seat swivelled and he spun himself round to look at the rest of the store. Sue was looking at shelves. She reached up and pulled a packet down, then squealed with disgust as the packet split and the bright yellow contents cascaded across the floor and her feet – an exclamation of colour against the dust and grime of the floorboards.

"Christ!" she squealed and dropped the packet on the floor. She kicked it out of the way and then joined Jerry at the counter. "This place is like a museum," she complained.

"I wouldn't say museum, maybe just a little old-fashioned for you folks from the Basin." The voice came from behind them and Jerry spun round to face the speaker. He was an old man with grey hair and a lined face. Jerry stared at him for a long moment, fascinated by the wrinkles and marks that showed the man's age. Didn't they have treatments out here? Jerry found himself subconsciously stroking his own face, feeling the firm unlined flesh. He knew he would have as many treatments as he needed when the time came, once they got away.

"How did you know we was from the Basin?" Sue asked. Jerry felt her move to stand next to him. She seemed unsettled by the old guy. Jerry thought he looked harmless, the sort of guy that wouldn't cause any trouble.

"Most folks that pass through here are from the Basin," the old man said. "Not many people going in the other direction these days."

Jerry looked around the store again, taking in the dusty shelves and the old-fashioned stock. He looked back at the old man.

"You get many people in here then?" he said, not bothering to keep the sarcasm out of his voice. "Bet it's a regular stop-off point."

Sue laughed.

The old man smiled and started to wipe down the counter with a large stained rag.

"You would be surprised at who we see in here. The lost, the strayed. People running away from things – even a few folks running towards things. A real mixture," he said. "I've seen lots of folks like you – don't know where you're going, don't really care – "

"We're going east," Sue snapped, her nasal whine cutting across the old man's long, slow drawl.

"Yeah, east," Jerry said. The old man was making him feel uncomfortable. What business of his was it where they were going? "We gotta travel. We need to eat."

"East is good," the old man said, smiling. He suddenly became more serious and rubbed his hands on the cloth he had been using to clean the counter. "What can I get you folks?"

Jerry looked at Sue and waved her onto a stool. They both leant on the counter.

"Well," he said slowly. "Can you do breakfast? Coffee?"

The old man smiled and nodded. "Sure, I'm told we do the best eggs in the county. Two breakfasts coming right up." He went through the swing doors at the back of the counter. Jerry caught a glimpse of black shining metal and then the doors swung shut. The old man had better be quick.

Jerry laughed to himself – breakfast and coffee! It would be rehashed proteins and that thick sludge you got in every diner in the Basin. At the thought, his stomach rumbled – even rehashed protein sounded good after ten hours on the road.

"What's up with that guy?" Sue asked, dragging Jerry's thoughts away from the imminent food.

"What do you mean?" Jerry said. He glanced around the store again, his gaze lingering this time, examining all the details. Sue was right – this place was like a museum. He ran his hand along the counter. He could swear that this was real aluminium, not some cheap plastic imitation.

"Well, acting like this was some great place and that we weren't the first people he'd seen for a year!"

Jerry sighed. There was Sue doing people down again. Why couldn't she just accept people as they were – she always measured everyone against herself. Jerry was happy to treat people as they wanted to be treated – unless that meant not getting what he wanted. But that went without saying – look after number one his

dad had told him, just before he died. Jerry had taken that advice
to heart.

"The old man seems harmless enough," Jerry said.

"Harmless?" Sue laughed. "Of course he's harmless – what's he
going to do to us? We got half the Basin looking for us – no old
man is going to give us trouble." She slipped off her stool and
walked to the front of the store. She returned with a magazine
which she spread over the counter.

"I haven't seen one of these things since I was a little girl!" she
said with delight. "He's got a whole rack."

Jerry flipped over the pages to show the front cover.

"Hey – I was looking at that!" Sue said, snatching the magazine
back.

Jerry shook his head; the magazine was dated forty years ago but
seemed like new – just how old was the stock in this place? His dad
had carried magazines like this when Jerry was a kid. You never
saw them nowadays.

The doors to the kitchen banged open and the old man backed
out, holding a tray. A delicious smell of bacon and eggs followed
him and Jerry sniffed appreciatively. The old man put two cups
down in front of them and a big jug of coffee. He poured a measure
into each cup and pushed the mugs over to Jerry and Sue.

"Drink it while it's hot; the breakfast will be a few minutes." He
picked up the tray and disappeared through the kitchen door.

Jerry picked up the cup of coffee and held it under his nose –
taking in the smell. He sipped it gingerly. It was coffee, real coffee.
He gulped down a mouthful of the hot liquid. He gasped as it
burnt his mouth and the hot liquid flowed down to his stomach.
But it tasted terrific. Coffee this good was worth stopping for.

Sue looked at him and, when he nodded, she picked up her mug
and sipped it.

"It's real good," she said.

"Do you know how much a cup of this would cost in the Basin?"
Jerry said, his mouth now cool enough to speak.

Sue didn't reply, she was lost in the magazine in front of her,
turning each page slowly and alternating the page-turning with
sips of coffee.

Jerry picked up his cup and slid off the stool. He wandered through the store, looking at the packets of beans, instant potato, soap powder and other things he couldn't identify. A lot of the stock seemed as old as the magazine. None of it was the usual rehashed protein that covered the shelves of his local mart.

As Sue had said, the front of the store had a long rack of magazines. He picked up a couple and thumbed through the glossy white pages. Headlines and photographs of people he had never heard of flashed past his eyes. He dropped them on the floor in disgust.

A garish cover caught his eye and he picked up the magazine. It had a picture of a flying saucer on the cover and a girl in a chromium bra. He started to flick through it. It brought back memories of days spent lying behind the counter of his dad's store, reading the latest issues of similar mags. Occasionally he'd be called upon to help serve a customer, but mostly he spent that time lost in the worlds outside the Basin and the four walls of the pokey little corner store. That had been before the robbery. He hadn't read much afterwards.

Movement at the back of the store caught his eye and he looked up. Breakfast had arrived.

Jerry took his place at the counter as the old man was serving up two large plates of breakfast. The plates had eggs, bacon, hash browns, tomatoes (fresh red ones – not the mushy green types you usually saw in the Basin) and thick slices of white bread. Jerry's mouth watered just looking at it.

"This is great," Sue said through a mouthful.

"Good. Tuck in," the old man said to Jerry who was still sitting, looking at the plate – taking in the picture of the most perfect breakfast he had ever seen.

Jerry didn't need a second prompting and shovelled the food into his mouth. Sue was right, it was great : the bacon was crispy and shattered in your mouth; the eggs were just the right side of runny; the bread was crusty but warm and soft on the inside. And the hash browns were crisp on the outside but soft and creamy in the middle.

Both of them ate without talking and wiped the plates clean with the remains of the bread. Jerry sat back, belched and then took a large slurp of coffee.

"That was amazing," he said. "Where did you get all that stuff?" he asked the old man, who was now standing behind the counter, flicking through the magazine Jerry had been looking at.

The old man looked up and smiled. "Oh, just from folks around here," he said. "Most folks help each other out in Cooper's Creek."

"Jerry – we'd better get going." Sue was looking at her watch – the big, chunky man's watch she'd stripped off the car's former owner. "They're bound to be looking."

"Yeah, guess you're right." Lulled by the breakfast and the coffee and the general relaxed atmosphere, Jerry had almost forgotten they were on the run. They'd have a good head start on the Basin cops, until they found the dead guy, but the highway would be tagging their progress. Jerry hadn't been able to disable the car's identity – there hadn't been enough time in the escape. There was never enough time.

"There's plenty of time yet," the old man said, cutting into Jerry's thoughts. "I'm sure you folks could wait a while longer."

"No, we've gotta go," Sue said, pulling her bag out from under the counter. "We'd better take some supplies with us, Jerry."

"Yeah." Jerry laughed. "Shame we can't take you and your breakfast along."

The old man smiled and then rang up a sale on the old cash register at one end of the counter.

He pulled out a slip of paper, scribbled on it and passed it across to Jerry.

"What's this?" Jerry asked. He crumpled the paper in his fist and then dropped it on floor. "We don't pay bills." He walked round the counter and stood next to the old man. He was annoyed that this old guy had just ruined a perfect moment. Sue watched him, her eyes shining and tongue between her lips. She fumbled in her bag.

"Read the bill," the old man said. He stepped back from Jerry. "Everyone has to pay something, Jerry. In the end, everyone has to pay back what they've taken. But, take your time." He reached beneath the counter.

What did he mean – pay back? Jerry hated it when people tried to tell him what to do – everyone since the robbery had been telling him things. Relatives, social workers, police. None of them had helped.

"It's okay, Jerry, I'll handle him," Sue said from behind Jerry and he turned to see her point a pistol in their direction. That stupid old antique he had let her keep from the fat guy's apartment.

"Sue, no!" He jumped out of the way and heard the crack of a shot and saw the old man spin behind the counter.

"He was reaching for something, Jerry, I swear," Sue said. The pistol hung in her shaking hand and she dropped it. It clattered on the floor and slid under the counter.

Jerry walked around the end of the counter and reached beneath it. His hand closed on a cool, metal object. He pulled it out and slammed it down on the counter. "It's a tray, you stupid bitch!" he shouted. "A fucking tray – that's all!"

He knelt next to the old guy. A dark pool was slowly spreading across the dusty floorboards beneath the man's chest. The old man was out cold, but Jerry could see that he was still breathing.

"Let's go, Jerry, someone might have heard the shot!" Sue was also behind the counter now, stepping over the old man like he was just a piece of furniture. She scooped some food and bottles into a bag and then slung it over her shoulder.

Jerry lifted the old man into an upright position and pressed on the wound. The blood oozed, hot and thick, past his fingers. It was slowing now and Jerry pressed harder.

That had been the first thing he saw after the robbery – the man knelt over his father. The pool of blood across the grey floor – Jerry had been surprised at how bright it was – spread out from his father's body. The crowd of strangers standing in hushed silence around the aisles of the store. The wail of sirens as the police arrived too late. All those things had stuck with him and came rushing back now.

"Jerry!" Sue said again. She looked down at him and waved in the direction of the door. Jerry lowered the guy back to the ground. He was still breathing in slow, shallow gasps. Jerry stood and wiped his hands on his trousers. The blood left dark finger marks on the yellow fabric.

"I've got to stay," he said.

"What?"

"I've got to stay – I can't leave him like this."

"Jerry!" Sue screamed at him again. "What about us? What about the money?" That ugly, shrill cry that he hated so much. He fumbled in a pocket and threw the finger across to her. It dropped on the floor between them, the vital print at one end and the white of the bone protruding from the other.

"Take that – you'll need it," he said. "I'll catch you up somehow. The cops won't stop here."

Sue bent and picked up the finger. "Jerry," she pleaded. He shook his head. She turned and left the store. The screen door bounced behind her and Jerry heard the car start up and the whine of the hover motors as it drifted across the uneven gravel and onto the tarmac. Then there was silence. Jerry shrugged. She didn't matter now.

There was a phone behind the counter – the old-fashioned type without a screen. Jerry lifted the handset, but there was no dial tone. Just silence. He dropped the phone back on the hook and looked down at the old man.

He was still out cold, though the bleeding seemed to have stopped. Jerry picked him up and carried him through the double doors behind the counter. He stopped inside the doors and let out a low whistle of surprise. The room was a kitchen, but not the grubby, tired old kitchen he had envisaged. The walls were lined with modern metallic appliances, some of them unfamiliar.

Jerry noticed the stairs to the left and carried the old man over to them. Shifting the man's weight, he staggered one step at a time up the creaking stairs and onto a landing. He had a choice of three doors. He picked the nearest one and pushed it open with his foot. Once inside, he thankfully lay the man down on the small bed that occupied most of the room. Dust rose in a cloud from the bedspread and Jerry sneezed loudly. The old man stirred slightly and mumbled something. Jerry put his head close to the man's lips.

"Water," the old man said.

Jerry looked round the room but there was nothing but a dust-covered dressing table and chair. He went back onto the landing and pushed open another door. This was another small bedroom – almost an exact mirror copy of the room he had just left. This room was a little neater and though there was dust on the surfaces the bed looked clean.

A bathroom lay behind the third door and Jerry filled a glass at the sink. He returned to the old man and held his head as he sipped. The old man lay back with a sigh.

"I was like you," he whispered, his words so faint that Jerry had to strain to hear them. "Looking for something. I found it too." He lay silent for a moment.

"Found what?" Jerry asked quietly.

"This," the old man said. "This place or it found me – I was never quite sure."

"This place?" Jerry said. The old man was clearly rambling now.

"Yes. Cooper's Creek. It found me and now, it's found you."

"It hasn't found me!" Jerry said scornfully.

"So why are you still here?"

"I'll be gone in the morning, catch up with Sue just as soon as I know you're okay. My dad ran a store once you know?" Jerry said.

"I know," the old man whispered back and then was silent. Jerry could hear the slow rasp of his breath – he was asleep.

Jerry put the glass down by the bed and then went back downstairs. He found a packet of biscuits and a picture magazine in the store. He lay on the old man's bed flicking through the magazine. Eventually he fell asleep.

The old man died in the night. Jerry went to check on him and found him cold. His face had settled into a peaceful smile.

Jerry buried him in the yard behind the shop. It was a small, dirt area with a single tree in the middle. Jerry dug a shallow grave beneath the tree. As he returned to the shop after filling in the hole, he noticed a pile of boxes by the back door.

There were eggs, bacon, tomatoes, coffee and an assortment of biscuits. There was no note. Jerry smiled as he remembered the old man's words.

After cooking breakfast, he looked through the old man's cupboards upstairs and found a uniform, with a pair of red trousers, checked shirt, apron and small white hat. Jerry looked at the clean cloth and at the fading yellow grime of his own clothing. He took off his clothes and put on the uniform.

Back downstairs, he wandered around the store for a while, straightening the stock and then cleaned up the counter – wiping off the bloodstain on the wall. He swept the floor and bent to pick up a crumpled piece of paper as he did so.

He stood behind the counter and smoothed the paper out. It was the bill he had dropped earlier. Written across it in a thick scrawl of pencil were the words – *Whatever you can afford.*

Jerry smiled and put the paper in his pocket. He straightened his hat and wiped the counter down again. Already, he felt at home.

The Mountain

Michael Moorcock

The last two men alive came out of the Lapp tent they had just raided for provisions.

"She's been here before us," said Nilsson. "It looks like she got the best of what there was."

Hallner shrugged. He had eaten so little for so long that food no longer held any great importance for him.

He looked about him. Lapp *kata* wigwams of wood and hides were spread around the immediate area of dry ground. Valuable skins had been left out to cure, reindeer horns to bleach, the doors unfastened so that anyone might enter the deserted homes.

Hallner rather regretted the passing of the Lapps. They had had no part in the catastrophe, no interest in wars or violence or competition. Yet they had been herded to the shelters with everyone else. And, like everyone else, they had perished either by direct bombing, radiation poisoning or asphyxiation.

He and Nilsson had been in a forgotten meteorological station close to the Norwegian border. When they finally repaired their radio, the worst was over. Fallout had by this time finished off the tribesmen in Indonesian jungles, the workers in remote districts of China, the hillbillies in the Rockies, the crofters in Scotland. Only freak weather conditions, which had been part of their reason for visiting the station earlier in the year, had so far prevented the lethal rain from falling in this area of Swedish Lappland.

They had known themselves, perhaps instinctively, to be the last two human beings alive, until Nilsson found the girl's tracks coming from the south and heading north. Who she was, how she'd escaped, they couldn't guess, but they had changed their direction from north-east to north and begun to follow. Two days later they had found the Lapp camp.

Now they stared ahead of them at the range of ancient mountains. It was three a.m., but the sun still hung a bloody spread on the horizon for it was summer – the six-week summer of the Arctic when the sun never fully set, when the snows of the mountains melted and ran down to form the rivers, lakes and marshes of the lowlands where only the occasional Lapp camp, or the muddy scar of a broad reindeer path, told of the presence of the few men who lived here during the winter months.

Suddenly, as he looked away from the range, the camp aroused some emotion akin to pity in Hallner's mind. He remembered the despair of the dying man who had told them, on his radio, what had happened to the world.

Nilsson had entered another hut and came out shaking a packet of raisins. "Just what we need," he said.

"Good," said Hallner, and he sighed inaudibly. The clean, orderly nature of the little primitive village was spoiled for him by the sight he had witnessed earlier at the stream which ran through the camp. There had been simple drinking cups of clay or bone side by side with an aluminium dish and an empty Chase and Sanborne coffee jar, a cheap plastic plate and a broken toy car.

"Shall we go?" Nilsson said, and began to make his way out of the camp.

Not without a certain trepidation, Hallner followed behind his friend who marched towards the mountains without looking back or even from side to side.

Nilsson had a goal and, rather than sit down, brood and die when the inescapable finally happened, Hallner was prepared to go along with him on this quest for the girl.

And, he admitted, there was a faint chance that if the winds continued to favour them, they might have a chance of life. In which case there was a logical reason for Nilsson's obsessional tracking of the woman.

His friend was impatient of his wish to walk slowly and savour the atmosphere of the country which seemed so detached and removed, uninvolved with him, disdainful. That there were things which had no emotional relationship with him, had given him a slight surprise at first, and even now he walked the marshy ground with a feeling of abusing privacy, of destroying the sanctity of a place where there was so little hint of humanity; where men had been rare and had not been numerous or frequent enough visitors to have left the aura of their passing behind them.

So it was with a certain shock that he later observed the print of small rubber soles on the flat mud near a river.

"She's still ahead of us," said Nilsson, pleased at this sign, "and not so very far ahead. Little more than a day. We're catching up."

Suddenly, he realized that he was displeased by the presence of the bootprints, almost resentful of Nilsson's recognition of their being there when, alone, he might have ignored them. He reflected that Nilsson's complete acceptance of the sex of the boots' wearer was entirely founded on his own wishes.

The river poured down towards the flat lake on their left, clear, bright melted snow from the mountains. Brown sun-dried rocks stood out of it, irregularly spaced, irregularly contoured, affording them a means of crossing the swift waters.

There were many such rivers, running down the slopes of the foothills like silver veins to fill the lakes and spread them further over the marshland. There were hills on the plateau where trees crowded together, fir and silver birch, like survivors of a flood jostling for a place on the high ground. There were ridges which sometimes hid sight of the tall mountains in front of them, green with grass and reeds, studded with gorse.

He had never been so far into mountain country before and this range was one of the oldest in the world; there were no sharp peaks as in the Alps. These were worn and solid and they had lived through aeons of change and metamorphosis to have earned their right to solitude, to permanency.

Snow still spattered their sides like galaxies against the grey-green moss and rock. Snow-fields softened their lines.

Nilsson was already crossing the river, jumping nimbly from rock to rock, his film-star's profile sometimes silhouetted against the clear, sharp sky, the pack on his back like Christian's load in *The Pilgrim's Progress*. Hallner smiled to himself. Only indirectly was Nilsson heading for salvation.

Now he followed.

He balanced himself in his flat, leather-soled boots and sprang from the first rock to the second, righted his balance again and sprang to the next. The river boiled around the rocks, rushing towards the lake, to lose itself in the larger waters. He jumped again, slipped and was up to his knees in the ice-cold torrent. He raised his small knapsack over his head and, careless now, did not bother to clamber back to the rocks, but pushed on, waist-deep, through the freezing river. He came gasping to the bank and was helped to dry land by Nilsson who shook his head and laughed.

"You're hopeless!"

"It's all right," he said, "the sun will dry me out soon."

But both had walked a considerable distance and both were tiring. The sun had now risen, round and hazy red in the pale, cold sky, but it was still difficult to gauge the passage of the hours. This, also, added to the detached air of timelessness which the mountains and the plateaux possessed. There was no night – only a slight alteration in the quality of the day. And although the heat was ninety degrees Fahrenheit, the sky still looked cold, for it took more than the brief six weeks of summer to change the character of this wintry Jotunheim.

He thought of Jotunheim, the Land of Giants, and understood the better the myths of his ancestors with their accent on man's impermanency – the mortality of their very gods, their bleak worship of the forces of nature. Only here could he appreciate that the life-span of the world itself might be infinite, but the life-span of its denizens was necessarily subject to inevitable metamorphosis and eventual death. And, as he thought, his impression of the country changed so that instead of the feeling of invading sanctified ground, he felt as if a privilege had been granted him and he had been allowed, for a few moments of his short life, to experience eternity.

The mountains themselves might crumble in time, the planet cease to exist, but that it would be reincarnated he was certain. And this gave him humility and hope for his own life and, for the first time, he began to think that he might have a purpose in continuing to live, after all.

He did not dwell on the idea, since there was no need to.

They came with relief to a dry place where they lighted a fire and cooked the last of their bacon in their strong metal frying pan. They ate their food and cleaned the pan with ashes from the fire, and he took it down to the nearest river and rinsed it, stooping to drink a little, not too much, since he had learned from his mistake earlier, for the water could be like a drug so that one craved to drink more and more until exhausted.

He realized, vaguely, that they had to keep as fit as possible. For one of them to come to harm could mean danger for them both. But the thought meant little. There was no sense of danger here.

He slept and, before he fell into a deep, dreamless sleep, he had a peculiar impression of being at once vast and tiny. His eyes closed, his body relaxed, he felt so big that the atoms of his body, in relation to the universe, hardly had existence, that the universe had become an unobservable electron, present but unseen. And yet, intratemporally, he had the impression that he was as small as an electron so that he existed in a gulf, a vacuum containing no matter whatsoever.

A mystic, perhaps, would have taken this for some holy experience, but he could do no more than accept it, feeling no need to interpret it. Then he slept.

Next morning, Nilsson showed him a map he had found in the village.

"That's where she's going," he said, pointing at a mountain in the distance. "It's the highest in this section and the second highest in the entire range. Wonder why she'd want to climb a mountain?"

Hallner shook his head.

Nilsson frowned. "You're in a funny mood. Think you won't

have a chance with the girl?" When Hallner didn't answer, Nilsson said impatiently, "Maybe she's got some idea that she's safer on top of a mountain. With luck, we'll find out soon. Ready to go?"

Hallner nodded.

They moved on in silence.

The range was discernibly closer, now, and Hallner could look at individual mountains. Although looming over the others, the one they headed for looked squat, solid, somehow older than the rest, even.

For a while they were forced to concentrate on the ground immediately in front of them, for it had become little more than thick mud which oozed over their boots and threatened to pull them down, to join, perhaps, the remains of prehistoric saurians which lay many feet below.

Nilsson said little and Hallner was glad that no demands were made on him.

It was as if the edge of the world lay beyond the last ragged pile of mountains, or as if they had left Earth and were in a concave saucer surrounded by mountains, containing only the trees and the lakes, marshes and hills.

He had the feeling that this place was so inviolable, so invulnerable, miles from the habitation of men, that for the first time he fully realized that men had ceased to exist along with their artefacts. It was as if they had never really existed at all or that their spell of dominance had appeared and disappeared in practically the same moment of time.

But now, for the first time since he had heard the hysterical voice on the radio, he felt some stirring of his old feeling return as he stared at the great mountain, heavy and huge against the ice-blue sky. But it was transformed. Ambition had become the summit, reward the silence, the peace that waited at the peak. Curiosity was the desire to discover the cause of a freakish colouring halfway up the mountain and fear did not exist, for in these enigmatic mountains there was no uncertainty. A vast, wall-less womb with the infinite sky curving above and the richly coloured scenery, blues, whites, browns and greens, surrounding them, complete, cutting them off from even the sight of the ruined outside world.

It was a snow-splashed paradise, where well-fed wolves left the carcasses of their prey to lap at the pure water of the rivers. A wilderness replete with life, with lemming, reindeer, wolverine, wolf and even bear, with lakes swarming with freshwater herring and the air a silent gulf above them to set off the smack of a hawk's wing. Night could not fall and so the potential dangers of savage wild-life, which could not be felt in the vastness of a world where there was room for everything, could never be realized.

Occasionally, they would discover a slain reindeer, bones dull and white, its hide tattered and perishing, and they would feel no horror, no emotion at all, for although its obvious killer, the wolverine, was a cruel beast, destroying often for the sake of destroying, the wolverine was not aware of its crime and therefore it was no crime at all.

Everything here was self-sufficient, moulded by fate, by circumstance, but since it did not analyse, since it accepted itself and its conditions without question, it was therefore more complete than the men who walked and stumbled across its uncompromising terrain.

At length they came to the sloping, grass-covered roots of the mountain and he trembled with emotion to see it rising so high above him, the grass fading, parting to reveal the tumbled rock and the rock vanishing higher up beneath banks of snow.

"She will have taken the easiest face," Nilsson decided, looking at the map he had found in the camp. "It will mean crossing two snow-fields."

They rested on the last of the grass. And he looked down over the country through which they had passed, unable to talk or describe his feelings. It possessed no horizon, for mountains were on all sides, and within the mountains he saw rivers and lakes, tree-covered hills, all of which had taken on fresh, brighter colourings, the lakes reflecting the red of the sun and the blue of the sky and giving them subtly different qualities.

He was glad they were taking the easiest face for he felt no need, here, to test or to temper himself.

For a while he felt complete with the country, ready to climb upwards because he would rather do so and, because the view from the peak would also be different, add, perhaps to the fullness of his experience.

He realized, as they got up, that this was not what Nilsson was feeling. Hallner had almost forgotten about the girl.

They began to climb. It was tiring, but not difficult, for initially the slope was gradual, less than forty-five degrees. They came to the first snow-field which was slightly below them, climbed downwards carefully, but with relief.

Nilsson had taken a stick from the Lapp camp. He took a step forward, pressing the stick into the snow ahead of him, took another step, pressed the stick down again.

Hallner followed, treading cautiously in his friend's footsteps, little pieces of frozen snow falling into his boots. He knew that Nilsson was trying to judge the snow-field's thickness. Below it a deep river coursed and he thought he heard its musical rushing beneath his feet. He noted, also, that his feet now felt frozen and uncomfortable.

Very slowly they crossed the snow-field and, after a long time, they were safely across and sat down to rest for a while, preparing for the steeper climb ahead.

Nilsson eased his pack off his shoulders and leaned against it, staring back at the field.

"No tracks," he mused. "Perhaps she crossed further down."

"Perhaps she didn't come here after all." Hallner spoke with effort. He was not really interested.

"Don't be a fool." Nilsson rose and hefted his pack onto his back again.

They climbed over the sharp rocks separating the two snow-fields and once again underwent the danger of crossing the second field.

Hallner sat down to rest again, but Nilsson climbed on. After a few moments, Hallner followed and saw that Nilsson had stopped and was frowning at the folded map in his hand.

When he reached Nilsson he saw that the mountain now curved upwards around a deep, wide indentation. Across this, a similar curve went up towards the summit. It looked a decidedly easier climb than the one that faced them.

Nilsson swore.

"The damned map's misled us – or else the position of the fields has altered. We've climbed the wrong face."

"Should we go back down again?" Hallner asked uninterestedly.

"No – there's not much difference – we'd have still lost a lot of time."

Where the two curves joined, there was a ridge high above them which would take them across to the face that they should have climbed. This was getting close to the peak, so that, in fact, there would be no advantage even when they reached the other side.

"No wonder we missed her tracks," Nilsson said pettishly. "She'll be at the summit by now."

"How do you know she climbed this mountain?" Hallner wondered why he had not considered this earlier.

Nilsson waved the map. "You don't think Lapps need these? No – *she* left it behind."

"Oh . . ." Hallner stared down at the raw, tumbling rocks which formed an almost sheer drop beneath his feet.

"No more resting," Nilsson said. "We've got a lot of time to make up."

He followed behind Nilsson who foolishly expended his energy in swift, savage ascents and was showing obvious signs of exhaustion before they ever reached the ridge.

Unperturbed by the changed situation, Hallner climbed after him, slowly and steadily. The ascent was taking longer, was more difficult and he, also, was tired, but he possessed no sense of despair.

Panting, Nilsson waited for him on a rock close to the ridge, which formed a narrow strip of jumbled rocks slanting upwards towards the peak. On one side of it was an almost sheer drop going down more than a hundred feet, and on the other the rocky sides sloped steeply down to be submerged in a dazzling expanse of faintly creaking ice – a glacier.

"I'm going to have to leave you behind if you don't move faster," Nilsson panted.

Hallner put his head slightly on one side and peered up the mountain. Silently, he pointed.

"God! Everything's against us, today," Nilsson kicked at a loose piece of rock and sent it out into space. It curved and plummeted down, but they could not see or hear it fall.

The mist, which Hallner had noted, came rolling swiftly towards them, obscuring the other peaks, boiling in across the range.

"Will it affect us?" Hallner asked.

"It's sure to!"

"How long will it stay?"

"A few minutes or several hours, it's impossible to tell. If we stay where we are we could very well freeze to death. If we go on there's a chance of reaching the summit and getting above it. Willing to risk it?"

This last remark was a sneering challenge.

"Why yes, of course," Hallner said.

Now that the fact had been mentioned, he noted for the first time that he was cold. But the coldness was not uncomfortable.

They had no ropes, no climbing equipment of any kind, and even his boots were flat-soled city boots. As the mist poured in, its grey, shifting mass limiting vision almost utterly at times, they climbed on, keeping together by shouts.

Once, he could hardly see at all, reached a rock, felt about it with his boot, put his weight on the rock, slipped, clung to the rock and felt both feet go sliding free in space just as the mist parted momentarily to show him the creaking glacier far below him. And something else – a black, spread-out shadow blemishing the pure expanse of ice.

He scrabbled at the rock with his toes, trying to swing himself back to the main part of the ridge, got an insecure toehold and flung himself sideways to the comparative safety of the narrow causeway. He breathed quickly and shallowly and shook with reaction. Then he arose and continued on up the slanting ridge.

A while later, when the main thickness of the mist had rolled past and now lay above the glacier, he saw that they had crossed the ridge and were on the other side without his having realized it.

He could now see Nilsson climbing with obvious difficulty towards what he had called the "false summit". The real summit could not be seen, was hidden by the other, but there was now only another hundred feet to climb.

They rested on the false summit, unable to see much that was below them for, although the mist was thinner, it was thick enough to hide most of the surrounding mountains. Sometimes it would part so that they could see fragments of mountains, patches of distant lakes, but little else.

Hallner looked at Nilsson. The other man's handsome face had taken on a set, obstinate look. One hand was bleeding badly.

"Are you all right?" Hallner nodded his head towards the bleeding hand.

"Yes!"

Hallner lost interest since it was evident he could not help Nilsson in his present mood.

He noted that the mist had penetrated his thin jacket and his whole body was damp and chilled. His own hands were torn and grazed and his body was bruised, aching, but he was still not discomforted. He allowed Nilsson to start off first and then forced himself on the last stage of the climb.

By the time he reached the snowless summit, the air was bright, the mist had disappeared and the sun shone in the clear sky.

He flung himself down close to Nilsson who was again peering at his map.

He lay panting, sprawled awkwardly on the rock and stared out over the world.

There was nothing to say. The scene itself, although magnificent, was not what stopped him from talking, stopped his mind from reasoning, as if time had come to a standstill, as if the passage of the planet through space had been halted. He existed, like a monument, petrified, unreasoning, absorbing. He drank in eternity.

Why hadn't the dead human race realized this? It was only necessary to exist, not to be trying constantly to prove you existed when the fact was plain.

Plain to him, he realized, because he had climbed a mountain. This knowledge was his reward. He had not received any ability to think with greater clarity, or a vision to reveal the secret of the universe, or an experience of ecstasy. He had been given, by himself, by his own action, insensate peace, the infinite tranquillity of *existing*.

Nilsson's harsh, disappointed tones invaded this peace.

"I could have sworn she would climb up here. Maybe she did. Maybe we were too late and she's gone back down again?"

Hallner remembered the mark he had seen on the glacier. Now he knew what it had been.

"I saw something back on the ridge," he said. "On the glacier. A human figure, I think."

"What? Why didn't you tell me?"

"I don't know."

"Was she alive? Think of the importance of this – if she is alive we can start the human race all over again. What's the matter with you, Hallner? Have you gone crazy with shock or something? *Was she alive?*"

"Perhaps – I don't know."

"You don't – " Nilsson snarled in disbelief and began scrabbling back the way he had come.

"You heartless bastard! Supposing she's hurt – injured!"

Hallner watched Nilsson go cursing and stumbling, sometimes falling, on his over-rapid descent of the mountain. He saw him rip off his pack and fling it aside, nearly staggering over the ridge as he began to climb down it.

Hallner thought dispassionately that Nilsson would kill himself if he continued so heedlessly.

Then he returned his gaze to the distant lakes and trees below him.

He lay on the peak of the mountain, sharing its existence. He was immobile, he did not even blink as he took in the view. It seemed that he was part of the rock, part of the mountain itself.

A little later there came an aching yell which died away into the silence. But Hallner did not hear it.

Not Responsible! Park and Lock It!

John Kessel

David Baker was born in the backseat of his parents' Chevy in the great mechanized lot at mile 1.375×10^{25}. "George, we need to stop," his mother Polly said. "I'm having pains." She was a week early.

They had been cruising along pretty well at twilight, his father concentrating on getting in another fifty miles before dark, when they were cut off by the big two-toned Mercury and George had to swerve four lanes over into the far right. George and Polly later decided that the near-accident was the cause of the premature birth. They even managed to laugh at the incident in retrospect – they ruefully retold the story many times, so that it was one of the family fables David grew up with – but David always suspected his father pined after those lost fifty miles. In return he'd gotten a son.

"Not responsible! Park and lock it!" the loudspeakers at the tops of the poles in the vast asphalt field shouted, over and over. For a first birth Polly's labour was surprisingly short, and the robot doctor emerged from the Chevy in the gathering evening with a healthy seven-pound boy. George Baker flipped his cigarette away nervously, the butt glowing as it spun into the night. He smiled.

In the morning George stepped into the bar at the first rest stop, had a quick one, and registered his name: David John Baker. Born 8:15 Standard Westbound Time, June 13 . . .

"What year is it?" George asked the bartender.

"802,701." The robot smiled benignly. It could not do otherwise.

"802,701." George repeated it aloud and punched the keys of the terminal. "Eight hundred two thousand, seven hundred and one." The numbers spun themselves out like a song. Eight-oh-two, seven-oh-one.

David's mother had smiled weakly, reclining in the passenger's seat, when they'd started again. Her smile had never been strong. David slept on her breast.

Much later Polly told David what a good baby he'd been, not like his younger sister Caroline, who had the colic. David took satisfaction in that: he was the good one. It made the competition between him and Caroline even more intense. But that was later. As a baby David slept to the steady thrumming of the V-8 engine, the gentle rocking of the car. He was cooed at by the android attendants at the camps where they pulled over at the end of the day. His father would chat with the machine that came over to check the odometer and validate their mileage card. George would tell about any of the interesting things that had happened on the road – and he always seemed to have something – while Polly fixed supper at one of the grills and the ladies from the other cars sat around in a circle in front of the komfy kabins and talked about their children, their husbands, about their pregnancies and how often they got to drive. David sat on Polly's lap or played with the other kids. Once past the toddler stage he followed his dad around and watched, a little scared, as the greasy self-assured robots busied themselves about the service station. They were large and composed. The young single drivers tried hard to compete with their mechanical self-containment. David hung on everything his dad said.

"The common driving man," George Baker said, hands on the wheel, "the good average driver – doesn't know his asshole from a tailpipe."

Polly would draw David to her, as if to blot out the words. "George – "

"All right. The kid will know whether you want him to or not."

But David didn't know, and they wouldn't tell him. That was the way of parents: they never told you even when they thought they were explaining everything, and so David was left to wonder and learn as best he could. He watched the land speed by long before he had words to say what he saw; he listened to his father tell his mother what was wrong and right with the world. And the sun set every night at the other end of that world, far ahead of them still, beyond the gas stations and the wash-and-brushup buildings and the quietly deferential androids that always seemed the same no matter how far they'd gone that day, Westbound.

When David was six he got to sit on George's lap, hold the wheel in his hands, and "drive the car." With what great chasms of anticipation and awe did he look forward to those moments! His father would say suddenly, after hours of driving in silence, "Come sit on my lap, David. You can drive."

Polly would protest feebly that he was too young. It was dangerous. David would clamber into his dad's lap and grab the wheel. How warm it felt, how large, and how far apart he had to put his hands! The indentations on the back were too wide for his fingers, so that two of his fit into the space meant for one adult's. George would move the seat up and scrunch his thin legs together so that David could see over the hood of the car. His father operated the pedals and gearshift, and most of the time he kept his left hand on the wheel too – but then he would slowly take it away and David would be steering all by himself. His heart had beaten fast. At those moments the car had seemed so large. The promise and threat of its speed had been almost overwhelming. He knew that by a turn of the wheel he could be in the high-speed lane; he knew, even more amazingly, that he held in his hands the potential to steer them off the road, into the gully, and death. The responsibility was great, and David took it seriously. He didn't want to do anything foolish, he didn't want to make George think him any less a man. He knew his mother was watching. Whether she had love or fear in her eyes he could not know, because he couldn't take his eyes from the road to see.

When David was seven there was a song on the radio Polly sang to him, "We all drive on." That was his song. David sang it back

to her, and his father laughed and sang it too, badly, voice hoarse
and off-key, not like his mother, whose voice was sweet. "We all
drive on," they sang together.

> "You and me and everyone
> Never ending, just begun
> Driving, driving on."

"Goddamn right we drive on," George said. "Goddamn pack
of maniacs."

David remembered clearly the first time he became aware of the
knapsack and the notebook. It was one evening after they'd eaten
supper and were waiting for Polly to get the cabin ready for bed.
George went around to the trunk to check the spare, and this time
he took a green knapsack out and, in the darkness near the edge
of the campground, secretively opened it.

"Watch, David, and keep your mouth shut about what you
see."

David watched.

"This is for emergencies." George, one by one, set the things
on the ground: first a rolled oilcloth, which he spread out, then a
line of tools, then a gun and boxes of bullets, a first-aid kit, some
packages of crackers and dried fruit, and some things David didn't
know. One thing had a light and a thick wire and batteries.

"This is a metal detector, David. I made it myself." George took
a black book from the sack. "This is my notebook." He handed it
to David. It was heavy and smelled of the trunk.

"Maps of the Median, and – "

"George!" Polly's voice was a harsh whisper, and David jumped
a foot. She grabbed his arm. George looked exasperated and a
little guilty – though David did not identify his father's reaction as
guilt until he thought about it much later. He was too busy trying
to avoid the licking he thought was coming. His mother marched
him back to the cabin after giving George her best withering gaze.

"But, Mom – "

"To sleep! Don't puzzle yourself about things you aren't meant
to know, young man."

David puzzled himself. At times the knapsack and the notebook filled his thoughts. His father would give him a curious glance and tantalizingly vague answers whenever he asked about them – safely out of earshot of Polly.

Shortly after that Caroline was born. This time the Bakers were not caught by surprise, and Caroline came into the world at the hospital at mile 1.375×10^{25}, where they stopped for three whole days for Polly's lying in. Nobody stopped for three whole days, for anything. David was impatient. They'd never *get* anywhere waiting, and the androids in the hospital were all boring, and the comic books in the motionless waiting room he had all read before.

This time the birth was a hard one. George sat hunched forward in a plastic chair, and David paced around, stomping on the cracks in the linoleum. He leaned on the windowsill and watched all the cars fly by on the highway, Westbound, and in the distance, beyond the barbed wire, sentry towers and minefields, mysterious, ever unattainable – Eastbound.

After what seemed like a very long time, the white porcelain doctoroid came back to them. George stood up as soon as he appeared. "Is she – "

"Both fine. A little girl. Seven pounds, five ounces," the doctoroid reported, grille gleaming.

George didn't say anything then, just sat down in the chair. After a while he came over to David, put his hand on the boy's shoulder, and they both watched the cars moving by, the light of the bright midsummer's sun flashing off the windshields as they passed, blinding them.

David was nine when they bought the Nash. It had a big chrome grille that stretched like a bridge across the front, the vertical bars bulging outward in the middle, so that, with the headlights, the car looked to be grinning a big nasty grin.

David went with George through the car lot while Polly sat with Caroline in the lounge of the dealership. He watched his father dicker with the bow-tied salesdroid. George acted as if he seriously meant to buy a new car, when in fact his yearly mileage average would entitle him to no more than a second-hand, second-rank sedan, unless he intended for them all to go hungry. He wouldn't have done that, however. Whatever else Polly might say about her husband, she could not say he wasn't a good provider.

"So why don't you show us a good used car," George said, running his hand through his thinning hair. "Mind you, don't show us any piece of junk."

The salesdroid was, like his brothers, enthusiastic and unreadable. "Got just the little thing for you, Mr Baker – a snappy number. C'mon," it said, rolling down toward the back of the lot.

"Here you go." It opened the door of the blue Nash with its amazingly dextrous hand. David's father got in. "Feel that genuine vinyl upholstery. Not none of your cheap plastics, that'll crack in a week of direct sun." The salesdroid winked its glassy eye at David. "Hop in, son. See how you like it."

David started to, then saw the look of warning on George's face.

"Let's have a look at the engine," George said.

"Righto." The droid rolled around the fat front fender, reached through the grille, and tripped the latch. The engine was clean as a whistle, the cylinder heads painted cherry red, the spark plug leads numbered for easy changes. It was like the pictures out of David's schoolbooks.

The droid started up the Nash; the motor gave out a rumble and vibrated ever so slightly. David smelled the clean tang of evaporating gasoline.

"Only one owner," the droid said, volume turned up now so it could be heard over the sound of the engine.

George looked uncertain.

"How much?"

"Book says it's worth 200,000 validated miles. You can drive her out, with your Chevy in trade, for . . . let me calculate . . . 174,900."

Just then David noticed something in the engine compartment. On either side over the wheel wells there were cracks in the metal that had been painted over so you could only see them from the reflection of the sunlight where the angle of the surface changed. That was where the shocks connected up with the car's body.

He tugged at his father's sleeve. "Dad," he said, pointing.

George ran a hand over the metal. He looked serious. David thought he was going to get mad. Instead he straightened up and smiled.

"How much did you say?"

The android stood stock still. "150,000 miles."

"But, Dad – "

"Shut up, David," he said. "I'll tell you what, Mr Sixty. 100,000. And you reweld those wheel wells before we drive it an inch."

That was how they bought the Nash. The first thing George said when they were on their way again was, "Polly, that boy of ours is smart as a whip. The shocks were about to rip through the body-work, and we'd of been scraping down the highway with our nose to the ground like a basset. David, you're a born driver, or else too smart to waste yourself on it."

David didn't quite follow that, but it made him a little more content to move into the backseat. At first he resented it that Caroline had taken his place in the front. She got all the attention, and David only got to sit and look out at where they had been, or what they were going by, never getting a good look at where they were going. If he leaned over the back of the front seat, his father would say, "Quit breathing down my neck, David. Sit down and behave yourself. Do your homework."

After a while he wouldn't have moved into the front if they'd asked him to: that was for babies. Instead he watched raptly out the left side-window for fleeting glimpses of Eastbound, wondering always about what it was, how it got there, and about the no-man's-land and the people they said had died trying to cross. He asked George about it, and that started up the biggest thing they were ever to share together.

"They've told you about Eastbound in school, have they?"

"They told us we can't go there. Nobody can."

"Did they tell you why?"

"No."

His father laughed. "That's because they don't know why! Isn't that incredible, David? They teach a thing in school, and everybody believes it, and nobody knows why or even thinks to ask. But you wonder, don't you? I've seen it."

He did wonder. It scared him that his father would talk about it.

"Men are slipstreamers, David. Did you ever see a car follow close behind a big truck to take advantage of the windbreak – to make the driving easier? That's the way people are. They'll follow so close they can't see six inches beyond their noses, as long as it makes things easier. And the schools and the teachers are the biggest windbreaks of all. You remember that. Do you remember the knapsack in the trunk?"

"*George*," Polly said.

"Be quiet, Polly. The boy's growing up." To David he said, "You know what it's for. You know what's inside."

"To go across . . ." David hesitated, his heart leaping.

"To cross the Median! We can do it. We don't have to be like everybody else, and when the time comes, when we need to get away the most, when things are really bad – we can do it! I'm prepared to do it."

Polly tried to shush him, and it became an argument. But David was thrilled at the new world that had opened. His father was a criminal – but he was right! From then on they worked on the preparations together. They would have long talks on what they would do and how they would do it. David drew maps on graph paper, and sometimes he and George would climb to the highest spot available by the roadside at the day's end, to puzzle out once again the defences of the Median.

"Don't tell your mother about this," George would say. "You know she doesn't understand."

Each morning, before they had gone very far at all, David's father would stop the car and let David out at a bus stop to be picked up by the school bus, and eight hours later the bus would let him out again some hundreds of miles farther west. Soon his parents would be there to pick him up, if they were not there already when he got off with the other kids. More than once David overheard drivers at the camps in the evening complaining about how having kids really slowed a man down in his career, so he'd never get as far as he would have if he'd had the sense to stay single. Whenever some young man whined about waiting around half his life for a school bus, George Baker would only light another cigarette and be very quiet.

In school David learned the principles of the internal combustion engine. Internal Combustion was his favourite class. Other boys and girls would shoot paperclips at each other over the backseats of the bus, or fall asleep staring out the windows, but David sat in a middle seat (he would not move to the front and be accused of being teacher's pet) and, for the most part, paid good attention. His favourite textbook was one they used both in history and social studies; it had a blue cloth cover. The title, pressed into the cover in faded yellow, was *Heroes of the Road*. On the bus, during recess, David and the other boys argued about who was the greatest driver of them all.

To most of them Alan "Lucky" Totter was the only driver. He'd made 10,220,796 miles when he tried to pass a Winnebago on the right at 85 miles per hour in a blinding snowstorm. Some people thought that showed a lack of judgement, but Lucky Totter didn't give a damn for judgement, or anything else. Totter was the classic lone-wolf driver. Born to respectable middle-class parents who drove a Buick with holes in its sides, Totter devoured all he could find out about cars. At the age of thirteen he deserted his parents at a rest stop at mile. 1.375×10^{25}, hot-wired a Bugatti-Smith that the owner had left unlocked, and made 8,000 miles before the Trooperbots brought him to justice. After six months in the paddy wagon he came out with a new resolve. He worked for a month at a service station at jobs even the androids would shun, getting nowhere. At the end of that time he'd rebuilt a junked Whippet roadster and was on his way, hell-bent for leather. Every extra mile he drove he ploughed back into financing a newer and faster car. Tirelessly, it seemed, Totter kept his two-tones to the floorboards, and the pavement fairly flew beneath his wheels. No time for a wife or family, 1,000 miles a day was his only satisfaction, other than the quick comforts of any of the fast women he might pick up who wanted a chance to say they'd been for a ride with Lucky

Totter. The solitary male to the end, it was a style guaranteed to earn him the hero worship of boys all along the world.

But Totter was not the all-time mileage champion. That pinnacle of glory was held by Charles Van Huyser, at a seemingly unassailable 11,315,201 miles. It was hard to see how anyone could do better, for Van Huyser was the driver who had everything: good reflexes, a keen eye, iron constitution, wherewithal and devilish good looks. He was a child of the privileged classes, scion of the famous Van Huyser drivers, and had enjoyed all the advantages the boys on a middle-lane bus like David's would never see. His father had been one of the premier drivers of his generation, and had made more than seven million miles himself, placing him a respectable twelfth on the all-time list. Van Huyser rode the most exclusive of preparatory buses, and was outfitted from the beginning with the best made-to-order Mercedes that android hands could fashion. He was in a lane by himself. Old-timers would tell stories of the time they had been passed by the Van Huyser limo and the distinguished, immaculately tailored man who sat behind the wheel. Perhaps he had even tipped his homburg as he flashed by. Spartan in his daily regimen, invariably kind, if a little condescending, to lesser drivers, he never forgot his position in society, and died at the respectable age of eighty-six, peacefully, in the private washroom of the Drivers' Club dining room at mile 1.375×10^{25}.

There were scores of others in *Heroes of the Road*, all of their stories inspiring, challenging, even puzzling. There was Ailene Stanford, at six-million-plus miles the greatest female driver ever, carmaker and mother and credit to her sex. And Reuben Jefferson, and the Kosciusco brothers, and the mysterious trance driving of Akira Tedeki. The chapter "Detours" held frightening tales of abject failure, and of those who had wasted their substance and their lives trying to cross the Median.

"You can't believe everything you read, David," George told him. "They'll tell you Steve Macready was a great man."

It was like George Baker to make statements like that and then never explain what he meant. It got on David's nerves sometimes, though he figured his dad did it because he had more important things on his mind.

But Steve Macready was David's personal favourite. Macready was third on the all-time list behind Van Huyser and Totter, at 8,444,892 miles. Macready hadn't had the advantages of Van Huyser, and he scorned the reckless irresponsibility of Totter. He was an average man, to all intents and purposes, and he showed just how much an average guy could do if he had the willpower. Born into an impoverished hundred-mile-a-day family that couldn't seem to keep a car on the road three days in a row before it broke down, one of eight brothers and sisters, Macready studied quietly when he could, watched the ways of the road with an intelligent eye, and helped his father and mother keep the family rolling. Compelled to leave school early because the family couldn't keep up with the slowest of school buses, he worked on his own, managed to get hold of an old junker that he put on the road, and set off at the age of sixteen, taking two of his sisters with him. In those first years his mileage totals were anything but spectacular. But he kept plugging away, taking care of his sisters, seeing them married off to two respectable young drivers along the way, never hurrying. At the comparatively late age of thirty he married a simple girl from a family of Ford owners and fathered four children. He saw to his boys' educations. He drove on, making a steady 500 miles a day, and 200 on each Saturday and Sunday. He did not push himself or his machine; he did not lag behind. Steadiness was his watchword. His sons grew up to be fine drivers themselves, always ready to lend the helping hand to the unfortunate motorist. When he died at the age of eighty-two, survived by his wife, children, eighteen grandchildren, and twenty-six great-grandchildren, drivers all, he had become something of a legend in his own quiet time. Steve Macready.

George Baker never said much when David talked about the arguments the kids had over Macready and the other drivers. When he talked about his own youth, he would give only the most tantalizing hints of the many cars he had driven before he picked up Polly, of the many places he'd stopped and people he'd ridden with. David's grandfather had been something of an inventor, he gathered, and had modified his pickup with an extra-large tank and a small, efficient engine to get the most mileage for his driving time. George didn't say much about his mother or brothers, though he said some things that indicated that his father's plans for big miles never panned out, and about how it was not always pleasant to ride in the back of an open pickup with three brothers and a sick mother.

Eventually David saw that the miles were taking something out of his father. George Baker conversed less with Polly and the kids, and talked more at them.

Once, in a heavy rainstorm after three days of rolling hill country, forests that encroached on the edges of the pavement and fell like a dark wall between Westbound and forgotten Eastbound, the front end of the Nash jumped suddenly into a mad vibration that threw David's heart into his throat.

"George!" Polly shouted.

"Shut up!" he yelled, trying to steer the bucking car to the road-side.

And then they were stopped, and breathing heavily, and the only sound was the drumming of the rain, the ticking of the car as it settled into motionlessness, and the hissing of the cars that still sped by them over the wet pavement. David's father, slow and bearlike, opened the door and pulled himself out. David got out too. Under the hood they saw where the rewelded wheel well had given way; and the shock was ripping through the metal. "Shit," George muttered.

As they stood there a gunmetal-grey Cadillac pulled over to stop behind them, its flashing amber signal warm as fire under the leaden skies. A stocky man in an expensive raincoat got out. "Can I help you?" he asked.

George stared at him for a good ten seconds. He looked back at the Cadillac, looked at the man again.

"No thanks," he said.

The man hesitated, then turned, went back to his car and drove off.

So they had to wait three hours in the broken-down Nash as darkness fell and George trudged off down the highway for the next rest stop. He returned with an android serviceman, and they were towed to the nearest station. David, never patient at his best, grew more and more angry. His father offered not a word of explanation, and his mother tried to keep David from getting after him about his refusing help. But David finally challenged his father on the plain stupidity of his actions, which would mystify any sensible driver.

At first George acted as if he didn't hear David. Then he exploded.

"Don't tell me about sensible drivers! I don't need it, David! Don't tell me about your Van Huysers, and don't give me any of that Steve Macready crap, either. Your Van Huysers never did anything for the common driving man, despite all their extra miles. Nobody gives it away. That's just the way this road works."

"What about Macready?" David asked. He didn't understand what his father was talking about. You didn't have to run someone else down in order to be right. "Look at what Macready did."

"You don't know what you're talking about," George said. "You get older, but you still think like a kid. Macready sucked up to every tinman on the road. I wouldn't stoop so low as that. Half the time he let his *wife* drive! They don't tell you about that in that damn school, do they?

"Wake up and look at this road the way it is, David. People will use you like a chamois if you don't. Take my word for it. *Damn* it! If I could just get a couple of good months out of this heap and get back on my feet. A couple of good months!" He laughed scornfully.

It was no use arguing with George when he was in that mood. David shut up, inwardly fuming.

"Follow the herd!" George yelled. "That's all people ever do. Never had an original thought in their life."

"George, you don't need to shout at the boy," Polly said.

"Shout! I'm not shouting!" he shouted. George looked at her as if she were a hitchhiker. "Why don't you shut up. The boy and I were just having an intelligent conversation. A fat lot you know about it." He gripped the wheel as if he meant to grind it into powder. A deadly silence ensued.

"I need to stop," he said a couple of miles later, pulling off the road into a bar and grill.

They sat in the car, ears ringing.

"I'm hungry," Caroline said.

"Let's get something to eat, then." Polly leapt at the opportunity to do something normal. "Come on, David. Let's go in."

"You go ahead. I'll be there in a minute."

After they left David stared out the car window for a while. He reached under the seat and took out the notebook, which he had moved there a long time before. The spine was almost broken through now, with some of the leaves loose and waterstained. The paper was worn with writing and rewriting. David leafed through the sketches of watchtowers, the maps, the calculations. In the margin of page six his father had written, in handwriting so faded now that it was like the pale voice of years speaking, from far away, "Keep your ass down. Low profile."

David was sixteen. His knees were crowded by the back of the car's front seat, and he stared sullenly out the window at the rolling countryside and the gathering night.

Caroline, having just concluded her fight with him with a belligerent "Oh, yeah!" was leaning forward, her forearms flat against the top of the front seat, her chin resting on them as she stared grimly ahead. Polly was knitting a cover for the box of Kleenex that rested on the dashboard, muffling the radio speaker.

"I'm tired," George said. "I'm going to stop here for a quick one." He pulled the ancient Nash over into the exit lane, downshifted, and the car lurched forward more slowly, the engine rattling in protest of the increased rpms. David could have done it better himself.

They pulled into the parking lot of Fast Ed's Bar and Grill. "You go back and order a fish fry," George said, slamming the car door and turning his back on them. Polly put aside the knitting, picked up her purse, and took them in the side door to the dining room. There was no one else there, but they could hear the TV and the loud conversations from the front. After a while a waitress robot rolled back to them. Its porcelain finish was chipped, and the hands were stained rusty brown, like an old bathtub.

They ordered, the food came, and they ate. Still George did not return from the bar.

"Go get your father, David," his mother said. He could tell she was mad.

"I'll go, Ma," Caroline said.

"Stay still! It's bad enough he takes us to his gin mills, without you becoming a barfly's pet. Go ahead, David."

David went. His father was sitting at the far end of the bar, near the windows that faced the highway. The late afternoon sun gleamed along the polished wood, glinted harshly from the bottles racked on the shelves behind it, turned the mirror against the wall and the brass spigots of the taps into fire. George Baker was talking loudly with two other middle-aged drivers. His legs looked amazingly scrawny as he perched on the stool. Suddenly David was very angry.

"Are you going to come and eat?" he demanded.

George turned to him, his sloppy good humour stiffening to ire.

"What do you want?"

"We're eating. Mom's waiting."

He leaned over to the man on the next stool. "See what I mean?" he said. To David he said, much more boldly, "Go and eat. I'm not hungry." He picked up his shot, downed it in one swallow, and took another draw on the beer setup.

Rage and humiliation burned in David. He did not recognize the man at the bar as his father – and then, shuddering, he did.

"Are you coming?" David could hardly speak. The other men at the bar were quiet now. Only the television continued to babble.

"Go away," his father said.

David wanted to kick over the stool and see him sprawled on the floor. Instead he turned and walked stiffly back to the dining room, past the table where his mother and sister sat. He stalked out to the lot, slamming the screen door behind him. He stood looking at the beat-up Nash in the red and white light of Fast Ed's sign. The sign buzzed, and night was coming, and clouds of insects swarmed around the neon in the darkness. A hundred yards away, on the highway, the drivers had their lights on, fanning before them. The air smelled of exhaust.

He couldn't go back into the bar. He would never step back into a place like that again. The world seemed all at once immensely old, immensely cheap, immensely tawdry. David looked over his shoulder at the vast woods that started just beyond back of Fast Ed's. Then he walked to the front of the lot and stared across the highway toward the distant lights that marked Eastbound. How very far away they seemed.

David went back to the car and got the knapsack out of the trunk. He stepped over the rail at the edge of the lot, crossed the gully beside the road, and waiting for his chance, dashed across the twelve lanes of Westbound to the Median. A hundred yards ahead of him lay the beginning of no-man's-land. Beyond that, where those distant lights swept by in their retrograde motion – what?

But he would never get into a car with George Baker again.

There were three levels of defences between Westbound and Eastbound, or so they had surmised. The first was biological, the second was mechanical, and the third and most important, psychological.

As David moved farther from the highway the ground, which was more or less level near the shoulders, grew uneven. The field was unmowed, thick with nettles and coarse grass, and in the increasing darkness he stumbled more than once. Because the land sloped downward as he advanced, the lights ahead of him became obscured by the foliage.

He thought once that he heard his name called above the faint rushing of the cars behind him, but when he turned he could see nothing but Westbound. It seemed remarkably far away already. His progress became slower. He knew there were snakes in the open fields. The mines could not be far ahead. He could be in the minefield at that very moment.

He stopped, heart racing. Suddenly he knew he was in a minefield, and his next step would blow him to pieces. He saw the shadow of the first line of barbed wire ahead of him, and for the first time he considered going back. But the thought of his father and his mother stopped him. They would be glad to take him back and smother him.

David crouched, swung the pack from his shoulder, and took out the metal detector. Sweeping it a few inches above the ground in front of him, he crawled forward on his hands and knees. It was slow going. There was something funny about the air: he didn't smell anything but field and earth – no people, no rubber, no gasoline. He eyed the nearest watchtower, where he knew infrared scanners swept the Median and automatic rifles nosed about incuriously. Whenever the light in his palm went red, David slid slowly to one side or the other and went on. Once he had to flatten himself suddenly to the earth as some object – an animal or search mech – rustled through the dry grass not ten yards away. He waited for the bullet in his neck.

He came to the first line of barbed wire. It was rusty and overgrown. Weeds had used it for a trellis, and when David clipped through the wire the overgrowth held the gap closed. He had to tear the opening wider with his hands, and the cheap work gloves he wore were next to no protection.

He lay in the dark, sweating. He would never last at this rate. He decided to take the chance of moving ahead in short, crouching runs, ignoring the mines. For a while it seemed to ease the pressure, until his foot slipped on some metal object and he leapt away, crying aloud, waiting for the blast that didn't come. Crouched in the grass, panting, he saw that he had stepped on a hubcap.

David began to wonder why the machines hadn't spotted him yet. He was far beyond the point any right-thinking driver might pass. Then he realized that he could hear nothing of either Westbound or Eastbound. He had no idea how long it had been since he'd left the parking lot, but the gibbous moon was coming down through the clouds. David wondered what his mother had done after he'd taken the pack and left; he could imagine his father's drunken amazement as she told him. Maybe even Caroline was worried. He was far beyond them now. He was getting away, amazed at how easy it was, once you made up your mind, amazed at how few had the guts to try it. If they'd even told him the truth.

A perverse idea hit him: maybe the teachers and drivers, like sheep huddled in their trailer beds, had never tried to see what lay in the Median. Maybe all the servodefences had rotted like the barbed wire, and it was only the pressure of their dead traditions that kept people glued to their westward course. Suddenly twelve lanes, which had seemed a whole world to him all his life, shrank to the merest thread. Who could say what Eastbound might be? Who could predict how much better men had done for themselves there? Maybe it was the Eastbounders who had built the roads, who had created the defences and myths that kept them all penned in filthy Nashes, rolling west.

David laughed aloud. He stood up. He slung the pack over his shoulder again, and this time boldly struck out for the new world.

"Halt!"

A figure stood erect before him, and a blinding light shone from its head. The confidence drained from David instantly; he dropped to the ground.

"Please stand." David was pinned in the centre of the search beam. He reached into the knapsack for the revolver. "This is a restricted area, intruder," the machine said. "Please return to your assigned role."

David blinked in the glare. He could see nothing of the thing's form. "Role?"

"I am sure that the first thing they taught you was that entry into this area is forbidden. Am I right?"

"What?" David had never heard this kind of talk from a machine.

"Your elders have said that you should not come here. That is one very good reason why you should not be here. I'm sure you'll agree. The requests of the society that, in a significant way, created us, if not unreasonable, ought to be given considerable thought before we reject them. This is the result of evolution. The men and women who went before you had to concern themselves with survival in order to live long enough to bear the children who eventually became the present generation. Their rules are engineering-tested. Such experience, let alone your intelligence working *within* the framework of evolution, ought not to be lightly discarded. We are not born into a vacuum. Am I right?"

David wasn't sure the gun was going to do him any good. "I guess so. I never thought about it."

"Precisely. Think about it."

David thought. "Wait a minute! How do I know *people* made the rules? I don't have any proof. I never see people making rules now."

"On the contrary, intruder, you see it every day. Every act a person performs is an act of definition. We create what we are from moment to moment. The future before us is merely the emptiness of time that does not exist without events to fill it. The greatest of changes is possible: in theory you are just as likely to turn into an aimless collection of molecules in this next instant as you are to remain a human being. That is, unless you believe that human beings are fated and possess no free will . . ."

"People have free will." David knew that, if he knew anything. "And they ought to use it."

"That's right." The machine's light was as steady as the sun. "You wouldn't be in a forbidden area if people did not have free will. You yourself, intruder, are a proof of mankind's freedom."

"Okay. Now let me go by – "

"So we have established that human beings have free will. We will assume that they follow rules. Now, having free will, and assuming that by some mischance one of these rules is distasteful to them – we leave aside for the moment who made the rule – then one would expect people to disobey it. They need not even have an active purpose to disobey; in the course of a long enough time many people will break this burdensome rule for the best – or worst – of reasons. The more unacceptable the rule, the greater the number of people who will discard it at one time or another. They will, as individuals or groups, consciously or unconsciously, create a new rule. This is change through human free will. So, even if the rules were not originated by humans, in time change would ensue given the merits of the 'system', as we may call it, and the system will *become* human-created. My earlier evolutionary argument then follows as the night the day. Am I right?"

If a robot could sound triumphant, this one did.

"Ah – "

"So one good reason for doing only what you're told is that you have the free will to do otherwise. Another good reason is God."

"God?"

"The Supreme Being, the Life Force, that ineluctable, unde-finable spiritual presence that lies – or perhaps lurks – within the substance of things. The Holy Father, the First – "

"What about him?"

"God doesn't want you to cross the Median."

"I bet he doesn't," David said sarcastically.

"Have you ever seen an automobile accident?"

The robot was going too fast, and the light made it hard for David to think. He closed his eyes and tried to fight back. "Everybody's seen accidents. People get killed. Don't go telling me God killed them because they did something wrong."

"Don't be absurd!" the robot said. "You must try to stretch your mind, intruder; this is not some game we're playing. This is real life. Not only do actions have consequences, but consequences are pregnant with Meaning.

"In the auto accident we have a peculiar sequence of events. The physicist tells us that heat and vibration cause a weakening of the molecular bonds between certain long-chain hydrocarbons that comprise the substance of the tyre of a car travelling at sixty miles per hour. The tyre blows. As a result of the sudden change in the moment of inertia of this wheel, certain complex analysable oscillations occur. The car swerves to the left, rolls over six times, tossing its three passengers, a man and two women, about like tomatoes in a blender, and collides with a bridge abutment, exploding into flame. To the scientist, this is a simple cause-and-effect chain. The accident has a rational explanation: the tyre blew."

David felt queasy. His hand, in the knapsack, clutched the gun.

"You see right away what's wrong with this explanation. It explains nothing. We know the rational explanation is inadequate without having to be able to say how we know. Such knowledge is the doing of God. God and His merciful Providence set the purpose behind the fact of our existence, and is it possible to believe that a sparrow can fall without His holy cognizance and will?"

"I don't believe in God."

"What does that matter, intruder?" The thing's voice now oozed angelic understanding. "Need you believe in gravity for it to be an inescapable fact of your existence? God does not demand your belief; He merely requests that you, of your own inviolate free will and through the undeserved gift of His grace, come to acknowledge and obey Him. Who can understand the mysteries of faith? Certainly not I, a humble mechanism. *Knowledge* is what matters, and if you open yourself to the currents that flow through the interstices of the material and immaterial universe, that knowledge will be vouchsafed *you*, intruder. You do not belong here. God knows who you are, and He saw what you did. Am I right?"

David was getting mad. "What has this got to do with car accidents?"

"The auto accident does not occur without the knowledge and permission of the Lord. This doesn't mean that He is responsible for it. He accepts the responsibility without accepting the Responsibility. This is a mystery."

"Bull!" David had heard enough talk. It was time to act.

"Be silent, intruder! Where were you when He laid the asphalt of Westbound? Who set up the mileage markers, and who painted the line upon it? On what foundation was its reinforced concrete sunk, and who made the komfy kabins, when the morning stars sang together, and all the droids and servos shouted for joy?"

It was his chance. The machine was still motionless, its mad light trained on him. A mist had sprung from the no-man's-land. Poison gas? He had no gas mask; speed was his only hope. He couldn't move. He hefted the gun. He felt dizzy, a little numb, steeling himself to move. He had to be stronger than the robot! It was just a machine!

"So that is the second good reason why you should not proceed with your ill-advised adventure," it droned on. "God is telling you to go back."

God. Rifles. He had to go! Now! Still he couldn't move. The fog grew, and its smell was strangely pungent. Once past the robot, who knew what he could find. But the machine's voice exuded self-confidence.

"A third and final good reason why you should return to your assigned role, intruder, is this:

"If you take another step, I will kill you."

David woke. He was cold, and he was being shaken by a sobbing man. It was his father.

"Not responsible! Park and lock it!" For the first time in as long as he could remember, David actually heard the crying of the loudspeakers in the parking lot. He struggled to sit up. His mouth tasted like a thousand miles of road grime.

George Baker held his shoulders and looked into his face. He didn't say anything. He stood up and went to stand by the car. Shakily, he lit a cigarette. David's mother crouched over him. "David – David, are you all right?"

"What happened?"

"Your father went after you. We didn't know what happened, and I was so afraid I'd lose both of you – and then he came back carrying you in his arms."

"Carrying me? That's ridiculous." George wasn't capable of carrying a wheel hub fifty yards. David looked at the potbellied man leaning against the front fender of their car. His father was staring off across the lot. Suddenly David felt ashamed of himself. He didn't know what it was in his chest striving to express itself, but sitting there in the parking lot at mile 1.375×10^{25}, looking at the middle-aged man who was his father, he began to cry.

George never said a word to David after that day about how he had managed to follow his son into the Median, about what a struggle it must have been to make himself do that, about how and where he had found the boy, and how he had managed to bring him back, or about what it all meant to him. David never told his father about the robot and what it had said. It was all a little unreal to him. The boy who had stood there, desperately trying to get somewhere else, and the words the robot had spoken, all seemed terribly remote, as if the whole incident were something he had read about. It was a fantasy that could not have occurred in the real world of pavement and gasoline.

Father and son did not speak about it. They didn't say anything much at first, as they tentatively felt out the boundaries of what seemed to be a new relationship. Even Caroline recognized that a change had taken place, and she didn't taunt David the way she had before. Unstated was the fact that David was no longer a boy.

A month later and many thousand miles farther along, George nervously broached the subject of buying David a car. It was a shock for David to hear that, and he knew they could hardly afford it, but he also knew there was a rightness to it. And so they found themselves in the lot of Gears MacDougal's New and Used Autos.

George was too loud, too jocular. "How about this Chevy, David? A Chevy's a good driving man's car." He looked embarrassed.

David got down and felt a tyre. "She's got good rubber on her."

The salesdroid was rolling up to greet them as George opened the hood of the Chevy. "Looks pretty clean," he said.

"They clean them all up."

"They sure do. You can't trust them as far as you'd . . . ah, hello."

"Good morning," the droid said, coming to rest beside them. "That's just the little thing for you. One owner, and between you and me, he didn't drive her too hard. He wasn't much of a driver."

George looked at the machine soberly. "Is that so."

"That is so, sir."

"My son's buying this car, not me," George said suddenly, loudly, as if shaking away the dust of his thoughts. "You should talk to him. And don't try to put anything over on him; he knows his stuff and . . . well, you just talk to him, not me, see?"

"Certainly, sir." The droid rolled between them and told David about the Chevy's V-8. David hardly listened. He watched his father step quietly to the side and light a cigarette. George stood with Polly and Caroline and looked ill at ease, quieter than David could ever remember. As the robot took David around the car, pointing out its extras, it came to him just what his father was: not a strong man, not a special man, not a particularly smart man. He was the same man he had been when David had sat on his lap years before; he was the same man who had taken him on his strolls around the rest stops so many times. He was the drunk who had slouched on the stool in Fast Ed's. He was a good driving man.

"I'll take it," David said, breaking off the salesdroid in mid-sentence.

"Righto," the machine said, its hard smile unvarying. It did not miss a beat. Within seconds a hard copy of the title had emerged from the slot in its chest. Within minutes the papers had been signed, the mileage validated and subtracted from George Baker's yearly total, and David stood beside his car. It was not a very good car to start out with, but many had started with less, and it was the best his father could do. Polly hugged him and cried. Caroline reached up and kissed him on the cheek; she cried too. George shook his hand, and did not seem to want to let go.

"Remember now, take it easy for the first thousand or so, until you get the feel of her. Check the oil, see if it burns oil. I don't think it will. It's got a good spare, doesn't it?"

"It does, Dad."

"Good. That's good." George stood silent for a moment, looking up at his son. The day was bright, and the breeze disarrayed the thinning hair he had combed over his bald spot. "Goodbye, David. Maybe we'll see you on the road?"

"Sure you will."

David got into the Chevy and turned the key in the ignition. The motor started immediately and breathed its low and steady rumble. The seat was very hot against his back. The windshield was spotless, and beyond the nose of the car stretched the access ramp to Westbound. The highway swarmed with the cars that were moving while they dawdled there still. David put the car in gear; stepped slowly on the accelerator, released the clutch, and moved smoothly down the ramp, gathering speed. He shifted up, moving faster, and then quickly once again. The force of the wind streaming in through the window increased from a breeze to a gale, and its sound became a continuous buffeting as it whipped his hair about his ear. Flicking the turn signal, David merged into the flow of traffic, the sunlight flashing off the hood ornament that led him on toward the distant horizon, just out of his reach, but attainable he knew, as he pressed his foot to the accelerator, hurrying on past mile 1.375×10^{25}.

The Myth of Fingerprints

Roxane Gay

It is said that no two fingerprints are alike . . . whorls, loops and arches of flesh that separate one person's identity from another. I leave fingerprints everywhere. In the elevator, I press the doughy pads of my fingertips against the walls, the cool metal railing, leaving an oily smudge behind. In stores I gently massage sales counters and merchandise racks. I'm afraid that my life is going unnoticed.

I once read that if you dream of fingerprints, bad things lie ahead. Last night I dreamt of fingerprints, so I've decided to go for a drive.

My mother always tells me to make sure I'm wearing good underwear when I go out – just in case. I'm not quite sure what just in case is but it is also said that mother knows best. So this morning, I wear my good underwear, with no holes, or worn threads of elastic hanging from the waistband. The other underwear – the bad underwear, which has misbehaved in some way – hides in the back of my top dresser drawer.

I take one duffel bag, and my father's old atlas. It's encased in faded brown leather – one of those old-fashioned atlases that fold open and snap shut. You can follow the vacations my family took when I was a child by the deep creases on the middle states and the coffee stains marking where we got lost, somewhere north of

Cleveland, Ohio. As I lock the door to my apartment, I wrap my fingers around the doorknob, just in case.

I should probably call my mother but I don't. I can picture my father, who is recently retired, slouching in a kitchen chair, idly scratching his chest, as my mother invents new and exciting ways for him to occupy his time and not hers. They are probably bickering, even at this ungodly hour. I decide to call her later, instead.

It's November, and as I step outside, the air is sharp, my lungs aching as I breathe. My car, twelve years old, has seen better years. The front bumper is non-existent, and a rusty dent has disabled the driver's side door. She's named Matilda, because she reminds me of a lumbering Australian farm wife – sturdy, and low to the ground. I open the back door, and toss my duffel bag onto the seat, muttering under my breath as I crawl into the front seat, my knee banging against the gear shift.

Matilda sputters to life, and while I wait for her to warm up, I empty the ashtray overflowing with cigarette butts that hold my fingerprints onto the parking lot pavement. Soon, the wind will pick up, and they'll be blown away, and some disgruntled environmentalists will curse all smokers.

After filling the car with gas, I head east on the interstate – away from Lincoln. I keep one eye on the road, while I stare at my fingers. In college, I majored in architecture, and my hands bear the scars thereof. Across the first knuckle of my right index finger is a corrugated scar born from a razor blade at three in the morning. From the pinky to the middle finger of my left hand is a jagged, fading line, created by a different razor blade, at the same time of morning. My fingertips are similarly scarred, pale marks of varying sizes interrupting the natural sequence.

In an hour, I will be late for my job, a good job by most people's standards. I have a cubicle with 3.75 walls and just enough space to perform a pirouette, but that would be entirely out of character so I use the space pretending to work. Most of my co-workers try to add personal flair to the sterility of their workspaces, but I'm lazy, apathetic by most people's standards. The only thing lining my 3.75 walls are lines I've cut into them, one for each day I've worked there. Today would have brought the grand total to 972, but today I'm not going to work.

The cup of coffee I inhaled at the gas station is engaged in a battle with the lining of my stomach, so I turn the radio on. I need distraction. Matilda's antenna has broken in half, so I'm forced to listen to an evangelical AM station, 1040 KRST. Sister Mary Jo Butler of the Jesus Loves You Too Ministry is offering her seven listeners the inspirational tale of how she was saved by our lord, Jesus Christ.

"I hit bottom," Mary Jo sobs. "I lay on the floor, cradling an empty bottle of Jack Daniels, when suddenly I saw a light. I felt warm all over and I knew it was him. I've been saved ever since."

I shiver slightly pondering this notion of lasting salvation. The tremulous passion in her voice irks me because I have little faith that there is anything in this world worth sharing with people who listen to AM radio. I am further irked by her need to share that passion. Her confession is so personal, so exposed; something better left to intimate conferences between parishioner and priest. Maybe it's that I'm jealous. If left to the narrow darkness of a confessional, I would have nothing to say. And as I listen to Mary Jo, I wonder what bottom looks like. Is it cold, dark, hard? Or is it warm, full of celebratory people waiting for another to fall?

I'm having an affair with my boss, Bert, short for Bertrand, and I'm not sure why. He's a tight, asthmatic little man, with incomplete features and an unfortunate wardrobe. One night, while working late, he stood just outside my cubicle, rubbing his invisible chin as he watched me sketch an arched entryway for a new medical complex. Stretching my leg, I pushed a box of pilfered office supplies out of his line of sight and tapped my fingers against my desk. He muttered something about my hair and when I turned around, he was gone.

Later, waiting for the elevator, he slithered towards me, wheezing slightly, as he adjusted and re-adjusted his wrinkled grey slacks. I nodded politely, pressing my fingertips against the metal up and down buttons, and the elevator doors. Again, he muttered something. I stared at him trying to muster a polite smile of indifference. When he said, "Great, let me get my coat," I nodded, wondering what was so great. Two years later, I'm still wondering.

"If you have a story of how you were saved, call now; again that number is 593-SAVE," Mary Jo says.

I grope the passenger's seat before remembering that I don't have a cell phone. I don't have a story to share with Mary Jo, but I do have questions. No one calls. Traffic is light, and the road feels bland, empty. There is no scenery, only mile after mile of corn or wheat or soybeans, I can't tell which after a while. As I enter Illinois, the radio crackles, and I sigh, relieved. I am no longer receiving the ministry of KRST. My back aches, and my eyes are watering. I can feel a burning sensation between my thighs, but I'm lazy enough to debate stopping, because I simply don't have the energy to get out of the car

A few miles down the road, I come across a truck stop, just outside of Joliet. I've never been to Joliet, but I've always liked the name. It reminds me of Shakespeare. Quickly, I climb into the backseat, again banging my knee against the gear shift. I don't stop to wince, because I really have to go. I stutter towards the dirty glass doors, my thighs dancing around each other, holding back the tide. I try not to breathe as I sit on the lukewarm toilet seat. The odour is that of the rank industrial disinfectant that wipes away the memories of the people who pass through here.

Before I wash my hands, I leave my mark against the chipping surface of the stall door, and the ceramic sink basin. In the lobby of the truck stop, there is a large map with a bright red star over Joliet. **You are here.** I pretend to study the map as I press my fingertips along the route I'll be taking to wherever I'm going. I whisper softly, "I am here," again and again. After grabbing an overcooked hotdog swaddled in grease and more coffee, I light a cigarette and return to my car, feeling refreshed, but hot.

Spending time with Bert is like attending the opera – all an acquired taste. Once you overlook his symphony of bad habits, and his aggravating penchant for wheezing and adjusting his pants, he is almost tolerable. The first time we made love was as accidental as our first date. I was wearing good underwear, just in case, and he had walked me to my door after an evening at Sizzler. He shifted from foot to foot, as he looked up at me, an almost sheepish smile on his face. I stared at the numbers on my front door, trying to make out the faint lines of fingerprints, pulling back slightly, as I felt his hand slide around my waist. Tilting my head, I forced a smile, waiting for the inevitable.

Bert kept clearing his throat, pulling his hand away to adjust his pants, occasionally switching the routine up, by running a hand through what's left of his hair. I finally tired of his fumbling, and leaned down, kissing him softly. His body froze for an instant. His lips were thin, but soft, briefly comforting. Then his arms flew around me and Bert moved his head vigorously from side to side. I do not think he realized that he should probably move his lips as well. Standing there hunched over, because Bert is five inches shorter, I remember thinking *so this is what pursed lips feel like.* He tasted like dinner mints and cheap cigars.

Later that night as we lay in my bed, I stared at his sleeping form, wishing for a marker with which I could add the facial features he seemed to be missing – a strong chin, two eyebrows, a fuller nose. Maybe a scar or two, because I like scars; they tell tales.

I'm on the Indiana Turnpike now, but little has changed in the way of scenery. Every fifty miles or so, there is a convenient rest area replete with greasy fast food and overpriced souvenirs. I refuse to stop at any of these, because they are inundated by irritable travellers, tired children and bored employees, none of whom I have the patience to deal with. Between cigarettes and fiddling with the radio, I clasp and unclasp my fingers around the steering wheel. I've done this so many times over the years that the steering wheel is now embedded with deep inward curves. If I look hard enough, I can see my fingerprints interlaced into an indefinable pattern. I remember that I should call someone, but I don't. I think about Bert for a moment and conclude that he's merely convenient, like the rest areas and replete with annoyances.

The workday is almost ending, and I doubt anyone has noticed that I didn't come in today. Bert won't be getting laid tonight, and by now I'm sure he's left a nasally message on my voice mail, wondering if I'm shutting him out again, assuring me that it's okay that I missed work. Bert took a few psychology classes in college, and thinks that he can analyse me. In many ways, I'm his pet project. He wants to reach me. He wants to understand me. He'll often suggest that I'm emotionally detached. I know that the problem is more that I have yet to find something or someone I care to attach my emotions to. He'll say that I need to open up to him, for our relationship to grow. But Bert is married and I know that there is nowhere for our relationship to grow.

Every now and then I'll turn my head, my neck stiff, my shoulders tight, to watch people in other cars. It's fascinating to watch lips moving in conversation or singing. I try to imagine what is being said, and find myself joining in these private exchanges. It's something to break the monotony of the cold asphalt and the waning sun.

If I had friends, they'd tell me that I could do so much better than Bert. They'd tell me that I'm selling myself short. And I would nod, and pretend to agree, but I wouldn't really care. My mother and I discuss Bert every now and then. She says that he is the colour of tap water. She doesn't bother telling me what this really means or that I could do better, because she doesn't like to state the obvious. Instead, she reminds me that he is nice, for a married man, and because she claims to understand me, she doesn't judge.

Bert's been married forever. I've never met his wife, Brenda, but it is said that she's a real gem of a woman. I picture her with an aquiline nose and watery blue eyes, over-processed hair, and a fashion sense rivalling Bert's. They have no children, only a pet poodle named Cookie that they dote on lovingly, and a country club membership that keeps Brenda in tip-top social shape.

I've just passed through Cleveland. We came here once, when I was a child, but I don't remember anything about that trip, save for getting lost in the middle of the night. I sat staring at the darkness as my parents fought in the front seat. My mother was trying to navigate, my father was certain we were heading in the right direction. He got so angry that he slammed his fist against the dashboard, sending a styrofoam cup of coffee flying across the atlas. While he wiped the atlas with the tails of his shirt, pretending that his hand didn't hurt, my mother crossed her arms across her chest, looking smug.

I don't think I've ever felt this sore. Even my fingertips ache. I wonder why I'm so out of shape, but I shouldn't be surprised. I smoke two packs a day, drink too much coffee, and don't know how to cook, so my diet consists of pre-packaged ham sandwiches from the convenience mart near my apartment, and a wide variety of frozen pizzas. My idea of exercise is walking the short distance from any given door to my car. At home, I spend my time reading. I feel the tinge of reclusive glamour as I curl into my couch, poring over a worn book, burning holes into my clothing with forgotten cigarettes. My favourite is *The Catcher in the Rye*. I am enchanted with its irreverence.

I'm a few miles away from the Ohio/Pennsylvania border and a migraine is lurking behind my eyes. I'm sorely tempted to drive my car right off the road. The next exit promises a plethora of motels, so, stifling a yawn, I pull off the interstate, and settle on the sleaziest-looking one. I like sleazy motels, because they remind me of Bert. While we've never frequented one, our relationship has that taint, with him scurrying home to his wife as I change my sheets, and scrub his scent from my skin.

I don't bother with my duffel. All I need is my cigarettes and a flat surface. The *Vacancy* sign blinks intermittently, and I throw a rock at it as I enter the small office. It's about the size of my cubicle at work, with bright floral print wallpaper and matching shag carpet. Again, I smell industrial disinfectant, so I make sure to press my fingers against the counter while I fill out the card with my licence plate number and address. The bored clerk throws a key in my direction, and rolling my eyes, I head for my room.

The decor in the room matches that of the office. The double bed, with a stained bedspread, sags in the middle, tattling on previous occupants. There's no remote control, so I ignore the television. I've forgotten how to turn one on manually. Before I lie down, I creep along the walls of the room, leaving my fingerprints. My breathing is harsh and ragged. I can feel tiny beads of sweat forming on my forehead. My hands are sore, very sore, but I don't want to leave an inch of this room unmarked.

It is said that the FBI has millions of fingerprints on file, but I've never committed a crime. I often wonder what would happen, if someone came upon my fingerprints. My complicity with the law has rendered the whorls, loops, and arches meaningless. Before I leave, the next morning, I throw the ashes from the cigarettes I've smoked against the walls and the end table, smiling as they reveal my fingerprints, however meaningless they may be.

I can feel a familiar ache in my body as I sit behind the steering wheel and head into upstate New York. This region of the state is wine country, and on all sides I can see the harvested vines withering. From the large billboards screaming at me, I know Niagara Falls is near. I've never been there either. In fact, I've never been this far from home. I live ten minutes from the house I grew up in, and my parents will probably die in that house, because like me, they are apathetic by most people's standards, including mine. I suppose, rather, I am like them. They appreciate the comfort of an existence that doesn't require much effort. When they've had one whiskey sour too many, they'll babble about moving to Florida, but when they've sobered up, they're still sitting in the kitchen, my father scratching his chest, as my mother reviews her recipe collection.

My parents met in high school, and got married because it seemed like the right thing to do. They aren't particularly enamoured of each other and they love to fight, but they stay together, because a divorce would require some amount of passion. I get the impression that I was an afterthought, because I am an only child, and my parents only took notice of me, because my mother was in labour for eighteen hours. She never lets me forget that fact. When I was nine, I'd go to Sunday School where Mrs Frink often talked about purgatory, this mythical place where our souls were cleansed before moving on to Heaven. One morning, I raised my hand, and asked if purgatory was living. My conclusion made good sense to me. Mrs Frink frowned, and after class, she gave me a note for my parents, patting me on the shoulder. But she never answered my question. I still wonder what that note said, but I threw it away without showing it to my parents.

I've decided to drive to New York City. Gotham beckons. Three hundred miles to go. My knowledge of New York is limited to what I've seen in movies, or read in books, so my goal, now that I have one, is to reach the fabled Brooklyn Bridge just as the sun is setting. If I were a romantic person, I'd go to the Empire State Building, or take a few rides at Coney Island, but I'm not. I'd like to be that kind of person, but I don't know how.

I've realized lately that my body feels lonely. I need to commit the act of touch with someone that means something to me. But I don't have that someone, so I continue to yearn. I can imagine what my parents are doing right now. My father is staring at the TV, drinking a sweaty bottle of beer. My mother is in the kitchen, cooking. Later, they will sit side by side eating dinner, exchanging nary a word. They will watch more television until ten, and then they'll go to sleep, wrapped around the edges of the bed, a wide expanse of emptiness between them. It's how Bert and I sleep, when Brenda is visiting her mother in Palm Beach or her sister in Chicago. Sometimes I want to reach across the bed and touch him, to remind myself that he's in my life. I want to feel the pale, thin skin that covers his bones. I want to feel *something* for him. My hand slowly inches across the sheets, but I always stop with my fingertips a whisper away from the sharp slope of his back, gentle words dangling from my lower lip. If he stirs, I immediately pull my hand away, pressing my fingertips against the bed frame, listening as he resumes his steady snore. And then my hand will slide back across the bed, fat tears sliding silently down my cheeks, because I cannot reach far enough.

Once I get where I'm going, I'll give my parents a call. Or maybe I'll wait, because it will be a few days before they realize that I haven't called. They have their routines, and today, I doubt that I am on the agenda. I remember coming downstairs every morning to find my father sprawled in his favourite chair, snoring gently. His lips would part slightly, a thin strand of saliva swaying back and forth with every breath. And his clothes were always the same, a dark tie hanging limply around his neck, and a short-sleeved dress shirt, the armpits stained with sweat and ineptitude. His cheap polyester pants would cling to his body in disarray. In my worn Spiderman pyjamas, I would tiptoe around the room, picking up his discarded beer bottles, before my mother could wake only to find that he had drunk himself into a stupor, yet again.

I never knew why I did this. Everything I knew about my father, my mother knew as well. We had a pact, my mother and I, to avoid the truth at all costs, besides which, some nights, she lay right next to him, cradling a bottle of cooking sherry or an empty box of wine.

I remember watching my father come home from work, heading directly to the refrigerator for a cold beer, and every time I approached him, I could feel . . . I could smell the indifference. I would sit at his feet, staring at the cheap black leather shoes with worn tassels, watching his legs cross, then uncross, as he stared at the television screen. At times, I wanted to reach out, resting my small hand against his thigh, but there was that smell that told me I shouldn't. I invented stories that might grab his attention, chattered about my day at school. But he would pat my head indifferently, and reach for the remote.

So I would patter into my mother's sewing room, and sit at her feet, staring at the wrinkled nylons sagging around her ankles, watching as she made a Halloween costume or Christmas decorations. Sometimes I was content with surrounding myself with the smell of her jasmine perfume, and face powder. Other times I would sit so close to my mother that only a breath of air sat between us. But we never touched. I would only sit, telling my mother the same stories, hoping that sooner or later, she would look up from the needle she was threading. Instead, she would tap her foot, listening to Jimmy Buffet, a thimble on her finger and a vacant expression on her face.

It's late afternoon and I've reached *the city*. My father's old atlas has new creases and stains. After passing through the Holland Tunnel into Manhattan, I toss the atlas out the window. I've never seen traffic like this, an endless stream of cars engulfed by monstrous buildings. My window is rolled down, and a painful blend of radios, voices and horns interrupt the silence I've been surrounded by for the past two days. I'm driving in the middle lane, slowly, and angry drivers pass me on both sides. I'm not lost, but I feel misplaced. I want to pull over and leave a fingerprint somewhere . . . anywhere, but there are so many cars around me. There's nowhere to go, but forward.

A while later, I've negotiated the city traffic and I'm at the Brooklyn Bridge. I park my car in a deserted lot, and grabbing my cigarettes, I walk to the anchorage located in the pilings on the Brooklyn side of the bridge. The chambers are vaulted like cathedrals, with unbelievably high ceilings. The place is overrun with tourists and their sticky children, high-pitched voices echoing back and forth. Closing my eyes, I run my hands along the walls, careful to leave my fingerprints. I remember reading about this bridge in an architecture class. It was hailed as arguably the most influential bridge in American history, and mentioned something about the architect dying during its construction. For some reason, I find that poetic.

As I leave the anchorage and head for the walkway in the centre of the bridge, I have to admire its elegant structure. The bridge is anchored across the lower East River by two neo-Gothic towers and a delicate lacework of steel wire cables. Squinting, I stare up at the soaring lines of the bridge, jostled back and forth by nameless people with somewhere to be. My hands fumble along the railing, as I leave a trail of fingerprints. Only this railing and about a foot and a half of thin wooden planks separate me from the river. I notice a few people staring at me, but I ignore them, looking down at the water. It looks dirty and cold; dark yet calm.

I wonder if water holds fingerprints.

Again, I close my eyes, lighting a fresh cigarette. I'm tired and thirsty and cold. I ache.

I want . . .

I want to scream . . . say something, say anything, but my throat is dry, so instead I take a long drag on my cigarette, the acrid smoke burning its way into my lungs.

I think of Bert sitting at his desk, chewing his nails furiously and the office supplies still hidden under my desk and Brenda playing tennis at the country club while Cookie the pet poodle has a manicure. I think of my parents – I never did call them and I realize that I forgot to lock my car.

Passers-by move past me, and my cigarette hangs from my dry lips while my hands dance along every surface I can find and I'm thankful that I'm wearing my good underwear. The air sluicing around me feels like ice.

I slowly realize that nothing momentous is going to happen here. I want to go home. Shoving my hands into my pockets, I spit my cigarette out, watching it float in the air beside me, before falling into the churning river. For a brief moment, I wonder . . .

And then I'm walking back to my car, almost running.

I pull out of the abandoned parking lot and drive onto the bridge. Again, the traffic is overwhelming. My car is barely moving forward. I look around me, remembering the dark calm of the river. I slam on the brakes, and as the blare of horns assaults me, I crawl out of the car and stand right in front of it. Cars stop. A few drivers roll their windows down, yelling as they veer around me. Sooner or later the police will come, and my fingerprints will become attached to my name. I light another cigarette and place a foot on the hood of my car and then I'm on the cold roof sitting, my legs crossed, smoking, rocking back and forth, whispering, "I am here."

How I Got Away

Leslie What

The temperature was up around a hundred the night my little sister disowned me. I was dressed in black jeans, a black T-shirt, black nail polish, black lipstick, black horn-rimmed sunglasses, and a black beret – and not, like my little sister thought, because I was a wannabe Monica, but because my roots needed retouching, and frankly, who had the time? I admit it was a stupid fashion choice for summer, but I looked great.

I stood on the sidewalk to dig through my black handbag for my car keys. Dang, but it was hot, even after dinnertime, even in the shade. Just then, some neighbour whose name I had forgotten came back from the corner grocery. He saw me getting ready to leave and said, "You sure had some wild times up there, didn't you?" He was about my age – a couple too many years past thirty – and wearing those rubber yellow flip-flop shoes that made embarrassing farting noises with every step.

I had on leather shoes, black, of course. Open-toed platforms. The kind that screamed SEX but without needing to moan. There was nothing like walking around the block on cowhide when you needed an extra lift, and I needed the extra lift after all that had happened. It had been the worst day of my life, or just about. The only thing I could say in my defence was that at least my shoes didn't fart when I walked. Not that anybody I knew cared about my good points, and who could blame them?

The neighbour whose name I forgot opened up his grocery bag, handed me a Coors, and said, "One for the road, babe. Good luck and happy trails."

I thanked him, and right away started drinking because I was so upset I already couldn't see straight. Besides, beer usually helped to clarify things. The more beer the better, at least that's what I always said.

My little sister came out onto her apartment balcony to yell down at me, "How could you do this to me, you bitch? You slut!"

She was talking about her husband. About how she thought he'd been unfaithful, and with me.

Technically, he wasn't and we didn't, but this wasn't a courtroom and I wasn't going to be set free because of any technicality. When she called me a slut it hurt my feelings. "You're making a mistake," I told her. "It's not what you think! It didn't mean a thing! Really!" But my little sister kept on adding more significance like she was sprinkling salt on Brussels sprouts to make them edible.

The neighbour whose name I didn't know was giving me the eye. "Wanna go out sometime?" he asked, and I took a card from my purse that said:

> Rev. Deb Mortenson
> Church of Arnold
> Oracle and Priestess

and handed it to him.

I'd earned my mail-order degree in divinity and had started up my own church, a church that believed in everything I did, which really made it easy to belong. The chapel was in the front seat of my car, a black Coupe De Ville. "Call me sometime," I said, not that I had a phone number anymore, or even a phone.

Meanwhile, my sister was screaming her head off. Her face turned bloody-Mary-red; she called me a slut again. "Get out!" she screamed. "I never want to see you again."

I still wasn't sure just how serious she was. Our parents were dead; she was my only family. I was hoping she'd get over it.

"Can I call you later?" I yelled. "Don't worry. Not collect!" My poor sister was making a fool of herself in front of everyone. I couldn't help but feel badly for her. Yet nobody had ever called me a slut before and I wasn't so sure what to make of it.

"See you around?" said the neighbour whose name I didn't know.

"Unlikely," I said, but smiled enough that he couldn't tell I was making fun of him. In my line of work, in the ministry, it was important to master that technique early on or you didn't get far.

My vintage Cadillac was parked beneath the avocado tree that had croaked the previous summer, during that big heat wave when we weren't allowed to water our yards, and practically everything had died. To keep my butt from blistering I sat down on top of a beach towel with a likeness of my personal saint, Arnold Schwarzenegger, who I believed was the strongest man on earth.

Maybe if I had spent my summer like a normal woman – in a bikini, with my towel spread out on Newport Beach and my lips smooching Arnold's terry cloth mouth – I wouldn't have been in so much trouble. Instead, I had stayed with my little sister and her two-timing husband, and now here I was, acting tough while covering up Saint Arnold's face with my ass. It was an awkward position, to say the least.

"Get the fuck out of my life!" shrieked my little sister. "Go away!" She was making a fool out of herself and it was embarrassing.

"Going," I said, still unsure just how serious she was, but beginning to get the idea.

I held my breath while turning the key. Lucky for me, the engine started. I unrolled all the power windows. Even though it was a hundred degrees out, my old car needed warming up. Life was so weird in that way. The Coors, ice cold when I'd first got it, warmed up before the car. Couldn't understand where the cold went. Not inside me; I was hotter than a Branch Davidian.

A cool breeze blew against the back of my neck, making the weather *almost* tolerable. Maybe wind was where cold went once it floated away from your beer. I got to thinking about the Heaven's Gate cult, and how that guy, Do (only he pronounced it, "dough"), got so many people to join. Probably had air conditioning in his mansion. An AC was all it would have taken to get me into any cult or mansion, that's how hot it was. I was ready to become an apostate in my own church, which should have given me a clue about the sincerity of my faith.

Too bad Do had died before getting famous enough to give seminars on the secrets of successful cult management to wannabes like me. He could have made a lot of money on the lecture circuit. Probably more than in the cult circuit. I hoped Do had made it into heaven, like he planned. I thought about what a drag it would have been to kill yourself and all your followers and then not even get into heaven! Talk about irony!

That was the chance Do took, being a visionary; who was I to say my pathway was any more direct? So far, I was the only member of my church, which made fundraising rather difficult; I was always broke. My church needed air conditioning if we had any hope of expanding. I decided to make air conditioning one of our central tenets, starting tomorrow.

I took one last look at my sister. Her curls were plastered against her face like broken veins. She looked so skinny it was pathetic. She was pale and tiny, someone I should have wanted to protect. When she noticed me watching, she gave me the finger.

I shrugged, waved goodbye. It pained me to look at her. "Sorry you feel that way," I yelled. I was pretty sure I really meant it. The engine stopped sputtering in preparation for takeoff. "Okay, I'm history," I said, ready to leave.

At that very moment, my little sister ran back into her apartment. She returned two seconds later with the goose down comforter I had given her for her wedding. She screamed, "Bitch!" and tossed the quilt over the edge.

I guess there was no point being comforted when you suspected your husband of porking your older sister, but it was quality down, and I was a bit surprised at her carelessness. I got out of the car and stuffed the whole shebang in the trunk beside my suitcases. "I'll send it back later," I said.

"Fuck you," my little sister answered.

I drove away then, filled with regret because of the terrible misunderstanding. I hadn't the slightest idea of how to make things right. At the first "Stop" sign, I stopped to take off my beret and wrap my hair in a black silk scarf to keep it from blowing all over the freeway. That was all I needed – to get busted for littering hair – on top of everything else. Littering hair was probably a felony in Southern California. Man. I missed Nevada, where a white girl could do practically anything without ever worrying about breaking the law.

At the last gas station before the turnoff, I spent the last of my money on gas. It wouldn't get me far enough, but I figured anywhere was better than here. I didn't know where to go next. If I had believed in God I would have asked Him for directions. But because I was an atheist with a bad attitude and a church to support my unique way of thinking, I prayed to my personal saint. "Rescue me, Saint Arnold," I said and got back into traffic. And somehow I ended up on Highway 101 heading north. Hallelujah! My faith was restored.

My sister had accused me of being jealous of her happiness. Ha! Showed how little she knew. Happiness! She didn't know the meaning of the word. She was still stuck with her no-good two-timing husband while I was free of them both, on top of the world, or at least on top of Saint Arnold.

I was thinking of checking out the Bay Area, where I might be able to find work in one of those drive-through tarot card readings and cappuccino stands. I had been an amateur fortune teller for fifteen years now and was pretty good at it. Maybe it was time to get serious. Maybe the whole thing with my little sister's husband was fate's way of giving me a kick in the butt to change my course. And if my career in fortune telling didn't take off, well I would always have my church to fall back on. The Bay Area was as bereft of spiritual guidance as anywhere.

Despite my plans, I couldn't help but worry about my predicament.

For one thing, I was broke. I had taken the summer off to stay with my sister and I was almost out of savings. Actually, ever since filling up at the gas station, I *was* totally out of savings. I gave myself a pep talk, but lost my confidence pretty quickly. "Okay, Saint Arnold," I prayed, "where to now?"

He answered me like always, in what a non-believer would have said was only my imagination, in his thoughtful and loud authoritarian voice. He said, "I WILL PROVIDE," coincidentally, exactly what I wanted to hear.

Lucky for me, I saw a clean-looking hitchhiker leaning on the freeway's shoulder. I had been a part-time idiot for most of my adult life, but I knew better than to pick up guys like Charlie Manson: guys with satanic tattoos or hairy bellies or chewed-up clothes. Guys like that lacked people skills, that much was obvious. If they'd had people skills they'd have been able to charm some co-dependent lady into mending their zippers. I knew from my work in the ministry that any guy without people skills was doomed to resort to a life of crime and safety pins holding up his pants.

No way would I ever let myself become a victim.

I considered myself the worldly type, the type who could sit on the Terminator's face and be proud of it. But even a blind, deaf, and dumb idiot with leprosy and only three days to live would have known that this clean hitchhiker guy posed no threat to life, liberty, or limb whatsoever. At least that's what I thought at the time.

The clean guy wore brown corduroy pants and a beige T-shirt with a drawing of a fish eating a fish with legs on it. His backpack was full and his Reeboks were clean. Either his shoes were brand-new or else the clean guy didn't get out very often. I had *nothing* to fear from him. Nothing. It could *not* have been more obvious.

I pulled over onto the shoulder. The clean guy ran the hundred-yard dash to my car, opened the passenger side door and hopped in. He tossed his backpack down, politely asked, "Where you headed?"

"North," I said. "Can you spare something for gas?"

Lucky for me, he wasn't too experienced in the hitchhiker department. He pulled out his sporty nylon wallet and gave me twenty dollars. I did some quick calculations. At my present rate, I was at least five hitchhikers short of San Francisco.

But then he let me see he had a lot more money and even some credit cards. I decided to be just nice enough to get him to take me out to dinner next time I got hungry.

I pulled back onto the highway. The wind blasted me like a dozen hair dryers; in a couple more minutes my lips felt freeze-dried, and I got scared they might fall off onto the highway. Getting busted for littering lips would be even more embarrassing than getting busted for littering hair. I managed to patch my lips back together with two coats of gloss while I tried to think about what I was gonna do next.

The clean guy shifted about like he needed to go to the bathroom. I recognized that signal. He was getting up the nerve to talk. Shit, I thought. Here it comes. Probably wants a blow job. Like so many of them. My sister's husband, for one. But when he finally did talk, it was even worse.

"Coupe De Ville," he said. "De Ville. The luxury car of the devil. Lady," he said. "Do you know Jesus?"

Why he thought I would want to talk religion with him I will never know. I was just about to tell him about the Church of Arnold and all we stood for, which was nothing, when he said, "Christ loves you."

Before I could answer, he opened his pack to take out a Holy Bible. He read something from a page marked with a silver clip, but the wind was almost too loud to hear him.

"Je-sus," I screamed. "You're not preaching to me, are you?" That was all I needed, on top of everything else. I didn't believe in any religion I couldn't control. That was why me and Saint Arnold got along so well.

"Lady," he said, and this time I did hear. "Don't you worry about Hell?"

"Je-sus," I said. I should have stopped my car and shoved his lumpy ass over onto the freeway, where it would fry like scrambled eggs in a hot wok.

Lucky for him, I wasn't that type of woman. "In my religion, we don't believe in Hell," I said, hoping to shut him up.

"You must be one of the Chosen People," he said, and I said, "No, I'm an Arnoldist," and finally he did shut up, but only for a while.

Evangelists were such a pain in the butt! What gave them the right to think they knew God's will any better than the rest of us? As if our relationship weren't bad enough, he had to go and make it worse.

"Even a whore can be saved by the love of Jesus," said the clean guy.

"What did you say?" I screamed. I struggled to keep my car in the lane and almost lost the fight to a blue Volvo.

"I was talking about Jesus," said the clean guy.

I forced myself not to scream. "I do not want to hear about it," I said.

A whore was a woman who sold her most precious possession to the highest bidder. No way was I a whore. My sister's low-life husband had never given me a dime, and I could prove it with my cheque register.

I'd never even had sex with my sister's husband, not really. That a-hole had crawled into my bed, tried to seduce me, then fallen asleep before it hardly started. We'd all been drinking margaritas and he was so drunk his penis had withered in my hand like a zucchini left too long on the vine. If my sister had let me explain before she kicked me out, she might have laughed about the whole thing. Because nothing had happened, when you thought about it. Nothing! It was all a big mistake and my sister's throwing me out of the house was more punishment than I deserved.

Arnold said, "CALM DOWN," but I was trembling. First my sister had called me a slut and now this hitchhiker had upped that to a whore. If I didn't know any better I'd have thought they were trying to tell me something. Lucky for me, there was this other hitchhiker. I noticed how this hitchhiker *did* resemble Charlie Manson, but I didn't give a damn anymore, and swerved to pick him up.

The Manson hitchhiker was missing two teeth and had long straggly hair and a bushy beard. His knapsack was dog filthy and held together with safety pins. He was wearing a leather vest with no shirt underneath and skin-tight blue jeans that bulged like he carried grenades in his pockets. A cartoon drawing of Satan on a Harley was tattooed in red on his forearm.

He was scary, but I didn't mind, so long as he rescued me from the Jesus freak.

The clean guy wiped sweat fmm his brow and said, "I'll hop in back." Probably afraid of having Charlie Manson behind him where he couldn't see him. I understood how he felt. There were times I felt uncomfortable sitting on Saint Arnold.

Charlie let the clean guy out and took his place. "Nice car," said Charlie in that tone of voice that let me know he was thinking about stealing it. "Where you going?"

"North," I said. "Where you headed?"

"Anywhere but here," said Charlie.

I didn't like the sound of that coming from someone else.

"You got twenty bucks for gas?" I asked.

"Sure," said Charlie. He took out his wallet. He had much more than that. Much much more.

I took this as a sign: my personal saint had provided an outlaw with money. "Way to go, Arnold," I whispered.

"Nice scarf," Charlie said, pointing like he was aiming a trigger at my head. "You have excellent taste."

"Thanks." I felt my cheeks flush because I liked this evil hitch-hiker, even though I knew he'd rob me the first chance he got. Worse thing was, I wanted him to like me. My constant need for approval sometimes made me want to barf.

I pulled back into traffic. The next thing I knew, Charlie took out a bag of marijuana. He bent way down out of the wind to roll himself a joint. He lit the joint, took a few tokes, sat up to offer it to me.

"No thanks," I yelled. "Maybe later." I didn't even smoke pot; I just didn't want to offend his sensibilities.

Meanwhile, the clean guy was screaming Scripture from the back.

"Jesus," said Charlie. "Not this shit." Charlie yelled at the clean guy and told him to shut up. That didn't work. After a few minutes Charlie said, "Pull over. Let's get rid of him."

Not like I hadn't thought that myself! Though it was different having someone else tell me what to do. And what exactly did Charlie mean by, "Let's get rid of him?" Coming from a serial killer, it had an ominous ring. Lucky for the clean guy, I was sitting on my conscience.

I heard Arnold yell, "DON'T STARE HELPLESSLY IN THE FACE OF EVIL!" and that made me take action.

"He can stay," I said. "It's my car."

Charlie looked pissed. "Okay," he said. "For now." He sounded annoyed and that got me worried.

I spaced out for a while but snapped out of it when the freeway lights crackled on as colour drained from daylight and the world began to fade and change to the black and white of evening. Twilight was one part of day I did not understand. The air was still hotter than a pizza oven, but growing darkness made it seem cool enough to trick my body, for a minute, anyway. For a minute I felt totally at peace.

"Help me out here, Saint Arnold," I said. Much to my surprise, my prayers were immediately answered.

All of a sudden, a police car, sirens blasting, pulled up behind me.

"Jesus," said Charlie. He bent down to eat his dope, plastic bag and all.

"Jesus," said the clean guy. "We'll be arrested."

Well, that was all I needed, on top of everything else. Just my luck they'd throw in a charge for attempted adultery, which was probably a capital offence within a four-hundred-mile radius of Orange County. How could Saint Arnold do this to me? Once again, I found myself struggling to keep my faith.

The police car pulled ahead of me and an officer gestured that he wanted me to stop.

I did and so did he.

The police officer walked up to the passenger side to talk to Charlie. "Step out of the car," he said. He made Charlie put his arms behind his back and stand facing the car. Another officer took down my licence number, then came up beside me to ask for my driver's licence and registration. He told me to go over on the shoulder so we wouldn't get run over.

"Do you know this man?" he asked, nodding at Charlie.

Charlie may have been a drug addict and murderer, but at least he was an honest one. He said, "I was just hitchhiking. This woman gave me a lift. We're complete strangers. She's innocent."

"I never met either of them before tonight," said the clean guy, thumping his Bible.

The policeman believed us. He took a long look inside the car and wrote down my name and – even though I no longer had an address – my address. The other one led Charlie away.

"Go on," said my police officer. "You'd better be more careful in the future if you want to stay out of trouble."

"Don't I know it," I said.

The clean guy pointed straight ahead and said, "That way lies Satan."

I stuck out my tongue and told him, "No, that way lies Oxnard." Too bad for him, I knew how to read a map.

He gave me a dirty look. "You'll be sorry for all you've done. I'm out of here," he said, and left without saying thank you for all I had done for him.

I hated it when strangers thought they knew more about my future than I did and gave him the finger. So I had made a few mistakes, so what? I now had forty dollars in my pocket and Saint Arnold beneath me and what did the clean guy have except a new story to tell his friends? And who had given him that story? Me, that's who! Instead of trying to lecture me he ought to have been grateful, maybe even made a bigger donation to my church. Besides, even a serial killer had sworn I was innocent.

"I SENT TWO ANGELS YET YOU DID NOT HEED THEIR MESSAGES," said Saint Arnold, out of the blue.

"Those guys were angels?" I said, but the more I thought about it, the more sense that scenario made. The whole evening was nothing if not a miracle.

Then I noticed something sticking out between the seat-cushion and the front seat where Charlie had been sitting and I turned on the dome light to get a better look. I reached over, pulled out a big silver buck knife with a carved bone handle. "Je-sus," I said. Something sticky covered the handle. So Charlie had killed somebody, then hidden the evidence where no one could find it.

Wasn't that what we all tried once we realized our mistakes?

I examined the knife for blood or hair, touched the blade with my fingertip. A pasty white film covered the metal, probably flesh or bone. When I sniffed the paste I knew it wasn't flesh or bone, but Jack Cheese. Fortunately, my Charlie Manson hitchhiker had only killed Jack Cheese, which was something I could live with. I could have sighed from relief if greed hadn't overcome me.

He had probably robbed a delicatessen. I stuck my fingers down the cushions and felt around some more in case there was some money. Poked myself with a safety pin, got popcorn under my nails, found some gum wrappers and a dime. Should have quit while I was ahead. Of course I didn't. Found a picture, taken years ago, before all the trouble, of me and my little sister. She'd always been the popular one, pretty and smart. Unlike me, she'd always had boyfriends and ambitions, always tried to help me when she could. It wasn't fair, the way I had always had to compete with her for attention.

I shoved the knife inside the cushion, flashed my lights and left them on, then pulled back onto the freeway and drove away as fast as I could. I was trembling like a Chihuahua, faint from heat, maybe some shame. My teeth began to tap dance in my mouth. I thought about turning around and going home, wherever *that* was. I could apologize to my sister for ruining her life by letting her husband almost pork me.

Except that I was feeling so guilty even my lungs hurt. I thought I was going to die and if that happened, I didn't want it to be in California. Maybe the clean guy was right and I was a whore. For the first time since the night before, I asked myself, why hadn't I thought to shove my little sister's husband out of my bed? Sure, he was drunk, but I was only sleepy.

And before I could duck, it hit me that maybe I had been flirting with the guy for months. I didn't like the truth of that. Maybe it wasn't all my sister's husband's fault the way I wanted it to be. If that was the case, how could I ask my sister to forgive me?

For once I didn't feel all that tough sitting on top of Saint Arnold. I mean, here I was, in the middle of Highway Confession, showing utter disrespect to my personal saint. I felt so sorry for myself, I could have cried except I wasn't the type. I was better at forgetting and moving on. I drove in a daze.

Too late I saw a desperate-looking lady on the side of the road with her thumb stuck out and my headlights reflecting off her eyeballs like she was some terrified deer. Not that any deer would be caught dead bumming a ride from someone like me. Deer might not have known where they were headed but at least they knew enough to get there on their own four legs.

It was dangerous for a lady to hitchhike, didn't she read the papers? She must have been deranged, carrying on like that. If that lady wasn't careful she'd end up raped or dead, at least sorry for all she had done. Stupid woman! Some people never worried about danger till too late.

Yet in a sick way, knowing there was someone potentially worse off than me cheered me up. Knowing there was someone with less assets than me gave me strength and a sense of direction. I decided to stop and help her out. Only before I could, I'd accidentally driven way past her. Oh well, and that was that. Sometimes, when you made a mistake, there was just no going back. I vowed to myself to stop and help the next time I saw a woman in need.

I heard a buzzing in my ears: Arnold, screaming, "TURN AROUND, YOU IDIOT!" and guilt coursed through me like embalming fluid. No matter what anyone tells you, this conscience thing was a pain in the butt. I slowed down to take the next exit, turned left, got on the freeway going the other way. Pulled off at the first off-ramp, turned left, got back on. My heart was thundering and I was sweating like Nixon at the hearings.

After five or six minutes I was right where I'd started. Too late. Got there just as the lady climbed into a car driven by a man with Hannibal Lecter hair. I screamed, "No!" and honked my horn. I shouted for her to get out and run to me. She didn't hear me or maybe Hannibal wouldn't let her out. Either way, she was on her own now. But not me. I had Saint Arnold watching over me, or vice versa.

I felt pretty bad but I had done my best to make things right by rescuing that safety-challenged lady. There wasn't any more that could be done, and if there was, I couldn't think of it. I had gone back for her, had tried to make things up. What did that clean guy know about me, anyway? No whore would have tried to help another person, so there! I gritted my teeth, held my head up and faced the wind, challenged it to cool me off.

Then Arnold had to go and ruin everything. "ADMITTING

YOUR MISTAKES IS THE FIRST STEP," Arnold said and I thought, Oh great! My personal saint was versed in twelve-step. "GO ON," Arnold said. "I TOLD YOU. ADMIT YOUR MISTAKE."

I was not about to admit anything, least of all to someone who already knew. I did not need any saint-in-a-towel giving me advice. I yanked Arnold out from under me and almost dumped him over the side of my car the way my sister had thrown away my comforter. Instead, I held him under my arm in a death lock.

"Eat Right Guard, sucker," I said, feeling Captain Kirk smug about the whole arrangement.

But something stopped me from committing Arnocide. Maybe it was the breeze that came from nowhere to hiss against my neck and whisper to me not to give up. For the first time all day I started to worry if there was any hope for me after all I'd done? The one thing I had forgotten to think up when I thought up the tenets to my church was whether a person could do anything so terrible they could never be forgiven. I was afraid to think about that now, because if the answer was No, I didn't want to know it.

I wrapped Saint Arnold around my shoulders and sat there for a long while, considering. I didn't know the words to use on my little sister to make things right. The right words had to exist, sure as I had a patron saint and my own church to back Him up. As soon as I had the chance I was gonna pray for words powerful enough to get my sister to forgive me. And that would be that.

I felt a lot better having thought up a workable plan.

Eventually, the hot night dried all evidence of tears. One thing I'd never understood was why wind always hit a person from behind, like it was afraid to face her? Maybe coming from behind was the only way to deal with life when things got too hot.

It took a while, but that while passed, and all my guilt lifted. I felt a sense of calm wash over me like a goodnight kiss. I didn't know what to do next, but I was certain to figure out something. I was an oracle and a priestess, who once upon a time, might even find some decent followers to believe in me. I tucked Saint Arnold back in his pew and started up the car. I slid back into traffic on Highway 101. And then I headed north until I got there.

Miles To Go Before I Weep

Brian Hodge

The air conditioner in Dickory Doc's wheezed like a horse ready for a bullet in the head, and we were all sweating our drinks out as fast as we could pour them down. The heat makes people crazy . . . but then, for most, it's not too hard a push.

This seemed as righteous a truth as any I'd thought lately, one of those things to cross your mind for no good reason, then before too many ticks of the clock, along comes somebody to prove it. I'll watch, not often one to ignore a good object lesson.

"See those two?" This newfound friend and confidant that I'd never see again after a few more drinks pointed along the bar. His finger was aimed at a blonde barmaid and a redheaded customer who looked to be having a race to see who could grow their roots out quicker. Likely this wasn't the source of the aggravation mounting between them, but my new bleary-eyed friend and I sat too far away, and the jukebox wept too loud with lament over no-good lovers gone away, so we didn't have a clue what it was all about. Just didn't much like breathing each other's air, I guess.

My friend, forgotten name and all, waggled his finger at the bar in front of us. "Next round says those two'll be scratching eyes out inside of five minutes. Okay?"

"Bet," I nodded, but knew the loss would be mine, because I just had to lay it down once more in favour of human decency. It was a faith thing, and some days we all need a little of that sort of exercise in our lives.

So we settled in for the wait, see what five minutes really feels like when you're waiting for something to break, be it the peace, a window, or a bone. Feels like eternity, and, not for the first time, I wondered why we couldn't all just live out our days five minutes at a time. Why, we'd all feel like we had forever in front of us.

Though I'll concede that, for some, that might be the very worst thing to stare them in the face each morning.

So we waited and mopped our sweat with napkins already soggy from the bottles and our foreheads, all that tension like a loaded gun at the other end of the bar and only a handful of us aware of it at all. The others in their own little lost paradises, desert rats and cowboys and bikers, and their women. They converged here like the varied breeds that come to a watering hole on the African savannah: drink, for drink you must, but drink knowing you run the risk of turning into somebody's lunch.

As much a charm school dropout as the redhead already looked, she started to look meaner still over some new volley of insults exchanged across the bar, tried to get in the last word once the blonde's back was turned by throwing one of those little pickled cherries at her. It missed by a foot, splatted into the wall where it popped like a devil's eye.

"Too damn hot is all," I said. "Now if we were in Canada, say, this wouldn't even be happening."

"If we were in Canada," said my friend, "she'd've thrown a moose pie."

"Sorry, I beg to differ. A cooler climate leads to cooler heads. Eskimos? They don't even have a word for war." I paused with my bottle at my mouth, reasoning this through. "You know . . . another Ice Age just might go a long way towards world peace."

"Vikings," he said, and rather resembled one himself. "You forgot about Vikings. There goes your whole theory right there."

"Damn," I said, and wasn't it always just this way? Brutal facts intruding on what seemed for the moment like a revelation, perfect and honest. It wasn't any easy thing, saving the world.

And I was truly sorry a minute later when my friend won his bet, when the whole stewpot of strife and bad blood at the other end of the bar came to its inevitable boiling head, and the rest of the scenario played out uglier than a haemorrhoid.

Harsh words led to a shove, the shove led to a slap, and the slap was the pin on the grenade. The redhead decided to try using the blonde to wipe her own bar, and glass went crashing while men grabbed to salvage what drinks they could, then cleared aside to give them room to fight it out. Dickory Doc's roused with a mighty roar by the time the blonde landed a solid punch to the redhead's jaw and went scrambling across the bar.

I've never yet seen a catfight that wasn't a spectacle of awe and horror. This is, I suspect, because such fights wear the masks of both comedy and tragedy. There isn't the brute strength of men out to bust a head – often a lack of the finer coordinations – so it's almost funny, those wild roundhouse swings and the feral faces that only furious women can make, and when the makeup goes, it only exaggerates things more. But then again, there's all the pure animal viciousness of tooth and claw, and that dark red-eyed bloodlust to not give up until one tears out the other's throat, and maybe drinks harsh foaming whiskey from the loser's skull.

They kicked and they gouged, tore loose flaps in each other's clothes, bit when they could. When they weren't grunting in fierce rage, they called each other names that no man could employ and get away with. In time they flung each other out the door to land beneath the sky of this burning Newby, California night. The air was still and only the bravest stars showed through LA's leftover smog, the city's only bequest to this desert town where rivers and dreams and old dogs came to die.

"I don't guess anybody calls the sheriff, do they?" I asked.

My friend shrugged his big Viking shoulders. "Friday night, no high school football, now what do you think?"

Desperate people with desperate hopes cheered as those four mean little fists pummelled away, or yanked out a dangling scrap of dark-rooted hair and flung it aside like a puny scalp. Locked in a deathgrip, the beautiful sweaty harridans went rolling across the gravel lot, through a dirty oil slick left by some heaving engine, and came out looking like negatives shot at a Kabuki theatre.

When she gave her rival's head a good knock against the lot, I thought the blonde might've been able to snatch victory from what was looking like defeat, but then the redhead reached up to bum a cigarette from some burly truck jockey, and went to work on the blonde's shoulder. She burned in one tight round hole after another, through the tattered T-shirt and then skin, and the blonde barmaid started to yelp as if she'd only just discovered what true pain really is. For the redhead it was like scenting fresh-spilled blood, and her fingers jabbed forward, going for one wide blue eye but missing by a fraction, hissing out the cigarette against the blonde's cheekbone.

There was no shortage of admiring cheers for that trick, although if my voice was heard at all, it would've been a groan of sickness. There was no comedy left, only tragedy, and I felt it all the way down to my gut; deeper, even, in some dark place where the soul cowers, protected in its final refuge. And I remembered when I used to try to intervene at such times as this, playing the peacemaker, before I got taught the true value of a smile and an empty hand.

It didn't take long for the redhead to finish things, all open-handed slaps and bitter bloody grins and rabbit punches. Two final kicks in the ribs, and the blonde curled up like a question mark at the end of her life's sentence. She lay in the gravel and the dust and the oil, not moving except for the labour of sore ribs as she tried to breathe. The redhead was up and swaggering back to the bar to nurse her own wounds, drink her just rewards, celebrate victory. Something to tell her grandkids about someday, on lazy Sunday afternoons at the trailer park.

The sated crowd was swift to break, following its champion back inside. All of them like chickens with their pecking order, strutting away to leave a bird-sized lump of feathers and blood heaped in the dirt. To the rest I guess she didn't exist anymore, barmaid or not. Peculiar, but then I'd never much liked Newby, coming through here. I always get the feeling I should've stayed at the motel.

I paid off my bar mate and told him he'd have to drink the spoils of war alone, and he didn't seem insulted as he went back inside with an unsteady saunter, and next thing I knew the lot was empty but for the final two of us, breathing the ghost of a smelly breeze from the west. I crunched over to where the blonde lay in her pain and defeat, went down on one knee.

"Do you need any help?" I asked, as gently as I could.

She lay in shadows, and her eyes didn't open. After a moment her backhand flashed with clumsy accuracy and a big chip of gravel ricocheted off my forehead.

"We'll put my eye out next time." I fumed a few seconds, even if her pride was the last thing she had to guard. "Anybody I can call for you, then?"

She struggled a moment, raised on one elbow, and started to snicker when she saw me covering my face with crossed arms. That little bit of a laugh did her face some good, battered as it was. Nothing but tangled hair and dirty scrapes, trickles of blood and swelling, and that crusty hole on her cheek like a wound from a .22.

"No. Not a soul," she said, looking as if she wished she'd never gotten up that morning, maybe all year. "Pretty sad, huh?"

I'd lowered my arms by now, and pulled a red kerchief from my pocket that I sometimes used as a bandanna. "It's clean," I said, and gave it to her. She went scooting backward to sit against a dusty fender and dab away at the damage.

"You know, what I can't figure out is, how come nobody moved in to stop it, you coming from behind the bar." We both knew what I meant. In every bar I'd ever been in, with any personality – good or bad – was the Eleventh Commandment: thou shalt not mess with the barmaid. Break it and unshaven angels would be dancing on your head in seconds, if only to save themselves from prolonged thirst.

The battered woman gave a spiteful look at the closed door. "Loretta? She's local. I'm not," and that said it all. "You must not be either, if you didn't know."

I shook my head. "No. I'm not."

She huffed with a short low whiskey laugh. "Well, looks like your IQ just shot up by forty points."

I grinned down at the gravel. "You're sure there's nothing you need?"

Her hand dropped to her side, came up with another big pebble that she held as if deciding whether or not to throw it. No fire behind it this time, just a quiet stubborn pride and a smile too painful to let loose.

I nodded, started across the lot against a backbeat of bass, thumping like a sick heart inside the bar. I got in my van and backed out, angled for escape, and when I stopped to put it into drive there came a frantic thumping up along the side of the van. Then her splayed hand slapping glass, and there she was in my window, more life in her than I'd thought she had left. I rolled the window down.

"I just saw your licence plate."

Florida plate, picture of a manatee in the centre. "And?"

"You wouldn't happen to be going back there, would you?" And the hope in her voice, her eyes . . . they lit up bright as fireworks, put all that damage in the dim background. I would imagine the sad faces of orphans are the same, whenever kind-looking parents tour the home. *"Would you?"*

"I'm leaving tomorrow morning."

"Can I ride along?" The fingers of both hands were curling over the edge of my door, fierce as eagle claws. "Only as far as Mississippi. I'll go halves on gas."

The last thing I wanted was an argument, her on the one side and my conscience on the other, both of them telling me the very same thing. At least my conscience wouldn't start throwing rocks.

"Mississippi?" I said, and then what must've sounded to both of us like yes. Probably not the best decision I'd ever made.

But the heat does make people crazy, and crazy never runs out of ways to show its face.

I didn't even get her name until the next morning, after I'd followed her directions to a half-size trailer she was renting. It sat on a flat slab of desert browns and scruffy chaparral, a tin can that had been kicked from one edge of town to the other.

Allison. She was Allison Willoughby, and everything she owned looked to fit in two suitcases and a purse as big as a saddlebag.

The back of the van, as empty now as it had been full on my way west, swallowed her luggage, and as strangers we bid a welcome goodbye to this weeping lesion of a town. Allison's middle fingers popped up like a pair of switchblades and with a demented ecstasy she jammed both arms out the window, and I believe if we'd known each other better she'd have jammed her bare ass instead.

"Worst month of my life," she told me, before one last bitter lunge out the window: "Fuck you all and the inbred horses you fell off of!"

She laughed then, laughed like a woman freed of unimaginably heavy weights, a woman ready to spread wings and soar. She tumbled back into the seat, radiant with relief. Propping her feet against the dashboard in their cowboy boots, and bare-legged up to faded cutoffs and a purple shirt tied off at her stomach. Last night's blood and oil and grime were washed away, leaving only the black eye, the bruises, the burn. She'd swept her hair down and to one side to hide the worst but it was poor camouflage. Pretty enough, under it all, but the set of her eyes and the tiny lines were like a map of whatever rugged road she'd travelled. One wrong word and her face could go hard enough to dull an axe blade.

"All that hatred in just one month," I said.

"Yeah, well, I didn't sleep much, so it felt like two."

"I'm guessing it wasn't by choice?"

"Real Rhodes Scholar, aren't you?" When she looked at me, her clear eye going to a slit, I felt chastised. "I'm almost afraid to ask what brought you there."

"Just business."

Which amused her. "What business in that godforsaken urinal could've brought you all the way from Florida?"

"You must know the cycle shop there. Coyote's Paw Harley?"

"Naturally." Allison grew a bit more respectful.

"It's the end of a route I drive two or three times a year. I stop at places all across the south, east to west. I make clothes and things, and shops like that are usually my best markets."

She was nodding, a cockeyed smile working its way around the puffier spots on her lips. "A genuine craftsman. Don't see many of those anymore."

This was true. I belonged to an increasingly obsolete breed, and even though the money could get tight at times, the freedom was more than compensation enough. And I liked being master of my own life, lackey to no boss, with a couple of people working for me back in Panama City. Liked to take a stretch of leather and shape it to fit an idea born in my head, or discover the idea sunk into the leather already, speak its language and hear what it had to say for itself. I could look at a rack of vests and jackets, chaps and belts, hats and odd one-off pieces, originals all, see them hanging there and feel that I'd taken something dead and made it live again.

Pitiful consolation, however, for the sad-eyed noble cows.

While steering, I groped around the floor among my strewn belongings, came up with a folder and gave it to her. She flipped through the pages, sketches I'd made over the past few months; new designs, variations on old. I told her that while I could save the van and myself a lot of hard mileage by shipping my wares out by UPS, there was something meaningful in seeing where they ended up. Where they hung, the people that'd be looking them over, wearing them; the ways they were all different, the ways they were all the same. It gave me a better idea what people might like, whenever I could call some new stranger to mind when I took up the sketch pad and pencil.

"Any of these do anything for you?"

Some did, some didn't. She slid one from the stack and held it up, an eyebrow cocked. The paper showed a vest, its origins half-biker, half-bondage. "Seriously?" she asked.

I shrugged. "Some people like a lot of straps."

"Some people *need* a lot of straps," and it sounded like the voice of experience.

I wondered how she'd come to be stuck in Newby for a month, and it took another hundred miles of desert and carrion before the story began to tiptoe out of her. Allison had spent the last couple of years in Las Vegas with a guy named Boyd, a name she pronounced as if it were synonymous with twisted birthmarks and siring by jackals. Boyd suddenly became possessed of the certainty that his destiny lay in Los Angeles, and off they went. Boyd soon lamented that all destiny was subject to mechanical cooperation, as dismayed as she to find them stranded in Newby with a thrown rod. A grinning mechanic eyeballed a four-day estimate on the car, then turned around and had it driveable in three. This she did not find out until the fourth morning.

"Boyd must've received a new message that his destiny no longer included me," she admitted. "And that's just fine with me, but all the same, I hope his destiny now includes syphilis."

I was getting the idea that Allison Willoughby knew how to nurse a grudge and never wean it.

"So my main priority became saving up for a bus ticket home to Mississippi."

"Must've been a lean month, if you couldn't even scrape up enough tip money for a ticket." This brought a glaze of defensive irritation that I thought I recognized: the money had gone someplace else, some higher priority. "Your family in Mississippi couldn't have sent you ticket money?"

"I only said it was home. Who said anything about a family?"

You did. It's written all over your face, I thought, deciding against pressing further. Sometimes, blood or not, a family isn't anything to be proud of, a burden to be shouldered, a last resort for the broken and the lost.

That place where you trade your pride for a few more days of hoping for a miracle.

We were into New Mexico when we pulled off to pass the night. I got a motel room with two beds, thinking surely that would suit everyone's needs, not learning it didn't until after we'd eaten, then sat sipping a couple of contemplative beers while staring off at the moonlit desert in that easy silence that comes when you no longer feel as if you have to prove anything. Little did I know.

"I'll sleep in the van," Allison told me when we got back to the motel.

"There's no reason for that. Look, it's not a handout. I'd've had to get a motel room whether you came along or not."

She planted herself on the parking lot, those bare, booted legs steady as pillars, arms defiant across her chest. "I've slept worse places than that, I'll be plenty comfortable in the van."

"For crissake, you don't owe me anything. I got the receipt and it's a tax deduction, so quit being so damned stubborn and get a decent night's sleep, why don't you."

But stubborn she was, so stubborn that if you threw her from an airplane she'd fall up just to spite you. I argued a minute longer because conscience demanded it, then gave up, and it wasn't until I'd gone inside, then brought her a pillow and blanket from the unused bed, that I caught a completely different look in her eyes. Allison staring beyond me through the open doorway, a basic mistrust of four walls and a door that she wasn't able to conceal quickly enough. Five hundred miles of shimmering road just hadn't quite done the trick: I'd not yet proved myself, overcome whatever she'd endured to prefer the hard van floor to the risk I posed.

"If you change your mind," I told her, "just knock."

But the knock never came, as I knew it wouldn't, and sleep mostly teased. It often does, in a bed slept in by successions of strangers, our only connection the same mattress. Their lives taunted me, kept worrying at my mind and heart.

I got up in the middle of the night to check on Allison, a task neither asked for nor seemingly required, so perhaps it was curiosity more than anything. Beyond the motel squatting at its lip, the desert breathed and hummed, full of life brought out by the moon. I stepped to the windows in the back of the van and peered in.

This was the second night in a row I'd seen her curled up, and while Allison looked far more serene this time, it didn't come without a price. In her makeshift nest of pillow and blanket, surrounded by a protective wall of luggage, she slept with a hand loosely folded around a snub-nosed revolver. Its nickel plating shone with a lethal gleam of moonlight silver. She touched it the way a girl twenty years younger would touch a teddy bear.

I stood watching her for a moment, watching the peace it gave her, and I felt too many things for this late at night. Too many conflicting aches and confusing impulses, but convinced above all that the sooner she was out of my life, the better.

Of course that was logic talking, and logic I'd never been all that eager to listen to.

So when we could argue no longer I went back inside to sleep through as much of the night as would have me.

After my morning shower I offered to go get breakfast in a bag for us while she grabbed her own shower. While Allison agreed to that, our eyes held a few beats longer than needed, an unspoken understanding between us that we both knew I was making myself scarce for her benefit. The revolver was nowhere to be seen but I suspected it lurked close at hand, in that giant purse.

I wondered who or what had prompted her to carry it. If it was something she'd owned a while, or had bought only after finding herself stranded in Newby. The latter would, at least, explain why she hadn't even managed the bus fare over the month.

Allison looked a lot fresher when we returned to the road, carrying with her that fine clean smell of a woman with all the taint of the world washed away. Her hair blew wild and free about her face and shoulders, and I imagined what it must feel like between stroking fingers.

"Hey, hey, Tom, guess what *I* found last night," she said, her voice almost sing-song.

"You tell me." But as soon as she went digging through my stuff on the floor I knew what it had to be. The blush started at the soles of my feet, went up from there.

She opened a little flat box and began to pull out books that were just as little, just as flat, and brought them to her lap. As she flipped through them she read the titles aloud: "*Baby Animals. Bobby Meets the Dinosaurs. The Jolly Barnyard. Little Bear Goes to the Moon. Mr Putter and Tabby Pour the Tea. The Ever-Living Tree.* Hmm. I think *The Jolly Barnyard* was also the name of a porn flick that Boyd tried to force me to watch once. These belong to your kids?"

I shrugged uneasily behind the wheel. "Yes and no."

"Either they do or they don't. I can't make it any clearer than that."

"I don't *have* any kids," I growled, the first time I'd raised my voice to her. "But someday . . . if I do, if I'm lucky enough . . . then these books, well . . . they'll belong to them then. Is that clear enough for you?"

She looked closely at me, but it was more than that. *Watching* me, looking through me; past the scar that creased the corner of one eye, past the black hair that was showing dabs of grey before I'd even left my mid-thirties. Allison looked and saw all this as if it were new, watched me with that type of wonder on her face that can go so many ways, from slow tears to withering laughter.

"You buy these," she said softly, "and you hang onto them? You just . . . hang onto them?"

I was wishing she'd go ahead and laugh. Maybe she could tell from my face that I picked them up all across the country during these trips; that I read them, over and over, but no matter how many times I read one it still hurt a little, because there was no one I was reading it to, and I was truly beginning to fear there never would be.

She aligned the books in her hands, with unexpected grace, and returned them to their box. "I think that must be the single sweetest act of faith I've ever heard."

"And probably the most futile," I admitted. "What the hell, I'd make a lousy father anyway."

"Think so? You don't *know* about lousy fathers."

"Oh, I don't, huh? Any law says *you* get to have a monopoly on them?"

She rolled her eyes, as if she regretted opening her mouth. "No. No law." Turning the spotlight back on me like an accusation: "What's your problem, you don't have enough faith in yourself to get past the shitty example he set for you?"

"Maybe I'd know the answer to that if he'd stuck around long enough to set an example in the first place." And I didn't want to talk about this. *My* van, seemed that I retained that right, and just maybe *she* had more to answer for than I did. "Now suppose in the middle of the night I'd gotten an urge to read *Mr Putter and Tabby Pour the Tea* before I could get back to sleep. Would you have shot me?"

Allison glared then; how she did glare, as if I'd crossed a threshold better left uncrossed, entered a room I should've passed by. "You came out to watch me, is that how you spent your night?"

"Right, leaving tongue-prints down the windows, that's just the highlight of my trip." I shook my head and scowled, making a list of all the things I hated right then. I hated this break in the routine I was used to, hated the town of Newby and myself for stopping there, hated that solitary rut I'd dug for myself back home, and probably hated Allison, too, for dredging this all up fresh and making it look so pathetic.

We were quiet for several minutes, during which I refused to look her way . . . except out of the corner of my eye, and that didn't count. She stared out the window most of the time, head on hand and elbow on upraised knee, and when I finally saw her face again it didn't look hard anymore. She'd lost herself out in the passing desert, haunted by old ghosts. That's the trouble with ghosts: one place is as good as another when they're of a mind to follow you.

"I wish *my* father hadn't stuck around," was all she said, and no more for hours, but it was enough, and I knew that she'd never outpace the ghosts no matter how far or how fast she ran.

East, always east, with that highway whine forever in our ears like a mosquito. At last leaving the desert behind somewhere in west Texas, east Texas a different state even if the map said otherwise. It was green here, a land whose lush hills and shaded bowers owed more to the south than the west.

I don't know if it was because of the cross words we'd spoken earlier, or something else, but the more the land blossomed and deepened around us, the more Allison drew herself up inside a dark cloak of mysteries. As though the ghosts were no longer content to walk the backdrop of whatever landscape we travelled, instead shaping it and painting it to suit themselves.

We were getting closer to her home, and when home fires burn cold in your heart, old haunts can stoke up the worst within you.

She broke her silence once we started listening to the blues, tapes that she dug from her bag and handled with reverence, well-played tapes that must have seen a hundred rooms, a thousand bottles. Old music, as primitive and powerful as the elements, those hounded, aching voices made tinny by the funnel of decades. Her favourite was a collection of historic recordings made on the old southern state pen work farms and plantations. Nameless black men singing with fevered hearts, for it was all the freedom they had left.

"Listen," Allison commanded, and I tuned in.

"It ain't but the one thing I done wrong,
I stayed in Mississippi just a day too long . . ."

"I have an idea how he might've felt," she said. "How come it's the innocent that get locked up in the worst prisons?"

"You're asking the wrong guy." I held to the wheel until I decided she deserved something more than that. "Maybe it's because the innocent are the first ones to run out of people to fight for them."

"That's justice for you," she said. "A lot of them down here believe in original sin, as I remember. No one's innocent, they preach at you. But the way I see it, it's just something they've convinced themselves of so they won't go crazy. It's a lot easier to stay sane when you think you're getting what you deserve."

"I've heard a few of those sermons myself. Or slept through, at least."

"But then you have to wonder what kind of prisons those good neighbours believe eight-, ten-year-old girls deserve. Especially when their fathers are holding the keys. In their cold hands." I noticed her jaw tightening as she spoke, the words squeezed past clenched teeth. "What do you want to bet they don't spend too much time trying to fit that into their system?"

I wasn't going to argue with her there.

And the more we stopped, the more it seemed people everywhere were intent on proving her right. Gas stations and truck stops and roadside diners, we'd walk in and gazes would flicker our way. You always check out the newcomers, over coffee or a cold drink, with a lazy eye and feigned disinterest. They'd see us and let their minds fill in the rest, grasping for the explanations that were closest at hand. We were one thing but most would see another.

The bruises on Allison's face had, over the past two days, deepened into richer colours, as bruises will do. The purple of royalty, the yellow of sunrise. And on too many of those assessing faces I saw the same reaction, at stop after stop. A welcome to a brutal brotherhood in the eyes of too many men; a grim recognition in those of too many women.

This was not lost on Allison, either. "Maybe I should wear a sign around my neck: *He didn't do it.*"

"Then I'd lose their hard-won respect for me," I deadpanned.

"Look at them. Some loss." She laughed and nudged my shoulder and it was the first time we'd touched, a nice warm circle on my arm glowing with vibrant new life. "Can you read lips? You know what they're saying, don't you?"

"Oh sure," and I didn't really need any special talent. "The bitch must've had it coming."

Maybe we'd achieved a breakthrough in trust, or maybe it was just that the steamier heat made Allison a little crazy too, but she decided she didn't need the van to go to sleep that night. We slept beneath the same roof, lullabyed by an air conditioner that roared and wept cool oily tears onto a soggy carpet.

I didn't ask about the gun, didn't see it. Laid awake in the noisy dark, wondering if her head rested atop a nickel-plated lump in her pillow. I'd hear her shift in sleep, imagining her hand straying to touch its cold comfort, just in case, just in case.

I'm sure she'd trusted her father too, once upon a time.

And the next night?

We'd travelled and we'd talked, we'd opened up what we dared of our lives, and I don't suppose a man and woman can spend every moment of three days together without each at least entertaining the question of what the other must be like to love, if only for a night. The wounded and the wrongly imprisoned are no different, and maybe even need the answers more. Need desperately to believe that the whole world isn't conspiring against them, that there really is a place of justice and grace for them out there after all. That two can find it more easily than one.

If only for a night.

We made love and made of it those things we most needed – a look into the future, a bid to bury the ghosts. A road toward all that was missing from our lives. A week from now would we even remember each other's names? Would we even want to, need to?

We made love and made of it what we could, as good as we knew how, the best parts still locked inside the prisons of our bodies and our hearts. Life builds us that way, and the hell of it is, it so often takes an act of faith or blood or both to unlock the cell door and set us free.

"I won't see you after tomorrow, I guess." Allison seemed to mourn the inevitable as she sat on the bed, ankles crossed and her arms wrapped around both drawn-up legs. The cigarette burns on her bare shoulder looked, in the gloom, like black holes punched clean through to her soul.

"What am I taking you back to, Allison?"

She dodged it, pointing instead to my middle, where a thick scar curled around my left side just over the hipbone. "How'd you get that? It looks like someone tried to cut you in half."

That. My good samaritan badge of honour. "I tried to interfere in a family fight once. To keep somebody from doing something stupid. How was I supposed to know one of them had been laying new flooring . . . and still had his linoleum knife."

I remembered the blade, dull silver, its wicked curve like a stubby scimitar. Remembered the slippery loop of gut that slid free before I could get my hands over the spillway. But I had to laugh. That'd teach me to pick on carpenters and their sons.

Allison looked away. "Your life seems to have this habit of entwining itself with others that can only hurt you."

"Yeah, but think of the stories I get to tell." I let a moment pass and what she'd said still seemed to demand attention. "Are you trying to tell me you're no different?"

She bowed her head, bruises veiled behind a blonde curtain. When she raised back up, I had my awful answer without her saying a word.

"Tell me what I'm taking you back home to. You owe me that much."

"Why, because you did me the great favour of sleeping with me? Your magic semen is a healing balm, is that the way you see it?"

"No!" I shouted. "Because you haven't kicked in one dime for gas all day, and I wasn't even going to mention it!"

She blinked at me, then we both sputtered with laughter, the kind of laughter that tolerates few secrets, no lies, and when the truth came, there in the night, I wasn't surprised.

"I'm going to kill him. I'm going to put a bullet in him and see if that doesn't unlock this door I've been trying to rattle open for years."

"Your father," I said, and she nodded, as solemn as a judge. "You figure that'll do the trick."

"I've tried everything, Tom, good and bad. This is all that's left, the last thing I know to try. And the reason it feels right is because it's the one thing he most deserves."

While my first impulse was to try talking her out of it, the main problem with that was that it was night out, when ghosts are strongest. There's no talking redemption into someone besieged by darkness inside and out. You can only stay beside them, hoping the light isn't too far away.

Allison opened the small, flat box resting on a table, took out the books it contained, running her hand along covers showing worlds where children could ride dinosaurs, where gentle old men lived new lives blessed by old cats, where sweet-faced animals would never harm a soul.

"When I was a little girl," she told me, "I had a book like this that my aunt gave me. About a horse. I thought if I read the book enough, and said my prayers, then one day I'd wake up and the horse would be waiting for me outside. I must've run downstairs every morning at full gallop for six months before . . ."

Allison stopped, pulled herself back to now; the awful now.

"It's never like the books say it is, is it? If only, just once . . ." She couldn't finish, or didn't have the words for it, but still I knew exactly what she meant. Allison held the books to her chest, tightly, while I held her to mine.

And though I knew we all have to grow up and learn the truth of things someday, I wondered why some are forced to learn it so much sooner than the rest, and from the very ones who are supposed to protect them from it.

We rode those last miles through shadows and valleys, the sun burning through green treetop lattices. Miles that felt seeped through with a soul cursed the colour of an old barn fallen to decay. Polite little towns that simmered in their own dark secrets watched us pass, and while we weren't their business they watched all the same, for one never knows when another's secret may become public property.

She was going through with it, and nothing I could say made a bit of difference. Her face was set with the anticipation of this day of reckoning, and she rode holding the gun in her lap as if it were the one telling both of us what to do, where to go.

Everything, I suppose, but how to live with it.

Now and then we'd roll past a bus station or a shady inviting kerb and I'd wonder why I didn't just put her out to finish the trip alone. Mississippi, after all; my promise was fulfilled. So I'd tell myself that as the voice of reason and harmony only my presence could dissuade her in the end. Then just as readily I'd curse myself, deservedly so, for a liar and a fool.

What I really should've been asking was whether my desire to see her get away afterward was worth being an accessory to murder.

I tried to see the justice of the situation. Very few details had she provided, which made it painfully easy for me to imagine what her father had done. Silent as a ghost, staring from her bedroom doorway until she felt him over her shoulder, felt the force of his compelling smile, his hunger, long before she felt the press of his hands and body. The closer we got the stronger it all rose in my mind; and the deeper it ached. Men in love, or approaching love, have a burning need to torture themselves with what they know of a woman's past. Must be why love and pain are never that far apart.

We reached the house when shadows were begining to stretch

and good Baptist families were sitting down to dinner. A humble and unassuming place, two storeys of peeling paint and loose shutters, behind disinterested trees. Allison had me circle the block once, sitting there assailed by the reek of memory.

"How many years has it been?" I asked after we'd parked.

"Almost thirteen," she breathed. "I ran away a couple months after I turned seventeen. And I've never been back. Not even when Mama died."

"How do you know he's still here, then?"

"I've got a cousin down in Natchez I never lost touch with. Believe me, he's here. By now he should have at least two bottles of Dixie emptied and the *TV Guide* folded back to tonight's shows."

Well, I thought, and dared not say it, *sounds like a man who needs killing*.

And as we walked together up the weedy path I was hoping the years hadn't been kind to him. That he'd answer the door and just the sight of a withered, age-racked man would be enough to restore Allison's sense of justice. That she'd see what he had become and realize he could never compare with the omnipotent son of a bitch who lived only in the past.

Porch steps creaked like screaming souls, and she knocked on the screen door just as bold as Saint Paul could preach.

While we waited, her hand went fishing in her bag.

I heard the scrape of the knob, watched the inside door swing open, heard the chatter of his TV before I saw him standing there trying to make sense of us: two strangers, or maybe one stranger beside his own problematic ghost, returned to flesh after thirteen years. What does go through the head of a man like that?

"Hey, Daddy," and she was flat and neutral as a hangman.

He stared and blinked. "Well, girl. Always did expect you to find your way back one day." Then he turned his head to one side and spat what may have been a fleck of tobacco. "But I'll give you this much: I always expected you'd be alone and crawling."

"Well, that's two more things you got wrong, isn't it? Maybe you'd just better give up on trying to figure me out."

He started to laugh, a liquid rumbling in his chest and the seams of his face pulling back taut. They already drooped in such a way as to give him a look as sour as curdled milk. Willoughby must've been around sixty-five, with the latter-day bearing of a man who'd been as stout as hickory in his prime. He still had the arms, the shoulders, and if he now carried himself with a bit of a stoop he would apologize to no one for it. His hair was a dirty white, thinned well back along his crown, and hadn't seen a comb since morning. When he stepped back from the door to let us in, I saw the tube snaking from beneath his thread-worn shirt, and what it connected with.

A mean old man holding a colostomy bag. I was going to Hell for sure.

Allison barely waited for the door to latch behind us when her hand cleared the purse and the revolver gleamed, the brightest thing in the dingy living room. I shut my eyes until I realized she wasn't going to shoot him first thing.

"Well, lord have mercy, what's *this*?" Willoughby said, staring at the gun pointed at his chest. After an initial wary look, he seemed more amused than anything, as though it were all some game of bluff and bravado, love and hate, jealousy and concession, that only fathers and daughters could understand.

"One bullet for you," she said in a small firm voice, "and four more for each of your friends you whored me out to."

I felt a sudden plunging surge, all manner of new scenes that I never wanted to imagine. A chamber's worth of tortures that could last for years.

"That's five," he said with fresh contempt. "Who's the last one for – you, or your witness here?"

Allison gave it a few seconds' thought, antagonized, not to be outdone. With smug satisfaction she spun at the hip and put a bullet through the centre of the old man's television. His face went slack as noxious smoke poured from the hole and fogged to the ceiling.

"Aw hell," he moaned, genuinely remorseful, and sighed. Then he slowly turned and made for the adjacent dining room. An aged oblong table stood there on tired gryphon's feet, and had seen a hundred thousand dinners if it had seen a single one. "Well, I'm gonna sit. You can shoot me in the back if you can't wait for me to get situated."

When he was in his chair, colostomy bag slung from one of the spindles, Willoughby gave me a thorough once-over. "Now where's your manners, girl? Who's your fella?"

"His name's Tom St John," as we joined him at the table. "And he's almost restored my faith that the male of the species isn't entirely made of what's leaking out of you into the little bag you drag around."

Willoughby snorted. "Leaves your face looking like that and still he's Sir Galahad? Now that *is* a wonder."

"He didn't do this. Tom's never laid so much as an unkind finger on me in all the time we've known each other."

"Well, congratulations." The old man winked and thrust his hand across the table for a shake. I let it pass, still dwelling on the bag. "Ain't she something? Now most girls, they'd get a man stirred up to do their killing for 'em, but not this one, no sir. She'll dirty her own hands, won't you, princess? That's . . . *still* the makings of your plan, isn't it?"

"You shut up, Daddy. You don't think I'll do it?"

He waved her down and kept his eye on me, a shrewd old poker player who couldn't be bluffed. "How 'bout *you*, Tom St John? Could you put a bullet through your poor old daddy's chest? Right there at his own supper table?"

"I'd have to track him down first." I was trying my best to stand hard, not let Allison see pity and disgust get the most of me. If she saw that, I feared she'd toughen up for the both of us and there'd be no turning her back. "After that, well, whatever happened next I don't think I could be responsible."

"Ran rabbit on you, did he?" Willoughby mused. "Bet he took off on you when you were just a little bitty tyke, didn't he?"

"If he was anything like you," Allison said, "he did Tom the biggest favour of his life."

"Well, now, maybe that could be true, but you still can't stop wondering about him, can you, son?" And the old man smirked at me with his seamed face and his crinkled snake's eyes. "Maybe he just wasn't ready to be a father yet, had a few bushels of wild oats yet spilling out his pants. Got that business taken care of then who knows, maybe he prospered some since. Started over like young Tom St John never even drew breath at all."

Allison's whisper was like a whipcrack. "*Shut* up, Daddy."

Willoughby scowled at her. "Now what'd I teach you, girl? You don't go interrupting a couple of gentlemen trying to get to the bottom of a matter of some importance." Another wink for me. "How about you, Tom St John? Any young whelps, bastards or otherwise, wondering where you've got off to this fine evening?"

"I wouldn't be here if there were."

Willoughby reeled back in his chair. "Not a *one*? You don't say!" He hunkered forward again, and I could just feel him drawing me in, seeking someplace raw and bare to sting. "Not a problem, is there? Lordy, sure hate to think of that following you around for life, and the reason I ask, Tom, looks like grey in your hair already, and it makes a man look some long in the tooth for not even being started in his family ways."

And I was actually glad when Allison pulled the trigger when she did. Shoved the gun out from her chest and fired, and the old man jumped as, behind him, a big fan of brown splattered across the tired old wallpaper, then ran in rivulets for the baseboard. Willoughby gazed upon the ruin of his dripping colostomy bag and shook his head, and it only took until the smell hit for me to wish she'd at least chosen another target.

"Now that hurt," he said, and some dignity leaked with it.

Two shots so far – had the neighbours heard? No sirens yet, drawn by the first. These old houses were built solid, to hold well their secrets. Certainly this one had held a terrible few. Maybe it could hold this one more.

As we sat in the stench and the after-ring of the gunshot, Willoughby seemed to have gone a shade paler, his bold wrinkles and wattles tightened up as he understood he may have misjudged his daughter. I don't believe he'd taken her seriously until this moment.

"I expect I must be quite the joke to you now," he said, quite humble. "Gotta carry 'round this sack of my own droppings."

"A joke? A *joke*?" Allison was steadying herself, gun in both hands, lean brown arms outstretched and her cascade of hair going damp with sweat. "Do you see me laughing, Daddy? Did you *ever* see me laugh? I always thought I'd start laughing again once I could stand on your grave, but I just can't wait any more for you to die on your own."

"God's own time, princess."

She brandished the revolver. "This is all the god you need to worry about now." Allison took a deep breath, gagged on the stink and choked it down. Glanced toward the front door. "Do you still do it? Are there any little neighbourhood girls you coax in here?"

"No. It was . . . just you." Every seam and crinkle loosening and sagging, so limp they nearly slid right off his face. His eyes grew misty, one hand creeping forward atop the table, as though he were groping for some beautiful thing that lived only in his mind, in his dark and twisted heart. Pierced by roses' thorns, where old regrets and older desires nestle deep and turn to cancer. "There was never any other but for you."

Her head started shaking, tiny backs and forths, as Allison slumped in the chair, the gun a nickelled lump at the end of her arm. She still loved him, or a tiny sliver of her still did, some deep ember of love that Willoughby and his friends, for all their grotesque snuffling grunts, had never managed to extinguish.

And I was past knowing whether this was good news or bad.

"Daddy," she breathed, then groaned and turned to me, forcing the gun into my hands. "Just hold it on him," and then she was out of her chair. Convulsions squeezed at her middle as Allison went scrambling down a hallway, disappearing behind a slammed door. I could barely hear her getting explosively sick.

"Girl always did have a tender stomach," Willoughby observed, "even as a little bitty thing. Always getting carsick." Staring at me then, with strange eyes, like a man ready to howl with laughter at a joke that only he has understood all along. "Now as I recall, *you* were never that way. Good settled stomach on little Tom-Tom."

"What . . . ?"

"Now, no need to play dumb for my sake, son. Allison's busy, can't hear us." Shaking an admiring head. "Yes, sir, most men'd let surprise get the best of 'em, walk in ready to blast an old man and who do they see but their *own* old man, more than thirty years gone. You got some jim-dandy self-control, I'll give you that."

"No, no, no, no," and while I was hearing what he was saying, I couldn't believe it, didn't want to believe it, "that's just impossible, *my* father's gone forever . . ."

"And where the hell do you think he's gone *to*, Tom-Tom?" The old man smiled at me and chuckled as I'd always imagined my own father would; so superior, a bastard who's got the world figured out. "A man can move to Mississippi and call himself Willoughby, as easy as he can call himself St John. Though I don't believe he *ever* expects to see his kids find one another by pure chance."

I stared into his face, a desperate search for any trace of flesh or bone that I could match with some old picture I'd not seen for more years than I could remember. Or something I could align with what I saw in the mirror . . . although I'd always taken after my mother, and if Allison did likewise . . .

No. No, damn it. It just couldn't be.

Willoughby narrowed his rattler's eyes. "Don't know what your intentions are with the girl, but unless you got her fooled as to what a fine man you are . . . why, Tom, you might want to rethink them. Especially if you got thoughts of family going through your head. How do you think it'd affect the poor girl, she finds out her own half-brother's sired her a little mongoloid baby?" He ogled down the hall at a final dim sound of retching. "I don't believe she'd bear up so well, myself."

I felt the house contract around me, like a vast stomach that digested all the hopes and potential out of whoever walked in. All I could think about was running out the door and finding some fine honest shade beneath a tree, where I could lie in cool grass and think all this through, come up with the arguments that would show this man for the conniving liar he was.

But what if . . . ?

"I don't believe a damn word of it," I said.

He shrugged. "Face value, I wouldn't expect so. But if it's proof you're needing, well, son, see that Bible on that shelf over there? Hand it over and we'll get down to some proof business."

I looked over, saw it – an heirloom, maybe. A fat leatherbound Bible with a strap holding it shut, big enough to gag a crocodile.

"Swear on a Bible, you think that'll prove anything to me?"

Willoughby sneered and rolled his yellowed eyes. "What kind of idjit did you grow into, Tom? You're telling me you never heard of a Bible's got a family tree written up in it?"

I looked at it again, sitting on its dusty shelf, waiting to be cracked and its secrets of birth and life and death revealed. I could've left it there and always hoped. But always wondered. Yet what if I saw my name, thirty-six-year-old ink scratched in by Willoughby's hand? He'd know as long as we never looked, I could never truly rest.

I stepped across to the shelf, gun in hand, brought the Bible back and slid it over. Willoughby gave me a simpering grin as I sat, and his fingers worked at the old leather strap.

"I'm calling your bluff."

He nodded, flushed with some kind of twisted paternal pride. "I'd never expect any less from any son of mine."

Willoughby propped the Bible against the table's edge, canted at a preacher's angle. Cracked the cover back and stroked one hand down the pages, then brought it back up, and of all the surprises I never expected this Good Book to yield, a pistol was at the top of the list.

I wasn't even thinking as I scuttled backward in the chair, wood scraping against wood, and fumbled Allison's gun level. But Willoughby's quick-draw days, if ever he'd lived them at all, were behind him. I shot twice across the table into his chest, then clenched the gun in both hands, shaking like a man with chills . . .

Waiting for a dead man to make another move.

That quick? It was over that quick?

I stood, grabbed the Bible to stare down into its dessicated pages, cut out with a pistol-shaped hollow, and still I flipped from Old Testament to New with my heart squeezing up the back of my throat, in case I still found that family tree.

"Tom? *Tom?* You . . ."

Hands on walls, Allison braced herself steady in the doorway, an expression on her face as if she'd walked into the wrong room where everyone looked the same, but wasn't.

"He . . . he wanted his Bible," I whispered. "I didn't know."

"No atheists in foxholes?" She walked slowly over, stepping around the blood and the shit, staring at the man she called her father, slumped in the chair with his grey-whiskered chin drooping to his chest. "No, not him. Never him."

And I'll never truly know what Allison was feeling as she brushed her fingertips over his stilled skull, his face, his hard wide shoulders. She looked relieved and cheated but not quite sure how she should feel about either.

I tossed the revolver across the table to where she stood and it landed with a sharp clatter, to spin slowly, like the bottle in a much more innocent game.

"Two left. He won't feel them anymore." I chewed at the side of my lip. "But . . . you still might."

She took gun in hand, thinking, thinking fiercely as I turned my back on what had to remain just between the two of them, hoping I wouldn't jump like a scared rabbit when the hammer fell.

Waiting until she told me I could turn around again.

When we left the house, we left with neither ceremony nor accusation, nothing of importance left to say for the time being. It seemed enough to watch the sweltering streets on our way out of town, holding our breath at the sight of a police car, then easing out the biggest sigh of all as we rolled past an old sign bidding us goodbye, come again, you have family here.

Silence dogged us to the highway, but I knew the time for words would come later. A night's worth, or a week's, or even a lifetime's, depending on how we chose to live with this evening.

And yet for all we'd shared, there were still those dark regions of the heart where each of us would remain forever alone.

Her father had made sure of that.

He'd played each of us like a pro, divide and conquer, his instincts as shrewd as any mean old son of a bitch's could be. As we lit out for the east, then the south, then tomorrow, I told myself that all Willoughby had wanted was to rob us of anything and everything he could.

Maybe he'd known she really would've done it and forced my hand instead to deny her that last redemption. Or maybe he'd known she couldn't, but was ready to die anyway, and by my hand was as good as any. Or maybe he'd have shot us both.

Only one thing was sure: he'd taken me from a man who'd hoped to save his life and turned me into his killer. And self-defence doesn't cut much ice with me, not when you walk into a man's house the way we did.

The highway whined, and I imagined Willoughby and the Devil were laughing so hard by now they had to hold each other up.

Allison and I, we couldn't be related. This I told myself over and over again. He was just trying to steal the future, if indeed we had one. He was just trying to get to the gun.

I think.

As we fled the sunset into the deeper night I watched Allison sitting curled and pensive in the seat. Looked for some tell-tale cast to her face that I'd worn all my life. Knew that if I saw it, I'd just argue it away as a trick of dying light. And then watch for the next. And the next.

I watched as she started to cry, at the end of this long and bloody road, and when she opened up the small flat box, held the small flat books, Allison wept over them like a woman crying over a chest of lost gold.

And if I couldn't yet believe in happily-ever-afters, well, that was fine for now, because I knew that I was at least ready to turn the page.

Thy Blood Like Milk

Ian Watson

This tale is for the sun god, Tezcatlipoca, with my curses, and for you, Marina – whom I never knew enough to love – with apologies and blessings, somewhat tardy.

Have you ever screamed at your nurse to go away – to leave you in peace – and hated her, as bitterly as you've ever hated anybody? And begged her, as you never begged anyone in your proud life before?

Ten of us lay in the ward in plastic webbing imprisoning us, yet only three of us really counted, Shanahan, Grocholski, and me, for we were the only presidents. Yet a big haul for them, indeed, three presidents! How cleverly the hospital distinguished between us and the ordinary runners: the extra dose of nerve sensitizer in the syringe, the absence of any opiates. We hung on the raw edge of pain, gritting our teeth as the taps were spun and at times – when your bloodstreams burned like second nervous systems on fire in our bodies, and it seemed we were being roasted on a gridiron, from our insides outwards – at such times we let go and screamed. Whereas when the runners were being drained they moaned but did not need to scream. Mixed in with their quarter-pint soup of drugs (anti-shock, anti-coagulant, vitamins, iron) they received the opiates that let them still catch the idea of pain, but be somewhat glassed off from it – while we three were locked up in bright tin boxes with the howl of a thumb-nail on slate a thousand times amplified. The nerve sensitizer wasn't merely sadistic, but meant to aid the nurse monitoring the effects of the milking on our bodies; the opiates were supposed to block off the worst of the sensations arising. I might say that according to the compensation laws we should have all had opiates. But that's how they ran a punishment ward. Idiot thinking. Shanahan, Grocholski, and I – we didn't hold each other's occasional screams and pleas against each other. The pain just happened to be unbearable. As simple as that. In the eyes of the runners our agony confirmed our presidencies. The Aztec priests were tortured by the Spaniards before their congregations. So the Aztec priests screamed and begged, when their turn came? The congregations still believed in them.

"You scum of the earth!" Marina hissed as she jabbed our tethered buttocks with that cruel syringe, an Ahab tormenting her own private whale over and over again. (But I did not know her, did not know *you* as Marina yet.) "Do you know what will happen to you today? We're going to take so much out of you and for so long that your brain will starve for oxygen, you'll be half way to an idiot, a drooling vegetable."

"You know that's illegal, you bitch," I snarled as you tickled my bare flesh with the syringe anticipatorily making my nerves try to crawl away.

"Anyone may make mistakes," her eyes gleamed.

Only a scare, a put-on. Panic. She wouldn't dare.

"You must be a pretty girl under that mask. Why do you hate us so bitter?"

"Why give you the satisfaction of knowing?"

"You gave me the satisfaction of knowing just then – there's something to know."

And the syringe hit my flesh hard, at that, and dug in.

The hot acid gruel washed into me. My veins now lavaflows cursed with a consciousness of their own heat and motion. The exquisite agony of being emptied out. The pain of my tortured body racing to make more and more blood as the metabolic drugs goaded it on.

And under and around this pain, the fear that as life-blood

flowed out through the taps, my brain was starving and impoverished, on the brink of becoming the brain of an animal, a toad, a stone –

"Bitch!" I screamed.

Out through one set of pipes flowed my rich blood, in through another the miserable substitute fluid that my body raced to build upon. And Marina (whom I did not know as Marina yet) danced the empty syringe before my eyes, to conduct the music of my torment – keeping an eye on the dials and gauges but pretending not to. Why did she hate us so bitter? Well, I hated her just as bitter! Why ask why. I knew it when I rode for the sun, I might end up here if they found one single excuse to lay their hands on me.

Then the pain got too bad to think about anything else.

No windows in the ward. What was there to look out on? We were outside any Fuller dome, in this hospital. The pollution crawling up and down the sides of the building, dark grey to pitch black. A general turbidity over the land: over the great plains where the braves of another age and world hunted buffalo; on the treeless hills, where it had long since snuffed out the pines; pressing soft on the Great Dead Lakes, and, further out, pressing soft on the dark cesspool of the North Atlantic. Pressing upon the superhighways where mostly automatic traffic crawled and where we had hunted in our packs for that rare bird of paradise, that dark orchid, the patch of clear sun – the "sunspot" that blooms mysteriously amid the murk, shafts of gold piercing a funnel of light down to earth whereby the clear sky could be briefly glimpsed and worshipped. Were not the deaths we caused on the highways only petty sacrifices to ensure the coming of the sun?

And the murk lay thickly on this hospital, Superhighway 31 Crash Hospital, Prison Wing, in whose ward we swooned in pain as we gave up our life-blood to recompense the beneficiaries of this murk, authors of the forever eclipse of the sun . . .

When did I set out upon the sun trail? When did I drive down my own superhighway of the spirit, choosing my own side of the split world, the zone of blood and the sun? Oh these years of hunting for the sun – down ten times a thousand miles of gloomy darkness, oily globules crawling on our windshields, eyes glazed by the green gleaming radar screens of our sun buggies as we swung them, steering blind, through the rivers of automated slave cars, slave trucks riding their guide lines! Brains blazing with the data stream from Meteorology Central – the temperature gradients, the shifting chemistry of the pollutants, the swirling shapes of air turbidity, the cat's cradle of contrails spied upon by the satellite stations high above! (Have you seen a picture of the Earth from satellite? The masked globe, in its gossamer spidery web of contrails, a mud of many shades of brown ochre grey stirred slowly, punctured in several magic shifting locations by the white walls of sunspots drilling their way to the barren ground or the dead seas or the great photophobic anaerobic algae beds (where, perversely, the light kills them) or the dots of Fuller domes where the wasp world lives out its memories of middle-class existence). Grabbing the data with our minds to make a gestalt of it that will lead us to the sun! These years of hunting for the sun – and finding it! Being first to reach those clear fresh zones of radiance, where the flash harvests green and bronze the earth, and tiny flowers rage and seed and die within the span of thirty minutes. Being the only men to see it. To know that nature was still fleetingly alive, in an accelerated abbreviated panic form, still mistress of a panic beauty. These years of discovering the sun and duelling for it on the highways, and ever in the back of our minds somewhere awareness of the Compensation Laws – the blood-debt to be settled.

"Hey," called Shanahan, as Marina came to him next in line with the syringe primed and loaded, a little bit of machismo on his part. "Why not come for a ride in my sun buggy after I get out of here? I'll drive you into the deep dark countryside and we won't hunt for no sunspots either. What we've got to do, we can do in the dark! Hey – but come to think of it – why not just come on a sun hunt with me? Put a blush of real genuine sunburn on those delicate white limbs of yours. Or could it be that you're just a wasp that buzzes about a sundome for her holidays, and never flies out?"

"Yes I'm a wasp, this is my sting."

And she stung Shanahan's quivering buttocks with the syringe, putting an abrupt end to his taunts. He hung in the white plastic webbing, twitching with pain, fat fly in a spider's web that he couldn't break out of. Marina spun the taps, spiderlike sucked him dry, until he howled.

Till he screamed like ice, like thumb-nails on slate.

And Marina – with what grim delight you watched him writhing.

With as much magic and mysticism in the hunt for the sun as there was meteorology, remember how we met together to plot strategies, when our own sun club – Smoking Mirror – first coalesced (later to be known as Considine's Commandos)? And the Indian runner, Marti, who said that his great-great-granddaddy had been an Indian magician, who stayed with Smoking Mirror till one black afternoon he pushed his buggy too fast, too wildly for a mere machine, down a highway crowded with slave traffic, perceptions throbbing with input, idea associations swarming, sense of time and space distraught – for he'd taken a peyotl pill to commune with his magical ancestry. Marti, who knew all the sun myths of all the Indians, South and North, of the Americas. Marti, who said the name we should call ourselves by – Smoking Mirror – alias of the savage wealthy treacherous Aztec sun god, Tezcatlipoca. Marti, who wore the obsidian knife round his neck on a leather thong. The same knife (stolen from a museum case) that the Aztec priests used to tear out the palpitating hearts of the prisoners sacrificed to Tezcatlipoca.

When we reached his smashed buggy and went out to it in our oxygen masks (we had a few minutes before the patrols arrived from the nearest emergency point, with their Compensation Laws to enforce on us, for the flanks of the highway were strewn with the wreckage of the slave cars Marti had collided with) we found the obsidian knife had turned, by a freak, as Marti struck the steering wheel, and driven itself into his chest.

I pulled it out and hung it in my buggy and never washed the blood off the blade. We met the sun that day, the next day, and for three days after – blazing sunspots drilling their way through the smog as we charted our crazy sad, angry course of mourning and celebration of Marti's spirit, across the continent, till even Meteorology Central sat up and took notice of the wild unstatistical improbability of our successes (a first sighting of a sunspot is a kind of scalp, see? a new brave's feather in our headdress) and the sun hordes came tracking us from all over the land to batten on us, converging, duelling, crashing towards us, driving our luck away – Tezcatlipoca would only reveal himself to us, to praise Marti who had named us in his honour.

Only after that when Marti had become history (though the dark-stained knife still hung in my buggy) the new name Considine's Commandos became known, and we settled down to a long period of reasonable successes, but never so successful as that one wild week after Marti died, sacrificed to the sun.

We duelled on the highways with the other clubs, skittering through the slave convoys where the wasps sat back in waspish disbelief with their windows blanked, lapping up video reruns and playing Scrabble, hearing occasionally the scream of tyres from the impossible Outside, brief nightmare intrusion on their security, banshees, werewolves, spooks haunting the wide open Darks between the Fuller domes.

One club that even called themselves the Banshees we tangled with on the southern highways, knowing them only by their radar blips, sneers and taunts over the radio, till one day – or night, where's the difference? – we all of us happened into the same bar at the same time, and I was carrying Marti's obsidian knife, beneath my shirt, or I would never have walked out of that bar to drive again. This time Marti had saved me, but the knife had other enemy blood on it now; and Marti's spirit seemed to disappear. At the cost of losing us the sun, he saved me. For weeks we hunted. For months. And nothing. We got to loathe the midnight roundup of the sunspot sightings from Met Central. Things were beginning to fall apart. Would have done, maybe, if we hadn't been cracked wide open, by the day that brought the Compensation Laws down on all our heads.

"You know what I'd do to that bitch if we were out of these plastic cocoons," Grocholski growled. "That bitch" was around the corner preparing our meals. "I'd rip off her sweet white mask and sweet white uniform, hook her up to this marvel of medical science and drain her whole damn bloodstream while I raped her as cool and clinical as you like, and put no liquid back in her but my seed – what's one fluid ounce to eight pints of the red stuff? – and I'd leave her hanging here in the web for her friends to find like veal in a slaughterhouse."

Vicious sentiments, Grocholski. But Grocholski had performed just as nasty at that – as cool and clinical, I had heard, though I hadn't met the man before the hospital threw us together here in the ward. He had pulled a girl's teeth out with pliers, one by one, for trying to walk out on him . . .

Vicious enough to bring Marina out, so genuinely distraught that she ripped off her white gauze mask and let us take a look at her full face for the first time – beautiful, I thought, amazed, though I hardly dared let myself admit it – not Barbi-dolly or Bambi-cute, but strong with a warp somewhere in it, maybe in the twist of the lips, that gave her the stamp of authenticity – being unlike the million other stereotypes from the same mould. And her green eyes blazed, till they boiled with tears that evaporated almost as she shed them, so hotly angry was she.

"I don't believe in any heaven. For you vicious beasts killed my man. My heaven was here on Earth! But now I believe in hell. And I know how to make a hell for you. Nobody will get any opiates from now on. Nobody. Thanks to your politeness."

"Hey," protested a runner from his white webbing. "You don't have the right to deprive us – that's illegal!"

"Isn't your people's philosophy outside the Law?"

I tried to tell her then, because suddenly I wanted her to know.

"We do have a code to follow, the same as you – it's a different code, is all . . ."

You didn't hear me, Marina, or you didn't seem to. For Shanahan was shouting:

"They always used the Indian women as torturers! The girls made the best!"

So he'd noticed, too, how high your cheek bones were, though masked and hidden partly by your rounded cheeks, the skin not pulled so tight – sealskin over a canoe frame – the way it had been with some Indian girls I'd known, riding for the sun with us, recognizing – and that was what I wanted you to understand, Marina – how we were the new buffalo hunters of the darkness, the new braves and warriors of the polluted darkened highways.

Then things got noisy in the ward. The act of freeing your mouth from the mask's embrace had freed all of our mouths too – but not so much for taunts and obscenities, for a while, till it turned ugly again, but for pointed remarks directed at a real and sexy – if hostile – woman.

With the mask off you became more real, and though we still hated you, we couldn't dismiss you as a perfect plastic wasp girl any more. At least I couldn't. You'd graduated to the status of an enemy.

Marina stared round the ward hotly, at the devils hanging in hell in their plastic wrappings, waiting helplessly to repay their debts to society – and made no move to put her mask back on.

She even answered a question.

"Why do I do this? I volunteered. It's not a popular job, dealing with your people. I volunteered, so I could hurt some of you the way that I've been hurt."

"How have you been hurt, Princess?" yawned Grocholski.

"Didn't you hear her saying we'd killed her man, Gr'olski?"

You gazed at me bitterly, yet in your unmasked gaze was a kind of salutation.

"How did it happen?"

"How do you think you kill good men? You ran him down in the dark, deliberately, while he was tending at an accident."

"Did you see it yourself?"

"Wasps can't see to fly in the dark," jeered Grocholski, carrying machismo further into the zone of his own personal viciousness.

"That's how I know," Marina told me icily, ignoring Grocholski who was thrashing about in his web simulating laughter. "Talk like that. Attitudes like that. Oh, he could see you coming on the radar screen before he stepped out of the ambulance. He could see. But he stayed out on the road to rescue a woman caught in a burning car. He was still foaming it down when you ran him over. You dragged him half a mile. They wouldn't let me see him, he was so smashed."

"Wouldn't *let* you see him?" Grocholski caught out of what she said – but he didn't press the point.

And I wanted her to know – to really understand, inside herself – what we people had, when we weren't being vicious beasts – how we were the real authentic people of our times, facing up to the dirt and dark outside instead of hiding in Fuller domes, hunting down the last glimpses of the natural world – the sun, the sky! How we were the last braves, the last hunters – how could I get that through to the Indian in you smothered in the plastic waspish flesh?

"The ambulance man saw it all on radar – how you changed course at the last moment, to hit him, out there on the road."

"Ambulance man probably hated us anyway – tell any sort of lie."

"Do you," in that frozen voice that I yearned to melt, "deny you run men down just for kicks?"

"You're not so kind yourself, are you? Why not ask yourself deep down what you're doing here torturing us – whether you aren't enjoying it? Revenge? A long revenge, hey! Something you're specializing in?" (Dared I say it yet – and expect you to accept at least a little bit of it – if not immediately, then later maybe when you were alone, lying awake in bed and worried because something had gone astray in your scheme of things?) "You're interested in us beasts. You took this job to be near us. Like a zoo visitor watches the tigers. Smell our musk, our fear, our reality."

Marina's hand cracked across my face, so hard my whole body rocked in its white cocoon.

I swallowed the taste of blood in my mouth and stared hard at her, whispered:

"True, it's true, think about it."

A look of horror came into her eyes, as she quickly pulled the gauze mask over nose and mouth again.

I suppose the Compensation Laws worked our way too. How else could it be, in a split society?

They bought our tacit support for the maintenance of "civilized" life – the deceits that otherwise we'd have done our best to explode, us sunclubbers, saboteurs, ghettopeople, all of us outlaws (whom it's plain ridiculous to call outlaw when full fifty per cent of the people live outside of wasp society). And the wasp world could only blast us out of existence by turning its own massive nuclear artillery upon itself – so, in return for the relative security of its slave super-highways, our own relative freedom to roam them. If the wasp world put too many feet wrong, explosives would go off in its highway tunnels, gatherings of the tribes pull down a Fuller dome, a satellite shuttle plane blasting off be met by a home-made missile with a home-made warhead on it. And if we put too many feet wrong (taking wasp lives with our sun buggies was one way) and if they caught us, there would be a blood debt to pay, hooked up to their milking machines, where we were not supposed to be hurt *too* much, or die, or get brain damage, but just *repay, repay* society. For they need red blood like vampires need it.

So I began working on your mind, Marina.

As for the others, well, Grocholski's thoughts were of tearing his enemies' teeth out with pincers, he knew nothing about minds. A king – but a stupid king, like many kings who must have triumphed over the stupidity of their subjects by a greater and crueller stupidity.

Shanahan was a subtler sort of president, had some idea what we stood for, could put it some way into words. Yet he couldn't see his way clear, as I could, into this woman's soul with all its possibilities.

And you worked on my body, Marina.

Neglected your promised cruelties to the others. Still treated Shanahan and Grocholski like dirt, but carelessly, indifferently, reserving your finest moments for me.

And I tried to grit my teeth through the pain and not scream out meaningless noises or empty curses, but always something that would drill the hole deeper and deeper into you – as the sun drills through the smog – till the protective layers were undercut and the egg of myself could be laid in your heart.

"Milkmaid with buckets of blood in your yoke, why not believe me?" I winced, as Marina thrust the gruel of drugs into the tender parts of my body. "We're hunting for something real in a dirty world – the dirt you wasps have spread around, till there's such a pile you have to hide yourselves away from it."

She drained the blood from me till I fainted, green eyes boring into me, doting on my pain . . .

The Myth of the Five Suns – how brightly Marti told it one day after a long fruitless race for the sun that took us near five hundred miles across the plains, till we pulled in tired and restless at a service area run by ghettopeople with their hair like headdresses, like black coronas around eclipsed suns.

"Five worlds there were," said Marti, the pupils of his eyes dilated to black marbles, his tight brown skin over small sharp bones like a rabbit sucked dry by ants, wizened by the desert sunshine that he had smarted under in his dreams. "In the First World men swam about like fishes under a Sun of Jewels. This world perished in a flamestorm brought about by the rising of the second sun, the Sun of Fire. The fishes changed into chickens and dogs that raced about in the great heat, unwilling to pause for their feet were burning. But this Sun of Fire died down in turn, gave way to the Sun of Darkness, whose people fed on pitch and resin. They in their turn were swallowed up by an earthquake and a Sun of Wind arose. The few survivors of the Sun of Darkness became airy dancing monkeys that lived on fruit. But the fifth sun was the Sun of Light – the one the ancient Mexicans knew. Which sun are we under now, can you riddle me that?"

"Sun of Darkness," answered one of the ghettopeople. "Here's your pitch and resin to eat." Dumping our plates of hamburgers, which may have been made from oil sludge or algae – so perhaps he was right in a way.

Then Snowflake – of the snub nose and blonde pigtails, with her worry beads of rock-hard dried chestnuts on a silver chain – who was riding with Marco in his buggy – wanted to tell a story herself, and Marti let her go ahead while we were consuming the burgers.

"There was this waspman, see, whose slave car broke down on the highway miles from town, and quite by chance in the midst of a sunspot. He'd lost all sense of time on the journey, watching video, so when the car stopped he thought he'd reached his destination – especially when he opened the car door and saw the sun shining and a blue sky overhead, like at home in the Fuller dome. He got out of the car, too busy with his briefcase to notice that under that sun and that blue sky the land stretched out black and devastated, a couple inches deep in sludge. An area where some light-hating plants had taken over, see, which had the trick of dissolving if the sun came out . . ."

"What?" cried Marco, indignant.

"Shut up, this is a story! At that moment the power came on in his car again and away it whisked leaving him standing there on the road. Other cars zipped by on either side. He waved his arms at them and held his briefcase up but all the passengers were watching video and had their windows opaqued. He got scared and leapt off the road into the sludge. However the sunspot was coming to a close now. The blue sky misted over and soon he was all alone in the darkness with cars zipping by on one side and a hand clutching down his throat for his lungs as the pollution flowed back, his eyes watering onion tears. And in the darkness, doubly blinded by tears, he wandered further and further away from the road into the sludge. Even the noise of the cars seemed to be coming four ways at once to him. But now it was dark again the sludge was coming together, shaping itself into fungi two feet high, and amoeba things as big as his foot, and wet mucous tendrils like snots ten feet long that coiled and writhed about . . . and all kinds of nameless nightmares were there in the darkness squelching and slobbering about him . . . So he went mad, I guess. Or maybe he was mad to start with."

A few runners, a few of the ghettopeople applauded, but Marco looked disgusted at her butting in – though our mouths had been full while she was doing the talking – and Marti expressed his annoyance at what he thought of as her sloppy nursery horror-comic world, preferring his horror neat like raw spirit, and religious and classical – and as we drank off our tart metallic beer (solution of iron filings) to wash the burgers down, he dwelt on the how and when of the Aztec sacrifices to the sun.

"Oh, handsome was the prisoner they taught to play the flute and smoke in a neat and elegant fashion and sing like Caruso. After a year of smoking and singing and playing the flute, four virgins were given to him to make love to. Ten days after that they took him out onto the last terrace of the temple. They opened his chest with one single slash of a knife. This knife." (He whirled the obsidian blade on the thong from around his neck, where he'd hung it when he left the buggy, flashed it at us.) "Unzipped him, tore out his heart!"

How strange, and remarkable, that the heartblood of the Aztecs' prisoner flowing for the sun should become our own heartblood pumped into storage bottles and refrigerated with glycerol at this hospital! A sacrifice of ice against a sacrifice of fire – both harshly painful – the one lasting as long as an iceberg melting, the other over and done with in a flash of time!

Waking up weak-headed but set in my purpose, growing sharper with each hour, I shouted for you to come to my web-side, as Shanahan and Grocholski stared at me bemused and grumbled to one another about this perversion of machismo.

"Nurse!"

And you drifted to my side, green eyes agleam, hate crystals in your Indian skull.

"What is it, Considine?"

"Mightn't you hurt me a bit more if I knew you were a person with a name? A nameless torturer never had much fun. Wouldn't you love to be begged for mercy by name – the way *he* called you by name, with emotion – the emotions of fear and anguish, if not of love? The victim begs to know his tormentor's name."

"So you're a victim are you?"

"We're all victims of this dirty world."

"No, you're not victims, not you people. You're here to pay because you made victims of other people. So that the lives of your future victims may be saved, by your own life-blood."

Almost as an afterthought, you added softly:

"My name's Marina, Considine."

"Ah."

Then I could let my forced attention unfocus and disperse into the foggy wool of fading pain . . .

★　★　★

And when she came again to plunge the bitter drugs into my body and spin the taps that recommenced the sacrifice of blood, she murmured, eyes agleam with the taunting of me:

"Your blood has saved two lives already, Considine – that must please you."

"Marina," I hissed before she had a chance to stick the syringe in me, "Marina, it's only a role in *our* game that you're playing, don't you realize? In our Sunhunter's game! For sure it's our game, *ours*, not *yours*!"

She held the syringe back, letting me see the cruel needle.

"You know the name of the game, Marina? No, of course you don't, in your white sterile uniform and your plastic waspish life, how could you ever know? But if you've really got Indian blood in your veins, that might help you understand . . ."

"What's there to understand, Considine? I see nothing to understand except you're scared of a little pain."

"Not scared," I lied. "The pain, the savagery – has to be. You have to hurt me, it's your destiny. Day by day you sacrifice me to the sun, my priestess!"

While she still hung back from me, listening in spite of herself, I told her something of Tezcatlipoca – of the giant in an ashen veil carrying his head in his hand, of the pouncing jaguar, of the dreadful shadow, of the bear with brilliant eyes. Of how he brought riches and death. Of the blood sacrifices on the last terrace of the temple. I told how Marti's knife had turned against his own bosom and how the sun had greeted us in splendour every day for a week thereafter. She went on listening, puzzled and angry, till the anger overcame the puzzlement in her, and she thrust the syringe home . . .

But of Tezcatlipoca the trickster I hadn't told her – nor of his deadly practical jokes.

How he arrived at a festival and sang a song (the song the prisoners were taught to sing) so entrancing that all the villagers followed him out of town, where he lured them onto a flimsy bridge, which collapsed, tossing hundreds of them down into the rocky gorge. How he walked into a village with a magic puppet dancing in his hand (the dance the prisoners were taught to dance) that lured the villagers closer and closer in their dumb amazement, till scores of them suffocated in the crush. How he pretended to be sorry, told the angry survivors that he couldn't guarantee his conduct, that they had better stone him to death to prevent more innocent victims succumbing to his tricks. And stone him to death they did. But his body stank so vilely, that many more people sickened and died before they could dispose of it.

As I lay there racked with pain, these stories spun through my head in vivid bloodstained pictures, and my mind sang the song that led the sun's victims onto the bridge, and my body danced the twitching dance that suffocated the survivors, and my sweat glands and my excrement stank them to death.

How would I, Considine, sun's Messenger, lead and dance and stink Marina out of this bright-lit ward, into the darkness that was my home?

When a doctor made his rounds of the blood dairy, he remarked how roughly I was being treated.

"Don't kill the goose that lays the golden egg!" he twinkled, to Marina. No doubt nurses had broken down on this hateful job before.

I smiled at her when he said that, for after a time assuredly the victim and the torturer became accomplices, and when that happens their roles are fast becoming interchangeable. I grinned the death-grin of Tezcatlipoca as he lay dead in the village and stank the villagers into vulture fodder for a joke . . .

So the doctor thought she might try to assassinate me, snuff me out! Surely the least likely outcome of our duel, by now.

The sacrifice was always preceded by a period of great sensual *indulgence* – a recompense for the pain to be suffered. Yet this victim here, myself, was tied down, bound in white plastic thongs, while his tormentor hung over him day by day replaying a feeble mimic spearthrust into his body, spilling his blood but replacing it again. Day by day it hurt rackingly, yet death never came. What could come? Only freedom – reversal of the sacrifice – over-whelming pleasure – triumph – and the sun! My pain-racked grin glowed confident, drove wild anguished discords through Marina's heart.

"Be careful, Nurse – this one's metabolic rate is far too high. He's burning himself up."

"Yes, yes," murmured Marina, distractedly, fleeing from me across the dark plateaux of her heart . . .

And, when more days had passed and I felt invincible in my agony, I commanded:

"Come to me, Marina."

Does the male spider command the female spider to come to him with her ruthless jaws? Does the male mantis command the female mantis who will wrench his head off with her sawblade elbows?

"Marina."

She came to my side, under the bemused gaze of Shanahan and Grocholski, who had given up trying to understand, and, unblessed by the presence of Tezcatlipoca in their skulls, were glad enough to lie back in their plastic webs relaxing from those first few days of machismo, happy enough that the heat was off them. They kept quiet and watched me wonderingly as I suffered and commanded.

"Marina."

"Yes, Considine?"

"The time's approaching, Marina."

"Time, Considine?"

"There has to be a climax. What climax can there be? Think!"

"I . . ."

"I'll make it easier for you. You can't drain me dry. Can't . . . terminate me. What satisfaction would there be in that? Who would you turn to then? To Shanahan? Grocholski? Look at them. Lying like slugs in their beds – great torpid bullies. What satisfaction would there be? Sure, Grocholski is a bastard, he'd pull your teeth out one by one with a pair of pliers. But has he any . . . spirit? Has the sun god whispered in his ear?"

Marina turned, watching the two presidents lolling in their white webs, shook her head – as though she understood the question.

Turning, she whispered:

"What climax, Considine?"

"I'll tell you tomorrow, Marina – unless you can tell me before then. Sleep on it, Marina, sleep on it . . ."

She came to me in the night like a sleepwalker – Lady with a Pencil Torch, whose beam she played over the webbing till she located the release tag, and there she rested her hand but didn't pull it yet-a-while.

As she knelt there bereft of her mask, her face level with mine, I gazed at her, not as avenging fury and priestess, but briefly as another human being passing in the dark. She knelt poised at the mid-point of a transformation in her role, for a brief time quietly happy in the lightening of the burden, the falling away of the robe of one office before the assumption of the next.

This pause must have lasted you an eternity, Marina.

I watched the long high planes of your cheeks in the back-wash of light off the plastic webbing, the hilltops of your cheekbones, sharper now in the contrast of dark and bright – and your eyes dark pools beyond the cheekbones, in shadow – and kept my peace.

Tezcatlipoca took the form of an ashen-veiled giant carrying his head in his hand and searched for the sunspot where he could be himself, the sun. The sight of him in the dark made nervous people fall dead with fear, the way the wasps in their slave cars shivered at our banshee wail as we passed them by on the highways, invisible, vindictive, reckless. Yet one brave man seized hold of the giant and held on to him – bound him in white plastic webbing, in spite of his screams and curses. Held him hour after hour till near morning when it was time for the sun to rise. Then the ashen giant began promising the brave man wealth and even omnipotence to let him go. At the promise of omnipotence the brave man agreed and tore out the giant's heart as a pledge before he let him go. Wrapping the heart up in his handkerchief, he took it home with him. When he opened it up to look at the heart, however, there was nothing but ashes in it. For the sun had already risen, and in his new omnipotence broke his promise and burned his pledge.

Take heed, Marina, hand on the release tag – take heed of the sun when he is free. You hold my heart now in your handkerchief,

blood drips into your bottles through the mesh, safely. The heart is
not yet ashes.

Her hand touching the webbing, her Indian face divided by a
watershed of light . . . at this brief pause in time could I have
afforded a little pity, a little affection . . . ?

"Is it time . . . ?"

She whispered into the darkness from which the sun must rise –
for the sun is time itself (or so I thought then) so far as our twenty-
four-hour clocks knew, so far as the circadian rhythms of our body
are aware.

What else is time, but the sun in the sky? But this is the Age
Without Time – for the travellers over the blackened prairies, for
the wasp refugees in the Fuller domes!

At the end of every fifty-two years, the fires were all quenched
throughout Mexico, and a fresh fire kindled on a living prisoner's
chest – to keep time on the move. What fire shall be kindled in
whose chest, to bring Time back into the world today?

"Yes, it's time to kindle the sun."

Marina's breast rose and fell convulsively as she pulled the tag.

Plastic thongs slid off my limbs in four directions at once like
frightened snakes and I slipped to the floor, free of the pain
hammock, knocking aside the sanitary facilities which she'd
forgotten to remove, with a noisy clatter that alerted Shanahan. He
craned his head against the tension of the web, as I sat massaging
life into my limbs.

"Considine," he called softly. A worried Marina flashed the
pencil of light across his face, and he blinked blindly at us.

"Considine, get me out of here – please!"

"Put him back to sleep, Marina." (Quietly.) "It's not his time for
release – Tezcatlipoca isn't with him." My feet prickling intoler-
ably with thawing-out frostbite.

She crept towards Shanahan, dazzling him with her pencil of
light; injected him with something, while he imagined his web was
being undone. By the time my legs were fit to stand on, he was calm
again.

She gripped my arm to steady me, helped me dress.

"Your car's in the ambulance sheds."

"Buggy," said I angrily. "Sun buggy."

"There's so much I have to learn."

"There isn't much," I assured her – and this, alas, was honest – as we slipped out of the ward towards the darkness of freedom.

"What is the sun really like?"

"A ball of incandescent gas . . ."

Of course Marina hadn't seen the sun. Except as a baby, long time ago, forgotten, maybe. Models of the sun were all. Hot yellow lamps hanging from the eggshells of the Fuller domes, switched on in the morning, switched off again at night. If a sunspot had ever bathed the hospital, she wouldn't have seen it through the solid walls.

As we crept into the ambulance sheds, she began to cough, grating explosive little coughs that she did her best to stifle with her hand.

A dull orange glow from standby lighting pervaded the gloom of the sheds, where half a dozen of the great sleek snubnosed ambulances were parked and a number of impounded buggies – beyond, light spilling from a window in the crew room door and the sound of muffled voices.

We climbed into my buggy – the key was in the lock – and I ran my hands gently over the controls, reuniting myself with them.

Tezcatlipoca's jaguar stencilled on my seat radiated confidence strength suppleness and savagery through my body . . .

Marina sat limply in the passenger seat looking around my world, stifling her cough – but the air was cleaner in my buggy, would get even cleaner once we were on the move.

"Who opens the doors?"

"We have to wait for an ambulance to leave, then chase it out. How soon till we see the sun, Considine?"

"Sooner than you think."

"How do you *know*?"

"What is the sun, Marina? A blazing yellow ball of gas radiating timelessly and forever at six thousand degrees Centigrade, too bright to look upon. A bear with bells on his ankles, striped face, blazing eyes. A magician with a puppet dancing in his hand. A smoking mirror. A giant in an ashen veil with his head in his hand. A G-type star out on the edge of the galaxy around which planets and other debris revolve. Your choice."

"I've seen movies of the sun – maybe it's no big thing after all."

"Oh it's big, Marina – it's the climax."

Then a siren went off in the shed, shockingly loud, and the lights came up full.

The ambulance crew spilled from their room, zipping their gear and fixing their masks as they ran. They took an ambulance two along the line from us.

Its monobeam flared out ahead, splashing a hole bright as the sun's disc on the door. Its turbines roared.

And the door flowed smoothly, swiftly, up into the roof.

As I started the buggy's engine a look of fear and terrible understanding came over Marina's face – sleepwalker wakening on the high cliff edge. She tore at the door handle. But naturally it was locked and she couldn't tell where to unlock it.

"Marina!" Using the voice that cuts through flesh to the bone. "Quit it!" A voice I'd never used to beg or plead with in the hospital. Authority voice of the Sun Priest. Obsidian voice. Voice that cuts flesh. Black, volcanic, harsh.

Her hand fell back upon the seat.

The ambulance, blinding the smog with its monobeam, sped through the doors – and us after it, before the doors dropped again.

Great Tezcatlipoca, Who Bringeth Wealth and War, Sunshine and Death, Sterility and Harvest! For Whom Blood Floweth Like Milk, That Milk May Flow!

The smog so thick outside. Even the great eye of the ambulance saw little. Undoubtedly they were relying on radar already, as I was – and wondering, doubtless, what the tiny blip behind their great blip represented, Remora riding on a shark . . . I dropped back, not to worry them.

When we got to the highway entry point, I took the other direction.

Whichever way I took, I knew it led to the sun.

Two hours down the highway, Marina sleeping on my shoulder, bored with the monotonous environment of the sun buggy (green radar no substitute for video), radio crackling out data from Met Central revealing total disarray among the air currents, turbid gas blowing everywhichways, absurd peaks and dips in the nitrogen oxides, crazy chemical transformations – a scene in disarray awaiting my touch, and what I brought it was the body of Marina, magnet to the iron filings of the everywhichways polluted sky.

Two hours down the highway, piloting with ever-greater certainty, careless of pursuit, I picked the radiophone up, tuned to the Sun Club waveband . . .

Nearby, voices of some charioteers of the sun.

"Considine calling you. Considine's Commandos. Smokey Mirror Sun Club. I'm heading straight for the sun. Anyone caring to join me is welcome. Vector in on my call sign . . ."

My voice woke Marina up, to the babble of voices answering over the radiophone.

"Considine?"

"How did you get out?"

"How do you *know*? Man?"

Who had ever dared call a hunt into being among sun runners other than his own? How great the risk he ran, of shame, revenge, contempt!

How did I know, indeed!

"Where are we?" yawned Marina. "What's going on?"

"We're hunting for the sun – I've cried fox and I'm calling the hounds in."

"Whose voices are those?"

"It hasn't been done before, what I'm doing. Those voices – the cry of the hounds."

"Considine, I'm hungry. Is there anything to eat in the car?"

"Hush – I've told you, *buggy* is the name. No eating now – it's time to fast. This is a religious moment."

A louder challenging voice that I recognized broke in on the waveband. The Magnificent Amberson's.

"Considine? This is Amberson. Congratulations on your breakout – how did you do it?"

"Thanks, Amberson. I got a nurse to spring me."

"A nurse?"

"She's with me now – she's part of it."

"Hope you know what you're doing, Considine. You really meaning to call a general hunt?"

"A gathering of the tribes. That's it, Amberson."

"Sure your head isn't screwed up by loss of blood? The weather data is chaos. Sure you haven't bought your way out of there by offering something in return – say, a gathering of the tribes in a certain location?"

"Screw you, Amberson – I'll settle with you for that slander after I've greeted the sun. Sun hounds, you coming chasing me?"

And a rabble of voices, from far and near, jammed the waveband.

Marina clutched my arm.

"It frightens me, Considine – who are they all? Where do they come from?"

"Some of the other half of the people in this land, Marina – just some of the other half of the people. The ones who stayed outside in the dark. The ones that weren't wasps. The Indians your ancestors would have understood. Spirit voices they are – gods of the land."

"Indians my ancestors?"

"Yes."

Green blips swam by me on the radar screen – slave cars that I sped by effortlessly. I paid no heed to the weather data. My gestalt, my mind-doll, was fully formed. Its embodiment hunched by me in the passenger seat, the curves and planes of Marina's body were the fronts and isobars and isohets of the surrounding dirt-darkened land. A message, she had been placed in the hospital for me to find, with pain the trigger to waken me to her meaning. So many forms a true message can take – a circle of giant stones of the megalith builders, a bunch of knotted strings of different lengths and colours (the *quipu* archives of the Incas) – a human body if need be. If the human body becomes a world unto the lover or the torturer, may

not the world itself with its dales and hillocks, its caves and coverts
and cliffs, be a body? Marina, my chart, on whom I read my
destination!

"Now you must take your clothes off, Marina, for you'll soon be
bathing in the sun – we'll soon be lovers."

"My clothes?"

"*Do so.*"

I used the Voice of the Sun, the Voice from the Sky. And, dazed,
she began to fumble at her nurse's uniform.

Her nudity clarified my mind – I knew exactly where to turn off
now, on to which decrepit smaller road.

"Sun hounds!" I sang. "Don't miss the turning."

Goosebumps marched across Marina's flesh and her nipples
stood out in the mental cold of her life's climax – the dawning
awareness that she had been inserted into life long ago and grown
into precisely this, and this, shape, as hidden marker for the
greatest future sunspot, burning spot of all burning spots that
might start the clouds of darkness rolling back across the land at
last, burning away the poisoned blackened soup from the Earth's
bowl in a flame-oven of renewal.

"Sun hounds!" I sang. "The Sun of Darkness is about to set. The
Sun of Fire comes next in turn. The men of this creation are to be
destroyed by a rain of fire, changed into hopping chickens and
dogs."

"Are you mad, Considine?" came Amberson's voice, nearer
now. "Look, I'm sorry I said what I did. I apologize. But, man – are
you mad!"

Now that I'd turned off to the east I was driving slower, yet the
buggy rocked and jolted over the broken-backed minor road,
tossing us about like fish in a scaling drum.

"It bruises me!" cried Marina, shipwrecked, clinging to her seat.

Your white nudity, Marina – and the Earth's dark nudity to be
explored, revealed!

"I give you the sun, you hounds and runners and presidents of
this land!" I hurled the words into the babbling radiophone. And
even Met Central was starting to show excitement, for they were

listening too, and beginning to feed out data rapidly that vectored in on me and my position.

As I stared through the windshield, the greyness ahead slowly lightened to a misty white that spiralled higher and higher into the upper air. We could see fifty yards, a hundred yards ahead. A great light bubble was forming in the dark. In wonder and gratitude, I slackened speed.

We stopped.

"Thank God for that," muttered Marina.

"Considine here, you sun hounds – you'd better come up fast, for I'm in the light-bubble now, it's rising, spiralling above, five minutes off the sun at most I'd say. It's *big,* this one."

"Is that the truth, Considine?" Amberson demanded.

"The truth? Who's nearest?" I called to the sun runners in general. And looked around. My buggy stood on a smashed stretch of road bandaging the blackened ground, at the base of a great funnel of strengthening light . . .

"Maybe I am." (Very loud, and breathlessly – as though running ahead of his buggy to catch me up.) "Harry Zammitt of Helios Hunters. I'm . . . coming into the fringes of it now. I see your buggy, Considine. The white whirlpool. Up and up! It's all true. Considine – I don't know how to say it. What you've done. Busting out, hunting down the sun in a matter of hours!"

As that first buggy bumped into the intensifying bubble of light, I piloted my own machine off the road onto the black ground.

We sat, watching the first rays of the sun burn through in golden shafts as the last mist melted.

And suddenly the day was on fire around us.

I squinted up through dark glasses and my windshield at a sun that seemed greater and brighter, a different colour even, from any I'd ever seen before, steely whiter – as if there was less separating me from the sun, that day.

"Out," I ordered Marina, leaning over her bare legs to flip the door-lock open.

She stepped out obediently into the sunshine, while I gathered the obsidian knife up by the thong from under my seat, dropped it in my pocket.

"But it hurts," she cried in surprise – the hopping chicken with burnt feet, exactly! "It's too hot."

"Naturally the sun is hot."

Yes it was hot, so very hot. The hard hot rays burning at my skin the moment I stepped outside, hot as a grill, a furnace.

Harry Zammitt moved closer in his buggy, and other buggies were rolling into the sunspot now.

"Marina – you must stand against the buggy – no, better bend your body back, sprawl backwards over the hood, lie on it – but keep your eyes closed or you'll be blinded."

"You can't make love to me across a car," she whined feebly, moving in a daze, wincing as her body touched the heating metal. "It hurts."

"It's a buggy," said I. "Lie back, damn you, lover. Across the hood of my buggy."

"You animal, you primitive animal," she mumbled, doing just as I said, spreading herself across the hood with her eyes screwed shut. For her this was the climax that confirmed all her fears and lusts for such scum as myself. Oh Marina!

For me the climax was different.

(Had I ever tried to warn you – had I? Who was I now, Considine the human being, or Considine the Priest of the Sun? Liar Considine, how you enjoyed being possessed – how you enjoyed the sanctification of your torture, in order to achieve the torture of sanctity – Marina!)

I, Considine, Priest of the Sun, snatched the obsidian knife from my pocket and brought it slashing down into your chest.

A pretty mess I made of you. The Aztecs must have had dozens of prisoners to practise on. At one blow! Monkeys maybe. Maybe they executed monkeys in the dark rooms under the temple pyramids. By the time I had hacked through the chaos of smashed ribs, torn breast muscle, flesh, that had been your body and my guide – by the time I had trapped the palpitating blood-sodden rag of your heart in my fist and wrenched it free – by that time I was vomiting onto the black soil.

(Soil that showed no signs of the flash harvest of grass and tiny blooms we all looked for, though it had been sprinkled with blood – as was I.)

My mouth putrid with bile, I turned, held your heart, Marina, high, dripping, to the blazing hurtful sun that blistered my skin raw as a flayed criminal's.

"What are you doing, Considine!" screamed the Magnificent Amberson, plunging towards me across the black earth – for he had finally got here, in the wake of some of his followers – sheltering himself under a sheet of metal.

"Sacrificing," said I. "As the sun god requires."

"Sun god?" he snarled.

"Tezcatlipoca has been reborn in the sky – surely you see?"

"Bloodthirsty maniac – I don't care about that – I can't see anything up there! Where has the ozone cover gone?"

I turned to Amberson then, blankly, still clutching the wet heart. "*What?*"

"The ozone layer in the upper air, don't you realize it's gone? Met Central is shouting murder about it. The hard radiation is getting through. You're burning to death if you stay out here. That's why there's no harvest, you fool. Scattering blood around isn't going to help!"

I dropped the heart on the ground, where it lay bubbling gently, tiny bubbles of blood, into the unresponsive warming soil.

Amberson snatched at me, maybe to drag me under the metal sheet with him, but I shook him off and jumped into my buggy, locking the doors, opaqued the windows.

And sat trembling there with the obsidian blade freshly blooded in my lap.

"Considine!" cried voices over the radiophone.

"Considine?" Amberson's voice – he was back in his sun buggy.

"Yes, I'm here."

"Now hear me, sun runners all, Considine led you here, and I admit I don't know how. But now maybe he'd like to explain why we can't go outside without being burnt, and where the harvest is?"

I said nothing.

"No? I'll tell you. Anyway, it's coming over Met Central. The ozone layer in the upper air has finally broken down – the pollution has got to it and changed it – and as the ozone layer just happens to be what filters out of the hard radiation from the sun, we had better get the hell out of here. Reflecting – as we do – on the demise of the honourable sport of the sun hunt. From now on anyone who spots the sun is going to wish himself a hundred miles away. So get going, sun runners. And bugger you, Considine. Let's all know this as Considine's Sunspot – the last sunspot anyone ever hunted for. A nice curse to remember a bloodthirsty fool by!"

Tezcatlipoca, why had you cheated me? Did her blood not flow like milk to your satisfaction? Was it because I botched the sacrifice so clumsily? Where the Aztec priest used one swift blow of the knife to unsheath the heart, I used twenty . . .

One thing Amberson was wrong about. The biggest thing of all. The thing that has given me my present role, more hated than Amberson could ever have dreamed as he uttered his curse upon me.

For Considine's Sunspot was not going to close up, ever. It carried on expanding, taking in more acres hour by hour.

Far more than the ozonosphere had altered in those chemical mutations of the past few hours. The pall of dirt that had blanketed the Earth so many years was swift to change, whatever new catalyst it was that had found a home in the smog; now, starting at one point and spreading outward, the catalyst preceding (swimming like a living thing – Snowflake's "childish" nightmare!) on a wave front from the point of light, the changed smog yielded to the hard radiations of the naked sun.

I was right – which is the horror of it – I was right. Tezcatlipoca is alive again, but no friend to man. Nor was he ever friend to man, but cheated and betrayed him systematically with his magic and his song, and his stink. Tezcatlipoca, vicious bear, hideous giant coming head in hand, bounding jaguar, using me as focus for his flames, as plainly as he used Marina (my lost love!) for his map.

Considine's Sunspot spreads rapidly from one day to the next, gathering strength, sterilizing further areas of the country, burning the earth clean. Algae beds consumed faster than they can be covered over. Fuller domes shrivelling, flimsy-fabricked.

Buildings in flames, so brittle. The asphalt motorways blazing fifty-mile-long tinder strips.

So let me be Priest of the Burning World then, since it is what I foretold and since, strangely (is it so strangely in these fear-crazed times?), the cult of Tezcatlipoca has revived, at least its ceremonies have, blood sacrifices carried out in the polluted zones beyond the encroaching flame front, in vain hopes of stemming it – oh, they only add fuel to the sun's fire! – with their cockerels and bullocks stolen from the zoo sheds . . . and people too, captive and volunteer – beating hearts torn out by far more expert hands than mine, tossed blindly at where the sun burns its way towards them. And, what no one will volunteer for, the flame kindled in the darkness on someone's writhing scream-torn body, to impress the god of fire – Xiuhtecuhtli – oh yes, modern scholarship is on our side! And after further scholarly researches (did not witchcraft almost win a World War?) babies are cooked alive, eaten in honour of Tlaloc, god of rains and springs, who waters the earth. Outlaws and inlaws, bandits and wasps – we are all in this together, now.

My fate, Wandering Jew of the burning roads, is to lurk outward and ever outward, casting around the perimeter of Sunspot Considine, buggy rationed and fuelled free of charge, with hatred, meeting up with my worshippers, torturers, meteorologists (has not meteorology absorbed all the other sciences?), time and again overcome by a craze of words bubbling from Tezcatlipoca's lips – taunts, demands, tricks and curses fluttering through my mouth from elsewhere, like captive birds set free, like the souls of his victims escaping into the sky.

And I ask:

Why *me*?

And:

Why you, Marina?

How I love you, in retrospect, having held your beating heart within my palm!

And the sunspot that bears my name, great tract of flame-land seared into the world, pre-Cambrian zone of sun-scarred earth sterile except for the bacteria lying in waiting for some million-year-to-come event – do you realize that logically the whole world will bear my name one day, if the sunspot expands to embrace it, though no one will be here to use the name – of Considine's Planet (as it may be known to the ghosts upon it) – why am I not allowed to drive in there and die? But the mad sun god will not allow it, while yet he holds me dangling on a string, jerking my vocal cords as it amuses him. Since I plucked her heart out I am his creature utterly. As she was mine, and earlier still as I was hers. So it rolls around.

Once I was a free man, sun hater, outlaw. Now a potential planet – and a slave. The empty gift of omnipotence! Considine's world – naked pre-Cambrian of some future society of insects, perhaps!

Marina.

Whose heart I felt flutter in my hand.

Thy blood like milk for me has flowed, hot as iron pouring from a furnace!

Marina and Considine.

Eve and Adam of the world's end, our non-love brought life to its close, victim and executioner of the vanishing smog-scape – which we all long for nowadays, passionately, and would sacrifice anything, or anyone to bring it back to us.

This tale is for the sun god, Tezcatlipoca, with my curses, and for you, Marina . . .

That'll Be The Day

Mark Timlin

I quit the band I was with after a disastrous gig in Sioux City, on the Iowa and Nebraska border, on the last day of January 1995. The temperature was sub zero outside and pretty much the same went for the atmosphere inside our dressing room. The fact was we were going nowhere fast. We had two ex-rock and roll stars who called the shots, and I just didn't fit in. Also the promoter was a jerk, who couldn't organize a piss-up in a brewery, hence the fact that we were playing a dump like Sioux City in winter, when we could have been in California catching some rays. I went back to the flea-bag motel he'd booked us into when we came off stage, packed some clothes into a bag, picked up the case containing my black and mother-of-pearl 1958 Rickenbacker bass with gold pick-ups and machine heads, and left town. I was wearing a Schott leather jacket over a blanket-lined Stormrider, a sweater, a flannel shirt, two T-shirts, Levi's 501 button-fly jeans, a pair of hand-tooled black cowboy boots that had cost me five hundred dollars, but were beginning to look a little the worse for wear, and a black woollen watch cap that I pulled down over my head. What I stood up in, the few bits and pieces in the bag, my guitar, my Rolex watch that had been a gift, five hundred and ninety-five dollars and change in cash, and a pack of cigarettes plus a Zippo lighter was all I owned in the world. Not much for a guy looking thirty-five in the teeth was it?

The bus station was closed, so I headed for the edge of town to try and get a hitch. I figured I'd head for Chicago where a buddy of mine from way back ran a club where I might get some pick-up work, look for sessions in the studios round town, and try and find an old girl friend of mine who had an apartment on the southside. I figured she might let me crash on her sofa, or if I was really lucky in her bed.

Jesus, but it was cold that night as I stood by the side of Highway 20 with my thumb up. Cars and trucks thundered by, giving me nothing for my pains but a draught of even colder air, until a battered pick-up truck with fat tyres pulled up on the hard shoulder with a screech of rubber and I ran to the passenger door.

The driver was a long hair of about twenty-five with a gun rack, a six-pack of beer between his legs and Nirvana on the stereo. Kurt Cobain, the singer with the band, had topped himself the previous April. The driver was wearing his suicide note printed on his T-shirt. Groovy.

"Thanks, man," I said as I climbed in beside him.

"S'nothin', dude," he said as he put his booted foot on the gas and we shot back onto the road. "Where you headin'?"

"Chi town eventually," I replied. "But outta this burg for starters."

"You don't come from around here?" It was a question, not a statement, and he wasn't far wrong by about five thousand miles.

"I'm English originally," I replied, accepting a can of Bud and offering him a Marlboro in return. "I married an American girl. We're divorced now, but I got to be an honorary Yank in the deal."

"Cool. You with a band?" He nodded at my guitar case and I figured this guy was no slouch when it came to observation.

"Used to be." I told him the story of my day.

"Hey, man," he said. "I was there tonight. I thought I recognized you. I don't blame you for splittin'. It wasn't too excellent a show."

I grinned in the darkness and took a hit on the beer. "You can say that again," I agreed.

He dropped me off in a place called Emmetsburg just before

dawn, when he turned off to get to the farm where he lived. It wasn't the fastest way to Chicago, as we'd taken a diversion onto 71, then 18, but I was in no great hurry and it was warm in the truck and the beer was cold. I stood just outside the city limits and watched the truck as it turned off onto a rural route and vanished into the darkness with a snarl from its exhaust.

I walked into town and found a diner just opening up and was served coffee by a yawning teenybopper with great legs. She saw my guitar case and said, "You in a band?" Same old same old, anywhere you go.

"Not any more," I replied, which pretty well brought that conversation to a halt. Maybe I should've said yes, told her a bunch of lies about my prospects, married the girl and settled down in Emmetsburg to raise a family. With what happened later, I think that *definitely* I should've.

After I'd eaten breakfast, she pointed me in the direction of the Greyhound station and I walked downtown. On the way I passed a used car lot with the slogan *BUD'S CHEAP AUTO'S – NO MONEY DOWN* printed on bunting that flapped in the cold wind off the prairie. I stopped and took a look around. They may have been cheap to some, but to me they were expensive, and I didn't believe that my credit rating was good enough for old Bud to let me sign paper for one.

As I was peering into the window of a late model Caddy, I felt a tap on my shoulder. I turned and saw a guy in his fifties wearing a black and red checkered jacket over black slacks and thick-soled boots. "Hi," he said. "Welcome to Bud's."

"Hi," I replied.

He took off one of the fleecy lined gloves he was wearing and pumped my hand. "And who do I have the pleasure of addressing?" he asked.

"My name's Max."

"Hi, Max. First customer of the day. And Bud always gives the first customer the best deal."

I shook my head. "I don't think I can afford anything here . . ."

"But you'd like to drive off the lot in a guaranteed, previously owned bargain, wouldn't you, Max?"

"Sure I would."

He took my arm and said, "So let's see what we can do. Where you headin', Max?"

"Chicago."

"You a musician?" He pointed his chin in the direction of my guitar case.

Like I told you. Same old same old.

I nodded back.

"Successful?" he asked.

"Would I be walking if I was?"

"But you could be some day?"

"Anything's possible."

"How much money you got to spend on a car, Max?"

"Five," I said.

"Five thousand. No problem."

"Five hundred," I corrected him.

His face fell. "I sure do get 'em," he said.

"So I think I'll just get on down to the bus station and get to Chicago that way."

"Don't despair, Max," said Bud. "Let's go round the back and see what we got. And I'll get Jenny-Lee to put on the coffee pot. You got the time?"

I told him I wasn't in any hurry, and obviously business wasn't booming for Bud, otherwise he wouldn't be wasting *his* time with me, and more coffee sounded good. So we went into the sales office where a tiny, white-haired lady who I took to be Jenny-Lee poured us a brew, and Bud lit a huge cigar after offering me one which I declined, lighting one of my last Marlboros instead.

"Let's take a look-see," he said when our cups were empty. "Where I keep my exchanges."

We went through to a walled yard next to a barn of a garage and Bud showed me round the collection of clunkers he's taken in part exchange on deals. But even they were too expensive for my slim wad of notes.

He shook his head sadly as he led me out front again through the garage which was piled high with junk, and right at the back a single car under an old tarpaulin.

"What's that?" I asked.

He sniggered. "That, son, is the worst deal I ever made. A '59 Mercury Monterey that I took in part exchange, and that died on me the minute the guy drove away in a late model Ford."

"Fifty-nine," I said. "A year younger than my guitar."

"Fifty-nine *model*," he corrected me. "Came out late '58. I was about sixteen at the time. I would dearly have loved one of those Mercurys, but all I had was my dad's old Oldsmobile to drive."

"Amazing," I said. "Mind if I take a look?"

"Help yourself. But the engine's dead, and the rest's not far behind. I dunno why I keep it around. Just nostalgia for better times, I guess."

I worked my way through the garbage that surrounded the car and pulled off the tarp. Underneath was a two-tone fifties automobile, red and white, where the rust, dust and cobwebs hadn't dimmed the colours to a vague khaki. One of the pair of front lights pointed towards the roof of the garage, one rear light was missing, the back bumper was attached to the chassis with wire, and all four white-walled tyres were almost on the rims. I opened the driver's door and got in behind the wheel. Inside, the car stank of damp and mildew, and the front bench seat had half collapsed. The driver's window was half open, and when I tried to close it, the handle came off in my grasp.

Bud walked over and looked in. "Told you, son," he said. "A wreck."

But something told me different. "Will it start?" I asked.

"Start. Hell no. It wouldn't start eight years ago when I pushed it in here, and it sure won't start now."

The key was in the ignition, and without thinking I turned it. The starter motor whined, the engine caught, died, caught again, and with a billow of black smoke from the exhaust, it kept running.

"Christ," said Bud and shook his head. "That's incredible."

"How much?" I asked, almost without thinking.

"You want to buy this thing, son? The wheel bearings have probably frozen solid. I doubt if it'll get you as far as the gas station on the next block."

"How much?" I asked again.

"Five hundred."

"Two fifty."

"I thought you had five hundred bucks."

"I do. But I need to run this thing to Chicago and get a motel room on the way. I can't do it on air."

"Three."

"Two-seven-five."

"No guarantee, no inspection sticker, no insurance. And if you get it outta here, I don't want to see it again, ever."

"Deal," I said.

And that's how I became the proud owner of a '59 Mercury Monterey, without even knowing why.

I paid Bud the two hundred and seventy-five dollars he wanted for the car, and he and I cleared the floor of junk in front of it. I got it started again, put it into gear and gingerly rolled it into the gas station next door where I got the jockey to clean the windows, check the oil, water, brake and transmission fluid levels which were all right down, top them up, and stick ten bucks worth of gas into the tank, before I pumped up the tyres at the air-hose. I checked the trunk, which by some miracle still locked, transferred my guitar and bag from the front seat where I'd thrown them, and after paying for my purchases and tipping the guy a couple of dollars for his trouble I headed out in the direction of Chicago. All the time he kept giving me looks that said he thought I was crazy driving that heap of shit. But what the hell, at least I was mobile again.

As I took 18 again, heading east, I switched on the old valve radio on the dash. Somehow the dial lit, and after it had warmed up I tuned into a hard rock AM station, and keeping well to the right on the highway, brought the car's speed up to fifty-five and relaxed back into what was left of the driver's seat.

I hadn't slept for a day or so, and before long I was yawning and my eyes started closing, and I knew I had to get some rest or else I was going to rack up the car and myself. So when I saw the sign for a place called Clear Lake I pulled off the main highway and went looking for a motel.

I found one right inside the city limits, between a K-Mart and another gas station. It had a diner attached, and looked to be just what I wanted. Under the neon sign out front that read *Lakeside Motel* in curly simulated handwriting, was another that read *Established 1945*, and under that was the most welcoming of all. In flashing red neon capital letters was the word VACANCIES.

I steered the Mercury into the parking lot and went into the office. There was an old guy behind the desk with a thinning flat top and a cardigan with holes in the elbows.

"Morning," he said.

"Morning," I replied. "Do you have a room?"

"That's what we're here for, young man," he said. "I'll give you the cream of the crop. Thirty-nine bucks a night, no finer value in the west." And he reached over behind him and took a key off a hook on the wall under the designation "1".

I signed in, took the key, ran the Merc round to the parking space also marked "1", took my gear out of the trunk and went into the room.

It was just another motel. Another suitcase, another hall, like the song goes. I'd been in a million of them. It contained a three-quarter-sized bed that had seen better days, a TV chained to the wall, a table, chair, nightstand and wardrobe. Inside the tiny en-suite bathroom was a john with a cellophane seal over the seat, to make me feel pampered, a wash basin and shower stall. I took a leak, shucked off my clothes, turned on the TV with the sound down and hit the sheets. I was asleep within a minute to the soft bleating of a daytime soap. When I woke up it was dark outside, and there was a game show on TV. I stretched, yawned, got up, went to the bathroom, cleaned my teeth and dressed in what I'd taken off except for clean socks and underpants. Years on the road had taught me that clean socks and underwear are a must every time you get dressed.

I suddenly realized that I was hungry and decided that a trip to the diner was in order. I went out past the car and saw that a big semi-trailer was parked on the otherwise deserted lot. I walked round to the front of the motel and into the lunch room next door. It was empty except for a waitress chatting through the hatch to the cook, and a guy with a baseball cap pulled down low over his face sitting at one table with the remains of a meal in front of him, and a coffee cup in one hand. I imagined he was the trucker and gave him a nod as I sat at a table by the window.

The waitress came over with a glass of iced water, and I ordered eggs over easy, links, home fries, toast and coffee. The food came quickly and I started to eat.

When I was about halfway through my meal, the trucker got up from his table, threw some bills next to his plate and walked towards the door. When he was next to my table, he said, "You the guy with the '59 Mercury?"

I looked up, puzzled for a moment, then realized that I was. "Yeah," I replied.

"Nice wheels," he said. "You keep it real good." Then with a wolfish grin that exposed two rows of very white teeth, he passed me by and out of the door. Sarcastic sod, I thought, and went back to my food.

When I'd finished and paid the check, I went back outside and walked towards my room.

As I went round the side of the building, I heard the starter motor on the semi grind, and with a roar the engine caught and the driver put all the brights and spots on full and pulled round towards the exit. As the light hit the Mercury I suddenly realized that the paintwork gleamed like new, both rear lights were whole, and that the back fender was attached to the chassis and shone like silver. The lights from the truck swept round and off the car, and a hand waved from the open driver's window, and it was gone.

I must've imagined it, I thought, but when I walked up to the car and put my hand on its flanks, the paintwork felt smooth and shiny. I went to the door of my room, opened it, switched on the light, and went to look at the Mercury in the splash of illumination from the doorway.

It wasn't the same car. Or at least it *was*, but something had happened to it whilst I'd been away. Where there'd been rust, the bodywork was whole, waxed metal. Where there'd been worn and stained whitewall tyres, were a quartet of factory-fresh rubber with sparkling white sides. Where one pair of front lights had pointed to the heavens, were two headlights perfectly aligned. And when

I reached into my pocket for the key, instead of one that was worn thin and battered from years of use, was a brand-new one on a leather fob. I opened the driver's door, and the interior light, that hadn't worked before, popped on to reveal upholstery and carpets that were pristine, and instead of the stink of mildew was that wonderful smell of new car.

I didn't know what was going on, so I went back to the room. The TV was still on, showing a re-run of *Gunsmoke* in black and white. But the room was different somehow. Newer, smarter, and the TV wasn't chained to the wall, and it wasn't a slimline Jap model either. But a bulbous domestic RCA in a wooden cabinet. James Arness shot three bad guys, then followed Miss Kitty into the saloon as the show went to a commercial break that was also in monochrome. The first ad was for Pepsodent, the second for some greasy kid's stuff haircream, and the last for the new Lincoln Continental. Fifty-nine, the man said. I couldn't believe what I was seeing. Was this some sort of crazy fifties theme night? I looked for the remote but it was nowhere to be seen, and the channel changer was actually on the front of the set. I switched across all four channels available, all in black and white again, and all showing programmes I'd seen before. I knew *very* weird things had happened to me in my travels before, but this was the weirdest and I didn't want to acknowledge what was happening. I picked up my guitar case and bag, put them in the trunk and went round to the office, where a young guy who looked vaguely familiar, in a letter cardigan with a blond flat top was behind the counter. He gave me a dirty look and said, "He'p you?"

"I'm round the corner in One," I said.

"Say what?"

I repeated myself slowly, and showed him my room key. He looked at it, then turned and looked at the board behind him. An identical key hung on the hook designated "1".

"Where'd you get that key, pal?" he demanded.

"The other guy gave it to me this morning."

"What *other* guy?"

"The other guy works here."

"I work here. My sister works here. My mom works here. That's it."

"No, man," I protested. "An older guy. Thinning hair, wearing a cardigan."

And I suddenly realized with a certainty that brooked no argument, that the older guy that I'd seen when I'd checked in that morning was this character in the future. Exactly where I was now I had no idea, except for a vague inkling.

"What's the date?" I asked.

"The date. What the hell's that got to do with it, you fag pinko? Where the hell have you been that your hair's so long? You look like a goddam girl. People like you should be shot. We didn't fight a war in Korea with the Commies where my old man died, so that people like you could walk round free. Now give me that key and get the hell outta here."

I dropped the key onto the desk and ran back to the Mercury. I jumped in behind the wheel and put the key into the ignition. The engine caught with a rich hum. I jammed the gear lever into drive and took off with a scream of tyres, out of the motel parking lot and back onto the highway. As I did, the radio, that I'd left on, warmed up. The hard rock I'd been listening to earlier had been replaced by an old tune by the Platters. For a minute I hoped I'd got a golden oldie station by mistake, until the song faded and the DJ announced, "That's it, cats and kittens. The number one song across the nation, 'Smoke Gets in Your Eyes', by the fabulous Platters. This is Kay-Why-Gee-Cee comin' attcha outta Mason City, I-Oh-Way, with your evenin' DJ Dave Dash spinnin' the discs for you. And now from the guys who're topping the bill at the Surf ballroom in Clear Lake tonight, February 2nd, 1959, let's hear from 1957, that golden goodie, that rave from the grave, 'That'll Be The Day', by Buddy Holly and the Crickets."

And the familiar opening guitar figure crashed out of the speaker. Jesus Christ, I thought. February 2nd, 1959. The day before the music died.

I stopped the car, switched off the radio, found my watch cap in the pocket of my jacket and pulled it on, pushing my long hair up under it, then checked my reflection in the car's rear-view mirror.

Not bad. Almost normal for the time. Then I spotted a young guy in a pea jacket, rolled-up jeans and baseball boots heading my way, and I rolled down the window. "Hey, pal," I called.

"Yeah?"

"Surf Ballroom, where's it at?"

"You gonna see Buddy Holly?"

"That's right."

"You're lucky. My folks won't let me go."

"That's tough luck. So where is it?"

"Down this drag, hang a right, take the second left and follow the crowds."

"Obliged," I said.

"Enjoy the show."

"I will." And I put the car into gear, gave him a wave and peeled off from the kerb.

I found the place easily and jammed the Mercury into a parking space next to the finest collection of classic Detroit iron outside *American Graffiti*. I fetched my guitar case and headed for the stage door.

There was a cop standing outside swinging his nightstick and talking to an old geezer in a veteran's cap who looked like he was in charge of the door, and making sure the fifty or so female teenagers in long, wide skirts and bobbysocks, holding records and autograph books who were crowded round didn't get inside and throw themselves on the rock and rollers.

He and the cop scoped me as I pushed through the crowd. I held up my guitar case and said, "Band." It had worked in New York in '81 getting backstage to see Deborah Harry, so I figured it would work in the boonies in '59 and I was right.

"You guys get any later and it'll be time to leave," said the cop.

"Sorry, sir," I said. "Had to try and find some new strings."

"In you go, young fella," said the vet, and he held the door for me. Nice manners, I thought. Things'll change.

I went into a long concrete corridor and stopped dead. Just coming out of a door up on my right was a familiar figure with black, curly hair, wearing a tight, dark suit, thick-rimmed black glasses, and holding a cherry-red Fender in one hand.

Jesus, I thought. It *is*. It's Buddy Holly.

"Mr Holly," I called.

The figure turned and grinned. "Hi," he said. "What can I do for you?"

As I walked up to him I racked my brains for anything I could remember about that day in 1959. Buddy Holly had long been an idol of mine. I'd read books about him and I'd watched *The Buddy Holly Story* on cable just a month or so before, for about the eighth time.

"My name's Max," I stuttered. "I play bass."

"We gotta bass player," said Buddy with another smile. "Great young guy called Waylon Jennings."

Jesus, I'd forgotten that he'd split from the original Crickets before the tour over contractual problems and had to form a pick-up band for the dates. "But you need a drummer," I said, remembering that the drummer he's been using had contracted frost-bite after their tour coach broke down on the freezing road the previous day.

"Sure do," said Buddy Holly. "Poor Carl. Those dam' buses are like iceboxes. This whole tour is a dam' disgrace. Carlo from the Belmonts stepped in for us on the first set. You play drums?"

I do as a matter of fact. Just a little. Most bass players do. "Sure," I said.

"Do you know our songs?"

Did I know Buddy Holly's songs? Sure I did. I'd owned about four copies of his greatest hits album, and I'd worn them white. "Sure," I said.

"Come in here," said Buddy, and he took me into an empty dressing room. He picked up a metal waste bin, emptied the contents on the floor and put it on a table upside down, next to an empty cardboard shoe box. He picked up a pair of drumsticks from an open bag on the floor, and handed them to me. Then said, "OK, Max. Play drums. Let's do 'Maybe Baby'."

It was easy. Whilst he picked out the chords on the unamplified Fender and sang along, I beat out the rhythm that I'd heard a million times before. He grinned at me as I hammered on the improvised drum kit and after a minute or so, he stopped playing and said, "You'll do, Max. I like your style. You can sit in on the second set with us."

"That's great, Mr Holly," I said.

"Call me Buddy. You're one of the band now. And hey, Max, what the hell is that accent you've got there?"

"English," I said.

"Is that so? Hey, I love England. We did a big tour there last year. Didja see us?"

I shook my head. Hell, I hadn't even been born when the tour took place.

"It's a shame none of your English bands ever had hits over here. We met some great guys while we were travelling around. Real talented."

"They will," I said, with absolute certainty. "They will."

"I sure hope I'm around to see it," he replied.

And then I had a great idea. Maybe he would. Maybe I'd been given a chance to change history and prevent Buddy Holly, the Big Bopper and Ritchie Valens catching that plane out of Mason City airport in a few hours' time, and save all their lives and the pilot's too. And maybe with my help they'd all be around to see those English bands invade America in the sixties.

"The show starts in a few minutes. The guys are already on stage doing backup for Ritchie. I'll let them know we've got a new drummer. It'll be a kick in the head."

We walked out of the dressing room, me still clutching the drumsticks in one hand, through a couple of fire doors and I heard screaming and applause from out front and the last few bars of "Donna", and a very young Hispanic-looking guy with bad skin ran past me, sweat pouring from his face. Man, I thought, this is insane. That's Ritchie Valens. I watched from the wings as Buddy Holly went and spoke to the three musicians on stage and pointed back at me. The guitarist shrugged, the bass player nodded, and the drummer hopped off his stool with a look of relief and walked off stage. "Good luck, fella," he said as he passed me. "I'm gonna get a cup of coffee."

From the other side of the curtains I heard the MC ranting on, building up the excitement for the last segment of the show featuring the star of the tour, and I walked on stage and Waylon Jennings shook my hand as Tommy Allsup, the other guitarist gave me a wave. "I hope you know what you're doing," said Waylon.

"Trust me," I said back. "I'm a bass player myself too. And I know this stuff like the back of my hand. We'll cook."

"I sure hope so," he said, as I sat at the recently vacated drum stool and ran round the tiny kit with my sticks. No problem, I thought and winked at Buddy who was plugging into the single, small amp the band were sharing.

Waylon shoved a set list into my hand, and as the screams grew louder out front the curtains parted.

It was great. A dream come true, playing with Buddy Holly that cold, snowy night in middle America. We only did a short set. They did in those days, and it flew past. Buddy opened with a solo version of "Gotta Travel On", then we joined him for "Peggy Sue", "Think It Over", "Rave On", "Everyday", and maybe half a dozen others. All my favourite Holly tunes, and although I say so myself I did pretty well. Waylon, Tommy and Buddy obviously agreed, as they kept looking back at me and grinning. We encored with "That'll Be The Day", and before I knew it, the curtains had closed and the guys gathered round shaking my hands and clapping me on the back. "Want to finish the tour with us?" asked Buddy. "Carl ain't gonna make it back."

"I'll have to think about it," I said.

"Well think fast, I'm taking a plane outta here pronto."

"Buddy," I said as we walked back to the dressing room, where he put on a scarf and shrugged into a heavy overcoat. Nice style it was too. Real fifties. Then I suppose it would have to be. "Why bother? I've got a brand-new Mercury Monterey outside. I'll drive you to the next gig. And anyone else who wants to come along."

"So you're coming with us. Great. But I'll pass on the ride, fella. I need to get my dry cleaning done and grab some real shut-eye before the Moorhead gig. We're flying to Fargo which is real close, and that's that."

"Well let me drive you to the airfield at least." I had some crazy idea about kidnapping him.

"It's OK, we've got a ride. Listen, Max, see you in Moorhead, I've gotta run. Ritchie and the Bopper will be waiting."

I followed his figure through to the stage door where he signed autographs and hustled over to a car and climbed in. Ritchie Valens and the Big Bopper were already aboard, and the car went off in a cloud of thin exhaust. I ran to the Mercury and followed them. It wasn't a long drive to Mason City airport, and I parked my car out of sight behind the small control tower next to an even smaller block of offices. Standing on the runway in front of the tower was a single-engined, red Beechcraft Bonanza four-seater, with a young guy leaning against the side.

I looked at the little plane and had an idea. If I could disable it, then the three musicians wouldn't be able to fly. They might not like it, but what the hell?

"You the pilot?" I asked, as I walked up to the kid leaning against the machine.

"Sure. You with the guys going to Fargo?"

I nodded. "Buddy wants to see you," I said. "He's in the office paying the fares."

The pilot shrugged and headed towards the office block.

I looked around and saw a tool box. I opened it, grabbed a huge monkey wrench and went to the tail of the plane and gave the rudder a hell of a whack.

"What in Christ's name?" I heard somebody bellow from inside the fuselage, and a huge figure came through the door and hit the tarmac running.

Shit, it was the Big Bopper and he was as mad as hell. I hadn't realized there was anyone inside. "You crazy fucker," he screamed. "What the shit do you think you're doing?" And ignoring the wrench in my hand he threw a great overhand right hook which hit me somewhere between my nose and my eye and took me out of the game.

I woke up at the side of the runway, lying in the tall grass to the sound of an aircraft engine, and as I lay in the frozen brush I saw the Beechcraft speed down the runway and take off. Two men were standing watching the plane, and I watched it too as it did a sharp left turn, then its lights vanished into the light snow that was falling over Mason City, and that's about all I *do* remember.

I woke up again inside the Mercury, parked on the side of a country road. How I'd got there I don't know. A low mist lay across the fields, and it was so cold that I could feel the ice in my three days' growth of beard. The snow had stopped.

I stretched painfully on the busted-down driver's seat, and the stink of mildew inside the car had permeated right through my clothes. I tried the engine but it was dead, and when I crawled outside I saw that all four worn and filthy whitewalls were flat. I kicked the bodywork and the toe of my boot went right through the rotten metal, and a shower of rust fell onto the blacktop. I tugged open the trunk, rescued my stuff and set off on foot. I managed to hitch a ride at a crossroads and got to Chicago late the next night, where I holed up in a fleabag hotel before moving on. I didn't look up the guy I knew, or the woman.

If you read the history books about Buddy Holly's last tour, and I have, they'll tell you that Carlo Mastrangelo, bass singer from the Belmonts played drums for the Crickets on that fateful night. They're right, and he did. But only for the first show. I know, because it was me behind the kit for the second and final set of the night. Indeed of Buddy Holly's life.

Not that I care about that. That's not what worries me. What *does* worry me. What still haunts me as I go from city to city, never being able to settle in one place for long, is whether or not something I did when I attacked that little plane whilst it was waiting to take off at Mason City airport, *did* damage something vital that the pilot didn't notice.

And the thought that wakes me screaming from some forgotten dream all these years later, is whether it was me that killed the pilot of the red Beechcraft Bonanza, and his passengers, J. P. Richardson, better known as the Big Bopper, Ritchie Valens, and Charles Edward "Buddy" Holly on the morning of the 3rd February, 1959, a few months before I was born, many thousands of miles away in London, England.